THE WINTI

JENNIFER ASH took the medieval part of "*Romancing Robin Hood*", written by her alter ego Jenny Kane, and turned it into the standalone novel "*The Outlaw's Ransom*" - the prequel to "*The Winter Outlaw*".

Whereas Jenny Kane writes cosy Sunday afternoon contemporary fiction with a hint of romance and a feel good factor, Jennifer Ash writes medieval mysteries with an edge of uncertainty - albeit with a touch of romance in the background.

"*The Winter Outlaw*" is the second novel in "*The Folville Chronicles*".

Book Three, "*Edward's Outlaw*", will be published at the end of 2018/early 2019.

JENNIFER ASH

THE
WINTER OUTLAW

COPYRIGHT

Littwitz Press
Dahl House, Brookside Crescent
Exeter EX4 8NE

Copyright © Jennifer Ash 2018
Jennifer Ash has asserted her rights to be identified
as the author of this work in accordance with the
Copyright, Designs and Patents Act 1988.

First published in Great Britain by Littwitz Press in 2018

www.littwitzpress.com

A CIP catalogue record for this book is available
from the British Library.

ISBN: 978-1-9998552-7-7

All rights reserved. No part of this book may be copied,
or transmitted in any form or by any means, electronic, electrostatic,
magnetic tape, mechanical, photocopying,
recording or otherwise, without the written permission of
the author: Jennifer Ash and Littwitz Press.

Acknowledgements

Once upon a time I fell in love with a television programme called *Robin of Sherwood*.

I would like to dedicate this book to everyone who played a part, large or small, in the creation of that television programme, over thirty years ago.

I'd specifically like to thank Barnaby Eaton Jones and Iain Matthews, for allowing me the opportunity to meet my heroes in the flesh in 2016. An experience that allowed me to thank in person, the actors, actresses, producers, script editors and casting directors, who had, without realising it, set my life upon a course to become a historian and a novelist. A path which has led to a life that I love.

Bakewell

DERBY

Ashby de la Zouch

Charnwood

N

NGHAM

■ Brokesby Field
Reresby
                    ■ Teigh
■ Ashby Folville
■Twyford

TER

~ *Prologue* ~

Winter 1329

Adam Calvin's vision blurred as his eyes streamed in the cold. His breath came in wheezing puffs. He needed to rest, but he daren't. Not yet.

It was only as the vague outline of a cluster of homes and workshops came into view in the distance that he realised where his legs had been taking him. Slowing his pace, but not stopping, Adam risked a glance over his shoulder. He'd expected to see dogs, horses and men chasing him, but there was nothing. No one.

Scanning the scene ahead, making sure he wasn't running into trouble as well as away from it, Adam exhaled heavily and aimed for a building he hoped was still standing.

The last time he'd visited the tiny village of Walesby there had been an old grain store on its outskirts. Built too close to the point where the frequently flooding Rivers Maun and Meden merged, the grain store had paid the price of a poor location. Long since abandoned in favour of a superior bake house, it was a perfect temporary hiding place for a man on the run.

Adam had no breath left with which to sigh for relief

when he saw the neglected grain store. Uttering a prayer of thanks to Our Lady for the fact the building hadn't been pulled down, he lifted the worn latch. He eased his way into the damp space, which was stuffed with rotting sacks containing all manner of rubbish.

Scrabbling awkwardly over the first few rows of musty sacks, Adam made himself a man-sized gap at the back of the room. Sinking down as far as he could, hoping both the sacks and the dark would shield him long enough for his cramped limbs to rest, he did his best to ignore the putrid stench and allowed his mind to catch up on events.

Only a few hours ago everything in Adam's life had been as it should be.

He'd been fast asleep in his cot in the small private room his status as steward to Lord John de Markham gave him.

Had given him.

Adam wasn't sure what time it had been when he'd been shaken to his senses from sleep by Ulric, the kitchen boy. He suspected it hadn't been much more than an hour after he'd bedded down for the night.

Ulric, who'd frantically reported that a hue and cry had been called to capture Adam, had urged his master to move quickly. The sheriff had unexpectedly arrived and there had been a brief meeting between him, the Lord Markham and one other unknown man. An anxious Ulric had said that rumours were flying around like snowflakes in the wind.

Some of the household staff were saying Adam had stolen something, some that there had been a death; a murder.

Either way, for his own safety, Steward Calvin had to leave. Fast.

Confused, scared and angry that his good name was being questioned; without having time to find out what was going on or defend himself, Adam had grabbed his scrip.

Pulling on his boots and cloak, with Ulric's help he'd headed through the manor via the servants' walkways.

The only item Adam hadn't been able to find to take with him was his knife. Contenting himself with lifting one from Cook's precious supplies as he ran through the kitchen, he'd left the manor that had been his home for the past twenty years.

With a fleeting nod of gratitude to his young helper, Adam had fled into the frosty night. Only minutes later he'd heard the calls of the hue and cry; echoes of the posse's footfalls thudding against the hard, icy earth.

Now, wiping tears of exhaustion away with the back of his hand, Adam strained his ears through the winter air. All he could hear was the busy work of the mice or rats who were taking as much advantage of the building as he was.

Glad of the water pouch Ulric had stuffed in his scrip, Adam took a tiny sip. He didn't know how long it would have to last him. Closing his eyes, he rested his head against the sacks that boxed him in and tried to think.

Had he outstripped the hue and cry? If they were nearby, taking the chance to rest while waiting for him to run again, then Adam was sure he'd have heard something - but there were no muttered voices, no horses panting and no hounds barking at his scent.

Adam managed to get his breathing under control. He'd been part of the hue and cry on occasions himself, and he knew such groups didn't tend to chase their quarry far, or for long. Especially not on a cold winter's night, when they could be tucked up in bed before the demands of the next working day.

With growing confidence that he'd chosen his bolthole well, Adam allowed himself to relax a fraction. Few people lived in Walesby since the most recent of many destructive floods, and its location meant he was only a few steps from the edge of Sherwood Forest. A desperate man could easily disappear into the woodland's depths.

As the hours ticked on, Adam became convinced that the pursuit had stopped. However, he knew that by the morning the hue and cry would be replaced with soldiers if the sheriff barked the order. His bolthole wouldn't stay safe for long.

Yet that wasn't what concerned Adam the most. He wanted to know what he was supposed to have done that warranted his midnight flight. How could he even begin to go about clearing his name if he didn't know what he was accused of?

In the meantime, where was he going to go?

~ *Chapter One* ~

The bells rang out the hour of Prime as Adam sank deeper into the straw. The clergy of England would be heading to early morning prayers, while the peasants and townsfolk rose from their slumber to tackle the day ahead.

He was getting used to bedding down in livestock sheds and shelters during the daylight hours. Over the past two weeks, moving by night and hiding by day, Adam had crossed the border from Nottinghamshire into Leicestershire.

Sleeping during the day wasn't the only major adjustment he been forced to make. He'd been amazed at how quickly he'd got used to being exhausted and afraid, to lurking in the shadows, to being unceasingly hungry. Then there was the ability to live with constantly rehashing the events which had led to his becoming a hunted man. That ritual filled Adam's walking hours and dominated his dreams; his nightmares.

In all of his forty-five years upon God's earth, Adam had never heard of the hue and cry being raised *before* a criminal had been confronted with their wrongdoings. Much of what had happened against him didn't ring true. Especially if, as Ulric had said, Sheriff Edmund de Cressy had arrived at the manor to assemble the posse against him before the cry was even given.

De Cressy's reputation for taking bribes was well known, but Adam couldn't begin to imagine what possible advantage there was for the sheriff in wasting time hunting for *him*. The county was overrun with corrupt knights and lords, and outlawry was becoming a concern across England. What honour could there possibly be in chasing an aging steward?

Hoping his theory that he'd be safer in another county was correct, Adam curled into a ball. The oblivion of sleep was the only time he could banish the growling of his empty stomach, but even that couldn't stop his unquiet mind. His dreams were increasingly full of images of betrayal and panic.

Adam had lost track of how many miles he'd travelled. Avoiding people where possible, he stole apples from stores, and pinched scraps of bread and meat where he could, simply to survive.

Each time he dared think he had left his troubles behind, he'd overhear a rumour of pursuers approaching and he'd travel on, further and further away from West Markham.

Whispers on the breeze said there had been a death at the home of his master, King's Sergeant, Lord John de Markham. But whose demise had occurred remained unspoken. Others only spoke of a betrayal by a trusted servant.

Ashamed that his name was probably being linked to those deeds, Adam closed his eyes against the growing daylight. What exactly had he been blamed for? Had Ulric been mistaken? Was he running from a pursuit that was chasing another man?

After five years fighting as a solider for the king, and twenty years of loyal service in the household of John de Markham, twelve of which had been as his steward, Adam had believed himself totally trusted. Thinking back, he could recall nothing unusual happening during the day he'd been forced to flee. In fact, the only ripples in the otherwise smooth running of the household in the weeks prior to his departure had been minor incidents; incidents he'd reported to Markham himself.

Two petty thefts from the manor, and a handful of unexplained breakages, had occurred over a period of two months. Surely, they couldn't be the crimes he was being accused of? Lord Markham had asked Adam himself to root out the culprit, but as the thefts had stopped as soon as he'd reported them to his master, he hadn't been able to bring the perpetrator to book.

He'd assumed the matter to be closed. Now that time with nothing to do but think had been thrust upon Adam, he saw that, perhaps, his previously easy relationship with his master had begun to corrode in recent months after all. He didn't know why, nor was he sure why he hadn't noticed earlier. Surely all those years of good service couldn't have been jeopardised just because of the unresolved theft of a belt and a ring?

It was the rumours of a death that worried Adam the most. If there had been a killing, then who was dead?

He was tired of repeatedly asking himself the same questions. He was tired of running. He wanted answers.

Adam sighed into the straw. Answers meant he couldn't afford to run any further from the scene of the crime.

First, he must build up his strength.

Then he'd have to go back.

Hoisting the basket over her arm, Sarah balanced the weight of the fabric she'd purchased across the food beneath. Once she was convinced it wasn't going to pitch onto the frost-hardened ground below, the housekeeper began to walk the mile from the market, towards the manor of Ashby Folville.

Humming quietly to herself, Sarah mentally planned how she'd cut the cloth in order to produce a wedding gown fit for a queen.

Mathilda of Twyford had come to the Folville household under the strangest of circumstances. In the summer just passed, the young woman had been taken hostage against a debt that her father had failed to pay off. During that time, Mathilda had stolen the heart of Robert de Folville - and, more remarkably, earned the respect of his brothers. Sarah smiled at the memory. That was not an easy thing to do when you found yourself thrust unceremoniously into the household of one of the most notorious families in the county, but Mathilda's quick wit and common sense had repeatedly proved her worth to them all.

Although Mathilda's father's debt to the Folvilles had been more than repaid by Mathilda's bravery in helping to uncover a murderer, she'd stayed within the household. And now, in a few weeks, during the forthcoming Winter Solstice celebrations, Mathilda was to marry Robert and become the mistress of the house.

Sarah had been reassured immediately after the announcement of the forthcoming union that her long-held position as the Folvilles' housekeeper, guide and confidant was not in jeopardy. She and Mathilda were to handle the welfare of Robert and his brothers between them.

'After all, with men such as these,' Mathilda had whispered when they were out of her future husband's earshot, 'the common sense of two women still isn't really enough.'

Used to travelling the semi-forested track between the market and the manor alone, secure in the knowledge that the fearsome reputation of the Folvilles would protect her, Sarah strode boldly along. Lost in her thoughts, she took the final turn in the narrowing road, her mind switching from gown design to the more immediate task of cooking for the day ahead.

She'd been weighing up the idea of using a few of the precious winter apples to make a pie, when a rustling noise made her turn sharply. Staring keenly left and right, the housekeeper shrugged off the sound that had so unexpectedly cut through the peace of the frost hinted morning and resumed her walk.

Two steps later, with only a few yards to go before she reached the gateway to Ashby Folville manor, Sarah cursed in shock as she was grabbed from behind.

'You never looked 'ard 'nough, woman.'

Before a scream could escape her throat, a dirty hand clamped over Sarah's mouth. Any opportunity to bite the attacker was instantly taken away from her as the man's thick fingers gripped her face tightly, making sure his chipped nails dug into her flesh.

Sarah struggled as a second pair of arms encircled her, squeezing her stomach so hard that all the air was knocked from her body. The housekeeper's basket was thrown from her grasp; the roll of fabric fell onto the slushy mud-soaked track with a heartbreaking squelch.

'We 'as got oursel's a right feisty un 'ere.'

Hot breath, stinking of ale, tickled Sarah's ear. She desperately tried to jerk away, but a sudden stinging smack against the opposite side of her head stopped her dead and forced a gasp of pain from her muffled lips.

'You is gonna deliver a message to your masters. Yes?'

The grip against her was lightened just enough for Sarah to nod in terrified agreement.

'Good. This be it.'

The last thing the housekeeper saw, before a gnarled fist knocked her into black oblivion, was the glinting edge of a freshly sharpened knife.

1300

'Where?'

'Beneath the rowan tree near the gatehouse.'

'We were intended to find him then.'

'Indeed, Father.'

Henry, the sub-prior of Launde, smoothed out his black and white habit and looked down at the baby with concern. Wrapped in a clean cloth, the boy had clearly been looked after. He was in good condition, fed and washed. A small smudge of salt on the child's forehead told of a hasty baptism.

'He's been cared for; but at what cost to the mother, I wonder.'

'She can't have left him long ago; he was still warm when he was found. There was no sign of anyone though. Brother Mark has a space in the almonry at Leicester Abbey, but we'd need a wet nurse.'

Henry nodded, 'Make the necessary arrangements. And then we'll baptise him.'

'My lord?'

'I know she has left the salt to tell us he's been baptised, but if this woman was desperate enough to abandon her child, she may have been desperate enough to risk his soul and make a pretence of his anointment in case we refused to take him. Better he is welcomed into Christ's arms twice than not at all.'

~ *Chapter Two* ~

The wound to Sarah's arm had only just stopped weeping blood.

It was two days since Allward, the kitchen boy, had discovered the housekeeper sprawled unconscious on the pathway, badly beaten, only a few moments walk from the entrance to the Folvilles' home. Found in a pool of blood, the gash to Sarah's left arm had been short but deep. A bruise on the left side of her face had already turned purple and was now heading towards a dull green. Her right eye was puffed up to twice the size it should have been.

'You're supposed to be resting.' Mathilda wasn't at all surprised to find Sarah in the kitchen before her, despite the dew of dawn still being crisp upon the winter earth outside.

'And let *them* win? Not likely.' Sarah held her head high as she winced during the simple act of chopping an apple.

'You've only just regained your wits.' Mathilda sat next to her friend. 'Whoever they are, they'll not win. Damaging your arm further by using it before it's mended won't help track them down.'

Sarah put aside her knife. 'You sounded just like my Lord Robert then.'

'Is that a compliment?'

The housekeeper raised a half-smile. 'I'm not at all

sure.' A sigh overtook her as she rubbed her elbow just below the wound. 'How am I going to make your wedding gown now?'

'Don't worry, I can do it.'

'Yes, but...' Sarah looked more stricken than Mathilda had ever seen her. For the first time since they'd met, Mathilda saw Sarah's forty-plus years shining through her usually youthful countenance.

Mathilda laid a gentle hand on her friend's shoulder, 'I know you wanted to make it, and you shall. By the time I've cut the cloth to your precise requirements, and tacked it into shape, you'll be healed enough to take over - or at least order the exact placing of my every stitch!'

'Are you saying I'm so bossy that I'd peer at your every needle-swipe?'

'I most certainly am!' Mathilda swept the apples, knife and bowl nearer, and began to peel them herself. 'Anyway, we have plenty of time until the ceremony. Perhaps it's as well we've had to wait so long for all of the brothers to be available to attend.

'Apart from the odious Richard.'

'The Rector of Teigh will not be missed.' Mathilda shivered. 'To think he tried to frame me and Robert for murder! Anyway, he's in France, fighting for the king.'

'And the treacherous French are welcome to him.'

Mathilda returned the conversation to more pleasurable things; scowling as memories of the reverend Folville's disloyalty made Sarah's beaten face crease with anxiety. 'Preparations are well in hand, so just concentrate on getting better. I'm sure Allward and I can keep everyone fed on our own for a few more days.'

Banging her good hand down on the table in frustration, Sarah whispered her embarrassment to Mathilda. 'I feel so useless. If only I'd been paying attention. I'm such a fool!'

'You are no such thing, Sarah, and never have been.'

The door to the kitchen opened and the speaker, Robert de Folville, dipped his head in acknowledgement to Mathilda as she rose to fetch her future husband some ale. 'If you were even remotely foolish Sarah, my brother the Lord John would never allow Mathilda to reside here prior to our wedding. My brothers trust you with her virtue.'

Mathilda laughed. 'I remain insulted that they believe me incapable of doing that all by myself!'

'They don't know you as well as I do, clearly.' Robert winked in a moment of levity before anger reclaimed him. Hurling himself onto the bench, he crashed his beaker onto the table with such a thud that the women both jumped.

Mathilda spoke calmly. 'If you keep doing that we'll have to ask my father to make us some new drinking cups.'

'Your father's potted vessels are sturdy enough to withstand my anger.'

'Which is just as well!' Mathilda pushed some bread towards Robert, knowing his ire would calm quicker once his belly was full.

Robert nodded his gratitude, 'How does your arm fare this morning, Sarah? I can see your face heals in an interestingly colourful fashion.'

'It heals, but too slowly for my liking.'

Harrumphing into his ale, Robert briefly considered admitting he'd been expecting something like this for a while but changed his mind. Despite everything, he hadn't predicted an attack so close to home. If he had, he'd never have let his brother Eustace borrow his small armed guard for his latest escapade.

Rumours had been running wild for some time about an outlaw in the area, but Robert wasn't convinced a lone outlaw was behind this attack. Anyone desperate enough to strike down a woman on the doorstep of the most notorious criminal families in the county would have stolen the food from Sarah's basket. They may even have taken the cloth to trade for food and drink.

Keeping his suspicions to himself, Robert asked Sarah yet again, 'Are you *sure* you can't recall anything about your attackers?'

Seeing the pain cross the housekeeper's face, Mathilda interceded. 'You know she doesn't, Robert. No amount of wishing is going to change that.'

'When the news of Sarah's assault reaches my brothers' ears in Huntingdon, there's going to be trouble. I wouldn't want to be whoever was responsible once Eustace, John and Walter, not to mention Thomas and Laurence, get hold of them.'

Ripping his bread in half, spraying crumbs across the table, Robert growled, 'Inches from my gateway. Inches! How dare he?'

'They,' corrected Mathilda. 'There had to be at least two of them.'

'Yes.' Robert concurred, 'At least two men. What gall brings outlaws so close to the gates of a Folville home?'

'I can't answer that, I wish I could.' Mathilda took a deep breath. 'There's something I need to tell you. I don't think it's connected, but...'

Mathilda got no further, for Allward was on the kitchen doorstep, his face flushed with anxiety. 'A messenger has ridden into the courtyard, my Lord. I would describe him as unafraid.'

Rising to her feet, Mathilda immediately adopted the role of future mistress of the manor. 'Will you go out to him, my Lord, or shall I call Steward Owen?' Catching the suspicious look on Robert's face, she added, 'Or will you receive this person in the hall?'

'Owen is out on a task for me.' Robert was already on his feet. 'Allward, please do as Mathilda suggests, and escort this messenger to before the fire in the hall.'

'What's wrong?' Mathilda didn't miss the way Robert's hand had slipped to the pommel of his dagger as they took their leave of a frowning Sarah. 'You are inviting this stranger into the heart of your home as a display of being unafraid?'

'Astute as ever.' Robert picked up Mathilda's hand, kissing the palm lightly while running his other hand over the exquisite leather girdle he'd given her as a testament of his intentions; the act of affection giving him strength. 'I have been expecting something like this. Perhaps I'm wrong, but the manner of Allward's delivery makes me think the moment has arrived.'

'Will you share your suspicions with me?'

'Your counsel will be welcome. Although I know many find it curious that I should consider your opinion worthwhile. However, if I'm correct - and in truth I pray I'm wrong - then I do not wish for this messenger to see you. Wait within earshot behind the tapestries. Listen hard.'

Memories of how she'd first encountered Robert, and how she'd eavesdropped on his conversations with his brothers from behind those very tapestries, came back to Mathilda. Then, like now, the only thing she could feel was the danger in the air. 'I will. Take care, my Lord.'

The messenger was as brazen as Allward had implied. Mathilda at once saw the wisdom of making it clear that the Folville manor was a domain in which anyone foolish enough to act without respect took a chance on leaving with fewer limbs than they'd entered with. An unspoken message this emissary could relay to whoever passed as his master.

'You are one of the younger Folvilles.'

'And you are presumptive. I am Lord Robert de Folville. Which master sends such an ill-mannered messenger to one of my family's manors?'

From her space behind the tapestry that separated Allward's sleeping cot from the hall, Mathilda leant as far forward as she dare. Placing an eye to the gap between the hangings, she could see the visitor holding out a roll of parchment.

As a rule, most lords sent stable boys or kitchen hands to deliver messages. This was a grown man with all the hallmarks of being a hired thug. His arms were thick with muscle, his face unshaven. His clothing was practical and worn. Mathilda wondered if she was observing an outlaw, or a man who worked for one.

Suddenly the memory of the wounds on Sarah's face, bruised and broken, rose in her mind like bile. *It has to have been him...*

It was all Mathilda could do to stop from rushing forward and knocking the senses from the man herself as his gruff voice echoed around the hall.

'My master's name is none of your concern. He sends you this as an adequate introduction.'

Robert took the proffered scroll and unrolled it. His face darkened with each word he read. There was a heavy silence before he eventually said, 'I am having trouble deciding if your master is an over-bold man or a coward.'

'How dare...'

Mathilda sent up a prayer to Our Lady as she saw the Robert's angry countenance, hoping he wouldn't do anything foolish.

'I dare because this is *my* home. You will kindly remember that I invited you in. While you are on my territory you will conduct yourself in a seemly manner no matter how *low* your normal standard of behaviour!'

'Low? You, a Folville, a man from a family of murderers and felons, accuse...'

'I accuse you of nothing but serving a man too spineless to deliver this threat himself.' A slow grin crossed Robert's face as he brandished the scroll beneath the larger man's nose. However, there was no humour in his voice whatsoever. 'I have no intension of discussing the contents of this missive with you. I suggest you leave before I give in to my instinct and have you imprisoned so that my brother Eustace can shake you warmly by the neck on his next visit.

'Rest assured, the *only* reason that isn't happening is because I'm convinced your master would enjoy some harm coming to you. It would provide him with a perfect excuse to invade this house or report your disappearance to the sheriff. A report that would lead the authorities straight to this manor.'

The messenger didn't move a muscle. Mathilda guessed from his fleeting expression of disquiet that what Robert had said was sinking in. Was he considering the notion that his master, far from giving him the honour of this duty, had expected him to be a sacrificial lamb?

Not replying to Robert's surmise, he said, 'And your reply to my master is?'

'Tell him to be careful what he wishes for.'

'Only that?'

'Precisely that.'

'And do you agree to what he asks?'

'I can't imagine anyone ever agreeing with him. I suspect he'd be disappointed if they did. It would remove his excuse for violent reprisal.'

The messenger snorted. 'Clever words won't change anything, Folville.'

'I will take that as you agreeing with me about your master's temperament.' Robert looked past the man's head. 'Allward, escort our visitor to the gates. He is leaving.'

Brushing his shovel-like hands together, the messenger turned on his heel. As he did so, Mathilda edged into the kitchen. Putting a finger to her lips to tell Sarah to remain quiet, she hovered in the doorway to watch the stranger leave. The confidence of the man was as unsettling as if he'd drawn the dagger he wore so boldly at his waist and waved it in her direction.

Mathilda drew out of the shadows a fraction as Allward led the man across the courtyard. Robert was keeping closer than he normally would, bringing up the rear as if to make sure that the messenger left as instructed.

Glad of her thick cloak as she waited in the doorway, Mathilda watched carefully as the messenger mounted his ride and steered it towards the gateway. A bay horse, well built to withhold the bulk of its rider. The man wore good boots, and his demeanour was more that of a well-fed steward than a desperate outlaw.

'You would do well to take note of the message, Folville. My master is not a patient man, and I'm sure you do not wish for another of your household to suffer damage.'

Robert had only got this sword halfway out of its scabbard before their unwanted guest swung his horse to face the kitchen doorway. The man stared straight at Mathilda, his face set in a leer.

'A fine woman, Folville.'

Seconds later, he was gone, leaving nothing but a pool of icy mud where his horse's hooves had churned the earth.

~ *Chapter Three* ~

Robert's anger that Mathilda had slipped into the sight of the visitor was capped only by the realisation that the messenger was responsible for harming Sarah. What tipped his anger into rage was that the poor excuse for a man had been in his home *and* left again in one piece.

'Tell me! Please, my Lord,' Mathilda stepped back as Robert slammed his sword into place, 'what was his message?'

Before he replied Robert called for Allward. 'You are to take this scroll to my elder brothers. Stop at Leicester first to see my Lord Eustace. Show him this and bid him give you food and ale to sustain you for the rest of your journey towards my Lord John in Huntingdon. It is John that the parchment is destined for, although I advise you to stand aside when Eustace reads it. He will explode like a thatched roof in a fire.'

'Yes, my Lord.'

Allward had already run from the kitchen to the stables when Robert called after him. 'Be careful, lad. Return safely.'

As soon as Allward had ridden from the courtyard, a thick cloak wrapped around his slight frame, Robert called to the stable boy. 'Daniel, you will attend to the household fires for Sarah until Allward's return. Go now, the hall blaze is failing.'

A mumbled, 'Yes my lord,' was lost in the boy's dash to the hallway as Robert returned to his seat on the bench at the kitchen table.

He was too calm. Far too calm. Mathilda could feel her shoulders tense as she and Sarah waited in expectant silence for Robert's outrage to erupt.

It didn't come. Instead a deadly peacefulness had settled on the Folville. He spoke with a deliberation that brooked no argument at all. 'Mathilda, I will need you to assist Sarah in the necessary household preparations. My brothers will be here within a day or two.'

'Certainly, my Lord.' Mathilda curtseyed, knowing when to hold her tongue.

Robert turned his attention to Sarah. 'You saw our visitor leave?'

'Yes, my Lord.'

'Have you ever seen him before?'

'No. He may have been one of my attackers, but I can't say for sure.' Sarah closed her eyes briefly to aid her thoughts. 'His hands were certainly big enough, I suppose. I recall, now I've seen him, that the hand over my mouth was large. It covered my lower face completely. The man who attacked me didn't talk so well, though. Your messenger was well-spoken. The outlaw I heard was not. I'm sorry my Lord, I've only just remembered. It's all such a blur.'

'Your wits were knocked from you; the apology is his to make, not yours.'

Mathilda took the cloak from her shoulders and wrapped it around the older woman, who shivered despite her clear attempts not to.

Robert regarded them both sternly. 'Neither of you are to

go out of this house alone. Do you understand? You do *not* go beyond the gate without an escort until I say otherwise.'

The women nodded.

Robert, not keen to share what was in the message, but knowing he'd get no peace from Mathilda until he did, said, 'Let us go into the hall and get Sarah by the fire. I'll explain as much as I can. But not one word, not a single word goes beyond this hall unless my brothers say so. Understood?'

Listening to the crackle of the newly topped-up hall fire, Mathilda took comfort in the heat of the flame as she helped Sarah onto a cushioned bench.

Waiting until Mathilda and Sarah were settled, Robert explained, 'You will have heard rumours of an outlaw in the area. Not unusual in these days of unrest. The chaos from London, which spreads with increasing speed across England, makes it inevitable that wolfshead activity will increase. How a country is supposed to function when King Edward is a puppet to the whims his mother, Isabella, I don't know.'

Catching the look of impatience in Mathilda's eye, Robert cut to the point. 'It seems the outlaw rumours were true. And I am not, in this case, referring to honourable men thrust outside the law in the style of Robyn Hode. Here we have a selfish, greedy, power-mad fool. That messenger was from the heart of that fool's very lair. It appears there is a contender for chief criminal retainer in the area.'

Mathilda's forehead creased pleasantly as she thought out loud, 'He didn't look like an outlaw, good or bad. What did the message say?'

'My family, *our* family, has been challenged. If the Folvilles don't agree to arrange to let them, whoever *they* are, share in all our...arrangements, there will be consequences.

Consequences which the message made clear would be far worse than the injury of a servant. I have been *instructed*, instructed you'll note rather than invited, to be at The Thwaite the evening after next. Once there, I am to discuss terms to surrender a large part of the Folvilles' retaining base.'

Sarah sucked in a painful breath as Mathilda leant her elbows upon the oak table, seeing precisely why Robert had summoned his brothers to arrive earlier than their wedding date.

'You are dying to speak, future wife; do so before the words boil from your mouth in front of Eustace. His amusement at how I allow your opinion to be heard will grate on my nerves today. Let's have it before he arrives.'

'The man's boots were good. New, even. And they fitted. It was as if they'd been made especially for him. Are you sure he is an outlaw, living in the forest? How could such a man afford that? A chance boot theft that resulted in so good a fit seems unlikely.'

'You do not believe he is living wild.'

'I know there is an outlaw hereabouts. He's been spotted, albeit fleetingly. But reports say he is alone. As the message itself establishes, our unwelcome visitor isn't a man alone. Nor does he speak for a reckless loner. He is a bully and speaks for another of his kind. Bullies rarely work without others backing them up.'

'A family?'

'Perhaps. Like the Coterels over in Derbyshire, maybe, but closer to home.'

Robert was thoughtful. 'If you're right, Mathilda, then this is more serious than a few desperate men trying to extort our connections from their woodland hideaway. The Coterels at least share values with us.'

'Robert!' The tone of Mathilda's voice cut, and Robert

had the good grace to look sheepish.

'Yes, I know, the Coterel brothers are no saints, but nor are my brothers and I. Yet neither they, nor we, would do this. Together we have targeted the basest of corrupt officials. The Coterels would not attack one of my servants on the doorstep. That was a cowardly act, and Nicholas and John Coterel are anything but cowards.'

'Not now, maybe... but perhaps in the past, when you were all testing your new-found influence? As a show of strength?' Mathilda spoke carefully, not wanting to offend.

Acknowledging the uncomfortable truth with a dip of his head, Robert said, 'If this is a noble family testing its mettle, then we need to be on our guard.' He rose to see if his steward, Owen, had returned, but Mathilda put out a hand to stop him.

'There's something else.'

Robert frowned. 'What do you mean?' What else do we need?'

'Someone has been taking food from the store in the night.'

'What?' Robert's shout echoed through the room 'Why didn't you say?'

'Are you going to stay calm long enough for me to tell you; because I don't think it has anything to do with what happened to Sarah, nor with the messenger. Yet it occurs to me that the soul it does concern is in danger of becoming a scapegoat for whatever else is going on around here.'

'What in Our Lady's name are you talking about Mathilda? I think you'd better start from the beginning.'

The afternoon of Sarah's attack, Mathilda reported, she had been working late in the kitchen, making a thin broth to tempt the housekeeper with once she'd come to her wits.

She thought she'd heard something moving outside. The yard had already been secured against the early winter night, so the slight shuffling sound had alerted her attention.

When Mathilda had gone to investigate, there had been no sign of anyone. On entering the stores however she'd discovered that a few apples had been knocked over. As she'd looked around she had wondered if everything else that should have been there, was there. Nothing was obviously missing, so she had assumed all she'd heard was the fall of badly balanced fruit. The following evening, though, she'd listened out on purpose, and again heard the soft shuffle of something that sounded very much like feet. Waiting until the noise had passed, her heart beating fast, Mathilda had gone to check, and found that two apples were missing.

At the time, she explained, she'd decided not to say anything to Robert, as he was already in a fury about Sarah's attack, and thinking that only the very desperate or very stupid would steal from the Folvilles, Mathilda had been convinced that someone with a score to settle against the family would have caused as much damage as possible, not just scrumped a few apples.

Convinced her instinct was correct, and that the minor theft from the store was nothing to do with Sarah's attack, Mathilda had kept her suspicions to herself.

'I decided to test my theory before I accused an innocent man of theft. So the following night I baked three extra loaves of bread, making a distinctive cross pattern in the top. I sprinkled them with flour and crept out into the store to leave them as tempting bait.'

Mathilda had spoken into the flames of the fire as she relayed what had happened until that moment. Now she squarely faced her future husband, 'I checked that Sarah was alright. Then I waited until the household was asleep, before hiding at the back of the store.'

Robert sighed. 'I ought to be angry. I *am* angry; yet at the same time... well, let's just say I'm sure you were born to be a member of this household.'

Touched and surprised by her future husband's calm acceptance of what she'd done, Mathilda took up her story again, 'The more I thought about it, and the fact that no damage had been done and only a tiny amount of food had been taken, convinced me that this thief isn't greedy. This is a person who needs to eat. This is a question of survival, and having found a good supply of unguarded food, they dived in and out at speed, taking what they could consume instantly, and hopefully, what won't be missed. I thought however, that the lure of fresh bread last night would be too hard for him to resist.'

'Last night!' This time Robert did shout, but Mathilda held up her hand placating him.

'Yes, last night. I crouched behind the barrels of cider. I didn't have to wait long. That was when I knew I should have told you, my Lord. I was anxious, and your comforting presence was missed. Especially when a shadowy figure sidled into the store. I could hardly even hear his breathing. This person had learnt to be careful.'

'Get to the crux, woman!' Robert barked in exasperation.

'The man hesitated in the doorway. He hadn't expected the loaves. His hand hovered over them for ages while his eyes stayed on the apples he'd evidently returned for. I guess he was weighing up if he could hope the missing loaf would be blamed on theft by a dog or some such.

'In the end I got fed up with waiting for him to do something. He was just stood there, staring longingly at the bread. So, *without* showing myself, I spoke to him.'

'Saying what? And I hope you truly did keep to the shadows that time!'

'I did, my Lord. I said, "You must be extremely hungry to invade this particular household." He ran to the door straight away, but I called after him. I said, "Enjoy the bread, I made it for you." That's when he stopped and turned to where I was crouched.

'He asked me why I'd baked for him. I told him only a desperate man steals from a Folville, so he must be truly in dire need of food. He stuttered, "A Folville…?", then he ran. I doubt he'll be back. He had no idea this was your manor, Robert, I'm sure of it. Which means this man is not connected with today's loathsome messenger.

'Why in the name of all that is Holy didn't you tell me? Why so reckless? Honestly, woman!'

'I was going to tell you this morning, but our conversation was interrupted by a messenger.'

Incensed that someone had dared steal from them, Robert threw his tankard of ale at the fire. 'There was a time when the Folville name was enough to keep the thieves away. Is the state of the country so bad that I have to employ a guard dog?'

Sarah, who had stared into the glow of the flames while Mathilda told her tale, wrapped the shawl tighter around her shoulders. 'You were reckless, Mathilda. I wish you hadn't done that. If anything had happened to you...'

Seeing the concern on Sarah's face, Mathilda relented. 'I'm sorry. I didn't mean to take risks, but I knew I was safe. Although now I'm not sure I could explain why I felt that way.'

'I remain unconvinced. With someone trying to muscle in on Folville rule, then...'

A clatter from outside the hall made Sarah start, and Robert jump to his feet.

'Forgive me, my Lord.' The steward walked with long purposeful strides to his master. 'Two new attacks on merchants passing through the area. I regret to report that your fears are looking well-founded.'

Mathilda's eyes narrowed as she looked at Robert. 'I am not the only one holding back news, then.'

'I was also going to tell you this morning.'

'But you were also interrupted by the messenger?'

Robert was about to respond, when he caught the steward's eye. 'I too have news, Owen. I will find you in the yard shortly.'

As the steward inclined his head in respect and left, Robert turned to Mathilda, 'Are you truly convinced our nighttime visitor is simply a hungry man on the run?'

'Yes.'

'Well, I'm not. The hours until the meeting at The Thwaite tomorrow night are thinning fast. Whether this man is connected to whoever I am to meet, there is a very real threat to the Folvilles' reputation here.'

Keeping her voice level, Mathilda reasoned, 'Which is why I'm sure our bread thief is not connected. As soon as he'd heard the Folville name he fled.

'And so he should!'

'I think you should go and find him.'

'What?'

'Go and find him, Robert, before your brothers arrive. If Eustace gets to the thief first, then all hell will break loose.'

1306

Closing his eyes obediently, the boy turned his worries into prayers as he knelt against his simple cot in the small stall that formed his only private place in the entire abbey.

He couldn't help thinking that Brother Mark was looking weary. It wasn't like him to lose his smile. Of all the Augustine brothers, he was usually both the calmest and the happiest.

I bet I know what's troubling him. But what if I'm wrong?

The boy had been warned about telling tales and speaking out of turn, and so he said nothing about his concerns for Brother Mark. He watched, though. And as he watched, despite being but six years old, he learnt; quickly.

There was a new pupil in the almonry; Richard. His family had paid for him to be educated in the Abbey. He hadn't been abandoned and made sure everyone knew it. There were no humiliating tales in his background.

Brother Mark said it was wrong to hate, but he couldn't help it. Richard inspired hate by laughing when bad things happened.

And he had cruel eyes.

~ *Chapter Four* ~

Following Robert to the yard, Mathilda continued to try and reason with him about the food thief. 'I truly believe you should go and find the man once you've spoken to Owen. He can't be that far away, and you know every inch of your land inside out.'

'All right, I'll go! But only so I can string him up and shut you up!' Robert sweetened his tone, 'you have a kind heart, Mathilda, but I can't help thinking that there has to be a connection between this thief and the upstart.'

Mathilda smiled up at Robert's annoyed face, taking his arm. 'And I remain unconvinced, but either way, we should help him. I think he might be useful to us.'

Stopping in his stride towards the stables, Robert studied Mathilda's expression more carefully, 'Useful? How?'

'Wouldn't an assistant be useful? A previously unknown assistant that you, and indeed the family as a whole, could use to help investigate the other matter?'

'You aren't making sense.' Robert gestured his thanks to Daniel as he led his horse from the stable.

Knowing she was losing his attention, as Robert began to check over his saddle and bridle, Mathilda spoke more urgently, 'A man who is hardy and strong, as this man must be to survive out on a winter's night on the run, could help us. We have to assume this threat to the Folville family has not set eyes on all of your brothers. The messenger's master will not yet be aware of what Eustace, John and the others look like. How would they know if they were talking to a true Folville or not while meeting in the wood at Thwaite?'

Robert spoke slowly. 'You think we should get this winter outlaw to pay for his food by posing as a Folville at the meeting tomorrow?'

Suddenly remembering her place, Mathilda said, 'only if you think the man suitable, my Lord; then he might be helpful, although I'm not sure exactly how yet.'

As they considered the potential benefits of Mathilda's idea, Robert called to Owen, 'You had news for us?'

'My Lord, Mistress Mathilda. My tidings are not good. A group of men invaded the town's tavern last night. Four barrels of Jacob Lock's ale were stolen and several of his men have sore heads from being knocked about with a cudgel.'

'Lock's?' Mathilda had never set foot in the inn at the corner of Market Street in Ashby Folville, but its reputation for being a popular place for the town's men folk to discuss the issues of the day over a flagon of Jacob's finest ale was well known.

Owen was solemn. 'They left a message saying that, as the tavern was on *their* land, Jacob had a duty to pay for that privilege. The men said they'd return to collect a tithe of four barrels of ale in lieu of rent at the beginning of every month.'

Robert and Mathilda exchanged glances, before telling Owen about their own unwanted visitor.

Placing a hunk of bread and some ale into his saddlebag, Robert explained to the steward about their other problem. 'It seems we also have a lone outlaw sheltering hereabouts. I'm away to track him down. You'll accompany me, Owen, and we'll discuss tactics to curb the scope of this would-be retainer.'

'You swear you gave no clue as to my identity or our whereabouts, Edgar?'

'I swear, my Lord.'

Rowan Leigh reclined against his sheepskin covered chair. He felt the familiar warm glow of power as his messenger called him 'my Lord.'

The confident smirk on his face was momentarily hidden by his tankard of ale, only to be revealed again so he could dismiss Edgar towards his next task.

Rowan placed the cup on his bench. Although he was satisfied that his orders had been fulfilled, he hadn't yet decided if he was pleased to see his messenger return.

He'd been convinced that the Folvilles would hold Edgar as their prisoner. Either they weren't as ruthless as their reputation foretold, or, whichever brother was in residence at the moment was brighter than he'd assumed and had realised that keeping Edgar hostage would invite an invasion of the manor.

'Well, all they've done is delay that invasion!' he muttered with determination.

Rowan Leigh had spent years working out how to achieve the status in life he craved - a status he believed he deserved. Now, he treated each step towards his goal with consideration, wary resolve and violent care.

He had toyed with the idea of changing his name. It's very meaning, *from the field*, rubbed in his unfairly humble origins. Leigh had dismissed the idea however. He'd discovered from an early age that it was easier to lie if you were surrounded by truths. Rowan sat back and reflected on his past.

Found as a newborn baby, abandoned in a field near a rowan tree, he'd been taken in by the Augustine monks of Launde Priory, before being taken to Leicester Abbey. Stuck there until the age of fourteen, when he'd been apprenticed to a carpenter working just outside Lubbesthorpe, Rowan had little love for the men who'd pushed their hard, prayer-filled, way of life upon him.

Yet, in his rare moments of gratitude, Rowan knew he should be thankful that he'd been taught to read and write as if he was a nobleman. Something he'd convinced himself from an early age he must be. He could not believe the monks' assertion that a wanton woman had found herself with child and, not wanting a fatherless baby, had left him to take his chances. Rowan had decided he was the loved child of a nobleman that had been kidnapped and left to die. In his mind that gave him bearing and the right to wealth and property.

As a child he had built up vivid images of his distraught parents searching for him in vain that he'd shared with his schoolmaster, Brother Mark.

Normally Brother Mark was the only kind face in the place, but Rowan had been shaken to the core when the monk had dismissed his happy imaginings as pure folly. The monk had had the front to tell Rowan that he was simply unwanted. Just like that. *Unwanted.* As if that was alright; as if it was nothing to worry about now he had a roof over his head and food in his belly.

It had been that moment, that smiling, dismissive crushing of his dreams, which had sown the seed of his future self. And once that seed had taken root, it had grown quickly, until the moment it had blossomed into full obsession. The total unwavering belief that he had been born deserving more.

Having learnt the trade of carpentry, Rowan had discovered something he was naturally gifted at, and soon built a reputation as an excellent carpenter. That was not his only reputation, however.

In his mind he'd been mistreated by the mother who left him, mistreated by the church that raised him, and bullied by his master. He told himself he'd been raised to see cruelty as the only means of progress, and that he'd use it only to get to where he intended to be.

Rowan had taken over the property on the outskirts of Lubbesthorpe from his deceased master's elder son, who had been killed fighting in France. Seeing this as a stroke of luck and a positive sign from God - who clearly supported his desire for respect and power by saving him having to murder the lad as he'd planned - Rowan had quickly made changes to the workshop. The small staff who'd worked there were dismissed, and Rowan slowly began to establish a different type of following.

Leigh had chosen his companions with care. All of them had reason to be grateful to him; he'd seen to that. Ex-soldiers, criminals, outlaws; his small but loyal retinue came from the scores of dispossessed men returning from the foreign wars with no work or families to go back to.

He grinned slowly. Word was quietly spreading. It was beginning to be whispered that there was a man with a group of followers in the area who would do anything - for the right price. If you knew where to find them.

Rowan took another slug from his tankard before getting to his feet and pulling an axe towards him. It was time to chop some logs into workable pieces of wood. It was a job he could have given to any of his men, but he liked to keep his strength up.

As the first swipe of the axe hit the carefully placed log

he replayed his plan through his head. If he was to prove that his retinue was more powerful than the Folvilles, then he was going to have to damage them publicly. He needed negative rumours about them to spread through the county.

Unlike the Folvilles, who worked by forming financially beneficial alliances beyond the family, Rowan was operating by keeping everyone he could as close to his side as possible; either via loyalty or blackmail. Because that was how a family worked, wasn't it? With one man in charge, preferably a lord, and everyone else obeying that man. And now the man they'd be obeying was him.

He'd been denied the rightful nobility of a family as a child, so he was going to have one now. In fact, Rowan Leigh was determined to have a lot of things that life had previously denied him. Expecting his men to call him 'my Lord' was just the start.

The second blow of the axe took his mind to the forthcoming meeting at The Thwaite. Rowan had no doubt that Robert de Folville would be there. His curiosity alone would spur him forward. However, none of the Folvilles were foolish. Rowan knew he was going to have to conduct his men with care. Not that he had any intention of attending the woodland meeting himself. The longer his face remained unknown, the better. The role of messenger this time was to go to Rowan's right arm, Gamelyn. At least, that's what he chose to call himself after hearing tales of his favourite outlaw hero. His real name had been left on a battlefield in Rouen, and no one was reckless enough to ask him why.

Gamelyn had been Rowan's luckiest find so far. An association he had to thank his benefactor for. It grated Rowan's nerves that he needed a benefactor at all, yet despite his illusions, he was realistic enough to know that he wasn't yet wealthy enough to go without noble backing. When he was, well, he'd cut his benefactor dead. Literally. Unless of course, he was willing to pay to keep his involvement with Rowan Leigh's enterprise quiet.

The promised collaboration would last until Rowan had removed the power of the Folvilles in the region and taken their lands. That was the deal. Which was fortunate, because that was all Rowan had required from his benefactor in the first place. It was essential that he took everything the Folvilles had acquired, the land they controlled and - most important of all - the officials they had in their pockets. A crooked smile crossed Rowan's face; perhaps, if Edgar's report had been correct, he'd acquire himself a wife. The young woman his messenger had noticed in the company of Robert de Folville sounded a most suitable candidate for the role.

~ *Chapter Five* ~

Robert and Owen reined in their horses. They'd been methodical in their search, visiting each known bolthole, shed, hut and abandoned building on the Ashby Folville estate from west to east.

'He could have fled, my Lord.'

Robert looked grim as he stared across the field before them. There was an abandoned sheep shelter against the far wall. 'I'm not so sure. I think he will leave now he knows whose land he's on, but not until nightfall. There have been no firm sightings of this elusive outlaw, so he has to be operating by night.'

Circling his horse around to face in the direction of the shelter, Robert gestured to Owen to copy the pattern they'd adopted at each of the other locations they'd searched that day. Approaching from either side so that escape routes were cut off, they walked their mounts slowly across the frost covered earth.

On arrival, Owen jumped lightly from his saddle and, tethering his horse to a nearby tree, crept forwards.

There was no door, just an opening in the wooden hut so that sheep could huddle together, covered against the worst of the winter weather. However, it had been years since any sheep had been kept in this field, which had been parcelled into strips of land for the locals to work - yet there was a heap of stale hay piled at the furthest point from the doorway. To Owen's expert eye, it was arranged in a way that didn't suggest its placing by Mother Nature alone.

A grave nod from Owen to his master saw Robert dismount. Walking together, both well practised in the art of moving without making a sound, the men closed in on the lump of hay. Silently they observed as the tiny telltale rise and fall of straw gave away the fact that someone was soundly asleep beneath the mouldy blanket.

Owen pointed to one side. A half-eaten loaf, liberally covered in flour, with a mark in the top that Robert knew to have been made by Mathilda, was carefully wrapped in a piece of fabric to be finished later.

Wasting no time, Robert crouched down and shook the sleeping man, shouting orders at him before he'd come to his senses.

'You will accompany us!'

Fear crossed the outlaw's face, before being replaced by a flash of relief, as if the people before him weren't the cause of his nightmares, before fearful caution wisely took control of his features.

Robert stood back, giving the older man time to rise to his feet. 'I would strongly advise you not to bolt. I promise you, whoever you're fleeing from; they are nothing compared to the peril of running from my family.'

Adam opened his mouth to speak, but Robert gestured to the flour that covered his hands in unspoken accusation.

'Your hands betray you, so I wouldn't bother denying that you stole from my food store.'

'I had no intention of denial.' Adam brushed his hands against his already dirty hose. 'Forgive me, my Lord Folville. I simply needed to eat.'

'You seem very sure that Lord Robert will find this man.'

'I am. He knows where to look.' Mathilda smiled at Sarah who was casting her critical eye over the roll of fabric which had been purchased for the wedding dress. Since being knocked into the mud by the attackers, it had been scrubbed three times, and at last it was looking as if the housekeeper was going to declare it clean enough to cut into shape.

'Had it occurred to you that this outlaw might be better off without Robert finding him?'

'Honestly, yes it has. However, with a greater danger rearing its head, I think any opportunity for extra help should be grasped with both hands.'

'And if he isn't the tragic figure of pity you have painted him to be?'

'Then Robert will deal with him or hand him to the sheriff's men.'

Sarah laughed. 'To think you were a terrified wee thing when you arrived here. Now you are throwing a man into the very dungeon you once occupied.'

Mathilda kept her eyes on the fabric, denying herself the flicker of apprehension she still felt at the memory of what could so easily have happened to her if the disgraced Rector of Teigh had managed to make things go his way. 'He will only end up in there if that is what he deserves.'

Further discussion on the point was halted when the unmistakeable sound of horses entering the courtyard made the women turn from the material.

Leaving Owen to resume his duties, Robert herded the resigned and tired outlaw into the manor. Mathilda saw that the bread thief's wrists had not been bound, and she hoped this was because her theory about him not being dangerous had proved correct.

Stood in the hall before the outlaw, Robert spoke. 'Your name?'

'I am Adam Calvin, my Lord. I was steward to Lord John de Markham of West Markham.'

Adam was older than Mathilda had expected. As she observed his quiet but clearly worried demeanour, she was again reminded of her own initial encounter with the Folvilles. This time she sat on the bench in the hall beside Robert, in front of the fire. That first time, she'd been the prisoner, until life had revealed it clearly had a different plan for her.

'West Markham is a good way from here. Beyond Nottingham. What brings you onto my land?'

Adam, obviously trying not to show he was frightened, opened his mouth to speak, but Robert, who'd been staring at his bedraggled figure, added a warning. 'I am sure you have heard of the Folvilles. Our reputation is not a forgiving one. I suggest, therefore, that it is an honest tale you tell. Begin.'

Stumbling over his words as first, Adam told his story.

He explained how he'd learnt to be careful, moving by night, and hiding by day as he made the long journey from West Markham in Nottinghamshire to the border of Leicestershire, eventually hiding in the abandoned hut where they'd found him.

It was there that he'd made the decision to stop running before he was too far from home to have any chance of clearing his name. But then he'd heard about an attack on a local woman, and afraid of being blamed for that as well, he'd continued to lay low. Only the desperate need for food had seen him venture from the shelter to find sustenance.

Until the attack he'd thought Ashby Folville might be

the town in which he could find work. A place to reinvent himself and regain his strength. It seemed far enough away from home to avoid detection, but close enough to be in the writ of the same sheriff, and therefore there was a chance of discovering what he was accused of - and who had accused him.

As soon as his strength had returned, Adam told them, he'd planned to equip himself to look more like a respectable man and not an outlaw on the run. He had decided he would pretend he was new to the area after time serving in France and was looking for work.

Mathilda listened with interest, relieved that her instincts had not let her down, but Robert was becoming fidgety at Adam's lack of getting to the point. 'You tell us that you are innocent, and that you wish to clear your name. You do not share with us what it was you are accused of?'

'Forgive me, but I truly do not know, my Lord. The first I knew of my reduced situation was when the kitchen lad, Ulric, woke me. In a right state he was; telling me the hue and cry had been called to capture me, and that I had to run.

'So I ran. I don't know what from, but the lad wasn't exaggerating. The pack was on my heels. I lost them and hid on the edge of Sherwood, and then worked my way through it. Not something I wish to have to do ever again.'

Mathilda looked at Robert, expecting him to make some reference to Robyn Hode, but on this occasion, he was holding his tongue on the subject of his outlaw hero. 'And no clue was given?'

'All I can think was that a few things had been going missing in the household. I myself reported them to my Lord Markham; but perhaps I was accused by someone of those thefts. Rumours of a death have also followed me, but whose death I don't know. I wish I did. It might help make sense of the situation.'

Adam shifted slightly closer to the fire. His damp clothes steamed in the heat. He was looking more anxious by the second as Robert stared him at, saying nothing.

Suddenly Robert called for his steward, and Owen, who'd obviously been ordered to be within hailing range beforehand, came to his lord's side. 'Take our visitor to the dungeon.'

Mathilda had to bite her tongue not to intervene as she saw Adam flinch.

'However, I am not inhuman. Master Calvin has been without food or drink for some time. You will give him some ale and broth and equip him with a blanket. I do not wish a death from cold on my hands at the moment. I need to consider the circumstances.'

As a confused Adam trailed after the grim-looking Owen, Robert turned to Mathilda. 'You think he's telling the truth, don't you.'

'I do, my Lord. I think his bemusement is very real. I think he has been wrongly accused as he claims; which means someone else is benefitting from that accusation.'

'What makes you so sure Calvin isn't simply a very good storyteller?'

'I've been there, remember. I stood where he stood. Accused of something I didn't do.'

'I'm hardly likely to forget, am I? But that isn't enough, is it, Mathilda? You're surely not naive enough to think that a woman's instinct, even if it's yours, is going to prove his worth to Eustace.'

'Is it enough for you?'

Holding her brave defiance in check, Robert spoke firmly. 'Calvin stays in the dungeon while *I* decide what to do. I was hoping for someone younger and fitter.'

'So was I, but he can't be that unfit, or he'd never have lasted this long having travelled so far on foot.'

Robert shook his head in a manner that announced that the discussion was closed. 'I can't see how Adam Calvin can be of any use to us at all. Now, if you'll excuse me, Mathilda, I need to talk to Owen about today's other unwanted visitor.'

1307

He couldn't stop shaking as he lay in his narrow cot. Why didn't Brother Mark believe him?

It had been Richard. It was always Richard.

Richard had been the one who'd dropped the ink - on purpose! Richard had torn the last piece of parchment in the school room.

This time Richard had hidden the last of the season's apples from the food store in his room, so he'd got the blame.

He was tired of seeing the very particular smug grin that appeared on Richard's face when he succeeded in getting others accused of the thefts he'd committed. It was a look Richard managed to magically hide the second one of the brothers turned in his direction. No blame ever landed on his shoulders. Richard gazed at the monks through wide innocent eyes; appearing as if he was an angel straight from heaven, even though all the pupils knew he was a demon straight from hell!

The only reason for Richard getting away with so much had to be because he came from a wealthy family. It had to be.

Before Richard had arrived and ruined his life, Brother Mark had always been on his side. He'd dared to secretly hope that he was Mark's favourite; although it was a sin to think like that and so he'd never shared his affection out loud. And then Richard had arrived. It was as if his cruelty and meanness were invisible to anyone over the age of sixteen.

Everything Richard did in public got praised.

Everything Richard did in private hurt someone else.

As they were so close in age, the monks had thought they'd be friends. The monks had thought wrong.

His black eye ached.

He'd told Brother Mark he'd fallen on the church steps. Richard had told him he had to, and he hadn't bothered to argue. He'd begun to believe that the monks would never accept the truth about Richard, even if they'd witnessed one of his cruelties with their own eyes.

~ *Chapter Six* ~

With her hands planted against her hips, her pale complexion blotched pink in frustration that her belief of Adam Calvin's innocence had been so easily brushed aside; Mathilda took three deep breaths before marching after Robert.

Taking care not to speak to him in front of Owen, as she had no wish to humiliate her future husband, Mathilda swallowed her anger and lowered her hands beseechingly. 'My Lord, if I could please say one more thing on the matter before assisting Sarah with the household tasks.'

The look of amusement on Robert's face annoyed Mathilda far more than it ought to. 'I knew you'd be darting after me like a ferret down a rabbit hole. Go on then. I warn you though, Mathilda, I am unlikely to change my mind. Calvin stays where he is until this other matter is over, then he can go.'

'Until it's over?' A glimmer of hope stirred in Mathilda's chest, 'So you don't think he's involved in Sarah's attack after all then.'

'No, I don't, but as I keep saying, I can't see how he can help us. He is safer where he is.'

Ashamed that she'd assumed Robert was ignoring her suspicions, Mathilda acknowledged the truth of what he said. 'Adam's bound to be considered involved if identified as a rogue outlaw. Especially if he's been helping himself to food from other people's stores as well as ours.'

'Indeed, not everyone is as forgiving at having their harvest depleted by men on the run as I am!'

Mathilda rolled her eyes but held her tongue as Robert continued.

'In my position, as head of the local manor, I *have* to be wary. I need to be sure. I can't simply trust your good nature, Mathilda. There is a chance that, although I'm sure you can't countenance such a thing, you may be wrong!'

With a smile, Mathilda said. 'I imagine you'd like some ale, husband-to-be?'

'I would.'

'I was right about that, then.'

Robert laughed, and taking advantage of the fact no one else was around, pulled Mathilda close and kissed the top of her braided red hair. 'Are you always going to be this disobedient, woman?'

'If I feel strongly about something, then yes.'

'I'm very pleased to hear it.' Robert felt Mathilda's slight frame mould against his, 'I'd better let go of you now, my beautiful girl, or there is a danger I won't be able to. Then Sarah would be after me with a zeal far more terrifying than anything my brothers could conjure.'

Reluctantly stepping away, patting her shawl into place after it had got caught on Robert's arm, Mathilda grinned, 'Sarah would defend my honour, I have no doubt. Sadly.'

'Mathilda of Twyford!'

The potter's daughter laughed at Robert's half disapproving, half hopeful expression, before returning to the issue of Adam and the messenger. 'So, what do you plan to do about our situation if you're reluctant to use the decoy that's fallen so helpfully into our laps?'

'Just when I thought you'd dropped the matter.' Robert took the cup of ale Mathilda had passed him. 'How do we know for sure this Calvin is not a spy sent to distract us and collect information for the man who sent the messenger?'

Thinking more seriously, Mathilda said, 'I concede that is possible, but I find it unlikely. I'm sure Adam Calvin is the outlaw we've heard of, pursued down from the north, just as he claims, but nothing more than that.'

'Even if you're right, I need a plan to present to my brothers, with or without the use of Calvin.'

'Well if you'll listen to me for a second, almost-husband, then I'll suggest one.'

Adam wasn't sure if he should feel more or less frightened than he had before. The chill of the cellar was insistent, and the damp was chilling his bones. On the other hand, his gaoler had provided him with a blanket which took the edge off the cold, and he'd had his first cup of hot broth to drink in weeks.

These mixed messages were not what he'd expected to find within the home of a Folville.

When he'd returned to his hiding place in the sheep shelter, on discovering that the bread he'd taken was from the Folville family store, Adam hadn't even had to think about what he had to do. It was obvious. He'd sleep there that night and the following day, staying in hiding in case the infamous brothers were keeping a look out for him. Then he would leave the area as fast as he could. It didn't occur to him that they'd actually hunt him out.

Trying to take comfort from the idea that, if they were going to kill him, surely, they'd have done it straight away and not wasted food on him, Adam let out a ragged sigh. Unless Robert de Folville was waiting for his older brothers to come and cast their judgement on him...

He shivered, and not just from the cold. He was suddenly more exhausted than he'd ever been. Being trapped, all decisions out of his control, he felt defeat and relief him flood him at the same time. However hopeless his situation was, at least his fate wasn't his decision to make any more.

'You'll come with me.'

Adam frowned as the household's steward waited in the open doorway of the dungeon. He squinted against the light. It seemed incredibly bright beyond the small stone space, even though it was the dead of winter and very little natural light could make its way through the manor's small windows.

Moving slowly, Adam kept the blanket around his shoulders as he followed the steward. Moments later he found himself in front of the hall fire again, his clothing steaming with damp.

The woman was still sat with the Folville. Of all the things he'd encountered in his short time in the household, the fact the lord took heed of the advice of his woman was the most surprising.

'Adam Calvin, I may have found a way in which you can repay my family for the trespass you committed against us.' Robert paused, watching the openly stunned expression on the older man's face. 'First, however, I must know more about your situation. I may decide you are not trustworthy enough for the task I have in mind.'

'My Lord.' Adam inclined his head in a short bow. He had no idea what else he was supposed to say.

Robert gestured for Owen to sit at the long wooden table with him and Mathilda, before pointing at Adam. 'You may also be seated, Calvin. Mathilda tells me that the gaol chills the bones very quickly. If you are to be of use to us it would be counterproductive to kill you with cold.'

More confused by the second, Adam gratefully sank onto the wooden bench next to Owen and took the mug of warmed honey water he was offered.

It was quickly clear that this was less an act of kindness from the younger Folville, and more a sensible move to keep his potential asset well. The stern expression on Robert's face as he spoke was not one Adam had any wish to argue with.

'Can you think of any reason, any reason at all, why Lord Markham should have turned on you?' As Robert asked the question, he played the point of his dagger along a groove in the table that his brother, Eustace, had made in a fit of anger some weeks before.

Adam kept his eyes on the line of the blade. There was no doubt who was in charge here. 'No, my Lord Folville, I have thought and thought, but I can think of no reason. As I said before, there had been a few petty thefts over the past few months and the occasional breakage in the kitchens, but I was the one who reported them, not the guilty party.'

'Theft is never petty.'

Adam looked down at his hands as they gripped his cup. The evidence of the flour from the loaf Mathilda had baked to trap him was still visible beneath his fingernails. 'You're right, my Lord. Theft isn't a petty matter. I am truly sorry that circumstances forced me to steal from you. Altogether I took three apples, a loaf and a small jug of cider. Once I've found work, you will be repaid. You have my word.'

'Your word. You want me to accept the word of a self-confessed thief?'

Adam swallowed in the face of the Folville's steely gaze, 'I'm sorry to say, my Lord, that my word is all I have left to offer.'

'And you have no other idea why you were made to flee without a chance to discover the facts? I find your tale of the hue and cry being summoned before an attempt to arrest you had been taken unlikely. You were a sleeping man. Surely no one is easier to capture than a man abed.'

'I can't explain, my Lord. I have asked myself the same question many times. I was loyal to my master always. I had served him as steward for twelve years, and as a servant before that. I had thought myself my Lord Markham's trusted man; his confidant. I was clearly wrong.'

The bewildered sadness that came from the prisoner touched Mathilda's heart, and for a moment she was ashamed of herself for suggesting he be used in a plan to gain the upper hand over the unwanted messenger's master. Surely now, though, Robert must believe that this was not a man in the employ of a ruthless outlaw.

Robert then asked the very question Mathilda hoped he would. 'And you swear to me upon your life that you are not part of an outlaw group?'

'A group? No. It is just me, as you found me. Alone and at a loss as to how to clear my name.'

Mathilda studied Adam's lined face as she asked, 'You intend to try and clear your name?'

'If I can find a way, my Lady.' Adam looked defeated. 'But I have travelled far. If I want to discover the truth, I'll have to return to the heart of my troubles.'

'You'll be killed.'

'Possibly. But if I don't try, then I'll never know who wronged me or why.'

Mathilda gave a sideways glance at Robert as she said, 'I'm not sure if that is a very brave thing to do, or if it's foolhardy.'

'As I said to my Lord Folville, my word is all I have

left. I don't want to meet my maker without at least trying to clear my name. I feel that everything I have ever said and done has been blackened and judged as a lie.'

'You are very brave, Master Calvin.'

'And you are kind, my Lady. If I'm honest, I'm simply tired of not knowing, and tired of running. I was not raised to run away. I fought the French and never ran. Whoever has wronged me in my own home will answer for what he's done.'

Robert's eyes narrowed. 'And how will you ensure that?'

'I don't know, my Lord. Not yet.' Dragging a large palm through his ragged greying hair, Adam sighed. 'I don't suppose it matters now I'm here.'

'You think we're going to kill you?' Robert spoke with no edge. It was not an unrealistic assumption.

'I think the matter is out of my hands, my Lord. Although I should thank you. The blanket, food and drink were most welcome. An act of kindness in an unfriendly land.'

'Don't waste your breath thanking me, Calvin. It is Mathilda to whom you owe thanks.'

Turning to face Mathilda, Adam bowed his head, 'Thank you, my Lady.'

For a few minutes the only sound in the hall was the crackle of the fire licking at its host of logs. Robert and Mathilda regarded their guest quietly as a gust of air down the chimney sent a cloud of smoke billowing into the room. The interruption seemed to bring Robert to a decision, and he laid down his dagger.

'We also have a situation that needs close and urgent attention. If you agree to assist us, Master Calvin, and *if* that help is successful, then I will help you discover who is behind the smearing of your reputation.'

Adam looked from Owen to Robert, to Mathilda, and

back to Robert again. 'You will, my Lord?'

'Do not thank me too hastily. The task we have in mind is not an easy one and the cost could be higher than you're willing to pay for discovering the truth.'

Adam was silent for a while, before saying, 'In doing what you ask, I would also be paying off the debt for my theft?'

'You would.'

'Then perhaps, my Lord, you'd tell me of your plans?'

Moved from the hall, Adam found himself locked in a small storeroom, which had been fitted with a makeshift mattress of straw. Thankful that it wasn't the dungeon, and that he'd been assured he was only there to think about his options, Adam closed his eyes and tried to make sense of what was happening.

Robert had told him that, to make amends for stealing from the Folvilles, he was going to have to commit a crime. In this matter he had no choice. The following evening, in front of a group of rival criminals, he was to pretend to be Simon de Folville; a cousin of the brothers. To add credence, if it was found necessary, he was to pretend to have an understanding with the Folvilles' injured housekeeper, Sarah.

Adam had listened as Robert had detailed the visit from the messenger to the manor and the raid upon the local tavern. The Folville had been careful to point out how easy it would be for people to blame Adam, as a lone, desperate outlaw, for what had happened, rather than to blame the real culprits.

Realising he'd blundered into a heated dispute, and that his own future now depended on helping cement the Folvilles' supremacy in the region, he thought hard. In return for finding out the truth, Robert de Folville wanted to use him in a potentially life-threatening scheme.

'It's a choice without a choice.' Adam rolled onto his back and stared at the stark ceiling.

'I'm as good as dead.'

~ *Chapter Seven* ~

John de Markham stabbed at his food with the point of his dagger.

'Are you sure, my Lord Sheriff?'

Edmund de Cressy had a satisfied grin on his face. His tone was gratingly calm. 'I looked into the matter as you instructed, my Lord. I know you don't want to believe the evidence I've uncovered against your man Calvin, but nonetheless, I *have* uncovered it. The missing objects were found in his cot.'

Markham laid down his knife. 'It isn't just my erstwhile steward I'm angry with, but with myself. I always believed I was a good judge of character. It makes my skin itch to think that he blinded me to the truth for so long.'

Holding his hand up as if to calm his friend, de Cressy said, 'You're not the first master to be treated with contempt by his servant, and I doubt you'll be the last. Adam Calvin knew you well. It was no work at all for him to dupe you. After all, we require our servants to know our thoughts and needs before we have them. Occasionally one or two of them are bound to take advantage.'

'Adam was always loyal and trustworthy, yet now he's gone the spate of thefts has gone with him.' Markham angrily picked up his knife and stuck it into the capon on his plate. The king's serjeant was far more annoyed by his steward's disloyalty than the thefts. 'I always considered Adam amongst the best. Yet, I can see your evidence is overwhelming, Edmund. Then there is the little matter of the weapon used on the body. I cannot deny that the knife you presented to me is Adam's knife.'

Helping himself to some meat, the sheriff said, 'I have instructed my men to keep up the hunt. I'll get justice for you, John. I have Calvin's guilt assured by a trusted approver. It is only a matter of time before the villain is within my net.'

Observing his dining companion shrewdly, John chewed the stringy meat. He spoke judiciously. 'I appreciate your efforts, Edmund, but Adam is no fool. He will be long gone by now. Surely you have far more pressing issues to attend to than pursuing my errant steward. Even with an approver to assure the conviction, I can't see that it's worth your while to chase a minor criminal across England for me.'

'You're a friend. I will not let the matter rest.'

'Why thank you, my Lord Sheriff.' John de Markham kept to himself his growing suspicions that there was more to this business than Adam stealing a few items from his household as he asked, 'So who is this approver of yours? He must have the eyes and ears of a hawk.'

Edmund laughed, reading the lawyer as easily as his steward had done. 'You are unsure of my motives? Come now, you have no reason to doubt me. I assure you the approver is a sound one; but I have promised him his secrecy, and as you have every reason to know, I keep my word when I give it.'

'Forgive me, I find I'm not willing to believe the obvious in this case.'

The sheriff nodded in understanding, 'We've worked

together many times, Markham, using bribes to secure convictions sometimes I admit, but only when we had no choice to get the necessary resolution to a problem. We've always acted for the greater good of all, you know that, John.'

'I do know that.' John's eyes narrowed, as he recalled their one, ill-handled case, when two murderers had ended up paying their way out of a visit to the hangman. An act he bitterly regretted. He wasn't quite sure how de Cressy had talked him into accepting the bribe in the first place. 'I know that very well, and it seems that you are determined not to let me forget it.'

John de Markham watched as the sheriff turned his horse in the stable yard and headed back to his own manor. The approver's name had remained unspoken, but the lawyer had his suspicions.

Muttering as he retired to his chambers, Markham made himself a private promise. 'If I find you've sent my man into a life of outlawry for your own means, de Cressy, then I will convict and send you to the gallows in his place.'

Sitting at his work table, deep in thought; he spoke into the sputtering flame of the candlelight. 'If Adam is the thief, then he'd have taken what he stole to sell so he had money to start a new life with. He would certainly not have left them in the first place anyone who wished to think ill of him would look.'

The king's serjeant sighed, Adam was sure to be a very long way away by now, so the chances of the truth ever being uncovered was slim. Still, he'd be keeping a closer eye on de Cressy. The man had all the castle constables, keepers of the forests, and the foresters themselves to administer, as well as the law of the land. If he was being so attentive over this business, then it was only because there was some profit in it for him. One thing Markham knew for sure; Edmund de Cressy liked profit. With every passing month of his sheriff-ship he seemed to become noticeably more driven – and greedier.

From the shadows, Wilkin Sayer watched as the sheriff rode from the manor house courtyard. Neither man had looked at each other. The risks involved in their working relationship were understood on either side.

The son of a Welsh cooper, Wilkin had been on the run from his home country for several months when he'd managed to wangle himself a position as a minor servant in De Cressy's household. Working carefully, making himself invaluable with his ability to pick up information without detection, and ensuring that work was noticed by his master, it wasn't long before Edmund de Cressy made Wilkin an offer he'd have been a fool to turn down.

Working as a spy and an approver, providing evidence of guilt against suspected criminals - sometimes more creatively than necessary - Wilkin had become very good at his job. He was no fool however; he knew there was a limited life expectancy in being a spy.

After a discussion with de Cressy some weeks ago, the sheriff had promised to find his loyal worker a more comfortable and safer long-term position, providing that he continued to keep his ears open within that household when required.

However, their conversation had taken place when the steward of Markham, Adam Calvin, had been visiting with a message from his master. Wilkin had been convinced that Adam had heard more than he should of the Welshman's working arrangement with de Cressy.

Both sheriff and spy had spotted the opportunity that was

presenting itself to them at the same time. Beyond the sheriff casually asking Sayer if he'd ever considered the post of steward as a career move, they hadn't discussed the idea. John de Markham was a man whom, Sayer had quickly judged, it shouldn't be too difficult to manipulate into looking for a possible replacement steward in the not-too-distant future.

The following day, Wilkin had arrived at the manor of West Markham asking if there was work, claiming his old Welsh lord had passed away, leaving no heir, and that he was a steward looking for a new position. Adam Calvin, not recognising the man from his visit to de Cressy, had liked him, and with a request to his master, had taken Sayer on as senior kitchen assistant in the ever-busy kitchen. A move which Markham, who was plagued with having to host guests with increasing frequency, had wholly approved of.

Within only two weeks Sayer had meticulously set about blackening Adam's name. He'd broken things to start with, items that only Adam was permitted to touch. Then he'd committed intermittent thefts that could easily be blamed on the steward when the time came. A few weeks after that, Wilkin had officially approved the steward to de Cressy, who was duty bound to report the matter to Markham; using the stack of evidence his spy had fabricated.

Seeing the post of steward as the perfect opportunity, with its many lucrative possibilities, to improve his own lot, Wilkin had operated slowly and carefully to avoid any chance of guilt being laid at his own door. His work as a spy had given him more insight than even Edmund de Cressy was aware of. Sayer had only survived this long by making sure he always had more information on the people he worked for than they had on him.

Wilkin hadn't yet told de Cressy that he'd discovered his

plans to increase his influence beyond his scope as sheriff, by retaining criminals. Now, Sayer judged, was the perfect time to let slip what he knew.

Not wanting to make any mistakes and end up like Adam Calvin, rather than accuse de Cressy of harbouring criminals, he added another level to the sheriff's regard for him. He introduced de Cressy to a man of growing underground power in the neighbouring county of Leicestershire. A man who had even more ambition than de Cressy himself.

A man who called himself Rowan Leigh.

~ *Chapter Eight* ~

Mathilda dismissed Daniel, the stable boy who'd accompanied her to Twyford. Leaping joyfully from her horse, she wrapped her arms around her father.

She didn't like to think about how close she had come to losing him and her brothers Matthew and Oswin. Nor did she dwell on the fact that the man she loved was partly responsible for the threat that had once touched her family. Each time she visited the pottery she felt a lightening of her cares, as relief and gratitude that she still had a family home to return to whenever she wished filled her heart.

'To what do we owe this visit, my girl?' Bertred of Twyford hugged his daughter. 'You're not in your finery, so it must be because you knew I'd be off to market and might need a hand. At least that's what I'm hoping.'

Mathilda laughed at his cheekily beaming face. Before she'd been taken as a hostage to his debts many months ago, Mathilda had feared she would never see her father smile again. 'That is precisely why I'm here. I thought it would be nice to travel up to Rotherby with you. Is that alright, Father? I could sell for you while you take orders for future works.'

Giving his daughter another hug, her father said, 'And?'
'And?'

'There must be another reason why you'd put up with sitting in my rickety cart of pots all the way to Rotherby? It's almost in Nottinghamshire, for goodness' sake.'

'It's a good market. I'm so glad you've expanded your selling area.'

'It's easier now your brother Matthew is such an accomplished potter in his own right. I was beginning to think that the family business would die with me.'

Mathilda squeezed her father's hand, not wanting to see his advancing years, as she turned to the cart he'd been loading. 'Shall I help?'

'Should a future lady of the manor concern herself with such menial tasks?'

'Are you teasing me, Father?' Mathilda laughed as she tucked her shawl into her leather girdle and picked up a stack of beautifully turned tankards.

'Yes.' He momentarily looked more solemn, 'I'm glad you've come, lass. Matthew and I miss you.'

'I miss you too. And Oswin.'

Bertred's face broke into a grin. 'He'll be home soon too.'

'He will?' Mathilda owed her younger brother so much. He'd gone into the service of the Folvilles' sometime associates, sometime rivals, the Coterels, and helped save her from the evil plans of Richard Folville, the disgraced rector of Teigh. A man who was now safely out of the way in France.

'Has Nicholas Coterel let Oswin leave his service?'

'The agreement was for four months' work. That is now over. I believe he was offered the chance to stay, but he has decided to come home to help me.'

Mathilda felt a knot of guilt in her stomach. 'I'm sorry I'm not here more often, Father. How are you managing with the house?'

'Don't you fret, child. We manage well enough, and I dare say Matthew or Oswin will take a wife soon enough to assume those duties.'

Adding a scattering of straw around the pots in the cart to help stop them cracking on the journey, Mathilda clambered on board. She decided not to tell her father that the decision to help him today wasn't entirely benevolent; nor had it been her idea.

Robert had been in the kitchen earlier than Sarah that morning. One look at his face had told Mathilda that he hadn't slept well, if he'd even bothered to go to bed at all. She hadn't wasted her breath asking him what was wrong. It was obvious that he'd have been planning how to play the meeting that evening in The Thwaite.

Over ale and bread he'd called a brief meeting between himself, Mathilda, Owen and Sarah. Robert had told them he'd worked out how Adam could help, and he was determined to honour his part of the bargain in return and find out who was blackening Adam's name. Robert had suggested that the next time Mathilda's father went north to a market, she should go with him; keeping her ears open to try to discover if the posse hunting Adam was still active. Knowing that the wait for nightfall to arrive would take forever, Mathilda had been grateful that Rotherby market was that day and had agreed to leave for Twyford at once. She might as well be busy and useful, rather than sitting around fretting.

Sarah, glad to have a moment to herself, scrubbed the immense table in the hall with her good arm. In just a few hours the entire family would arrive at the Ashby Folville manor.

The housekeeper stared at the wood she was lovingly cleaning. Eustace would no doubt make new grooves in the oak. Ever since he'd been old enough to own one, Eustace had always fiddled with his dagger. Lord John on the other hand would be calm, considering everything that was said before announcing what would be done in a way that brooked no argument. Sarah smiled as she thought of the boys she'd helped rise to adulthood. Walter, Thomas and Laurence, always similar in both looks and personality, would sit silently at the table, listening, each as eager for the next time they could act in retribution; each reserving their inbuilt rage until it was truly required.

Still nursing her bruises, she put down her brush and ran a tentative finger over the scar on her arm. It was knitting together well thanks to Mathilda's quick work with warm water, herbs and bandages, but it was unlikely she would ever be able to undertake the level of labour she'd managed before.

Allowing herself a rare sit down in the domain of the lords, Sarah sighed. What use could she be to the brothers if she was weakened? It was as if her wound had brought her advancing years into sharper focus. An unwanted and yet timely reminder of her own mortality. Once Mathilda was the lady of the house, would they want her around?

Pulling herself out of her moment of self-pity, she got to her feet. 'This won't do. This won't do at all!'

Returning to scrubbing the table she'd cleaned, polished and served food onto throughout her adult life, Sarah cast her mind to the roll of fabric she'd purchased for Mathilda's wedding dress. It would have to be pinned and adjusted on this table, the only one big enough for the task. She'd need to ask Robert's permission to use the main hall but felt safe in the knowledge that he'd agree.

With a last wipe of the ancient oak, Sarah straightened up. It was time to attend to the first of Robert's additional tasks of the day.

Heading to the kitchen to gather the food and drink she'd been told to take to their imprisoned guest, Sarah wasn't sure what use Adam Calvin could actually be. Yet to meet him herself, she had been assured that he'd be no threat to her, but she couldn't help feeling apprehensive. Then, crashing the trencher down on the kitchen table, she growled to herself. 'You were never afraid of anything before. Do NOT let those cowards rob you of your confidence. This is your home!'

Picking the small meal back up, along with the key to the storeroom, Sarah went to meet Adam Calvin for the very first time.

Mathilda had forgotten how much pleasure could be found in selling her father's pottery.

The December morning was buzzing with talk of the Christmas and Solstice celebrations that were just around the corner. The air was clear and crisp. A weak ray of sunshine was doing its best to light the market square.

It had been a very long time since Mathilda had sold for her father, but since the family's fortunes had improved, so had his pottery. Bertred's heavy-duty kitchenware was selling well alongside his new range of more delicate vessels and pots. As Mathilda held the bronze burnished sheen of the beakers up to the light, they shone enticingly. Customers came to look as the glazes caught the sunlight beguilingly.

'You haven't lost your touch with the public then.' Bertred beamed as the pots sold fast. The orders they'd taken for pre-Christmas cooking pots had mounted up to the point he'd had to stop taking requests for fear of not having enough firing time for them all.

'I'm just delighted that you're doing so well again, Father.'

Mathilda had buried herself in being busy, but now, as the earliest shoppers took their wares away, she found the concerns she had about the night ahead barging their way back into her head.

If Robert and his brothers couldn't see off this newcomer, Mathilda wasn't sure what would become of them all. It would only take a change of allegiance for the lawyers, foresters and officials that the Folvilles kept in their pockets, to ruin them all. Determined not to burden her father with her worries, she said, 'Father, would you mind if I had a wander around the other stalls? I want to find something for Robert as a wedding gift.'

'Of course, my girl. I think if you head towards the far end of the stalls you'll find a balladeer. You might even get to hear one of those Robyn Hode tales you're so keen on.'

Mathilda returned her father's smile as she hurried off in the direction he pointed. A Robyn Hode ballad was exactly what she needed to keep the fears at bay. Hoping her father was right, she wove through the bustle of people, keeping her ears wide open as she went.

It had been a long time since Sarah had been in the company of a man of roughly her years.

Adam Calvin hadn't been what she'd expected at all. Not a typical criminal, nor an ambitious noble; not a disillusioned younger son or a lazy man who'd do anything rather than a hard day's work. As she opened the door to the store, Sarah came face to face with someone underweight, badly in need of a wash, a shave, and clean clothes.

Mathilda had been right about this man. This was not a

natural outlaw. This was another of the new breed of outcasts the country was creating with frightening regularity. This was a man who'd been deliberately wronged and cast into the darkness to survive as best he could.

'Thank you.' He took the offered food graciously, his hand shaking slightly.

Sarah observed him with shrewd eyes, deciding to interpret Robert's instructions to prepare him for the night in her own way. 'You'll be needing to wash after you've eaten. I will return shortly with suitable clothes. How tall are you?'

A surprised Adam muttered, 'Six feet.'

Sarah bobbed her head curtly. 'I trust I will not need to relock this door?'

'No. I'll not flee.'

'I will return once I've heated you some water.' Sarah walked away, her mind full of questions she wanted to ask the cautiously gentle man she'd left eating the first bread she'd managed to bake by herself since the attack.

The words of the balladeer wrapped themselves around Mathilda like a comforting blanket. Memories of her late mother singing to her combined with Robert's appreciation of the stories. One of the first things she'd loved about him was how he viewed the fictional outlaw's sentiment as a good yardstick by which to live in these troubled times.

After a while Mathilda pushed herself deeper into the crowds, turning her ears from the melodiously words of the minstrel to those of the ever present rumour makers and gossip-mongers.

It didn't take long to pick up the thread of what she was listening for. The whispers criss-crossed over each other, but it was clear that general feeling had Edmund de Cressy, sheriff of Nottinghamshire and Leicestershire, on the warpath after a criminal had slipped through his fingers. The reason why he'd been harsher and more intent to capture and punish this lost felon remained unspoken, and so Mathilda returned to help her father.

Travelling home, earlier than planned and triumphant that all their wares had been sold, Mathilda's father told her to keep her eyes open for signs of danger. He told Mathilda that while she'd been looking for a gift for Robert, he had heard word that a felon had escaped from the sheriff's posse and was presumed on the run in the area.

While Mathilda cursed silently for having been away from the stall at precisely the time she needed to be there, her father added, 'I'm glad Robert has the sense to send you abroad escorted. Will the stable-hand be coming to collect you from the pottery? I don't want you travelling alone if there is a desperate felon on the loose.'

Not telling him that the desperate felon in question was living in her store cupboard and was not the man they should be worried about, Mathilda merely nodded. She'd allowed herself to become wrapped up in the pleasure of the day, but now reality and the task that awaited her future husband came rushing back.

Until that moment Mathilda hadn't let herself consider that Robert might not return from Thwaite Wood. There was no knowing what would happen. The wound on Sarah's arm had been severe enough to make it clear that this newcomer wasn't bluffing in his threats.

'Daniel will be there to collect me, Father, never fear. Robert takes good care of me.'

Daniel was helping Matthew stack the kiln with fresh pots while he waited for Mathilda. Anxious for news about getting help from the other Folville brothers, Mathilda made her excuses to leave her family rather faster than she'd intended.

As she and Daniel set off towards home, Mathilda asked, 'Are they coming?'

'Allward had not returned when I left, my Lady.'

As they rode, Mathilda felt foreboding chill her spine as, in unspoken understanding, they began to travel faster, pushing the trotting horses into a canter. The forest began to encroach on each side, and they pressed the horses further. Yet even when she was going at a gallop, Mathilda couldn't shake the feeling that she was being watched.

'My lord.'

'Gamelyn,' Rowan acknowledged his comrade as he tightened the girth of his horse's saddle. 'You followed her and have news.'

'My Lord, the woman that Edgar spoke of is called Mathilda. She left the house early and went to help her father, the potter at Twyford. She has spent the day with him at the market in Rotherby. She'll return to the Folville manor within the next hour.'

'So she may be at The Thwaite tonight.' Rowan spoke with satisfaction.

'Perhaps. I cannot be sure, but it would be in her nature to accompany her future husband. This particular Folville has found a bride as audacious as himself.'

'But not,' Rowan turned on Gamelyn briefly snarling, before calming his tone, 'as audacious as me. I will see this wench for myself.'

Gamelyn contained his surprise behind a deadpan expression, 'You're coming to Thwaite Wood this evening, my Lord?'

'Only to observe. It would not do to reveal myself yet. I

wish to see this female who is described as *the only woman of the group of any consequence...* then, when victory over the Folvilles is complete, we could celebrate with a marriage ceremony of our own.'

1309

He didn't care anymore. Life was a lot easier now he'd stopped caring. Not caring made you numb. And being numb meant nothing hurt anymore.

~ *Chapter Nine* ~

Robert strode into the courtyard as the sound of horse's hooves thundered across the manor threshold.

'Your countenance is bleak, Allward. Tell me, what news do you bring from Leicester?'

'Forgive me, my Lord, but I do not bring the tidings you hoped for.'

The lad looked fearful, as if he expected to be blamed for the news he had to impart. 'Come now, Allward, tell me all. My brothers are not with you?'

'That is the problem, my Lord. They will be on their way, but none were able to depart on the instant. Eustace is due before the magistrate tomorrow, and it would not serve our purpose if he failed to appear.'

Robert acknowledged the sense in this. If Eustace wasn't on the scene to either accept his fate or bribe the authorities for whatever it was he'd done this time, he'd be no use to the brothers for some time. It was important that, as Eustace was the main reason the family's reputation stayed fearsome and uncompromising in the public domain, he remained free.

'This is a blow indeed, but does not explain why my Lord John, and Walter, Thomas and Laurence are not travelling this way at once.'

'My Lord John is in the family manor at Huntingdon, and although I have sent word, I don't know how fast he'll arrive; although I'm assured he'll come by Lord Eustace's steward. The others I couldn't locate, my Lord. I'm sorry. I left as many messages as I could, but I knew you'd be awaiting my return before this evening.'

Allward wiped sweat from his forehead, and Robert registered for the first time just how hard the boy had ridden to bring him this ill news.

'You did well. The outcome of your mission is not your fault.' Robert took the exhausted mount to attend to himself. 'Go inside and tell Sarah I wish you to have a meal and drink. Then I need you to rest, Allward. I will require your help later.'

'I'm to come with you to The Thwaite, my Lord?'

'You have more than earned your place in my household, Allward. You've served me from a pup. Are you prepared to serve the Folvilles as a man now, rather than a boy?'

'Sir, I am.' Allward thought he might burst with pride as he unbuckled his dagger belt from his waist before going inside the house. 'I have other news, my Lord. Again, I wish it was better.'

Robert looked grave as he pointed towards the kitchen door, 'Time is growing short, let's join Owen in the kitchen to save you relaying your message twice.'

As they entered the housekeeper's domain both men stopped in their tracks at the sight before them. It wasn't just Owen and Sarah at the table; but Adam Calvin, his appearance much changed thanks to the gentle chivvying of the housekeeper.

'Before you explode, my Lord Robert,' Sarah had already pre-empted that her master would have an opinion on her allowing their prisoner out of his secure room, 'Adam is not going anywhere, nor is it in our interests, or his, for him to do so.'

Adam got to his feet and bowed in respect. 'I must thank you, my Lord.' He indicated the clothing that Sarah had found for him. 'I'm told these belonged to you, I'm very grateful for the loan and your kindness. I am more than willing to help you with this evening's endeavour, whether you can help me in return or not.'

'Fine words, Master Calvin, but you owe me anyway, if you remember.'

'I do indeed. I don't forget.'

Robert was silent for a moment before gesturing for them all to be seated. 'You have told our house guest about our run-in with this upstart, Sarah?'

'Little point in delaying if the man is going to help you.' The housekeeper raised her chin and braced her shoulders, giving Robert a glimpse of the Sarah of old.

'Indeed.' Robert sat down opposite his steward, 'No news of Mathilda yet?'

'She'll be home before nightfall. Daniel has gone to Twyford to collect her.'

'I'll be happier when she is back.' Robert glanced towards the courtyard. 'Until I know what we face I don't think, although it pains me to say it, that we can rely on the family reputation to keep our womenfolk safe.'

Allward, looking a little awkward at being afforded the same consideration as Owen by having a seat at the table, rather than standing behind it as usual, coughed politely. 'My Lord, I must tell you my news.'

'So you must.' Robert raised his hands in encouragement for all present to take heed. 'Allward has secured my brothers' help, but it won't be here until tomorrow. Until then we are on our own.'

Sarah's sharp intake of breath did nothing to improve Robert's mood, but he held his tongue, instead saying, 'He also has more news. Allward?'

'I rode through Melton on the journey home. There word reached me that a man, who rumour calls Leigh, and his followers, have thrown their weight around in a similar manner to the inn in Ashby.'

Robert's face coloured crimson. 'Melton? Our family has a longstanding arrangement with the landowner there. We've been dealing with trespassers for them for some years.'

'It would seem, by the chaos that this Leigh and his men caused at the inn, that their demands are far more severe than your family's, my Lord. They appear to have nothing to do with justice, and everything to do with greed and power. This Leigh is demanding a higher tax for all those who come to Melton market to trade, a cut from the inn and a monthly safety payment to all the residents.'

As one, Robert and Owen exchanged a look of understanding. It was the steward who spoke first.

'Allward, are you saying that there was physical evidence that these men, Leigh's men, had secured the cooperation of the authorities in Melton through violence rather than via careful explanation of the wisdom of adopting a protection scheme?'

'I am.'

'Then, according to the terms of the Folvilles' arrangement with the town, we should protect the folk of Melton. If these are not the sort of trespassers we swore to protect them from in exchange for a meagre payment every month, then I don't know who are.'

Robert was already on his feet. 'Owen, you're with me. Allward, I know you're far from rested, but I want you to ride out to Twyford and add to Mathilda's return party. Daniel alone may not be enough.' He spoke faster now, the act of being busy giving strength to Robert's resolve. 'Having a name to fix to this rogue's deeds helps, but we need to know more about this Leigh. I intend to discover more before the allotted hour of the meeting.

'In the meantime, Adam, Sarah, you will work together to prepare for this evening. The swords and daggers in the store need sharpening. Sarah will show you where this can be done, Adam. Sarah, we will need food on our return. Time grows short. If we do not come back before twilight, then you may assume we have gone straight to The Thwaite.'

'But, my Lord,' Sarah was horrified, 'you must return for your weaponry and your brothers may yet make it, even if it is only one of them. And Mathilda, of course.'

'I fear tomorrow is the best we can hope for concerning my brothers. Until then we are on our own - but perhaps not as on our own as I feared. Owen and I will see about rallying our allies in Melton. This Leigh is about to discover exactly what it means to go against the Folville family. As to Mathilda,' Robert turned to Adam, 'rather than accompany me to Thwaite, you will protect them; my future wife and my dear Sarah.'

'I will my Lord. You can depend on it.'

The kitchen felt very quiet once Owen, Allward and Robert had gone.

Adam looked at his hands. He had no idea if he was doing the right thing by staying. He knew there was no one here to stop him from walking out of the house, crossing the courtyard and running, never to come back. Yet if he stayed there was a chance, however slim, that he'd find out who had set him up in West Markham.

On the other hand, Adam also knew that if he did help these people he could end up murdered, or having his neck stretched by the authorities for simply being in the company of known felons.

'You're considering your position.' Sarah's sentence wasn't a question, but a frank statement made without judgement.

'I would be lying if I said I was unafraid of the life that presents itself to me.'

'And you would be unwise, foolish even, to believe you were safe. But if my Lord Robert has vouched that he'll try and help you in return for your assistance, then that is what he will do.'

Adam got to his feet. 'Then I had better get to work. Can you point me in direction of the sharpening strap?'

'I can.' Sarah ran an appraising eye over Adam's new appearance. Since his wash and shave, and the clipping of his previously shaggy beard and greying hair, the ex-steward looked like a different man. No wonder Robert had given him a double-take as he'd sat at the kitchen table.

As Adam reached the back door, he turned and looked at the housekeeper. 'I am remiss. I haven't asked how you fare today.'

Sarah was surprised. 'I'm mending well. Thank you.' She hurried the used flagons together into the water bucket to be cleaned. 'The strap is just inside the door of the external store.'

'She isn't back.'

Adam frowned as he put the small collection of sharpened swords and daggers on the table. Their blades gleamed almost as brightly as the glow of his labour flushed face.

'The Lady Mathilda?'

'Allward should have intercepted her and Daniel ages ago.'

'Was the lad who went for her accomplished?'

'Yes, but young. Normally Allward or Owen would go, but we don't have the household strength these days that we used to have. The family name meant that force of numbers wasn't necessary.'

'But now this Leigh has seen that over confidence and is using it as a chink in the Folville armour.'

Sarah sighed, allowing the concern she'd been holding at bay show on her face. 'If anything has happened to her, I'll never forgive myself.'

'If anything has happened to Mathilda it will not be of your making.'

'I should have been paying attention on the way home from the market that day, then I'd never have been taken by surprise. It's my fault. I was so deep in thought. Planning the wedding dress and...' Sarah broke off as if she remembered who she was talking to. 'That sort of talk won't help, will it?'

'Sometimes sharing a worry helps.' Adam stared at his reflection in the blades on the table. He was about to ask about the housekeeper's attack when the sound of hooves entering the yard propelled them both to their feet.

1310

It had been such a long time since he'd smiled that the gesture felt foreign to him.

He thought he'd imagined it at first, but the friendly clap on the shoulder in congratulations for a job well done that Brother Peter had given him was genuine.

For the first time since Richard had arrived in his life, he felt free. He'd finally found something he could do that would help him make a life for himself outside of the abbey.

He suddenly saw the wood he held in his hands as a gift from the God he'd stopped believing in. This was something he had total control over it. He could shape it, cut it, sand it and mould it into whatever he wished.

A warm glow had started inside him as Brother Peter had proudly announced that he had a special gift. No one had said he had a special anything before.

Better than that. This was his chance to escape the misery of his existence for a few hours a day while he learnt a trade.

~ *Chapter Ten* ~

The innkeeper was in the process of trying to put his tavern back together. As in Ashby Folville, Melton Mowbray's hub had been the spotlight of Leigh's determination to make an impression on the area.

The landlord took one look at Robert and Owen as they walked through the door, and his expression became infused with wariness.

Robert held up a hand in consolatory greeting, 'No, Elias, you have nothing to fear from the Folvilles today. The anger you see on my face is not aimed at you. Tell me, what happened here?'

'My Lord, we couldn't stop them.'

'I have no doubt. These jackals have hit Ashby Folville's tavern as well. Have they left a message, beyond turning your furniture into firewood?'

'Just that you were no longer in control of this demesne, and all rents and fees due to your family are to go to them.'

'And your reply was?'

'I made no reply, my Lord. I had no chance to speak. The man they called Edgar had a hand over my wife's mouth and a dagger at her throat. I said nothing. I daren't.'

'Edgar.' Robert turned to Owen who nodded in understanding.

'They're getting braver, my Lord, using names in front of people.'

'Unless they are getting overconfident. Let's hope it proves their undoing.' Robert turned to the innkeeper. 'This Edgar, large hands? Big man?'

'Yes, my Lord.' Elias frowned as he picked up a fallen chair and pushed it against a broken table.

'Good boots?'

'I'm sorry, my Lord?'

'I have also had a messenger, Elias. Not so violent, but nonetheless he made his presence felt. The man was attired like a workman, an outlaw maybe, but his boots were too good to belong to a villain, and too well-fitting to have been stolen.'

'I'm sorry my Lord, I did not notice such details, but he was certainly dressed as a workman. A tradesman. He was too strong not to have a profession that didn't involve heavy lifting.'

Robert gestured to the worried landlord to take a seat on the nearest unbroken piece of furniture. 'How much stock did they take?'

'None, my Lord. They said they'd be back when their current supplies ran dry.'

Owen looked at his master, 'Makes sense. Why carry heavy barrels when you don't need to? It would only slow them down. Their stores will be full of the stock from Ashby.'

Elias looked from the nobleman to the steward, 'My Lords, please, what will we do? I can't fight off these men if they come in quantity. They frightened my wife. Next time they might hurt her.'

'You are wise to be wary, but you haven't been abandoned, Master Tavernier. Now is the time when the money you've paid us for protection over the years shows its worth. Protection is what you are going to get. While I arrange that, I'm going to need the town's help. It's time to assemble the posse.'

'The posse, my Lord? Like the sheriff does?'

'Indeed, Elias. These men have committed a crime, haven't they? I have no doubt the sheriff would be glad of me sorting out the hue and cry for him.'

'Of course, my Lord.' Not wanting to ask if the Folvilles had the sheriff in their pocket as well, Elias picked up two pieces of wood that had once formed a single stool, and said, 'I'll call my stable lad and get the men together. But, if I may be so bold, my Lord, how are you going to keep us safe?'

'Eustace is coming.'

Elias's shoulders, which had been hunched with defeat, instantly lifted. 'Is he now? Then, God help any outlaw who tries to poach land here.'

'Quite.' Robert, trying not to mind that his brother could engender fear and respect by just the mention of his name, whereas he had to continually prove himself, said, 'We haven't much time Elias. Send the lad. We act tonight.'

The pub was full, but no ale flowed. The motley mix of men and boys sat, their faces grave, their voices unusually silent as Robert explained what lay ahead.

'This man who calls himself Leigh is hell bent on savaging my family's income - and worse, its reputation - to the benefit of himself and his men. Now, some of you may say, why shouldn't he? My family doesn't ever act out of kindness. Well - you'd be right in part. However, look around you. Look at what this Leigh got his men to do to Elias's place in just a few minutes. My family is not given to destroying the assets it wishes to make the best of. Nor do we shirk our responsibilities if our side of a bargain needs to be upheld. Like now.

'Tonight, I'm calling in some favours. I need a group of men to come with me and Owen to Thwaite Wood. This Leigh thinks he is about to issue me an ultimatum. To hand my family's influence over - or else. If he sees me with the very men he already believes to have been frightened into serving him and not my family, then he will have pause for thought. He'll see that we are not so easy to overcome. In return, my brothers will have their men stand guard here until this matter is resolved.'

'You mean until Leigh is dead?' Elias, who had become unofficial spokesman for the town, was frank.

'Dead, arrested, or banished. Yes.'

The air, which stank of ale, dust, and damp, hung heavy with an expectant hush, and so Robert pressed his point. 'I'm not going to insist you to come with Owen and myself, but we clearly stand more chance of releasing you from Leigh's demands with a greater number of men.

'However, having said that, I want some of you to remain here to watch over your womenfolk and children. I do not trust that Leigh will do what he says, so keeping a group here is sensible. My brother's men will be here tomorrow.' Mentally crossing his fingers, hoping Eustace would agree to the promise he'd just made on his behalf, Robert was acutely aware of the passing minutes. He'd never have time to get back to the manor and collect the extra weapons Adam had sharpened up. He just hoped the older steward was up to keeping Mathilda and Sarah safe.

Fed up with waiting for someone to speak, Owen pulled his great height up from the chair on which he'd perched and moved to Elias's side. 'So, Melton? Do you help yourselves, or do you wait for these wolves to return to do worse to your homes, your livestock and your children?'

Within minutes the men had split into two groups. Those staying on protection duty and those who were to travel with Robert and Owen.

'We must leave as soon as you've all found a weapon.' Robert expressed his thanks to the town, 'Seeing me with the very people that he thinks he has stolen from my family's alliance will quell this Leigh; even if for only long enough to us hear his demands, dismiss them, and then return home to make more long-lasting plans.'

Mounting his horse, Robert wheeled it round to face an already mounted Owen. 'I want you to ride to Ashby. I need to make sure all is well there.'

Owen frowned. 'But these men aren't battle-hardened, my Lord, you will have no one at your side without me - and don't forget, many have an axe to grind with the Folvilles as well as this Leigh, albeit a less sharpened one.'

'I know, Owen, and if I had a choice it would be different, but I've failed Sarah once already. And then there is Mathilda. If anything...'

'I'm on my way, my Lord.'

Issuing up a silent prayer to Our Lady to look after Mathilda and to bless their endeavour, Robert led his gang of townsmen through the dark winter's night. Each man wore a thick cloak and was well booted against the harshness of the night which threatened snow. They presented a daunting sight as they approached the thickening trees of The Thwaite, some on foot, others mounted, as midnight closed around them like a shroud.

Robert knew they'd reached the right place when he saw a single burly figure languishing, arrogant and unafraid, against the thick trunk of an oak tree.

Recognising him as having the same manner about him as the messenger Leigh had sent to his home, Robert asked,

'Is that one of the men who came to the inn, Elias?'

'Yes. He isn't the one they called Edgar, though. I expect he's skulking here somewhere though.'

'Then we have arrived.' Robert lowered his voice, 'Hold your tongue and listen hard. There will be messages to deliver too many quarters after this night's work is done; the more open ears the better. Let's give them the chance to talk themselves into knots if we can.'

Lazily, as if the matter was of little difference to him, the unknown man pulled himself away from the tree, and walked deeper into the wood.

'Are we to follow, my Lord?'

Frowning, Robert examined the narrowness of the pathway the outlaw had gone down. It would mean that his followers would have to ride or walk down it single file. He could only admire the thinking. Instantly Leigh would have the upper hand.

Rather than follow, Robert gathered his group around him and stayed exactly where he was. Then, in as loud a voice as possible, knowing well how sound carried in the dead of night, he called into the trees.

'We have come to The Thwaite. No precise location within the wood was detailed, and so, if you wish to talk to me, Leigh, you'll have to come here. If not, then we'll be on our way.'

Rowan Leigh had been sat in the bough of a tree, hidden behind the mass of men he'd gathered to form an impressive force to intimidate Folville. Now, as quiet as a mouse, he leapt from the tree and rounded on Gamelyn. 'He knows my name! Who spoke it? Who revealed me? A member of this family! Find out who.'

Stuttering for a second, before composing himself,

Leigh's henchman said, 'Not I, my Lord, but I will discover the culprit.'

'You will.' The statement spoke of a great many consequences if Gamelyn didn't oblige his master's request.

Silent for a second, Rowan moved to where his men were waiting. There was no point now in the subterfuge he'd hoped to continue for a few more days at least. Elbowing his way to the back of the group, so he could be heard but not seen, Rowan ordered his men forward before taunting his visitors.

'You show more sense that I credited you with, Robert Folville.'

'Flattery is not a weapon I'd have associated with you, Leigh. It's late, get to the point.' Robert ran his eyes over what he could see of the assembled group. They were much as he'd expected. Big men as a rule, muscular, employed for strength and not brains. Although that didn't seem to matter, as Leigh was clearly capable enough to do the thinking for all of them.

The cold became denser as they paused, like two mini-armies unsure if they were on the right battleground. Each side hovered in the heart of an outer thicket of Thwaite Wood, each waiting to see how the other would react. Each man with his hand on the hilt of a weapon.

Leigh's voice came from the darkness. Robert knew there was no point in craning to catch a glimpse of him. If he didn't wish to be seen then he'd never be spotted beneath the triple protection of the night, the trees and his men.

'My name is Rowan Leigh, and I'm here to issue a warning. You and your family have reached the end of your tenure as rulers of the area. You have one week to inform all of your associates and noble connections, that they now belong to me. Each of the properties and parcels of land involved will elect a representative, who will come to me at Melton's inn at this hour in one week. Should this not be done, then the consequences will not be kind.'

Rather than keeping his intentions short and to the point, Leigh kept talking, kept repeating himself. After the third time Robert heard him saying that his consequences would not be kind, a fresh suspicion ran through Robert's head. Why bring them here just to issue threats? Apart from the time point of a power exchange, none of this was news. It was as if the man simply enjoyed the act of crowing.

Unless...

An ice cold suspicion swept over Robert.

With a barked order to his men, he swung his horse round, leaving a laughing Rowan behind him.

Galloping to Ashby Folville, fear clutched at Robert's heart.

1310

It had been two years since he'd cried. Even then it had been in secret. But he cried now. Hard. Unrelenting angry open tears of sorrow and rage as he cradled the broken toy in his arms.

It had been a surprise for Brother Peter. A thank you present for taking him on as his apprentice in the abbey's carpentry workshop. He'd intended it to be a gift for Brother Peter to pass on to his nephew in the city.

It had taken weeks of loving attention to detail to make the spinning top. Not only that, but it was the first item he'd made completely alone. And now it was ruined.

Someone had sawed it crudely in half; and he knew who that someone was.

Richard had been in the warming room when he'd been stood with Brother Peter, as the monk had praised his skill with wood to Brother Mark.

Only an hour later; returning to the workshop to make sure all was tidy and ready for the following day as the carpenter's apprentice should, he'd found the wreckage of the gift.

Within an hour of hearing him being praised properly for the first time since in his life, Richard had destroyed not just his work, but his moment of happiness.

~ *Chapter Eleven* ~

Owen hadn't wanted to leave Robert behind, but he knew that until the rest of the family arrived with their retinues, they were vastly undermanned. What was the point of defending the family name and enterprises if the manor house was left vulnerable?

Riding hard, Owen kept his ears pricked for activity either side of him as the night air pinched at his ears and cheeks.

Slowing as he got nearer to the manor, Owen felt something was wrong, although he couldn't see anything amiss. The courtyard appeared to be empty. There were no unwelcome visitors barring his way as he walked his mount across the properties threshold.

Owen drew in his reins. The gate wasn't shut or barred. Surely Adam would have had the common sense to close the heavy wooden doors once Allward, Daniel and Mathilda had returned?

He strained his ears. Nothing. No unexpected footsteps. No breathing. No birdcalls where there should have been none. Just the silence of the pitch of night. Yet it felt too quiet.

Why hadn't Allward or Daniel, rushed out to take his horse?

A sensation of terror crept up Owen's spine as he dismounted and, leaving his horse to stand beside the doorway, slowly entered the manor.

As he went inside, he gave a ragged sigh of relief. Adam, Sarah, Mathilda and the stable lad were huddled around the table, deep in conversation. They looked up in surprise.

Owen frowned. 'Why isn't the gate barred? And where the hell is Allward? He should be guarding the courtyard.' He rounded on Adam. 'My Lord Robert charged you with the women's safety. Why the hell are you sat safe by the kitchen fire when you should be attending to your duties?'

'It's barred and bolted.' Adam's face went grey as he understood the meaning behind Owen's question. 'I made sure of it. Allward rode straight out to The Thwaite once he'd returned Mathilda to us. Lady Mathilda herself barred the entrance after him.'

Still on the alert, Owen asked, 'And none of you have been outside since he left?'

Adam was on his feet, and with Owen and Daniel, headed to the door. 'I saw it closed. I swear that the bar was across on the inside.'

Rounding on Adam, Owen's face darkened, 'And why should I believe you are not Leigh's man? You could have left us vulnerable for him. They could already be inside the manor.'

Sarah jumped to her feet, her hand over her mouth to stop the cry of fear. Mathilda immediately put an arm around her shoulder. This wasn't like the housekeeper. Only now did Mathilda see how much the attack had taken out her friend.

Stepping into the argument before it got out of hand, Mathilda said, 'Owen, I did bar the gate. Neither Adam nor Sarah or Daniel has opened it. We have sat here as it is the most sensible place to wait for Robert's return. Allward had given us a signal to listen for so we knew it was them to let back in.'

'When did Allward leave? I did not cross him on the road.'

A silence fell over the kitchen. Owen pulled his dagger from his belt as, in the same breath, they all realised they weren't alone.

Then the world exploded.

Robert was driven by pure rage as he urged his horse to move faster and faster.

Some of the men from Melton had followed him, while others returned to their town. Both groups were fearful of what they might find on their arrival.

With every second he'd allowed Leigh to speak, to issue the same ultimatum over and over again, Robert knew he'd put another second between himself and Mathilda's safety.

He tried not to think about what he'd find. Tried to push out of his head visions of the manor being reduced to splinter wood. Cursing the fact his brothers hadn't been able to come to his aid; trying not to feel as if they couldn't care less about their younger brother, Robert kept riding.

The gate wasn't splintered, but nor was it closed.

'My Lord?'

Robert was vaguely aware of Elias at his shoulder, dismounting alongside him just outside the courtyard. He pulled his sword, the other town's men closing in around him, each wary, each seeing the significance of the kitchen door being wide open across the other side of yard.

'Should we go in, my Lord?' The innkeeper went to step into the yard, but Robert put a hand across his stomach, preventing him from moving forward.

'The floor.'

Elias's gaze dropped to the frost covered ground. The swirl of horse's hooves, indents of boot prints and worse, the telltale marks of something being dragged across the floor, spoke of an altercation.

'Too many men to judge.' Robert felt his words coming from his mouth, but they seemed to be bypassing his brain altogether. His head was screaming at him to move. To make sure Mathilda was alright. At the same time, he couldn't move forward. Visions of her battered body. Her dead body...He hadn't realised how much he loved her until that moment. The memory of Eustace's warning that love would weaken his edge reared up in his mind and Robert snapped back to life.

'Do you see what I see, Elias?'

'I am afraid I do, my Lord. I have to return to Melton, if the same awaits me there...my wife...'

'Go quickly. Be safe.'

As the innkeeper turned his exhausted mount around, Robert gestured to the remaining men to dismount outside of the yard so that the hooves didn't mess with the evidence of the yard before the sheriff saw it.

'Keep to the sides. Follow me,' Robert whispered as he made his way with long strides to the kitchen door.

The kitchen table was on its side. Robert was instantly struck by how odd the room looked without its sturdy presence in its usual place. A noise ahead made Robert raise his sword, as he edged into the narrow corridor that joined the kitchen to the hall.

'My Lord, thank God!'

A tired and bloodied Adam was being cleaned up by a distraught Sarah, while he was trying to comfort her at the same time.

'Mathilda? Where's Mathilda?'

Adam tried to stand, but his leg wouldn't hold him. 'Gone. Owen... my Lord, he's...'

Two of the men from Melton had come into the hall, their faces told Robert what Adam had been about to say.

'Where is he?'

'In the stable, my Lord. His horse is wounded as well. It looks as though Owen intended to follow whoever has been here.'

Robert felt the world around him slowing down. He didn't know which direction to go in first. He'd always thought he'd want to move faster, to strike out instantly in this situation, but he felt leaden. 'Sarah, did they hurt her before they took her?'

'Not beyond bruises caused by firm hands. One of the men spoke of being ordered not to harm her.'

'And you, Sarah; are you injured further?'

'Only my pride and my heart for Owen and Mathilda.'

Adam's countenance was white. 'I couldn't stop them, I tried, I...'

'I can see you fought hard. Sarah is alive, that makes your wounds worthwhile.'

'But Owen...'

'I will see him now.'

Sarah tried to say something, anything that would help. 'My Lord, I...' but the words died on her lips.

Robert turned to the men from Melton. 'You should return to your homes. I thank you. My brothers will be with me soon. I will send reinforcements to Melton before nightfall tomorrow, as I promised. You will not speak of what has happened here. Gossip will play into Leigh's hands.'

The men left swiftly, each tight-lipped and shaken by what they'd witnessed.

Adam wheezed through his bloodied lips, 'Leigh's men

have left another message.'

'Tell me.'

'The taking of Mathilda was revenge for undermining the pact this Leigh had thrown upon Jacob Lock, the innkeeper at Ashby. I was to tell you that this is just a taste of what Leigh is prepared to do to your family.' Adam pointed towards the stable block, referring to the fallen steward. 'This new man seems to think he is untouchable. Someone big has to be protecting him, my Lord. They have to be.'

Owen was lying in a position that shouldn't have been possible. His neck was broken, his leg twisted beneath him. Robert breathed out slowly. He was waiting to feel the comfort of anger, to feel something, but numbness was consuming him.

His loyal steward had, if Robert judged the scene correctly, been pulled from his horse with some force. Owen's face was cut; the bruising on his cheek showed he'd been on the receiving end of more than one punch in his quest to pursue Mathilda.

'I'm sorry, my friend.' Robert spoke into the stagnant air of the stable. The horses weren't moving, their ears pricked, as if they knew that a horror had happened here.

Determination flooded through Robert's veins, taking over from where rage normally coursed. 'I'll find her, Owen. I'll get her back. Your sacrifice will always be remembered. Always.'

Closing the stable door, so that Owen was left in peace for the sheriff's men to see, Robert returned to Adam and Sarah, his purpose returning with every step.

'Sarah, will Adam heal?'

'Bruised, muscles pulled, minor cuts and a small dagger wound, but miraculously nothing is broken. He will mend.

Owen will not.' Robert noticed the way Sarah was looking at Adam. A fresh wave of pain pierced him as he wondered if Adam knew that Sarah had begun to care for him; or if she had even seen it herself yet.

'No, he will not.' Robert sat heavily next to his housekeeper. 'I can't find Allward. Am I to find my messenger and young friend dead too?'

Sarah and Adam's expressions clouded further, before the housekeeper asked, 'Isn't he with you, my Lord?'

'With me? No.'

Adam swallowed uneasily, 'Allward returned Mathilda and Daniel to us and then said he was heading to Thwaite to be at your side. 'Didn't he find you?'

'No, he...' Robert looked around the damaged kitchen, 'And where is Daniel?'

'I sent him to Leicester.' It was Sarah who spoke now. 'We need Eustace's presence sooner rather than later, my Lord. Just knowing your most feared kin is on his way will help our situation. Please don't take that as disrespect, my Lord, I had to do something and...'

'And you did the right thing. I just hope Daniel didn't run into trouble.'

Adam shifted his position with a slight wince, 'I told him to ride away from Thwaite, and to keep off any connecting roads. It'll take longer, but he will have more chance of getting there in one piece.'

'Wise. I just hope Allward has gone to ground somewhere safe for the night now he's realised he must have passed me on the road. We'll need him more than ever tomorrow. Was Daniel hurt before he set off?'

'No, the boy slipped through their fingers while Owen was being attacked.'

'How many men where there? Tell me everything. I need

details before we go after Mathilda.'

'But go where, my Lord? None of us know where this Leigh is.'

~ *Chapter Twelve* ~

'How many men?'

Gamelyn laughed, 'Men? None, my Lord. Folville is so arrogant that he believed an old man, the housekeeper, a stable boy and the Lady Mathilda were enough to hold down the manor house in his absence.'

Rowan shook his head in mock despair. 'How foolish, anything could have happened!'

Gamelyn drew his dagger from his belt to admire where the blood of the fallen steward clung to the blade. 'I did as you advised, my Lord. I had the men wait until I was sure that most people were away from the manor. I couldn't believe our luck when it was so empty.'

'And the result of what did happen should be here soon.' Rowan preened a hand through his hair, 'This Mathilda intrigues me. Is she aware that her steward is dead?'

'No. She'll know him to be injured though, as she saw him fall from his horse before we got her secured. There was more fight in her alone than all the others put together.'

'I like her more with every passing moment. She went to the Folvilles' in the first place as a ransom, I believe.'

'So the gossips say.'

'Then Mathilda of Twyford is no stranger to being a victim of kidnap.'

Gamelyn held his tongue, he wasn't quite sure if he could believe what his master was implying, or if he'd misunderstood the admiration in his voice.

'It will be interesting to discover if being prepared to marry a member of a group that, shall we say, works fractionally outside the law, is a habit she is willing to repeat, or if persuasion is going to be required.'

'My Lord?'

Rowan laughed at his companion as if he was stupid. 'There would be no point in bringing her here if I didn't intend to keep her.'

Mathilda tried to concentrate. She knew she would panic later, but not now. She daren't. Not if she ever wanted to see Ashby Folville again.

Trying to memorise the route the kidnappers were driving the cart she'd been stuffed into was impossible. Bound and gagged, with a hood over her head, Mathilda felt the fingers of terror start to take over from her determination not to cry. Her desperation not to let Robert down, and not to prove Eustace right about having a woman in his brother's life causing nothing but trouble, started to slip away.

This wasn't like when the Folville brothers had taken her from her father. That had been rough, clumsy, and frightening, but it had been meant to scare her father into paying his debts. She'd quickly realised that she was in no real physical danger. This time it was difference.

The violence of the attack had taken the small household by surprise. When it hit, it had happened very, very fast.

Allward had intercepted her and Daniel just as they'd ridden from the Twyford village boundary. Filling them in quickly on events at Melton, the lack of brotherly support until the following day and that Robert was out calling in debts to get a force of arms to accompany him to Thwaite, the three of them had journeyed with speed and care to the manor.

Vigilant as they travelled, Mathilda's palfrey between the two lads' bigger mounts; they'd peered into the trees at the sides of the road more than they'd watched the road itself.

As soon as they'd reached the courtyard, Allward had sent Mathilda and Daniel inside, while he stayed just outside the main entrance. He waited while they closed and barred the doors against him, then he turned his horse about ready to ride to Robert's aid.

'Please, Our Lady, take care of him. Let him have found Robert and safety. Let them all be safe.'

A frightened Mathilda muttered the prayer as she recalled Sarah's delighted face on her safe return. The older woman had fussed around her, making sure all was well while answering Mathilda's questions on the events in her absence.

Adam had remained quiet, his hand on a dagger. He'd explained how Robert had asked him to polish and sharpen all the weapons, just in case they were needed. The dagger he was keeping close while he was the elder male there.

Sat at the kitchen table, Mathilda had told Adam of the rumours in the market at Rotherby, about a felon who'd escaped from Sheriff de Cressy's posse and was presumed on the run in the area. The only other information was that the sheriff was on the warpath about this missing criminal and was being more ruthless than ever in his behaviour. It was just as well that she'd had no more information to impart on the matter as there'd been no further opportunity to speak.

Owen had appeared in the kitchen as if from nowhere, his face scarlet with rage at his discovery that the house was unsecured. Then there'd been chaos.

The men must have been in the house for hours, just waiting. The thought sent an additional trickle of fear down Mathilda's spine as the cart bumped along the track to wherever they were taking her. One of the hidden men had to have unbarred the gates that she herself had locked as soon as Allward had disappeared into the distance.

Closing her eyes, Mathilda remembered that Adam had sensed something was going to happen first, but only half a second after he'd stood up, dagger to hand, a huge hand had gripped her mouth. A hand that hadn't moved fast enough to prevent Mathilda from sinking her teeth into its foul-smelling flesh before it silenced her. The memory of its owner cursing her to hell was the only good thing that had happened since her return to Ashby Folville.

After that it had been a blur. Mathilda remembered Sarah being knocked to the floor and Daniel shouting and pushing at a man whose chest was as thick as a tree trunk. There had been a lot of noise, which now she thought about it, was probably falling furniture. Maybe four or five men had been waiting for them. At least three of them had homed in on her.

She had kicked, scratched and fought against her attackers as best she could. Mathilda, scared as she was, took some satisfaction in knowing that she hadn't made her removal from Ashby Folville an easy matter. Even when her hands were bound, and she could do nothing but allow them to drag her across the courtyard to a cart that was suddenly there, Mathilda hadn't made it simple for them, digging her heels into the frozen dirt of the courtyard floor. She wondered if Robert was back at the manor now. If he'd seen the drag pattern of her boots in the gravel and understood what they meant.

Owen had been behind her, but they'd overpowered him, while Adam and Sarah had been busy fighting off their own assailants.

Mathilda felt a sensation of cold that had nothing to do with the season or the lateness of the hour. They *were* alive. They had to be.

Could all this effort truly just be to deprive Robert and his family of everything they had, including her?

Laid upon a meagre bed of hay and covered by a thick blanket, her knees under her chin, her muscles cramped with their confinement, Mathilda listened to the cackles of the men above as they drove the horses. Confident they were safe from attack, clearly anticipating a reward from their master for gaining his prize, Mathilda realised with horror that the meeting at The Thwaite had only been arranged to make it easier to kidnap her.

Her fingers, trapped at her stomach, stroked the leather girdle Robert had given her; each cut-out butterfly shape giving her a little courage. She was to be a Folville. She would not let them down.

The Thwaite. She stopped trying to recall every twist and turn in the road and began to wonder what had happened there. Had Allward got to Robert? Were they alright? The thought they might not be was another place she didn't wish to dwell on. They may have got there and found no one waiting for them at all.

Mathilda closed her eyes against the cloak of darkness. *You are to be married soon. Robert is a fighter. He will fight. His brothers will fight. Sarah is making the wedding dress right now. You will get home. You will...*

The cart stopped.

The silence after the journey seemed even more threatening than the humourless laughter that had past between her guards as they'd driven her along.

She wanted to freeze time. To stop the cover of the cart from ever being lifted off. She didn't want to meet this man who called himself Leigh; the man who had designs on local supremacy whatever the consequences.

The choice was not hers to make. The blanket was off, and she was being hauled to her feet.

Blinking in the dark light, Mathilda found herself looking at the outside of a workshop and cottage. Its ordinary appearance felt wrong. It jarred with the sinister air of brutality and fear that hung around it.

Trying not to let the nausea rising in her throat get the better of her, Mathilda threw off the men holding her shoulders. 'I am perfectly capable of standing by myself.'

'That's the spirit.'

The voice came from behind her. It sounded amused but also satisfied. Mathilda felt as if she had passed some sort of test. She did not look round.

The man didn't say anything else as he came to stand before her. His small eyes peered out of a large face, which was baby-smooth. A total contrast to the roughness of the hands he was holding out in greeting. Hands she wouldn't have wanted to touch even if her wrists were unbound and she could reach out in supplication. They were covered in scars and calluses. Mathilda briefly wondered if his many blisters caused him pain. She hoped so. Mathilda knew dangerous and ruthless men when she saw them. She lived amongst them. She was going to marry one.

This man wasn't like Robert. He wasn't even like Eustace. The scrawny but muscular felon standing before her with an expression of self-satisfied contempt was never going to be dangerous or ruthless for the greater good. He wasn't even dangerous because he was greedy.

This man was dangerous because he enjoyed how it made him feel. He was ruthless because it was fun. Even if his very stance hadn't told Mathilda that, the look in his eyes did.

It was like being in the company of the Devil himself.

Mathilda felt the bile rise faster than she could stop it and greeted Rowan Leigh formally by being sick all over his sturdy leather boots.

~ *Chapter Thirteen* ~

Quickly shuttering the gates, Adam turned to Daniel. Half carrying and half propelling the lad as he slipped from the saddle, Adam bade him catch his breath before alerting Sarah, to the boy's arrival.

The lad was almost as exhausted as his horse. Calling over her shoulder for Robert, all formality between master and servants gone in the face of the new danger that surrounded the family, Sarah plied Daniel with bread and ale as she told Adam to put the boy by the kitchen fire.

'I'm truly glad to see you in one piece, lad.' Robert came into the kitchen, his face a queue of unanswered questions.

'They are on their way, my Lord.' Daniel's voice cracked, and he took a slug of drink before he went on. 'My Lord Eustace rallied his men immediately. He will go straight to Melton as you promised. My lords Walter, Laurence and Thomas are on their way here and my Lord John will arrive as soon as he can get away from the duties of the day.'

Robert laid a thankful hand on Daniel's shoulder. 'You achieved much in a short time. Thank you.'

'Not me alone, my Lord. Eustace sent men on to John, and I was fortunate that Walter, Thomas and Laurence are staying with my Lord Eustace. You can imagine how angry they were.'

Sarah snorted. 'I imagine Eustace has been foaming at the bit to get away ever since Allward told him the news.'

Daniel's high colour grew. 'Ummm. I'm sorry, my Lord.'

Robert's brow furrowed. 'Sorry?'

'Allward sir, he hasn't been to see Eustace. The other brothers hadn't seen him either. I can't say about my Lord John.'

Sarah and Adam stared at each other and then at Robert. No one spoke as what Daniel was saying sank in.

The boy was openly shaking now, whether from cold, fatigue, or the relief of offloading the news he'd been carrying, Sarah wasn't sure.

Robert opened his mouth to ask if Daniel was sure. To make sure he'd really heard what his stable boy had just said, or at least implied, about Allward, when the clatter of hooves heralded the arrival of one of the Folville brothers.

Eustace's presence filled the manor in seconds. Everything about the second-eldest Folville was large: his size, manner and temper. Accompanied by only two men, he sat at the table and slammed his fist down onto the table before Robert had had the chance to greet him.

'Before you comment, I have sent men onto Melton. Now brother, why had you not told me us about this upstart's invasion into our affairs before? Too ashamed that you couldn't keep the family manor safe all on your own?'

Grateful for the familiarity of his brother's ire, Robert felt himself respond in kind and his drive to act return. 'Don't be such a damn fool, Eustace. I sent word. It seems, however,' he glanced at Daniel, 'that it never reached you. If Adam hadn't had the sense to send young Daniel here out, then we would have continued to think you and the other family members were happy to leave us to our situation alone.'

'You sent who before?'

'Allward.'

'I have not seen him. Does this mean that he has betrayed us?'

Sarah interrupted before common sense could stop her, 'No, my Lord. He would not. He...'

Adam's hand came to her shoulder, 'Lass, I fear he may well have done. Someone let those savages into your home. Someone who said help was coming, when there was no help to come.'

'But Allward is so loyal. He and Owen were friends, he would never...' Sarah's voice cracked, and she couldn't finish the sentence.

'I think, little brother, you have much to tell me. Where is Owen, and who,' he pointed suspiciously at Adam, 'is this?'

Frustration was edging into Robert's mind. 'We don't have time to waste, Eustace. We need to find this Leigh's hideaway and get Mathilda back.'

'What did I tell you about having a woman in your life, Robert?'

'This is not the time for your lectures, Eustace! For Our Lady's sake! Mathilda has been kidnapped, and the family reputation dented. How many officials out there have been waiting for a moment like this? How many will be happy to blame us for the destruction at Melton and the murder of Owen? It's just the excuse they've been looking for to arrest us all and send us abroad, or worse, to have our necks stretched.'

Eustace saw Sarah's face go pale, and he knew he hadn't misheard what Robert had said. 'Owen is dead?'

'Murdered by the men who took Mathilda.'

'I'm truly saddened to hear that. He was a good man.'

'He was. I need to tell the coroner, but events have moved fast.'

'His body is still here?'

'The stables.'

Eustace nodded gravely, and with a wave to one of his men to accompany him, he headed to the courtyard. As he and Robert left the kitchen he said, 'Allward isn't the first servant to betray his master. He won't be the last. He'll be punished.'

'If he did betray us.'

'For pity's sake Robert. It's plain as the nose on your face! Mathilda is gone. Owen is dead. If it wasn't Allward on the inside, then it was Adam. What do you know about him?'

The sight of Owen's mangled body shut Eustace up for a moment. He crouched to his knees and looked closely at the family's former steward. Then, in a move that surprised his brother, Eustace took of his cloak and laid it over the fallen man.

'We need to talk to Ingram.'

Robert nodded, before saying, 'You think the old sheriff rather than the new one?'

'I do.' Eustace brushed his hands together, his eyes still on the body, 'we should heed his advice before we take action within the realms of the law.'

'I'll send Daniel once he's rested.'

'It needs doing now, brother.' Eustace turned to his man at arms, who understood the unspoken task placed upon him and left immediately. 'From what your boy said, this newcomer isn't going to hang around before he pushes his advantage; the advantage of having your future wife in his power.'

The vein in Robert's neck began to throb. 'If he's laid a

hand on her....'

'Brother, a hand is the very last thing you need to worry about. If he really wants to deprive you...'

'Don't say it.'

Eustace nodded. 'Mathilda is a strong one, Robert. And brave. Hold on to that. Keep that thought upmost.'

Unused to such consideration from any of his brothers, Robert acknowledged Eustace's words with a slap to his back. He retreated from the stable in time to see Walter, Laurence and Thomas thunder into the courtyard.

Robert took their bridles and bid them a brief welcome. 'Go to the hall. Best we go through this together now. We don't have time to wait for John. I have much news and it is bleak indeed.'

For once no one passed comment that Robert had invited Sarah and Adam to be present as the family sat in council.

The brothers listened gravely as Robert described the attack on Sarah, the messenger, the summons to Thwaite, the raid on Ashby Folville tavern and the further attack at Melton.

'And this man is?' Walter, usually so quiet, pointed meaningfully at Adam.

'Adam can answer for himself. If he hadn't been here, then it wouldn't have been just Owen's body left to greet me on my return from Thwaite.'

'Speak, Adam.' Eustace directed his gaze straight into the eyes of the older man.

'My lords, I am Adam Calvin. I was steward to John de Markham, king's serjeant and lawyer of West Markham in Nottinghamshire until I was wrongly accused of a crime. A crime which I did not even have time to establish the nature of before the hue and cry was raised and it was made clear to me I had to run for my life. I ran. I arrived here without knowledge of whose land I was hiding on. My Lord Robert found me.'

Eustace frowned. 'Why do I have the feeling that is only part of the tale?'

'Forgive me, my Lord, but my problems suddenly seem less important. Owen is dead, and the Lady Mathilda is gone. If I can help you before I return north to attempt to clear my name, I will.'

'And we're just expected to believe you did not attack Sarah, nor are you any part of this Leigh's band?'

'I can't prove something that didn't happen, my Lord. I had never heard of this Leigh before I arrived here. If I'd stumbled north instead of south while being pursued by de Cressy's men, then I'd never have heard of him even now.'

'De Cressy?' Eustace steepled his fingers. 'That new sheriff of ours is a fool. Too openly greedy for a man in power. There is no style to his thirst for power.'

'Forgive me, my Lords,' Sarah took the chance to speak. 'Before Mathilda was taken she was beginning to tell us about what she'd learnt while at Rotherby with her father. It was about de Cressy being on the warpath; being in pursuit of someone. Gossip had it that the sheriff is becoming openly corrupt and reckless.'

'Is that so?' Eustace and Robert exchanged glances, 'Then it is a good job we have sent for Ingram and not de Cressy isn't it.'

'Ingram is still corrupt, brother.' Thomas broke his silence, but his face was caught in a half-smile, 'But at least he is corrupt for us and not against us.'

Adam looked at Sarah, who nodded in response to the question he wisely didn't ask out loud. Ingram was in the Folvilles' pay. De Cressy was not.

Mathilda screamed in shook as the bucket of cold water was thrown at her. It almost knocked her to the floor as Leigh aimed it directly at her face. Washing the sickness from her mouth and down her body, it fell onto her boots and the ground beneath.

Every muscle in Leigh twitched. He was livid. He hadn't spoken. He hadn't yelled. He had just turned around, fetched a pail of ice-covered water from the corner of the yard and thrown it at her, ice and all.

Leigh looked Mathilda up and down as she stood, every garment soaked through. Her red hair was plastered to her face and neck. The trembling of fear that she'd been unable to prevent as she stood, semi-bound and helpless, was instantly diminished by the paralysing chill that engulfed her.

He called for a blanket, which he put around his own shoulders, before leading against a nearby wall. Crossing his arms, he just stood there and stared at her.

It appeared that Rowan Leigh was intent on punishing Mathilda for getting his shoes dirty by observing her die slowly of cold.

~ *Chapter Fourteen* ~

'We're going around in circles!'

Robert couldn't keep still. He had explained everything that had happened to his assembled brothers, but they couldn't agree on how to proceed. 'We need to find where they're hiding and find Mathilda!'

Eustace was carving a new line in the oak table with his dagger, 'We need to preserve our reputation first, brother. We've had that for years. Mathilda is but a new plaything.'

'How dare you! Mathilda has already saved this family's name once. Or had you forgotten that?'

Sarah looked from one brother to the other in disgust. 'Will you listen to yourselves!' Then, ignoring the warning glance from Adam, she got to her feet and yelled above the bickering. 'Stop it!'

The shock of the housekeeper, even one as opinionated as Sarah, forgetting her place and bellowing across the hall silenced them all. Every eye in the room glared as the woman who'd raised them in the absence of their mother, who'd always travelled with their father, clasped her hands to her hips.

'Mathilda is missing! The future lady of this house. She is to be a *Folville*. God help her! This *man*...' She spat the word with contempt, '...he sent his followers to stab me as a message. There was no warning first, no nobleman's acknowledgment of intent; he didn't even do the dirty work himself. And now if we are to believe he has managed to turn Allward against us, as some of you are suggesting, which I doubt very much, he would have done so in a way that gave the lad very little choice. Torture, even! Do I have to starve you all into using your common sense before you stop arguing and stand together to act?'

'Well said, Sarah. Sensible as always.'

The housekeeper blushed and curtseyed as Lord John Folville, head of the household, marched into his hall. 'Forgive my outburst, my Lord.'

'No need, Sarah.' John passed her his riding cloak as he swept into his seat at the head of the table. 'Forgive my delay. Daniel has informed me of everything while he tended to my horse. You have sent for Ingram?'

'We have.' Robert rose to his feet, 'I am pleased to see you, my Lord.'

John wasted no time in getting the point. 'Owen will be buried today. He was a good man. He does not deserve to be left lying like fallen cattle. Daniel has gone to Launde Priory to deliver a message from me to Prior Henry of Braunseton. He will arrange a place for Owen in the grounds of our church at St Mary's. Furthermore, I have sent my men into the woods surrounding this manor. If Leigh had this place under observation before, then there is no reason to believe he has stopped doing so.'

Robert put his head in his hands and groaned. 'It seems you may have been partly right, Eustace. Much as it pains me to say it. I was not thinking straight. Mathilda was too much in my mind. I should have left some of the Melton men in the woods. I'm sorry, John.'

'Sorry can wait until this is over. Daniel tells me you

have checked the area a few times, and you can't be everywhere at once. Now, how many men do we have between us?'

As the arguments morphed into tactical discussions, Sarah sat in her seat with a sigh of relief. She was shaking, although she hadn't noticed until now.

Adam frowned, mouthing silently in her direction, 'Are you alright?'

The housekeeper let the conversation wash over her as John took charge while Robert got a firmer grip of his feelings. She was relieved when Eustace asked her to go and fetch food and drink and she could escape to the sanctuary of her kitchen.

Seconds later she stopped dead. For a few precious minutes she'd forgotten that the table had been thrown onto its side. Jugs and pots lay smashed and abandoned on the floor. The water bucket had been kicked across the room and the aroma of apples hit her nostril, telling Sarah that at least one of the flagons of cider she kept on hand in the kitchen had been smashed.

'How could I have forgotten about this?'

Even if her arm and shoulder hadn't been weakened by her attack, Sarah couldn't right the table on her own. Rocking one of the table's two benches upright took all her effort and in a sudden rush of fatigue, everything that had happened hit her. Tears streamed down her cheeks, and nothing she could do would stop them.

Fear for Mathilda and Allward, combined with grief for Owen, consumed her in a confusion of worry. For the first time since she'd come to work for the family as a young woman appointed to look after the sons of Alice and John Folville, Sarah didn't feel safe. It was not a sensation she liked. The helplessness she felt made her cry silent angry tears all the harder.

'Hey now, lass, come on.' Adam had come into the room without Sarah noticing, 'The Folvilles are together in there. That is not a force of men I'd go up against lightly. This Leigh has no idea what he's taking on.'

Embarrassed at having been caught showing weakness, but grateful for Adam's common sense, Sarah wiped her tears away with her sleeve and pushed her shoulders back. 'Would you give me a hand?' She tilted her head towards the fallen table.

'I will, but it might take more than the two of us, it's a heavy table. I've come to collect the ale, Eustace is getting impatient.'

'Of course!' Sarah immediately bustled to the kitchen bench, thankful that it had been built in and so was not damaged beyond an arm sweeping its usual covering of items to the floor. 'What was I thinking? How is it going in there?'

'Lord John has the situation in hand. He has quite an effect on the brothers, doesn't he?'

Sarah allowed herself a proud affectionate smile through her grief. 'He does that. It's just as well, don't you think?'

'It's not my place to say. He may send me away. I suspect I'm in here helping you while they decide if I can be trusted.'

Instantly offended on Adam's behalf, Sarah said, 'But you saved my life and got Daniel to safety, so he could head out for help. If it hadn't been for you then Leigh's men would have returned to their lair in better shape, rather than with dagger cuts and bruises upon them!'

'I couldn't save Owen.'

'No.' Sarah squeezed Adam's arm lightly, 'But if you had saved him, then it could have been you we're mourning today. And possibly me and Daniel as well.'

Not trusting himself to reply, heartened by the touch of her hand on his arm, Adam bent to pick up the remaining bench, before gathering the shards of broken pottery. As he worked he listened to the sound of Sarah doing her best to put find enough undamaged beakers for the ale.

Straightening to his feet, Adam asked the housekeeper, 'Would you like me to go to the store for food? You'll not have had the chance to start the bread or stew for this evening's supper.'

Sarah shot him a grateful look. 'You are very kind. Thank you. I'm unforgivably behind in my daily tasks.'

'It is entirely forgivable. And anyway, I am ashamed to say I know my way around your store rather well.'

Robert pushed the pieces of apple in front of him around with the point of his dagger. He knew Sarah had done her best to prepare them a meal from the wreckage of her kitchen, but he couldn't eat. Every second that passed took Mathilda further into danger. There was no end to the horror Rowan Leigh could be inflicting on his future wife; the majority of which he didn't allow himself to consider.

His family were all in agreement on two points. First, Leigh had to be stopped and second, that he must be receiving support from someone of influence. There was no other way he could get away with being so brazenly felonious without so much of a sniff of the law being raised against him. Whoever his benefactor was must be discovered with as much haste as Mathilda must be recovered.

There was a third matter upon which they remained divided. The loyalty of Allward and Adam. Someone had to have let Leigh's men into the manor.

As Adam served ale and made sure the fire was kept at a

comfortable blaze, he saw Sarah signal from the corridor towards the kitchen.

Quietly heading to her summons, Adam found Daniel, mercifully unhurt, warming his hands by the kitchen fire.

'Daniel, what news?'

'Master Owen will be accepted at St Mary's. A litter will be sent for him before Vespers. I also intercepted my Lord Eustace's groom, John Pykehose, upon the road. He's met with the former sheriff. Lord Ingram will see the brothers today. Word is spreading. The gossip on the wind is that someone has the Folvilles by the heels.'

Sarah groaned. 'That's a rumour which will cost a few hides.'

'It will.' Daniel, wise for a boy of only eleven, added, 'We must go and talk to the Lords Folville. Ingram wants them to go to him, rather than him coming here.'

'Leave this place unguarded?' Sarah shuddered, and Adam had to restrain himself from putting his arm around her shoulders, a feeling that left even more questions in his head than he was already battling with.

Daniel shook his head, 'No Sarah, there are over a dozen men on guard by the front gate now. Haven't you been outside? Eustace's groom is a hefty chap and has a small band of his own. Plus, my Lord John's men are on their way as well. It will be like an army soon.'

'I haven't been out. There's so much to do here.' Sarah waved an arm around the kitchen, which still looked as though a herd of wild horses than invaded its confines.

'Eustace's groom says there are Folville men everywhere. Melton and Ashby are buzzing with the presence of Eustace's retinue. Not men that Leigh will want to argue with.'

A sense of relief sagged Sarah's shoulders, as she busied

herself with cooking a thick stew for supper. 'You shouldn't be keeping them waiting, Daniel. Go on, they won't mind the disruption for news they await.'

Daniel was on his feet when Adam asked him, 'Any word on Allward?'

'No. I'm sorry. I wish there was.'

Mathilda wasn't sure how much longer she could remain motionless. The fact she hadn't collapsed already was part miracle and part sheer bloody-mindedness at not wanting to show this man any weakness.

The cold had stopped now. Her clothes sucked against her clammy flesh, but all sensation had gone. She was completely numb. A voice far away in the recesses of her mind was telling Mathilda that this was bad, that not feeling cold anymore was bad. But not, said a conflicting voice, as bad as giving into this man. There were worse ways Rowan Leigh could kill her.

Mathilda couldn't see Leigh clearly anymore, due to the fading light and because her eyes had stopped focusing properly. She knew he was there though, so she stood, her feet firmly planted to the hard earth.

She was aware of people moving around her. Of whispering voices, of snorting laughter, but Mathilda paid no heed to any of it. In her mind she was at home with Sarah and Robert in front of the fire. Owen would be there soon, having secured the manor for the night, and they'd have a supper of stew and bread. In the confines of her mind, she was safe and well-fed.

The shout of triumph from the audience she'd attracted came like a whip crack through the night as the moment they'd all been waiting for finally happened.

Mathilda hit the dirty, slush-covered ground with a thud.

She was completely unconscious.

1311

He'd spent hours planning.

The thought of how he'd get his own back on Richard one day had kept him going for days, weeks, months.

Now, at last, he saw a way to get revenge on his tormentor.

~ *Chapter Fifteen* ~

'At last.' Robert muttered as he left the hall and went to find Adam.

'I think I've convinced them that you aren't one of Leigh's men. However, you will be watched. My brothers trust no one at the best of times; and this is far from the best of times.'

'It's no more than I expected, my Lord. I stole from you. They have no reason to trust me. In time, perhaps they will.'

Robert looked at Adam shrewdly, 'In time you hope to have your name cleared and return to West Markham, surely?'

Adam sighed. 'I don't see how that can be achieved, my Lord. The lands between here and there currently have bigger worries. If this Leigh is as ambitious as he appears to be, he isn't going to stop at usurping your influence in the county. He'll want to make a bigger name for himself than you did. He'll want to secure more power and take higher stakes.'

'You think he'll go for your master?'

'John de Markham is a lawyer and a king's serjeant. He has the ear of all the bailiffs, foresters and the sheriff himself.'

'So he does...' Robert was thoughtful for a moment.

'You don't think this is connected after all, do you? I mean, co-incidentally. You ran here, but do you think you were running because of Leigh?'

'I don't see how. No threats were made, no messages left. I was thrown out without reason or word. It was too underhand for this Leigh. I suspect he thinks his methods honourable because they are obvious.'

'However heavy handed.' Robert nodded. 'You're right. It was but a thought, what with Markham being so well-connected. Your old master may be a target later on. Do you want to warn him, Adam? You are loyal; I have learnt that very fast.'

'Once the Lady Mathilda is safe and I've repaid my debt to you, my Lord. Then maybe I will risk getting a word of warning to him. Until then, he is far enough north to be out of immediate danger, I think.'

'But is he? If only we knew where Leigh's base was. He could be in Nottinghamshire for all we know.'

'Wherever he is, he'll have left a trace. There will be a way to find him.'

'Eustace has already sent men out to scour the land. If he can follow us to our home, then we can follow him to his.' Robert called to some of the men in the courtyard for help and between them they righted the kitchen table. 'We ride to Leicester. Adam, I want you to stay here. You'll do Owen's job while you're here. And, sadly, that includes helping the monks who come for him to transport him from the stable to the litter. See Owen treated well for me.'

'I'd be honoured, my Lord.'

Leaving the manor guarded, and Sarah and Daniel doing their best to finish rescuing the kitchen while Adam prepared Owen for collection, Robert, Walter, Thomas, Laurence, Eustace and John took two armed men and, each using a different path, headed towards Leicester.

It was a few hours later, as Robert spotted the waterwheel denoting the outskirts of Leicester and its first fulling mill, when he remembered it was market day in the city. The main exchanges of the day would have been long over, but many of the market holders would still be there, especially those who'd travelled far for the privilege of selling their wares.

'Bertred.' He whispered the word. Robert had not told Mathilda's father of her kidnap because he hadn't wanted to worry him, but he'd forgotten about the market. Rumours would be flying and there was a chance that Bertred could have found out about his daughter already. Cursing, Robert was torn. Did he try and find his future father-in-law, or did he go straight to the meeting place?

The smell of the nearest tannery hit Robert's nostrils, making him screw his face up in disgust. Something about the acrid stench snapped him into making a decision. He had no choice. Calling to his nearest companion, he gave him instructions to go into the market and make discreet enquiries for a potter called Bertred of Twyford. If he was there, then he was to impart Robert's regrets at not being available to tell him what had happened in person. And that *everything* - absolutely everything - was being done to find Mathilda. Of that there was no question.

Then, with a heavy heart, he headed to the agreed meeting place, the outline of a plan forming in Robert's mind as he rode through the thickening crowds of people.

'My Lady? Mistress Matilda? Please, can you hear me?'

Mathilda was vaguely aware of a voice. Someone was possibly stroking her hair. Or she could be dreaming. If she was, then at least this was a nicer dream than the last one. That one had been more of a nightmare, with a great deal of running and shouting and broken pottery. She thought she'd smelt blood at one point. Now though, all see could smell was horses and hay.

'My Lady? Are you alright?'

Mathilda opened her eyes and then closed them again. The light hurt, and the view was all wrong. Where had her bed gone?

The hand was at her forehead again, wiping hair from her eyes. It wasn't Robert and it wasn't Sarah. The hand was the wrong size and texture for either of them.

'Please...'

It was the panic in the voice that threw her eyes to open again. 'Allward?'

'Oh, thank Our Lady! I thought he'd killed you.'

'Killed me?' Mathilda tried the words for size on her tongue, but they didn't ring true. She tried to turn around to see the source of the voice, but she felt heavy with the effort of movement, and suddenly the nightmare started to reform into fearfully clear reality. 'Allward, is that you?'

'Yes, yes, it's me. Don't try and move, you'll hurt yourself. Just lie there and rest.'

'Why? Where are we?' Despite Allward's warning Mathilda tried to turn her head. Immediately she regretted it. Her muscles thudded with pain and her neck jarred. Mathilda tried to lift a hand to her face, but her arms couldn't reach that far.

'Allward! What's happening?'

'Rowan Leigh, my Lady. Don't you remember?'

It came back in a landslide of horror. The attack on the house, being dragged from Sarah and Adam and then the water. The cold, relentless water... Mathilda began to shiver.

It was as if the memory of the cold was far worse than the cold itself had been.

She closed her eyes again. 'How did you get here? Are you tied up too?'

'Just my feet. Not as much as you, but then I'm not so valuable.' Allward's voice cracked with anxiety. 'I'm so sorry, I couldn't stop them. I did try, but there were too many of them.'

Trying to keep calm, telling herself she'd be alright and that Robert would be there soon, Mathilda asked, an edge of panic creeping into her voice. 'But how come you're here at all? And how am I tied exactly? I can't feel my legs.'

Shackled via a chain that was attached to his ankles, Allward shuffled as close to Mathilda as his restraint would allow him. 'We're in a stable. As far as I can tell it hasn't been used for a while. The straw is stale, and the horse smell isn't very strong.'

'Allward. I meant, where are we? I mean, where's this place? How far from Ashby Folville are we?'

'I don't know. Beyond Leicester. They hit me around the head, and after a while I must have blacked out because I don't remember much beyond passing the city.'

'They kidnapped you as well. I don't remember much.' Mathilda tried to sit up again. Moving slower, she felt Allward's hands come to her shoulders.

'Let me help you, my Lady. Go slowly. You hit your head when you fainted. '

'Fainted?' The feeling of falling swept over Mathilda as another set of shivers rocked her petite frame. 'He...he threw a bucket of water over me?'

'You were sick on him.'

The realisation of events from the evening before sent a clammy sweat across Mathilda's body as they swam into unwelcome clarity. 'I was scared. I didn't mean to.'

'That wouldn't matter to him. It was an insult and Leigh doesn't stand for anything other than total loyalty and respect.'

'How do you know this?'

'I listen. I've also made him think I admire him.'

'What!'

'Please, my Lady, don't be angry. This man is dangerous. We need him to trust me.'

'And yet he clearly doesn't. You're chained up in here with me.'

'Only one chain. I suspect I'm here, so I can report to him what you say when you wake up.'

Mathilda frowned. 'You think he'll challenge you about what I've said as a proof of your admiration and switch of loyalty?'

'I can't see how else we'll get out of here.' Allward tugged at his ankle chain in frustration, 'At first, it was only a plan to get myself free. I had no idea they'd captured you. When I saw you last night...' The lad swallowed carefully, his expression etched with distress, 'I couldn't get free to stop him! All I could do was watch what he was doing to you from here.'

Allward pointed to the small shuttered window above him. 'I couldn't believe it. I wanted to call out to you, to let you know there was a friend here, but...'

'But you couldn't. I'm glad you stayed silent. If they doubted you so soon I suspect you'd be dead already.'

'I suppose so. It didn't feel right, though.' Allward hung his head, 'Especially when they took your clothes.'

'What?' Mathilda felt her blood morph into ice as, very slowly, afraid to see, she peered at her chest. 'My clothes?'

'If they'd left you in the ones you'd had on, you'd have

died of cold by now. They had at first, but I made them take them off. I didn't think they'd... I thought they'd have women folk here, but....'

As Allward's sentence tailed off into thin air, Mathilda felt her earlier nausea racing back up her throat. 'Where are my clothes?'

She reached for her waist. 'No!'

'My lady, I'm sorry, they wouldn't listen. I said I'd do it. Better me than them. And I'd have shut my eyes and not leered like they did.'

The butterfly girdle was gone. The only present Robert had ever given her. Hand-crafted for her, it had been a token of his love and intent. And it was gone.

Allward saw the terror in her eyes. 'He took it. He said Robert would have to buy it back. I don't know if he meant the girdle, or...'

'Or me?'

'I'm sorry. The chain, it wouldn't...'

Mathilda opened her mouth, but no words would come out. She didn't even know how to ask the next question. A question she didn't even know if she wanted the answer to.

Understanding what Mathilda needed to ask, but wasn't sure how to, Allward said, 'As soon as you fainted he ordered you brought in here. You were unconscious. I pleaded with him. Told Leigh that if your virtue was questioned then you'd be worthless. That he'd lose what he had to trade with. Luckily he believed me.'

Mathilda hadn't realised she'd been holding her breath until that moment. Exhaling in a rush of relief that Rowan hadn't taken the maximum advantage of her while he could, she couldn't prevent a shudder at the thought of his hands being anywhere near her. 'Did... did he... was he the one who took my clothes off?'

'No. He made Gamelyn do it. It amused him to witness his henchman's discomfort as much as he enjoyed having you at his mercy. I don't think it mattered to Leigh that you weren't aware of what was going on.'

'He would have known you'd tell me.'

'I suppose so.' Allward looked at his feet in shame. 'He will probably want me to give him a detailed account of your reaction to the news.'

'Was I... did they... was I ever naked before you?'

'No, my Lady. They left your chemise. It was just your outer garments that were removed. If they hadn't, you'd be dead and then Leigh would have no bargain to strike with my Lord Robert.'

'That's why my outfit is cold and damp then.'

'Yes, but you are not frozen to a corpse. The dress and cloak they manhandled you into is thick wool. It probably saved your life.'

Mathilda ran the sides of her hands clumsily over the replacement clothes. They were rough, but Allward was right, they were bulky, and had made the difference between life and death. Swallowing down more bile, Mathilda closed her eyes against the realisation of the last few hours, 'How do you happen to be here in the first place, Allward?'

'I was on my way to help my Lord Robert at The Thwaite. Leigh had men watching the manor. I was scooped off the road a mile outside the village. Three men knocked me from my horse. They grabbed my horse to add to their stables here. I was lucky to only get bruises and a mild wound to my head.' He rubbed his short hair, and Mathilda could make out a gash over his temples. 'Is my Lord Robert on his way my Lady?'

Mathilda's face paled further. She shrugged, the act costing her a few seconds pain as some more of her muscles declared themselves to be more bruised than she'd previously realised. 'I can't see how. He has no idea where we are.'

Allward nodded gravely. 'Will you trust me, my Lady? It will sound like betrayal, but it might get me out. And if I can get out, then I can get help.'

'I will trust you; but be careful, Allward. One wrong move and we're both dead.'

~ *Chapter Sixteen* ~

'I'm sorry to hear about your steward, Folville. He was a good man.'

Robert Ingram, former Sheriff of Leicestershire and Nottinghamshire, had set up a council in a private room of one of the city's lesser populated taverns.

'Thank you, my Lord,' Robert bowed in agreement. 'Owen was loyal to the bone. He will be missed.'

'Yes, yes, Owen was a good man, but we have more pressing matters.' Eustace was as impatient as ever, but for once, Robert agreed with his brother's desire to act fast.

As the family congregated around the table, Ingram got straight to the point. 'I had reason to be thankful of our alliance during my time in power, my Lords Folville. What of my successor? I find it curious that you came to me and not de Cressy?'

John settled himself into the chair to Ingram's right side. 'No secret there. We trust you. We don't know him and so we don't trust him. The ink on his appointment is still wet and, as yet, we've had no reason to require a favour from him.'

'And, of course,' Thomas added as he unhooked his cloak and threw it over the back of his chair, 'he hides himself away in Nottingham, whereas you were always far more considerate in your locality.'

'Quite.' Ingram grimaced. He was well aware that the geographical convenience of residing in Leicester had played right into the Folvilles' hands. Their association hadn't always been an easy one, or one he wished to dwell on, yet between them many of the counties more corrupt officials had been dealt with, one way or another.

'What do you know of Rowan Leigh, my Lord?' Robert spread his palms out on the oak table, trying to calm his racing pulse. *Mathilda could be anywhere by now.*

'Beyond what I learnt from your lad Daniel and the information Eustace gave me on arrival, very little. I know someone has let it be known that there is a man within this county with a home for anyone who has served in the wars and returns homeless, who is willing to enter loyal service. I have to assume that man is Leigh.'

'Unusual. But giving employment to those without it is not a felonious arrangement?' John queried.

'True, and as a few of the area's more persistent ruffians have disappeared, I wondered at first if this man was doing the county a favour. Then I received a messenger; a man I had already met professionally. A felon called Edgar Waterman. He took great pleasure in informing me that my agreement with you gentlemen was at an end and that it was his master who would be controlling the region now.'

'When was this?' Robert wasn't surprised. It made sense that Ingram would be one of Leigh's first targets. Although he no longer held power, the former sheriff remained a man of influence. As a known associate of the Folvilles, obtaining his favour would be a major coup.

'Two days ago. The same day that Edgar and some friends, paid a visit to the tavern in Melton, I understand.'

'They've also greeted Jacob Lock's place in Ashby Folville a similar manner and they've paid two visits to our home. The first visit was informative, the second one...'

'I was sorry to hear about Mathilda.' Ingram ran a hand through his short beard. 'I have heard no more than rumour as to where these miscreants reside. However, if you met at Thwaite, and as they appear to have made the Hundred of Goscote their prime target area, then it is not unreasonable to assume that they hide within its boundaries. Why try and obtain the Folville family power if they don't live near enough to exploit it fully.'

'Our thoughts precisely.' John tapped his fingernails against the table, 'And yet no word has reached us as to where they are. Nothing at all.'

'Nor me.' Ingram rocked his chair onto two legs, stretching as he said pointedly, 'They were unsuccessful in securing my alliance, but they will try again.'

'You are sure of this?' Laurence broke his silence and leant forward a little in his seat.

'I am. I was informed there would be a future visit and that I'd be very unwise to refuse a second time.'

'Did they say when they'd be back?' Eustace started to play his dagger in his hands, 'We could wait and follow them. Or just skewer the bastards there and then.'

'Killing them may be inevitable, Eustace, but it's hardly helpful before we've tracked Leigh himself down,' Ingram steepled his fingers against his chin as he spoke, 'and no, I don't know when, but I can't imagine the wait will be long.'

Robert groaned. 'We can't wait at all. That fiend could be doing anything to Mathilda. She could be dead ... or worse.'

No one needed to ask what was worse than death. If Rowan really wanted to hurt Robert, then the way to do so was blindingly obvious. He'd force her into marriage, and it would probably be done in a brutal fashion.

'We need to be prepared for when they return.' John tilted his head towards their host. 'I propose two of our men stay with Ingram at all times. Eustace, do you have any expert trackers in your party?'

'I do, brother.' He acknowledged the wisdom of the suggestion. 'I'd do it myself, but there is a chance Leigh's men would know me on sight.'

'More than a chance, I'd say.' Ingram took over the proceedings, 'Additionally, a group of men should start to sweep the area. These men must be hiding in plain sight somewhere. No family name is being bandied about, so I doubt we have a noble connection - although I could be wrong - and although Edgar is a felon, he is not a fool. Whoever has employed his services is ambitious and clearly far from stupid. And again, I say Leigh must have someone supporting him. Someone who is affording him the courage to behave so brazenly with not a whiff of the hue and cry being raised...'

There was a moments silence as each brother understood exactly what it was that Robert Ingram was speculating.

'You think Edmund de Cressy is behind him?' John de Folville ran a hand through his tightly cropped hair. 'If you're right, my friend, then this has become much more interesting.'

'Interesting!' Robert almost spat the word, 'Mathilda is going through hell out there, how can you...' He stopped and frowned. 'Edmund de Cressy. He's the one who's had men chasing Adam across the county for a nonexistent crime.'

'Adam? The store thief?' Eustace's expression darkened. 'Have you been double-crossed after all, little brother?'

The former sheriff leant forward, his elbows on the table. 'Adam Calvin?'

Robert looked up in surprise. 'You know him?'

'Not personally, but I do know John de Markham.'

Every nerve in the room was on edge as each brother swivelled to look at Robert, who could only repeat what Mathilda so firmly believed. 'Adam isn't a traitor.'

Ingram's eyes narrowed as he appraised the younger Folville shrewdly. 'You aren't easily taken in, my Lord, and you may well be right. My Lord Markham isn't in your pay?'

John shook his head. 'Too far away. And what need do we have for lawyers? Things never go that far. We make sure of it.'

Snorting into his ale, Walter gave his eldest brother a hostile stare, 'Unless our lords and masters don't act on our behalf fast enough.'

'This,' Eustace glared at Walter, 'is not the time to debate previous errors of judgement. We have to think about the current situation. Is Adam Calvin a spy or not? Someone clearly helped Leigh's men into the manor. That door cannot be opened from the outside.'

Robert's fist landed on the table with a resounding thump. 'He saved Sarah's life! He protected Daniel. Adam got the word to Ingram here, and he fought tooth and nail to save Owen. If you think I've been fooled, think on this: Sarah is not so easily taken in, and she trusts him. And Mathilda...' He paused, swallowing carefully, 'She was utterly convinced Adam had been wronged. What's more, she was fearful that he'd be used as a scapegoat for Leigh's activity.'

Ingram sat back again. 'I recall Mathilda was astute when it came to the death of Master Hugo of Derby.'

Robert frowned at the thought of his friend's murder. 'She saw through the treachery of my reverend brother quickly. Mathilda is no fool, and she is brave. I hope these attributes are helping her now.'

Ingram inclined his head slowly. 'I have only heard of Adam Calvin because de Cressy is hunting him.'

'Adam told us he was. Although he doesn't know why, or what he is accused of.'

Ingram shrugged. 'What interests me more, is why the hunt is still going on. Calvin is only a steward; and there has been no outcry about any murder. I have heard rumours of a death, but there are rumours about everything, and it interested me that only the word death is used, not the word murder.'

Eustace's impatience was becoming a tangible presence in the room. 'So do you think Adam has lied, or not?'

The former sheriff, used to Eustace's temper, kept his tone calm. 'I couldn't say, but I would trust your womenfolk. Both are unusually bright for their nature and neither is easily tricked. However, I think I may go and visit my old friend de Markham. It isn't easy to pull the wool over his eyes either. I would like to know why Adam was made to flee without at least being accused or arrested. If de Cressy is abusing his position more than most, then the king will want to know, regardless of whether he's helping Leigh or not.'

Robert felt that at last progress was being made, even if it wasn't in the direction he'd hoped. 'I promised Adam that if he helped us, then I'd find out what he was accused of.'

'Then perhaps we had better ensure he helps us,' Thomas growled into the fireplace.

'He *is* helping us.'

Seeing another argument brewing, John cut in, 'Let's use Calvin's need for our protection as much as we can, while we can, then.'

Robert studied his eldest brother's expression, 'You've had an idea, John?'

'I have.'

'Well, go on then, brother!' Eustace prowled the small room, 'Speak your wisdom.'

'Sit down, Eustace!' John turned to address Ingram. 'We don't know where Leigh is and as time is short, I don't think we can rely on our men finding him quickly enough to avert disaster.'

'At last!' Robert said, 'Someone has noticed that my future's wife life is in peril.'

'And so is our reputation. And with every fresh piece of gossip it is further threatened.'

Robert muttered under his breath, but merely said out loud, 'Your idea, John?'

'We bring Leigh to us, or at least his men. The man likes to leave us messages. Let's leave him one.'

All eyes levelled on the lord of the manor as he spoke. 'With the life of the Lady Mathilda in jeopardy, Rowan Leigh will be expecting us to act soon. He may even believe he has the winning hand. I think we should encourage that belief, in the short term at least.'

'And?' Robert put his hand on the handle of his dagger, its presence reassuring.

'We leave a message at the taverns in Ashby and Melton. We know Leigh is going to send men to both places soon. Our message will demand a further meeting to discuss terms in The Thwaite. This meeting will take place on the understanding that Leigh brings Mathilda with him, so Robert can see she is cared for.'

'So we lull him into the belief that he has won. That we are willing to swap some influence for the girl?' Eustace sounded incredulous. 'Why wouldn't he see this is a trap?'

'It doesn't matter if he does. We will have achieved our aim by just getting him there. Leigh in person, not just this

Edgar or any of his other followers.'

'And what makes you think he'll come himself?' Robert asked.

'Because those will be the terms. That we are only willing to deal with the man in charge, not his hired hands.'

'And I take it we then follow Leigh to his lair?' Robert was trying to work out why Adam was needed for this, when their own men were already known to be good trackers.

'Naturally, although that is what he'll expect us to do.'

'So?'

'So we must ensure that Rowan Leigh's meeting at Thwaite will be the last one he ever attends.'

'Dangerous, but doable.' Eustace cast an eye towards the ex-sheriff as he added, 'But I don't think any of us would want to gamble with having our necks stretched for killing Leigh, however much of a public service we'd be performing.'

'Hence Adam Calvin,' interjected Ingram.

Robert looked from Eustace to Ingram to John. He didn't think Adam had the ability to kill anyone, but he held his tongue.

Eustace was looking pleased. 'That is a good plan, brother John, but there is one major question that remains unanswered.'

'Which is?'

'Where is Allward? If we believe that it wasn't Adam who let Leigh's men into our home, then it had to be him.'

1311

It wasn't fair

He kept telling himself he shouldn't have been surprised. That everything Richard did was designed to make his life worse.

Suddenly, he couldn't stop thinking about all the midnight visits when Richard had shaken him awake simply to tell him he was unwanted. He could see the relish on Richard's face as he told him that his mother must have hated him. That foundling was just another word for dumped.

Richard had told him over and over and over that children like him would only ever grow up to be servants or slaves. He'd even had him believing that once he was twelve years old the monks would sell him to the highest bidder. If, Richard had added with an evil grin, anyone had money to throw away on someone so weedy.

Some nights he had lain awake wondering if Richard could read his mind and see into the fearful recesses of his soul.

It had taken him so long to formulate a plan that would pay Richard back and show him and his family that having money wasn't an excuse to be cruel. And today was going to be the day he triggered that plan. The day he was going to strike...

But Richard's education was over. He had gone home.

~ *Chapter Seventeen* ~

Allward had been gone for nearly the whole morning. It had been bad enough being trapped with a friendly face by her side, but now she was alone, Mathilda's imagination had far too much free rein, and she was becoming increasingly scared.

Where is he?

Surely if they were going to torture information from him it wouldn't take this long or be this quiet? They weren't the sort of men who'd hang around when it came to acting on the threats they'd issued.

What was Allward telling them?

A voice at the back of Mathilda's head insisted that Allward wouldn't tell Leigh anything that could endanger her or the family, and yet...Why had Leigh's men bothered taking someone of such low status as Allward? He wasn't worth anything in monetary terms. They'd only taken her because Robert wanted her; otherwise she had no value at all.

Allward had been with the Folvilles since he was a boy, Mathilda was sure he wouldn't betray them lightly; but what if they tortured him? Rowan had already proved he was capable of that. She shuddered at the memory of the initial shock of the freezing water hitting her.

She ran her bound fingers over the space where her girdle should have been. The lack of its reassuring presence was fast becoming the hub for all her fears.

Would Robert want her now another man had stripped her? Worse, one man had touched her, while another had leered and laughed as they'd savoured her helplessness.

Somehow, the fact she had been unaware of what had happened, and that she couldn't have stopped it if she'd tried, didn't help. Thankful that Allward had been there to prevent them going further than they had, and strangely glad of the itchy fabric against her skin, Mathilda ignored the growl of her hungry belly. She made herself lie still and conserve energy while she waited for Allward's return.

If he did return.

Sarah squinted at the tiny stitches. The light was fading fast and as she held the newly-sewn seam up to the candle flame, she could feel the strain in her tired eyes. She wasn't going to stop, though. When she came home Mathilda would find her wedding gown ready and waiting for her. It would be exactly as they'd planned together, and it would be worn on the Winter Solstice. It *would* be worn.

'Sarah, lass, don't you think you should get some sleep?'

Adam sat next to the kitchen fire. He could see how desperately tired the housekeeper was as she stared at the scrubbed fabric. 'The house is secure. Daniel is abed. It's time you followed his example.'

'This material is so tricky to seam. It's so fine, you see. Lord Robert said cost was no object for Mathilda's dress.'

'I'm sure he did. And he will see her wear the dress, but I'm sure both of them would be distraught if they didn't have you at the wedding because you worked and worried yourself into an early grave.'

At this, Sarah did glance up. Her red-ringed eyes blinked as she took in Adam's concerned face. 'Lord Robert will bring her home, you know. He will.'

'Yes, he will; so you wearing your eyes out sewing when there is no light isn't going to make any difference to the situation, is it?'

The needle jabbed Sarah's finger. She winced, immediately sucking it so red droplets didn't smear the fabric that had already been through so much. 'Adam? Mathilda will come home, won't she?'

Despite everything, this was the first time Adam had seen Sarah look scared. 'I can't promise you that. I wish I could, but I can't.'

Sarah sounded resigned. 'I know.'

'I will do everything I can to help.' Adam found himself wanting to reach out, to put his arm around her, to comfort her, but he didn't move. It was unlikely the gesture would be welcomed, and he had no intention of adding to her worries.

'Afterwards,' Sarah began to smooth the fabric with her fingertips as she spoke, 'when this is over, one way or the other, what will you do? Will you return to West Markham?'

'I don't know.' Adam let a sigh escape, 'I need to go back if I want answers. But whether I can do so safely...'

'Master Robert said he would find out what happened.'

'I think he has bigger things to worry about now, Sarah. I wouldn't ask him to put himself out for me any more than he has already. I stole from him and yet he has let me stay here.'

'Lady Mathilda convinced him it was the right thing to do.'

'And if... forgive me, Sarah, if Mathilda does not come home... or even when she does, I can't imagine my Lord

Folville's mood will be a forgiving one. He won't want me around as a reminder of her kidnap or Owen's death.'

With her eyes fixed on the line of stitching that had secured the first sleeve in place, Sarah said, 'Robert won't rest until he finds her.'

'And I will help him.'

'So will I.' A tear escaped from the corner of the housekeeper's eyes. She scrubbed it away angrily before it too could fall on the gown. Not looking at her companion, she asked, 'Is there anyone at Markham who'll be worried for you? Missing you?'

'A family you mean?' Adam stared into the fires blaze. 'No. There's no one. I used to wish there was. Now I'm glad there isn't, or they'd be facing the shame of having a husband and father with an accusation of felony hanging over his head. May I ask; do you have a family?'

'This is my family. I bought up the Folville boys from a young age. All except Richard.'

'Richard?'

'He was sent into the church. Not the right choice for him. He is a cruel, vindictive man, just as he was a cruel and vindictive boy. If you think Eustace is violent and too quick to act or judge, then let me tell you that he is nothing compared to Richard, Rector of Teigh.'

'Where is Richard now?'

'France. Mathilda discovered he'd incited a man to commit murder. The brothers managed to keep him from the hangman's noose, but had Ingram send him into the King's service in France instead.'

'Then he may be dead.'

'He may; but the man has the luck of the Devil himself.'

Adam looked grave. 'He'll need it if he's over there.'

'You've been?'

'Briefly, and then I was sent to Scotland a few years before I was steward for Markham. It is not a period of my life I choose to think on.'

'I can't imagine you killing a man.'

'There were many who took pleasure in the slaughter. Many who enjoyed continuing to pillage between battles. I did not.' Adam looked thoughtfully into the flames for awhile. 'The boys had no mother?'

'They did, but Lady Alice spent most of her time travelling the lands with her husband, Lord John. She was a good mother when she was with them, but you can imagine what a handful the boys were. I helped then and I'm still helping now that their parents have gone.'

The silence stretched between them for a while as they became lost in their own thoughts. After a while, Adam got up and very gently took the needle, thread, and fabric out of Sarah's hands. Her fingers felt ice-cold as his hands brushed against them. 'When did you last eat?'

'I don't recall.'

'You must look after yourself. When Robert gets back he'll need you to be there for him. Food, drink, clothes, everything... it will all be required fast. To do that you have to be rested and fed. Not to mention having the energy to finish the dress and arrange the wedding feast.'

Sarah twisted her head towards the door. 'Where are they?'

'Leicester is a long way. I suspect they have stayed the night with Ingram. They'll have a plan to implement.'

'I should stay up in case they return.'

Adam shook his head kindly. 'Go to bed. I will sleep on Allward's cot in the kitchen. If they return tonight, I'll fetch you without delay.'

'I'm unlikely to sleep.'

'Yet your body will at least be rested.'

Sarah regarded Adam carefully. 'You are very kind.'

'Only sometimes. Now go to bed, woman.'

Getting up, her joints aching from sitting hunched over her work for so long, Sarah looked directly at the steward, blurting out the new fear that clouded the room. 'Do you think Allward betrayed us?'

'If he did, he will have been given no choice in the matter and we can't do a thing to change that. Rest now.'

~ *Chapter Eighteen* ~

Elias looked worried.

'Eustace's man, John Pykehose, will not leave you. Not for a moment. He has his own men. They are here, in the village.'

'Where?'

'Around. If they are needed they'll make their presence felt.'

Elias nodded; he could easily imagine men under the command of Eustace de Folville becoming a pack of wolves at the mere sniff of trouble. 'Alright, my Lord. And the message is?'

Robert passed a piece of parchment over to the innkeeper. 'I wrote it down. If Leigh wants to play at being a nobleman, let us see if he can read like one.'

'And if he can't?'

'Then you may recite it to him.'

'Umm, my Lord?' Elias looked blankly at the rolled message. 'I am no noble, nor did I receive an education beyond the correct measures of ale.'

'Forgive me,' Robert smiled, 'I'll read it out.

'The Folville family will agree to exchange the leases to lands and alliances formed in return for the life and freedom of Mathilda de Twyford, on the condition that Mathilda is bought to Thwaite Wood tonight at Vespers in the company of Rowan Leigh himself, to discuss terms.'

Elias paled. 'You're giving us all up, my Lord?'

'Not for a second, but if we're ever going to get close to this wolf's lair we have to get him to come out into the open.'

'So this is a lie.'

'This is a trap.'

The innkeeper grimaced as he surveyed his damaged domain. Several pieces of furniture sat to one side in a state of disrepair after Leigh's men's onslaught. 'Then I will deliver this gladly. Are you sure they'll come today?'

'I'm not sure they'll come here, and so the same message has been left at Ashby Folville inn, and also with several of the prime targets for Leigh's ambition. He is not going to let much more time pass before he makes another move. He's taken too many risks not to see this through to the end. He may not send a man here, but he'll send one somewhere and I intend to be ready.'

'Where can I get word to you, my Lord Robert? If they do come here?'

'You won't have to. Eustace's groom will see to everything. All you need to do is serve your ale.' Robert surveyed the tavern. How many stools were destroyed?'

'Three beyond hope, my Lord.'

'I'll make sure they are replaced when this is over.'

'Thank you, my Lord.'

Allward hadn't come back. Mathilda had given up waiting for him. Instead, all her concentration was focused on listening for his voice, or for the mention of his name on another man's lips.

He could be dead. But if he was, then surely these men

would have found that funny. They would have made Allward's murder obvious. Made it public, even. Enjoyed its cruelty.

Allward?

Mathilda's insides shrivelled at the thought that he might have been the one to let Leigh's men into the manor.

He wouldn't...

Her insides gave an involuntary growl. She hadn't been fed and her mouth was so dry from lack of water, that if someone didn't come to talk to her soon, she wasn't sure she'd be able to speak ever again.

Mathilda was convinced she was being held at a workshop, probably a carpenter's or a cooper's. The smell of sawdust was strong, and she could hear the sound of sawing and hammering coming from across the other side of the yard she'd been humiliated in the day before... or was it two days ago? Mathilda closed her eyes and tried to get a grip on time.

Robert. Where are you?

Sarah had made enough stew to feed an entire army, which was as well because it felt as though an army had moved into the manor. There hadn't been so many people in residence at the manor since the murder of the corrupt nobleman Belers by the family had necessitated a brief period of extra security.

Being busy however was balm to Sarah's soul. The housekeeper didn't want time to think. She just wanted industry to exhaust her into sleep and then for it to start all over again until Mathilda was found and the circumstances of Allward's disappearance were known.

Men had come for Owen's body in the early hours of the morning and having sent up a prayer for his safe keeping in Heaven, Sarah had dived into her preparations. With Daniel's help, she had set up dozens of extra sleeping cots around the edges of the main hall. Broth was bubbling over the fire, and the vegetables for a second batch of stew were already prepared.

Bread was rising in the warming oven, and as she wiped the sweat of labour from her forehead, Sarah turned her attention to making sure there were enough tankards left after Leigh's men had laid waste to her kitchen and larder. If not, she'd have to hazard Daniel's safety and send him over to Twyford to ask Mathilda's father for more.

Sarah was stirring the huge pot of broth over the fire when Adam came into the kitchen. 'Something smells good.'

'Stew for supper and broth to keep the men going. My Lord Robert is certain that today will be the day they bring Mathilda home. I don't want a single empty belly leaving this house before heading to face Our Lady knows what!'

Adam inhaled the aroma with appreciation. 'There are more men arriving by the moment. Your labours will be much appreciated, I'm sure.'

'In truth I care little whether they are or not. I just don't want time to stop and think.'

The stand-in steward acknowledged the truth of what the housekeeper said. 'I have all the horses stabled, but there is little room for the poor creatures to move, it's so full out there.'

'It won't be for long. Are they also fed and watered?'

'Daniel is doing a good job, but we miss the skills of Allward. Daniel tells me he is a good horseman, excellent at calming the beasts when they're skittish. They know something is wrong.'

Sarah put down the wooden spoon and poured Adam a

drink. 'I'm surprised Bertred's sons are not here.'

Adam sat for a moment, flexing his tired legs as he stole a few precious moments' rest. 'Eustace's man persuaded Bertred and Matthew to stay in Twyford. If Mathilda was taken, then her father and brother's may also be a target. And Oswin is still in service with the Coterel family in Derbyshire for a few more days, until the year's end.'

Sarah snorted, 'And God help anyone who attacks Oswin now he has the trust of the Coterels as well as the Folvilles. Facing off one criminal family is reckless enough, but two... Leigh isn't that much of a fool, I'm sure.'

'Perhaps.' Adam stared into his ale. 'I should get on. I want to make sure my Lord Robert has armour that is so polished, Leigh would be ashamed to strike at it.'

'I wish we knew for sure. I mean, Robert can't be positive that the messenger will get his letter to Leigh today. And if he does, then we can't be sure that the meeting will happen, or if it does, if it'll be tonight. And with every moment, Mathilda... What if Leigh... what if he makes her, against her will, and...?'

'He won't.'

'But you can't know that. He...'

Adam got up and put an arm around a sobbing Sarah. 'If he lays one finger on her, then he will not live to see tomorrow.'

Sarah, immediately angry at her tears, said, 'I have cried more in the last two days than in the whole of my life.'

'She is like a daughter to you, just as the boys are like sons.'

'She is. I never thought I'd see any of them married. And I really never thought I'd see one of them married to a girl I actually liked, rather than someone with the right sort of land or wealth. Mathilda is very special.'

'And she will be a beautiful bride.'

Footsteps at the kitchen door made them both turn around. 'She most certainly will.' Robert's expression was troubled but determined. 'The message has been delivered. We go to The Thwaite tonight.'

Gamelyn swung his horse into the workshop yard. The sound of sawing immediately stopped, and Rowan Leigh strode into the yard to greet his second-in-command.

From the shelter of her prison, Mathilda twisted towards the abrupt cessation of noise and listened as hard as she could.

'My Lord.' Gamelyn held out the roll of parchment. 'Folville had the nerve to leave you a written message. No doubt he believed you incapable of reading it.'

'No doubt.' Rowan snatched the paper. 'Was this read out to you?'

'The innkeeper at Melton has no letters, but he'd been told it contained a request to meet to discuss terms with Robert. May I ask, my Lord, if that is the case?'

'It is.' A satisfied smile broke out on Rowan's weasel face. 'I have been expecting this. They'll be going frantic trying to find the girl.'

'Where is the suggested meet?'

'Same place as before, and for tonight.' Rowan tapped the parchment against his hand. 'We are to take the girl with us.'

Mathilda tried to sit up straighter as she strained to hear properly. Then wished she hadn't as the ropes cut into her wrists. *Robert's coming...*

'Will we go?'

'Fetch the boy.' Rowan stamped his feet against the cold and wrapped his cloak tighter around his shoulders, 'I think he should be the one to deliver the reply, don't you.'

Gamelyn laughed. 'Certainly, master.'

Allward was before Leigh within seconds. 'My Lord, Leigh. You desire my help?'

'The time to prove your worth has arrived, Allward. As you predicted, the young Folville has asked to see Mathilda before he agrees to hand over any allegiances. You were right; it seems the man truly cares for the girl.'

'What do you wish me to do, my Lord?'

'Ride to Ashby Folville to tell Robert that I agree to his suggestion. The girl will be shown to him, but until I have proof that the Folvilles have truly withdrawn their control over the area in favour of me, then he will not get her back.'

'Yes, my Lord.' The young man bowed.

Allward was already striding purposefully towards the stables when Leigh called out, 'If you let me down, Allward, then I will kill her. But before I do, I'll have fun with her. And I will make you watch.'

The boy didn't even blink. 'I have given you my word, my Lord, as one foundling to another. I will return as soon as the message is delivered.'

A deathly silence dropped on the courtyard, before Leigh spoke again, 'One what?'

'My Lord, I too was left with neither mother nor father. I was taken in and raised by the Folvilles as a babe.'

Leigh's pallor became waxy. His words came out very slowly. 'Who told you that I was a *foundling*?'

Realising he'd overstepped some sort of invisible mark, Allward bowed low. 'Forgive me, my Lord. I meant no disrespect. I just meant that you should be proud of your achievements without the help of a family to support you.'

'*Who* told you?' Each word cracked like ice.

'I'm sorry, my Lord, I don't know. I overheard a conversation while I was within your holding cell. I saw no faces and recognised no voice.' Allward bowed again, 'Should I get on with delivering the message, my Lord?'

The venom as Leigh hissed, 'Go,' would haunt Mathilda for the rest of her life.

Mathilda was barely breathing. She hadn't been able to see the exchange, but even though the boy's name hadn't been used, she would have known Allward's voice anywhere.

He had warned her she wouldn't like what she heard. That she should trust him whatever. A violent shaking overtook Mathilda as she slouched into a position that eased the pressure on her wrist and ankle restraints.

Telling herself that whatever happened, she would be seeing Robert soon and that he'd have a plan, Mathilda clamped her eyes shut.

If Allward had betrayed them, then she might live; but the price for that would be to stay here with Leigh. If he was about to trick Leigh, then she might die as punishment...

There and then, with a muttered plea for understanding to Our Lady, Mathilda vowed that if Allward had caused this, she would kill him personally.

And then herself.

~ *Chapter Nineteen* ~

Rowan allowed himself another drink. Later he'd make sure he had a clear head, but for now he would indulge his urge to celebrate his progress so far and wash away the taste of betrayal. A betrayal he'd enjoy punishing when the time came.

Pouring out some more ale for himself and his master, Gamelyn added a new tankard to the table as Edgar came into the workshop. 'You have news?'

'My Lord, Gamelyn, I do.' Edgar wiped the sweat from his brow. He'd ridden hard, and the sun was high in the sky once more. 'De Cressy is due to arrive 'ere tomorrow to finalise an alliance 'tween us.'

'*Us?*'

'I apologise, my Lord. I meant 'tween you and 'im.'

'That's better.' Leigh's scowl widened into a grin, highlighting the smooth complexion which always seemed at odds with the coarseness of his nature. 'Then we have even more to celebrate. By the time our good sheriff comes to visit tomorrow, we'll have secured my control of the region and I will be able to announce my forthcoming marriage.'

Edgar and Gamelyn looked at each other but said nothing about Mathilda. Instead Edgar asked, 'Where be the turncoat?'

'Gone to deliver a message to his former master.' Leigh looked increasingly smug. 'We will soon see if young Allward is as loyal to me as he claims, or if he has an agenda all of his own.'

'You've had him followed?'

'Naturally.'

Gamelyn averted his eyes from Leigh's face. He was becoming increasingly uncomfortable with his master's premature confidence. 'Are we ready for the meeting tonight, my Lord?'

Rowan put down his drink and brushed his hands down his hose. 'Well, I am and the horses are. I have sent men into the wood already. Shall we go and see if our guest of honour is ready? I think perhaps a change of outfit might be in order. I'd hate the Folville scum to think we don't treat our womenfolk well.'

Leigh was two steps from the threshold when he turned to his men, 'Come on, then.'

'You wish us to help you dress your future wife, my Lord?' Gamelyn risked sounding as genuinely unsure about accompanying Leigh as he felt.

'And you'd be wise not to question that wish.' Rowan turned towards the stables. 'It would hardly be seemly for me to attend to Mathilda alone and we have no women here. That means you two will have to chaperone her.'

'Yes, my Lord.' Gamelyn felt the growl of his own stomach, which was more than ready for some food. 'Would you like me to find her some bread and water, my Lord? The girl will need strength to be a dutiful wife.'

'Well said. I will expect much of Mathilda.' Leigh wiped some stray sawdust from his cloak, 'Fetch her broth from the kitchen.'

Wishing he'd been the one to think of the excuse to leave his master for a few minutes, Edgar followed Rowan towards the stable, deep in thought. Leigh was usually so measured in his plans, but since the coup of capturing the girl he'd become less careful and now he was drunk on the very day he needed to keep his wits about him more than ever.

If he and Gamelyn didn't look out, Leigh would be sending them to hell via a faster route than the one they'd already resigned themselves to taking.

'It's no good going in with force of arms. Not if your description of the place is accurate.'

Eustace was in his element. He loved being in the thick of the action and it had been ages since life had justified him the opportunity for violence.

Robert could only agree. 'If Leigh has men well placed, and I'm sure he will have, then they'll be in the trees, hidden away. The entrance to the meeting place was narrow. It would be no hardship to pick off our men with arrows.'

'So why did you agree to the same location?' Walter was loitering by the kitchen door, fidgety to get going.

'Because it has to be close to where he is living and therefore near to Mathilda.'

'And yet it isn't safe.'

'Not for a big group. Or at least, a big visible group.'

Eustace was nodding in agreement. 'You are thinking we should play fire with fire. If Leigh is using underhand tactics against us, then we should as well - and do it better. We have, after all, more experience than him.'

'But do we?' Walter was frowning at the gathering of brothers. 'We don't know how old this man is or his background. We have no intelligence on him whatsoever. He can't have simply sprung from nowhere.'

Robert shrugged. 'We don't have time to send out for enquiries. Anyway, Mathilda is the best at that, and she can hardly go hunting for rumours, can she!'

Unaware that he'd picked a bad moment, Daniel ran into the hall, his face pink with the excursion of his work in the stables, 'My Lords! Allward is here.'

'Allward?' Robert turned his eyes to the doorway as Thomas came in, Allward's cloak twisted in his fists, a dagger at the boy's throat.

'The traitor returns, brothers.'

Allward looked desperate to speak, but with his cloak all but strangling him, there was no chance of him getting a word out.

'Let the boy go, Thomas.' John, who'd been sat by the fire, got silently to his feet. 'Come here, Allward.'

Rubbing his throat, Allward coughed as he took a step forward, and bowed to the assembled family.

'Where did you find him, Thomas?'

'He rode in here; bold as you like.'

John looked at Robert as he said, 'Hardly the act of a traitor.'

'Unless he is particularly daring and has an inflated sense of his own worth.' Thomas kept close to Allward, his dagger drawn.

'I assure you, Thomas, my mind is open to every possibility.' John studied the lad for a long time before asking, 'Where have you been, Allward?'

'Leigh kidnapped me. Please, my Lord, Mathilda is with him.'

Robert rounded on the boy, grabbing his arm and gripping it hard, 'She is alive? Unharmed?'

'Alive, yes. But unfed and thirsty and suffering from the

effects of cold.'

Robert felt his spirits lift and fall in quick succession. 'Where is she?'

'Lubbesthorpe, my Lord.'

'That's La Zouche's land.' John got to his feet, anger spitting from his teeth. 'He was loyal to us. His family have helped us many times. He's in France, though. At least, I thought he was.'

'He is, my Lord. He's not returned from hiding after his support for Despenser and Mortimer became known to the Crown.' Allward was shaking his head fast as he spoke. 'His daughter Joan holds the manor in his stead. She has been cowed by Leigh. It was a gradual, careful process. Leigh was taken on as the town carpenter after serving as apprentice to the previous one.

'Leigh has slowly risen and gathered about him men with nowhere to go but the battlefield or the gallows. I doubt my Lady la Zouche knew what was happening until she was caught fast in his web. Why would she question an apprentice taking over from a deceased master?'

Eustace played his dagger pommel in his palms. 'You think the Lady Joan would be rid of this stain on her lands now, though?'

'I do, my Lord.'

While Eustace was talking to Allward, Robert saw Adam had come to the doorway, the older man's expression was grave as he waited to hear what Allward had to say.

Robert pushed a cup of ale towards the boy. 'I hardly know what to ask you first, Allward, but the obvious must be addressed. You are alive. Owen is not. How is this possible?'

'My Lord Robert?' All the colour drained from the boy's face. 'Owen is dead?'

'You didn't know?'

Allward's stomach knotted with grief. 'He... he was my friend. He took me in, looked after me, taught me... they, they didn't say.'

'How come you escaped?'

'Escaped?' Allward looked confused, 'I didn't escape. I was sent. Leigh got your message. I have the reply. I have to go back, otherwise...'

The tension in the room was suddenly magnified.

'Otherwise what, Allward?' Robert already knew the answer to the question. 'Mathilda suffers?'

Allward whispered, 'Yes,' before wiping a mucky sleeve over his eyes. 'I'm doing my best to look after her, my Lords, I promise.'

After a moment of hush, John took charge. 'I think you'd better tell us what you were told to say, Allward. Then you had better explain your actions from the second you left this manor the night Mathilda was taken, to this very moment.' He paused with a heavy silence, 'I am sure there is no need to tell you, Allward, that all your years of loyal service will count for nothing if we find you have betrayed us.'

'My Lord, you have my word that I have not. They think I have, though. It's a plan.' Allward spoke fast, his voice suddenly eager, 'Mathilda knows about it. I was imprisoned with her for a while. We agreed I should do this. It seemed the only way to let you know where she was.'

Robert could easily believe that Mathilda would have thought up such a ruse, but simply said, 'So the message you have to deliver is what?'

'Leigh and Mathilda will be at The Thwaite as agreed. He says he will hand her over once he has proof of the alliance exchanges.'

'Do you believe he will keep his word?'

'That he will be there, yes. That you'll see Mathilda, probably. The rest... I couldn't say. I would expect treachery.'

'From him or from you?' Eustace had been regarding Allward with a shrewd stare.

'I can only give you my word of good intentions my Lord. I cannot prove them.'

Robert noticed the scar beneath Allward's fringe for the first time. 'You've been hurt?'

'I was pulled from my horse by Leigh's men when they took me. It was just after I left here after delivering Mathilda and Daniel home from Twyford. Lady Mathilda shuttered the gate behind me, and I rode out again. I intended to come to Thwaite to help you, my Lord Robert. To my shame however, I was intercepted within the mile and knocked of my wits. I awoke in the stables of the carpenter's workshop at Lubbesthorpe.'

'You knew where you were?'

'I've been there before, my Lord. When my Lord Roger la Zouche employed us to rid the world of the corrupt Belers, I was the boy in charge of the horses.'

'Indeed, you were.' Robert felt his palms itch. He wanted to believe Allward. He'd watched the lad grow from a pup in the care of Owen, but if he was lying... 'And Mathilda was bought to the stable as well?'

'By the morning she was with me. I couldn't believe it. If I'd known they intended to follow us from Twyford... for surely that must have been what happened.'

'It would seem likely.' Robert was thoughtful. 'We need to get to Lubbesthorpe before the meeting at Thwaite tonight. If we can get to Mathilda first, then Leigh's bargaining weapon is gone.' He got to his feet, 'Let's go!'

'Steady, little brother.' Eustace reached out to stem Robert's rush. 'If she isn't at Lubbesthorpe, then we could be racing off in the wrong direction.'

'But Allward said...'

'And yet someone *did* let Leigh's men into this manor. If it wasn't Adam, as you insist, and it clearly wasn't Sarah or Owen or Daniel, then who was it?'

Mathilda heard them coming. Her whole body felt weak and she knew that, if they'd decided to throw themselves on her, then she wouldn't be able to stop them.

'Our Lady, protect me. Please.'

1312

Brother Peter had hugged him.

He'd never received a hug before. He was ashamed at how he'd stiffened with fear before recognizing the gesture for the act of affection that it was.

Brother Peter had spoken to the Lord la Zouche on his behalf. The carpenter at the village of Lubbesthorpe needed an apprentice and it was to be him!

As he'd packed his few belongings into a sack, he'd looked down at his narrow sleeping cot for the last time. This was his chance. His chance to prove he was never going to be just a servant.

Richard had been gone for six months now, but the shadow he'd cast was long. With a determination that hardened his battered heart, he made a vow to himself as he walked away from the dormitory for the last time.

He was going to be the best carpenter in the land.

Then he'd make a new plan. A much better one.

~ *Chapter Twenty* ~

Edgar had been thankful for the partial reprieve from going into the stable. Rowan had sent him to fetch a roll of clothing waiting on the bed in the master's quarters.

Tied into a bundle by a piece of rope, Edgar recognised them as women's clothes, but he didn't want to guess where they'd come from. He took his time picking them up. The irony of the situation wasn't lost on him. The lack of women here had been a major factor in him deciding to stay with Rowan, but now his master was keen to take a wife, albeit just to prevent another man from having a person he loved.

A childhood spent being terrorised by an unholy set of nuns in a priory in the north of the country had sent Edgar fleeing into the arms of the King's army at a very early age. He'd kept a healthy distance from all womankind ever since. Their ability to look innocent in public and act like the Devil on earth in private, frightened Edgar in a way that a dagger at the throat or the thought of an arrow between the shoulders never could.

Everything about his master marrying Mathilda of Twyford set Edgar's alarm bells ringing. Why couldn't Rowan be content with slowly building his small empire? They were doing well until he'd listened to that cockroach, Edmund de Cressy.

The workshop had regular custom. Rowan's skill as a carpenter were superb, and his sideline in protection and taking tithes from travellers who strayed through Leicester Forest without their express permission was bringing him followers and giving him a wealth that he, as an orphan from the monastery, could never have aspired to.

Now though, the master had lost his satisfaction in sneaking the odd bit of money away from those too rich or stupid to stop them. He'd been shown a way to satisfy his inbuilt greed and cruelty. And even that would be tolerable if he would just stick to a land war. But a woman... a woman promised to a member of the Folville family... That was asking for the King himself to come calling, with a noose in one hand and an axe in the other.

Knowing he couldn't safely delay any longer, Edgar gathered up the bundle and headed towards the stable, hoping he'd intercept Gamelyn on the way so he didn't have to witness Rowan speak to Mathilda alone. Or worse, watch as he removed her layers. In Edgar's limited experience, women were even more dangerous when they had no clothes on.

At that moment, more than anything in the world, Mathilda wished she could stand up. The figure of Rowan Leigh would have been less imposing if he she could stand in front of him, face to face. She knew she'd still be scared, but at least she wouldn't feel small and scared.

'You must be hungry.'

'As you haven't seen fit to feed me or offer me refreshment, then you can assume you are correct.' Sounding far more confident and brave than she felt, Mathilda squared her shoulders as she added, 'It was not a difficult conclusion for you to reach.'

Crossing his hands over his chest, Rowan lounged

against the wall on the opposite side of the stall, scorn etched across his unsettlingly cherubic face. 'Are you always so disrespectful towards your host, or did you pick those manners up from Folville?'

'I usually have a choice in deciding which *host* I visit.'

'Ah, but that's not exactly true, is it. You had little say in the nature of your arrival at the Folville manor on your first visit there, did you?'

Mathilda held his stare. There was something not quite right about the way he could go so long without blinking.

'What is it, Mistress Twyford? Lost your desire to answer me back already?'

'I see little point in telling you things you already know.'

The sound of approaching footsteps outside made Rowan grin. Mathilda found herself thinking that he had too many teeth in his smile as he said, 'that will be your refreshment arriving. I trust you aren't going to say something stupid like you won't eat any food I offer?'

Holding his gaze, forcing herself to fight the instinct to turn away, Mathilda said, 'On the contrary, I wish to eat and drink. I will need all my strength to escape from this place.'

'You think you'll escape? Interesting.' Rowan turned to the doorway, 'Come in Edgar, Gamelyn. Mathilda is hungry.'

Although she wanted to ask what Leigh's plans were for her, what he intended to do with Allward and a million other questions, Mathilda held her tongue as she regarded the two men who entered the stable.

Immediately the space in the stable felt diminished. Both men dwarfed Leigh. They were tall and bulky against his slim sinewy frame. Their hands looked as if they'd been designed specially to wield swords, their arms to pull back longbows; the items they were holding looked incongruous in their grasp.

'Gamelyn, the food please.' Leigh gestured to the shorter of the two men.

Mathilda was surprised. 'Gamelyn? As in the outlaw hero? You should be ashamed to bear such a name. He'd never have kidnapped a woman.'

Gamelyn opened his mouth to respond but swallowed the unpleasant retort when he saw the blaze of rage that passed over his master's face. Instead he said nothing as he shoved a cup of stew and a beaker of water on the floor before the prisoner.

She hadn't missed the flash of rage in Rowan's face but pushed her luck anyway by sighing with heavy purpose. 'I am grateful for the food, but pray tell me how I'm supposed to drink or eat if my hands are bound?'

'For heaven's sake, man, untie the lady.'

As Gamelyn's thick fingers worried at the knots that held her wrists, Mathilda tried not to inhale the sickly aroma of sweat that hung around him, or the stench of his breath.

At last her wrists were free. Without bothering to rub the sores that had formed on her skin, Mathilda's hands grabbed the two vessels. With shaking limbs, she ate fast. Too fast at first, making herself choke, much to the amusement of the men present, all of whom appeared far more comfortable when she appeared vulnerable than when she was being brave.

It didn't take long for the stew to disappear. Until then, her tongue licking out the stew from the cup, all pride gone in the face of her hunger, Mathilda hadn't paid any attention to what the other man was carrying. Now she saw the fabric roll. She was instantly reminded of Sarah and how she'd been attacked, possibly by these very men, while carrying the roll of material for her wedding dress.

The thought made her feel weak. Would she ever wear that wedding dress?

Rowan, as if sensing he'd not lost face in front of his colleagues as much as he'd thought thanks to this woman, kicked the used pottery from her hands, making Mathilda jump and the cups smash against the wooden walls.

'I would strongly advise that, now you've had your food and your moment of mock bravery, that you do precisely what I tell you to.'

Trying not to throw up the food she was just digesting and thus earn another dousing, Mathilda echoed Rowan's words back at him. 'And what, precisely, will you be telling me to do?'

'Isn't it obvious? You were to be married and I hate to disappoint people.'

Mathilda's insides became as cold as her outsides as she studied the roll of fabric that was dropped next to her tethered ankles. Even in their rolled and creased state, the contents were unmistakable. It was a wedding gown and matching cloak.

'Aren't you keen to see what you'll be married in?' Rowan's tone was mocking as he bent to undo her restraints, so she could change her clothes, but at the same time, every word he uttered was heavy with unshakeable intent.

Fighting off the realisation of what he was saying to her, Mathilda crushed fistfuls of straw in her free hands, 'I know what I will be married in. Sarah, despite your best efforts to stop her, has the fabric for my dress and has made a start on its assembly.'

'In this you are mistaken. You merely know what you thought you'd be married in. But then, to be fair to you, Mathilda of Twyford, you *thought* you knew which man you were to be married to as well. And, again, you were mistaken.'

'Are you ready, my Lord?'

'Thank you, Wilkin. I have a few more documents to sign before you can return them to the Lord Markham. Then I will be on my way to Lubbesthorpe.'

Edmund de Cressy laid his quill on the desk and looked up at his approver. 'You're fitting into Adam Calvin's shoes well?'

'Indeed, my Lord. I thank you for recommending me to His Lordship.'

'It was the least I could do.' De Cressy picked the quill up and tapped the end over the inkpot. Tiny jet droplets rippled across the black liquid. 'And the thefts have stopped now Calvin has gone, I assume?'

'As you would expect after the removal of the chief suspect.'

'Indeed.' Edmund regarded Wilkin Sayer. 'You've come a long way since you crossed from the border of Wales; be careful you don't slip back again.'

'I'm always careful, my Lord.'

'I don't doubt it.' De Cressy smiled, 'You have been of good service to me. Your network of connections is wide and useful.'

'I simply pay attention to what's going on around me, my Lord.'

'And charge for passing that knowledge on.'

'The information I had wasn't always safe for me to know, my Lord.'

'Like the background to Rowan Leigh's childhood, for example.'

'If Leigh knew that anyone had information about his personal history, well... He sees his history as weakness. He doesn't want to be judged on how his life began.'

'A sensitive soul.' Edmund barked derisively. 'A *violent* sensitive soul.'

'He'll be useful to you, my Lord, but I would, if I may be so bold, continue to advise caution. Rowan Leigh is the most unpredictable man I've ever encountered.'

'As long as he helps me get rid of every cursed Folville in the country, and preferably beyond, he can be as unpredictable as he likes.'

~ *Chapter Twenty-one* ~

'So we're decided.' John Folville took his cloak from Adam. 'Eustace will go to Joan la Zouche and offer assistance. It is the least we can do for the daughter of a friend. With luck, she'll have had word from her father.'

Robert was thoughtful. 'Even if she hasn't, can we say that she had?'

'Clever little brother.' Eustace and John exchanged approving looks. 'Leigh would love to bag the help of the son of a baron, even if William la Zouche was a rogue of the style that makes us look like a spring breeze.'

Robert allowed himself a moment's satisfaction before continuing to lay out the immediate plan. 'Allward will return with our assurance that we intend to keep our word, but only on the safe return of Mathilda. In the meantime, we will continue to be vigilant in Melton Mowbray and Ashby Folville itself. The more we can learn about Leigh before Robert sees him this evening the better.'

'And you are convinced Allward's telling the truth about being on our side?' Eustace looked far from certain.

'He said it was Mathilda's idea. It sounds like her sort of scheme.'

Robert, Sarah, Adam and Eustace were sat around the kitchen table with John. Allward had been allowed to rest on his cot, but with a guard of Walter and Thomas looming over him, it was anybody's guess whether he'd actually get any sleep or not.

'And when I get to Rowan, brother, are you in agreement with the plan?' Robert knew what he wanted to do, but if he killed Leigh right there in front of his men, Mathilda's life would be in even more danger. Not to mention that it hadn't been long since his status as an outlaw had been lifted after the murder of Roger Belers. He didn't want to enter married life with a murder conviction hanging over his head.

'I am. That's when Adam will have the opportunity to prove his worth.' The elder Folville looked at the former steward. 'What say you, Calvin, can you do it?'

Sarah looked up from where she'd been sat at the end of the bench, listening to everything that was being discussed while stirring a pot of stewing apples, as Adam replied, 'I have already pledged by word, my Lord. If the opportunity we hope for arrives, then I will not hesitate to take it.'

'Well said. If we follow the plan we've made, then we should, at the very least, get Mathilda out of there. At best, we'll bring the man down before he gets a firmer grip on the region as well.' Robert paused and switched his attention to Eustace. 'You'd better find Zouche's girl. If Lady Joan has knowledge of Leigh's exact whereabouts, then we need to know, just in case this evening doesn't go to plan.'

Eustace was already on his feet. 'I've met Joan many times. The woman is an ogre, but an attractive one. Not easily swayed. If this Leigh is controlling her, she won't like it and is probably already plotting to remove him herself.'

'Then why hasn't she been to us for help before?' Robert mused, more to himself than the room, but Eustace replied anyway.

'Pride, brother. The woman is so stiff with it that it's a

miracle she can bend to dress. I will return soon.' With an inclination of his head to John, Eustace was gone.

'And now I must leave too, Robert.' John got up, 'I have business I can't miss in Huntingdon first thing in the morning. If I'm not there it will make the rumours of our sudden weakness appear more real.'

'And right now, appearances are everything.' Sarah spoke with approval of the lord's common sense.

'Indeed, Sarah.' John smiled at the housekeeper fondly. 'You are to keep these renegades safe for me, yes?'

'I will do my best, my Lord.'

'I know you will.' John put a hand on Robert's shoulder, 'I will see you at the wedding, brother.'

'You will.' Robert was grateful for the confidence in this brother's voice. 'Mathilda and I are looking forward to it.'

Sarah got to her feet as well. 'Which reminds me, if you'll excuse me, my Lords, I have a wedding dress to finish.'

Allward had dozed for a while, but now he lay wide awake behind his closed eyelids. He could hear Thomas and Walter discussing the benefits of stiffened leather over metal for armour and the sound of footsteps moving about the kitchen, only a short corridor away. Sarah was probably cooking. She was always cooking. He was sure Robert would be getting ready to meet Leigh.

Beyond some low-level chatter, it was very quiet. Allward wondered if John and Eustace had gone. If they had, then Robert would only have a few guards on patrol and not all of them would know to be looking out for him if he managed to slip away. Although the chances of easing past Thomas and Walter were slim.

There was no doubt that Leigh was paranoid, although

why, Allward wasn't yet sure. He suspected he was close to the mark with Leigh's foundling beginnings, but as he himself had been raised outside his original family, he couldn't see why it should have caused such ire to cross Leigh's face when he'd mentioned it. After all, there was no sin attached to the child or the mother in such cases and hadn't been for over a hundred years.

The thought of Mathilda stuck in the stable, possibly already the victim of Leigh's intentions to force her into marriage, came back to Allward. Mathilda had always been good to him. His heart felt heavy. He knew they didn't trust him here, nor did Leigh trust him there.

Taking a ragged breath, Allward swung his legs to the floor as he sat up and called to Thomas, 'I must speak to Lord Robert and then I must leave.'

Mathilda hardly heard Leigh speak. She couldn't pull her gaze from the bundle of clothes that had been dropped by her feet. The impact of what it meant made her head swim.

'Are you listening to me, woman?' The sharp edge to Rowan's voice made Mathilda snap her eyes away from the material and up to him.

She still said nothing. Words wouldn't form.

'If you don't put those garments on, then you will not see Robert when he comes to beg for your freedom tonight.'

Knowing what seeing her wearing a wedding dress in the company of another man, albeit under duress, would do to Robert, Mathilda did no more than run her fingers over the outer garment of the roll. It was soft. A thick white fur cloak. It must have cost a fortune.

'Let me put this another way.' Leigh was getting bored of waiting for his command to be obeyed, 'You will put those clothes on now, or I will do it for you.' He pulled a dagger from his belt and, crouching down, pointed it directly at her throat. 'You need to understand your situation more clearly, Mathilda. So that Robert lives.

'You are to get married, but not to Robert. If you care for him, I'm sure you'd rather sacrifice your life with him than see his blood spilt. That is the choice. It's very simple. You marry me and he lives. You marry me without a struggle and Allward will also live.'

'Allward?' Mathilda muttered the name back at him, 'But he's been working for you, why kill him when he's been useful?'

'You have answered your own question. He's *been* useful. His work is complete. He is no longer required.'

'You bastard!'

Leigh's face turned puce. He moved so fast that, afterwards, Mathilda couldn't recall how the back of his hand connected with her cheek; knocking her off balance so she hit her head on the wooden stable wall.

Faintly she heard Gamelyn and Edgar trying to calm Leigh. 'She doesn't know, my Lord, she's just angry at the loss of her servant.'

'It was a hasty word spoken, no more, my Lord.'

Gamelyn added with a hint of entreaty, 'My Lord, if you damage the girl she'll never be able to give you the heir you crave.'

This final sentence, spoken by one of his henchmen, made Mathilda shrivel up inside. He meant to keep her. Whatever Robert did, whatever Eustace had planned, however hard Sarah worked on her wedding dress, she was destined never to wear it.

If Robert saw her in the dress Leigh had dropped before her, he'd assume the worst. He'd have no choice but to turn away from her. He'd think she'd been raped into wedlock.

Personal pride and his pride in the family name would prevent Robert from doing anything other than abandon her. But if she didn't put the dress on, Allward would suffer for his brave double bluff. Mathilda was grateful for the dizzying fog of her banged head and allowed herself to sink into a fake concussion. If she was lucky, Leigh would leave her alone until she came around.

Leigh, however, was having none of it. He kicked her shin so hard that Mathilda yelped back to the reality of consciousness. 'Don't play games with me, girl, you'll find I'm a hell of a lot better at them than you are.'

'I won't marry you.'

'That is where you are mistaken.' Leigh folded his arms. 'Gamelyn, Edgar, undo her ankles. It's time my future wife and I got better acquainted.'

'Are you telling me I can't send men with you?' Robert wasn't sure how he wasn't shouting as Allward explained the situation.

'If you do, if they find I was followed, then both the Lady Mathilda and I are as good as dead. This Leigh, he wouldn't just kill us, he'd have fun with us first. Then finish it. But slowly. He's like a cat with a mouse. He enjoys observing the suffering he inflicts.'

'You can't expect me to do nothing, Allward.'

'I'd never expect that, my Lord. Come to the meeting as agreed. Until then, check all your other contacts. Leigh has a grudge with this family that I don't understand, but I suspect it has to do with his past; his childhood maybe. And I'm sure someone is exploiting that fact. I don't know who, but I intend to find out.'

Robert was quiet. 'Allward, you have been a good servant to this house, but I find myself wary of you. It is not a sensation I am enjoying.'

'Please, my Lord. I'm trying to help; but all the time I wait here, Mathilda is alone with those men. There are no other women there. Not one. I have to go so I can stand between her and them.'

Robert was on his feet. 'Go. Go now. Deliver the positive reply of my attendance. And add this. If Mathilda is hurt in any way at all, then Leigh will be kept alive *for ever*. Here. In an agony I will never, ever get bored of inflicting.'

~ *Chapter Twenty-two* ~

John Pykehose inclined his head and turned his horse to face the direction of Lubbesthorpe.

Robert said nothing as he watched the groom blend into the distance less than a minute behind Allward. The man was an expert tracker. Working for Eustace, he had to be.

'My Lord, may I ask what Allward said?' Sarah smoothed the silk out over the hall table as Robert walked in.

She'd added the second sleeve now, and as Robert peered closer, he found that, no matter how hard he looked, he couldn't see the stitching. 'How do you do that, Sarah? It looks as if the material hangs together like magic.'

'Years of patching your hose has given me a practiced eye, my Lord.'

Robert felt too full of nervous energy to sit down, but he made himself sit still anyway. 'Why is it so hard to preserve one's energy when you know that is the very best thing to do?'

'Because survival instincts kick in, I suppose.' Sarah laid down her needle and flexed her fingers. 'My Lord; I asked about Allward?'

'I have to trust him, Sarah. I don't see how I cannot.'

Quietly easing out her arm in a way Adam had explained

would help release the ache in the muscle that had been the target for Leigh's man's knife, Sarah said, 'Much as it pains me, my Lord, someone did let those men in. If it wasn't Allward then it had to be Owen. There is no other option. I was with Adam the whole time, and Daniel was within hailing distance. If he hadn't been, then he'd never have managed to sneak out the back way to get help.'

'Why would Owen have turned on us? It would have led to his death at our hands.'

'It led to his death either way.' Sarah rubbed her palms together in the firelight. 'He fought hard against the intruders. I don't think it was Owen.'

'You think it was Allward then?'

'I've worked for this family all of your life, my Lord. You've survived this long, despite your deeds, because of one essential trait. None of you trust anyone. Ever.'

Robert sighed. 'Except you, Sarah.'

'Thank you, my Lord. Perhaps I am simply the exception that proves the rule. I've relived the moment when those men came in over and over again. I've tried to recall who gave who what look and so on. No one mentioned Allward and I certainly never saw him. If he did let them in, then he'd have had to come around to the back door and sneak through the house to open it for them.'

Robert nodded slowly. 'Which would mean weaving through the kitchen unseen.'

'Impossible with Adam and myself in there.'

The corner of Robert's lips curled upwards. 'Forgive me, Sarah, but you and Adam couldn't have been distracted for a moment, perhaps?'

'Distracted, my Lord?'

'I'm not blind, Sarah. It's obvious you are fond of each other.'

The housekeeper blanched. 'I can assure you, my Lord that I merely find it pleasant to converse with a man of my own age. That is all. I would have known if Allward, or anyone else for that matter, had sneaked past us.'

'I'd be pleased for you to find happiness with someone, Sarah. I like Adam. I know I shouldn't, as our introduction was hardly conventional, but I do.'

A shine came to Sarah's eyes. 'Not unlike when you met Mathilda, I suppose. You shouldn't have got on with her either.'

Robert reached a hand out and stroked the sleeve of the dress. 'I didn't intend to fall in love with her. I didn't intend to fall in love with anyone. Too much to lose. And as Our Lady knows, loss is inevitable in the end. I hate to admit that Eustace is right, but Mathilda's kidnap has weakened me, and therefore us as a family.'

'Because you'd do anything to get her back safely.'

Silent for a while, trapped in his own thoughts, Robert pulled himself to his feet. 'I'll have to leave very soon. Allward will have delivered my message by now.'

'Are you still assuming he is innocent in this?'

'Let us just say that I've listened to your insights and until I know one way or another, I'm keeping an open mind.'

'Thank you, my Lord.' Sarah picked the needle up, 'If he has been part of this, you won't have to punish him, because I'll have already knocked him into hell myself.'

Robert got to his feet. 'I'm going to make sure Adam is ready.'

Sarah's face gave away nothing as she said, 'Bring him home safe as well, won't you.'

'God willing.'

Mathilda stared at Edgar. She could only bear to look at

him because the whole time he had hold of her, his eyes were tightly closed. Unlike Leigh and Gamelyn. They were examining her so intently that she wondered if their eyes might actually leap from their sockets and disappear down her slip.

As Leigh pulled away her cloak, Mathilda distanced herself from what was happening by considering what had happened to Edgar to make him less than pleased to be holding his master's prisoner at such a time.

While Gamelyn twisted Mathilda's arm more than necessary during the removal of her woollen dress, she thought about what could have happened to Edgar to make him more respectful of women, to the point of fear.

Mathilda felt detached as Leigh's hot breath assaulted her neck. His fingers had found the ties at her neck. The ties that kept her chemise in place.

He isn't going to take that off. He isn't.

Mathilda kept her neck twisted firmly to the right. She didn't shut her eyes even now. Instead, she kept up her observation of the man she suspected of stabbing her friend. Strange how Edgar could wound a woman but couldn't look upon her violation.

Violation.

That was the word. That was the unwanted reality that sank into Mathilda's mind. Robert wouldn't be able to marry her if this man, or these men, took her. Mathilda didn't need to lower her gaze to know that Leigh was more than ready to rape her into marriage.

'Robert.' The word came out despite herself, causing a bark of laughter from Leigh.

'You can plead for him all you like, but he can't help you now. Even if he knew where to look, then he'd never get near. Although maybe I'd let him watch. If the rumours about him and his friend Hugo are true, then he might need all the tips he can get.'

Keeping her chin tilted up and her lips clamped shut, Mathilda shrugged off the prickle of tears she could feel forming at the corners of her eyes. She wouldn't give him the satisfaction of seeing her cry.

Leigh pulled the ties open, and her chemise dropped to the floor.

Mathilda felt Edgar's flinch as she stood, her arms held back, her body encased in only a thin wrap of cotton. Never had she felt so vulnerable.

'You have got ye'self a beautiful piece 'ere, me Lord.'

'Indeed, Gamelyn.' Leigh took a step backwards. For a split second, Mathilda's hopes rose. Perhaps this had been about humiliating her and he'd stop now. But in fact, he was just adjusting his position, so he could get a better view of her in her semi-undressed state.

Mathilda could feel Edgar's grip tightening harder than Gamelyn's. She found herself hoping that he wouldn't add to her growing bruise collection, or when she came to marry Robert people would see the black and blue marks on her skin, rather than the dress Sarah was making for her.

Stupid thought. *He won't marry you now. Not now. Not after Leigh has...*

The tears came, but still Mathilda wouldn't give Leigh the satisfaction of begging him to keep her virtue intact.

Edgar coughed. 'Me Lord. A 'orse.'

Leigh dropped the hand that had been reaching out to rip away Mathilda's cotton. His head twisted towards the direction of the courtyard. 'The boy returned?'

'You didn't expect him to?' Gamelyn frowned.

'I wasn't sure.' Leigh seemed to have forgotten Mathilda was there. 'Gamelyn, go and make sure he hasn't been followed. Edgar, fetch the others.'

They'd gone. But they'd taken her clothes and the thick woollen cloak with them, leaving only the bundle of wedding garments in their place.

Mathilda's brain took a few seconds to register that they really had gone. Her hands were free, but it took a while to drop them to her sides.

She hadn't notice the coldness of the air while the men had been there. Now its insidious presence reminded Mathilda it was nearing the end of December. The shaking started. A combination of shock, cold and fear, consuming her with a measure of relief that they'd been interrupted thrown in for good measure.

If Allward had returned from the Folville house, then surely Robert would have followed. He'd be close now, waiting with force of arms to rescue her and wipe this Leigh from the face of the earth.

Pulling the clothing closer, struggling into the hated garments as fast as she could, Mathilda's trembling fingers were clumsy over the fastenings. She tried not to think about what the clothing might be seen to mean. It was more important to stay warm. Mathilda secured each buckle and tie tighter than she normally would, all the time thinking about how difficult she could make it for Leigh if he tried to invade her again. Yet she knew that, with two men holding her, there would be nothing she could do to stop Leigh taking her if he chose to do so.

'Robert, where are you?'

1316

He'd learnt so much from Brother Peter, and now from his new master. His gifts with wood were unparalleled. But it wasn't within the world of carpentry that he lived once his chisel and hammer were put down at the end of a long day.

He listened and he learned.

The local taverns were his main source of information. As he befriended the innkeepers he learnt much about the county as a whole and the people within it.

He never said much, nor asked questions. He knew there were folk in the village who viewed his habitual silence as odd, but most respected his taciturn manner.

Anyway, he'd learnt at an early age that it was safer to listen than to speak.

How else would you find out what was going on? Especially when there was something specific you wished to discover.

~ *Chapter Twenty-three* ~

'It seems Robert learned more during his time as a soldier than I credited.' Eustace greeted Daniel with a curt nod outside the gatehouse of the La Zouche manor. The Folville had been impressed as the boy explained how Robert had told him to stop at frequent intervals to collect messages and gather information on his return journey to Ashby Folville.

'This messenger system of his is one we should adopt as a matter of course. You can tell Robert that we have Lady Joan's support. It's as we thought, she was given little choice in the matter of turning a blind eye to Leigh's behaviour; the reasons are not important now. Although it should be said she had no idea how far his excesses had gone. My men now have the outskirts of Lubbesthorpe surrounded. They will not be seen.' Eustace passed a rolled parchment to Daniel, who immediately hid it within the folds of his cloak.

Adam and Sarah shared an anxious glance as they put the last pouch of ale on the table ready for the extended members of the Folvilles' retinue to put in their saddle bags.

The atmosphere was heavy with expectation - and getting heavier with every moment that passed.

Robert was issuing last minute instructions to those who were to accompany him and to those who were to stay and guard the manor.

A constant patrol of men was scanning the land between Ashby Folville, the manor and the roads beyond. No sign had been made of anyone who could be connected to Leigh. In fact, no one out of place had been seen at all.

Robert had ordered the villagers not to tend their strips until he said otherwise. None of them had been stupid enough to ask him why.

Rumour was rife. The Folvilles had a rival. A gang who'd stop at nothing to oust them from power. The locals, who'd lived in wariness of the family from Ashby Folville for years, privately fearing and complaining about the brothers, had their first opportunity to consider if the brothers were an afternoon in the sun compared to the cold gusts of hate that were blowing across their land now. The Folvilles didn't smash up taverns, for a start...

It was rare for gossip to warm Robert's heart, but hearing the local population, who generally took a step back when his family came by, saying they were happier with the danger on their doorstep that they understood, rather with having Satan himself as a master, gave him hope that maybe, if it came to it, the villagers would be on his side.

Robert knew that much of the recent softening of attitude towards his family was partly down to Mathilda. The community liked her. She spoke to everyone as an equal and walked amongst them without fear. And that was largely because she *was* their equal. A potter's daughter. It had provided the community with much amusement when it was made known that the nobleman at the manor had fallen for a commoner. Robert had been annoyed by the disrespect at the time. Now he was glad of the more approachable atmosphere that existed between his family and the villagers.

The sound of Sarah approaching from the kitchen

dragged Robert from his thoughts. 'It's time to leave, my Lord. The men are ready.'

'Adam?'

'Checking all the saddles.'

Robert regarded Sarah. 'Are you alright?'

'I will be when you are all home safely. Mathilda included.'

'You'll be safe here this time, Sarah. The manor is surrounded by the men John left behind. Walter and his men will stay to look after you as well.'

'Thank you, my Lord. I don't think the felons will come back here though. They were very specific last time. They wanted Mathilda. That was all. If they'd wanted to cause more suffering, they'd have burnt the manor down, or destroyed the food store at the very least.'

'You're a brave woman, Sarah.'

'I've had to be.' Sarah opened a wooden chest that sat within the archway that connected the kitchen corridor to the main hall. The partially finished wedding dress sat inside. It was folded with such precision that Robert could see how much love had gone into the simple act of storing the garment properly.

'You will work on the dress while I'm gone?'

'Yes.' Sarah bent to pick it up, 'My Lord, may I ask a question you won't want to hear, let alone answer?'

Something inside Robert chilled as he took in the expression on Sarah's face. It was beyond fearful.

'Go on.'

'If, and I pray to Our Lady that this is not the case, Leigh has violated her, will you take Mathilda back? Would you be able to love her if another had laid his hand upon her?'

Robert flinched to hear someone speak the fear he'd been trying to deny since Mathilda had been stolen from him. He opened his mouth to say that of course he would. If she was forced into anything it wasn't her doing. But the words wouldn't come out.

Understanding, the conflict crossing her master's face, Sarah said, 'Leigh may have married her. He may have done everything you dread, but don't forget, don't *ever* forget, Mathilda would never give in easily. She's brave and resilient.'

'I know.' The words were a whisper, 'but if he has... if he's...'

'Then you'd have to make her a widow, wouldn't you.'

They hadn't come back.

Despite having no bindings now, Mathilda hadn't moved from the huddled position she'd adopted after dressing in the hated clothes. She knew she could make a run for it, but every part of her ached. Most of all her heart.

Would Robert ever believe that Leigh hadn't gone further than humiliating her in front of his henchmen? Especially if Leigh told him he'd done more than he had. It would be Leigh's word against hers. And his word would be backed up by the purple stains that covered her body as fingertip-sized bruises blossomed over the insides of her wrists. They spoke of unwilling taking - but suggested taking had occurred nonetheless.

If Mathilda could visualise the fingers that had pushed so hard against her skin that they'd left shadows of the pressure upon her flesh, the dirty nails grazing her tender skin, then Robert would be able to do the same.

It had to have been Allward who she'd heard arrive with the message. He'd have bought Robert with him; she was sure help was close by. Robert and Owen were probably hidden in the tress that surrounded the village, waiting for her. So why wasn't she trying to creep out?

Mathilda knew it was the clothes.

The wedding garments. If she hadn't put them on, then she'd have slowly frozen to death. But if Robert saw her wearing them, especially if he spotted her before she'd had the chance to explain, he'd assume the worst. If others saw her in them, then word would spread and Robert, whether he wanted to or not, would have to reject her anyway. Would he even wait for her to explain why she was garbed in another man's wedding attire before he jumped to conclusions and left her to her fate? Mathilda knew that Robert wasn't the clearest thinker when he was angry.

Forcing herself to close her mind to the clothes themselves, picturing them just as pieces of material that were the difference between life and death, Mathilda tried to stand up. Her legs trembled, as if they'd forgotten how to support her weight. Despite the small cup of stew and the water, Mathilda was still hungry and very thirsty. She cursed Leigh's skill. He'd kept her so weak that he had no need to use ties now; she simply didn't have the strength to go very far or fast.

There hadn't been any conversations in the yard for some time. In fact, it was spookily quiet. No one was moving at all. Mathilda held onto the wooden wall beside her and tried to stand again. Heaving herself up, shuffling to the stable window, she took her first proper look at the place in which she'd been imprisoned.

She found her sore eyes blinking against the fading evening light. She hadn't even realised what the time of day was. Perhaps it wasn't so strange that it was quiet.

Pulling the hated fur cloak tighter around herself, Mathilda saw a fair-sized house with a small fenced garden. It stood on the other side of a courtyard, which was every bit as large as the one at Ashby Folville. Behind the house, Mathilda could see the roofs of other village houses set back, just beyond the range of any cry for help. To her right there was an open-fronted workshop, which was almost as large as the house itself.

The stable block she was in was empty. She wasn't sure if that meant that Leigh kept no horses, or if everyone was out.

Think.

Mathilda's brain started to work. The act of taking charge of her limbs again was making her mentally, if not physically, stronger.

There had been horses. She'd heard them come and go. That was how they'd known Allward had returned, by hearing hooves. Assuming it had been him.

Did that mean the men had all gone to meet with Robert? Should she stay where she was, so he could come and rescue her, or should she try to escape?

Mathilda studied the landscape harder. It was unlikely the house and workshop was as unguarded.

Daniel leapt from his horse and grabbed Eustace's message from his cloak.

At least twenty men were in Ashby Folville's courtyard. Horses and riders were circling, impatient to be off. The crisp early evening hung with expectation, as if everyone present was off to battle.

'My Lord Robert!' Daniel called above the hubbub, fighting his way through people who had little time in their lives for an errand boy. 'My Lord Robert?'

'Daniel?' It was Adam who saw the boy's blond head first. 'Over here.'

'Adam. Thank goodness. Is my Lord Robert still here?'

'In the stable.' Adam dropped the reigns of his own mount and followed Daniel, pushing the mercenaries to one side to help the boy through to their master. 'Robert!'

The younger Folville snapped his head around at being addressed so disrespectfully, but one glimpse of Adam's face stopped his admonishment. 'Daniel? Tell us.'

'Allward. Allward. I...'

'What boy, what about Allward?'

'Dead. My friend, he's...'

Adam swallowed hard as he looked at Robert. 'Not a traitor then.'

'Or if he was, a disposable one.' Robert took hold of Daniel's shaking shoulders. 'Where is Allward now, lad?'

'Not far away. Just beyond the point where our last lookout can see from the woods above the manor. I think... I think he was dumped there on purpose.'

Adam leant against the stable wall with a heavy growl. 'They're taunting us. Telling us they know we are watching them, and that we can't touch them.'

Daniel steadied himself against Adam as he struggled not to sob. 'They just left him in the middle of the road. I was meant to find him. I'm sure I was.'

'You think you were being followed?' Robert frowned.

'I didn't think so. I kept checking. I rode the long route round, doubled back on myself and everything, my Lord, as we discussed. But now I'm not so sure. They must have followed me.'

'Or,' Adam ruffled the boy's hair, 'they simply left Allward there because it's never long between someone coming to, or leaving, the manor. Anyone could have found Allward and delivered the message of his murder. The important thing for Leigh is telling us he's in control.'

Not liking the truth of what Adam was saying, Robert

called three men from the yard and sent them to fetch the body. He then sent two experienced mercenaries out towards where Eustace was waiting with this fresh wave of bad news.

Once the immediate practical things had been done, Robert allowed himself a moment of emotion. Punching the bales of hay stacked on the shelves high in the stable block, Robert then sank his hands between the folds of his cloak. Placing his palms against the reassuring presence of his dagger and sword handles, he cursed. 'Damn. Allward didn't deserve this.

'Adam, can you take Daniel to Sarah. Break the news to her gently. I don't want her hearing this from another.'

'Yes, my Lord.' Adam had moved only a step away before turning to ask, 'Do we go ahead tonight?'

'We do.' Robert tried to blank his mind to how many more of his men might be dead. Had Leigh's felons been picking them off as they lay in wait?

But there was no choice. He had to go.

Mathilda was waiting.

~ *Chapter Twenty-four* ~

Allward had been knocked from his horse and his throat cut. The wound was deep, neat and fatal. Robert had seen such injuries inflicted before, but only ever on the battlefield. Ingram's warning that Leigh had gathered men who had once been soldiers, leftovers from the wars that no one but the Crown had any time for; resounded in his head.

Thankful for the small mercy that death would have come quickly for Allward, Robert laid a hand on Sarah's shoulder as she cleaned the blood from the boy's body. Her back stiff, her breathing barely audible, she worked as though she had distanced herself from what she was doing.

Adam's voice came from the doorway. 'My lord? Robert?'

Robert's expression was unreadable. 'Is it time to go?'

'It is.'

'And?'

'Everyone else is accounted for. All the sentries are alive and in place.'

Robert released a long exhalation of air. 'It's no good trying to track down who did this.' He stroked the hair from Allward's forehead. 'It would have been an order to be obeyed like any other. The blame lies with the creature who gave that order.'

'Rowan Leigh.'

'He'll expect us to be shaken; thinking the death of another trusted soul will make us weaker. In that, Leigh is quite wrong. It has strengthened my resolve.'

'And mine, my Lord.' Adam coughed, 'and if I may; the word has spread around the villages. Allward was known and liked. I hadn't realised until the innkeeper, Jacob Lock, and his fellows arrived, that Allward grew in Ashby Folville.'

Robert was surprised. 'Jacob is here?'

'He says he was cousin to Allward's mother. He has come to avenge the lad.'

'Really? I had no idea there was a connection.' Robert shook his head sadly. 'My family took the boy in when he was a babe after his parents were killed.'

'Leigh isn't endearing himself to the locals, my Lord. His felonies aren't aimed at the rich or corrupt. They are hitting everyone. The people aren't happy with this newcomer any more than we are.'

'I had heard rumours to that effect and I dared to hope that would happen, but I feared I grew too arrogant in my grief.' With a final look at the fallen young man, a fresh resolve took hold of Robert. 'The people are truly on our side, Adam?'

'You can't be surprised, surely?' Sarah lifted her face from her work. 'Don't you recall the Robyn Hode tales you're so fond of? Didn't that singular outlaw have the population on his side against the evil and corrupt?'

'Bless you, Sarah. Indeed, he did.'

Adam smiled at Sarah, thankful for her encouragement. There's something else, my Lord.'

'Speak up then, Adam.'

'Jacob has two extra faces with him, who have added

themselves to the tails of his retinue. I think you should come and see. Men who champ at the bit to avenge Mathilda, Allward and Owen every bit as much as we do.'

Mathilda paused in the doorway of the stable. She'd expected it to creak as she pushed it open, but no sound had come from its hinges. Without the protection of the thick oak door the winter air was even more cutting.

The place was eerily quiet. They couldn't all have gone to meet Robert. Surely Leigh had left some guards. They must have expected her to try and run away. The question was, what would they do if they caught her? She couldn't believe for a second that whichever way she ran, she'd end up in some kind of trap.

Pushing away all other aims, Mathilda tried to work out the most likely chance of escape. They would have men in the woodland around the house. They had the advantage of knowing the landscape, whereas she didn't even know if she was within Leicestershire.

The logical action was to take the quickest route across the courtyard to the gateway. The fact that the gate had been left open sent all the nerves standing up on the back of Mathilda's neck. She felt like a fly being encouraged to walk into a spider's web.

Allward had told her that Robert was only willing to meet with Leigh to discuss terms if she was there as well, so he could see she'd come to no harm. Yet, they'd clearly gone without taking her.

The rustle of her outfit as she moved was another problem. There was no way she could creep anywhere unheard in the marriage outfit, but if she took it off, there was a chance she'd freeze. Feeling as though each problem she addressed was taking her around in circles, Mathilda considered staying where she was for Robert to arrive. But then the memory of Leigh's eyes leeching into her flesh decided her against that course of action. She couldn't rely on Allward turning up in the nick of time again.

Clamping her skirts to her body to eliminate as much sound as possible, Mathilda stopped thinking. It was getting her nowhere. It was time to move. She'd worry about where she was going if she ever got there.

'My Lord Coterel! Oswin!' Robert wrapped the newcomers in his arms.

Nicholas, the head of the Coterel family from neighbouring Derbyshire, greeted his occasional ally, tilting his head to his steward as he did so. 'Oswin is shortly to leave my service and return to the family business. Naturally, once he heard about his sister's abduction he was keen to find her.'

A man of few words, Oswin stepped forward. 'My sister appears to have slipped through your fingers, my Lord Folville.'

'To my shame and anger, she has. But that will not remain so for long.' Robert flushed in the presence of Mathilda's kin's anger. 'You are both most welcome here. I'd be grateful for your counsel and your help. You are alone?'

'Twelve of my men are exchanging news with your own.' Coterel's eyes scanned the activity of battle preparation around them. An impressive group of arms, Folville.'

'And thanks to you, even better now. My brothers will be as grateful as I am.'

Coterel looked solemn. 'Tales of this Leigh have reached us even in Bakewell. I don't like what I'm hearing.'

Robert ventured a half smile, 'A group of men that you can't use to your advantage, Nicholas?'

'I'll not disagree with that.' The bigger man snorted,

'But he'll give honest criminals like us a bad name if he isn't stopped soon.' Coterel placed a huge palm on Oswin's shoulder, 'I am unable to stay, as I have commitments in Bakewell, but I wished to hand Oswin back to Bertred in Twyford, so that he could see at least his son was still whole. You have a plan?'

'A plan I'm fast adjusting after recent events.'

'Tell me.'

'My steward, Owen, is dead. You've heard?' Coterel nodded, so Robert continued, 'My messenger and stable hand Allward has been murdered as well.'

Oswin gulped. 'Allward? No!'

'I'm sorry. Yes.' There was no time now for extra sympathy, so Robert went on, 'There has to be someone passing on information to Leigh from the village, if not from inside this manor itself. How else could Leigh be one step ahead of me all the way?'

'Men at arms alone aren't going to solve this, you mean.' Nicholas surveyed his expert eye over the assembled men. 'You'll not be able to act discreetly with such numbers, even though many have the skill to blend into the forests.'

'Blending into the trees is largely redundant here. We head to Lubbesthorpe, for that is where, Allward told us this felon hides. Eustace already has its outskirts surrounded. But the meeting with Leigh himself, I think that would be better with just a few of us. The place he has detailed is small and secluded; within Thwaite Wood.'

'Lubbesthorpe? You mean the rogue has taken advantage of Zouche's absence?'

'Exactly so. Eustace is with Lady Joan now.'

Coterel echoed the concern that Eustace had previously aired. 'You think Leigh wants you to take an army into The Thwaite, so he can pick you all off from the trees?'

'I do.'

'He could pick off a smaller group as well; more easily in fact.'

'I don't think Leigh will kill me. He's enjoying making me suffer too much.'

Adam and Oswin exchanged anxious looks, but it was Nicholas Coterel who spoke for them all. 'If you walk into that wood alone, Robert, you'll have no chance.'

'I've lost too many men to endanger others. And I won't be entirely alone. I'll just appear to be. My brother Thomas and his men will enter and protect the village. Eustace has sent word via Daniel that Lady Joan's men will remove Leigh's influence from the fringes of the manor should any of his followers try to disappear.'

Nicholas's indicated his approval of Robert's tactical thinking before asking. 'And here?'

'Walter and his followers will protect this place, while Laurence will stand guard with his men in Melton Mowbray.'

'Leigh attacked your holding in Melton?'

'He did.'

Nicholas put out his hand to Robert in a gesture of farewell, and good luck. 'I remain of the mind that, alone, Thwaite is too dangerous.'

'I have no choice.'

Two voices came from the deepening dark at the same time, 'You do.'

Oswin and Adam looked at each other; both had unshakable determination etched upon their faces.

Adam spoke first. 'I'm coming with you. Mathilda saved my life.'

'So am I.' Oswin placed his hands on his hips. 'She's my sister.'

Robert was touched, 'Which is why she needs you alive, Oswin. To help her recover from this. To be at our wedding. And Adam; Sarah would skin me alive if...'

'Do not even think of arguing, my Lord. You took me in and we had a deal. I would assist you in this undertaking, to rid the land of Leigh and you'd discover who blackened my name.'

Robert tried to argue, but even as he spoke, he knew that Adam would be unshakeable. 'If we stand before him together, Leigh will have you shot before we've even made out which shadow is his.'

'He won't, my Lord.' Adam squared his shoulders, his face etched with determination. 'Because it's him who won't see *me* until it's too late.'

~ *Chapter Twenty- five* ~

There were plenty of shadows. Mathilda, conscious that the pallid sheen of her clothing could reveal her at any moment, kept as deep into the gloom as she could.

With her back firmly against the wall of the house, she walked sideways, her eyes darting constantly in every direction. Her ears were as alert as her eyes, but although Mathilda heard and saw nothing, every instinct told her she was being watched.

You're just frightened. There's no one here.

Mathilda had decided that, rather than dash like a hunted hare across the courtyard, she would head to the workshop. Perhaps there she could pick up a weapon, and some discarded work clothes she could exchange for the hated wedding outfit.

The scent of sawdust was almost overpowering as she entered the carpenter's workplace. Hopeful of finding at least an apron to cover her dress, Mathilda left the shadows and dashed to the work bench.

The palm was around her mouth before she had taken two steps across the threshold.

She didn't need to see the owner of the palm to know that it belonged to Edgar. He'd held her like this before and his personal aroma of wood and sweat had a singular sickly sharpness.

Mathilda didn't fight. Edgar was too big and her strength was best saved. Bracing herself for the sound of him drawing his knife, Mathilda willed Robert, wherever he was, to move faster.

When it came, the swift swipe of the knife exiting its pouch made Mathilda simultaneously close her eyes and struggle. The sharp 'Shush!' that came from Edgar, made her freeze again, but her eyes stayed shut.

'Be quiet.' The pressure of the chunky fingers over her mouth eased a little. 'If you promise not to call out I'll free your mouth. Yes?'

Mathilda positively motioned her head as best she could within the vice-like grip of Edgar's arms. She hadn't believed he was going to loosen his hold until the tree branch of an arm that had been compressing her stomach moved up to her neck. Taking a heavy lungful of air Mathilda, her shoulders against Edgar's chest, could feel his stinking breath at the top of her unkempt hair.

'Why are you in here?'

Not sure she was actually supposed to answer, Mathilda paused, but a shake of her whole body via the one hand that now clamped itself around her neck made it clear that an answer was expected.

'I was running away.' She stuttered out the words. Hearing them sounded ridiculous. How had she dreamt, even for a second, that she'd get out of here?

'Then why run in 'ere? Ye could be gone, girl!'

Something about the tone of Edgar's voice gave Mathilda pause for thought. 'I, I thought it might be a trap. I thought a weapon...'

Edgar was no longer listening. He cut across her sentence. 'You could 'ave bin gone from 'ere. It would 'ave bin nice again.'

Mathilda felt his fingers form new bruises on her neck.

'It was good 'til 'ee 'eard 'bout you.'

Apart from the heaviness of Edgar's anxious breathing, and her shorter breaths, the workshop was eerily quiet. Not even the dust dared move. Mathilda's mind raced, searching for something to say that might provide some answers. As the silence stretched on, she could feel Edgar become increasingly tense. Leigh, she realised, had no idea what his man was doing.

'What was good?' She whispered the words, hoping that if Edgar objected to her talking, she could pretend he'd imagined her speaking.

'Us! This!' He gestured around the workshop with his free hand.

'Carpentry?'

'Yes! No! All of it.' Edgar cottoned on to the fact he'd started shouting, and snapped his mouth closed for a few seconds. Mathilda could hear the effort he was making to strain his ears to pick up the approach of anyone else.

Braving another comment, Mathilda asked, 'Where is everyone, Edgar?'

''unting.'

Mathilda's heart seemed to stop for a second. *Hunting Robert?* 'For food?'

'For power.' Edgar snorted, as though her question was completely stupid. 'Power.' He spat the word. 'That was fine, that was good. Climbing 'is way up into worthy society. But then 'e gets 'is 'ead turned...' The outlaw's anger at his master's behaviour translated itself through the increased pressure of his fingers.

Mathilda yelped in pain as Edgar pinched her neck. The fact he could snap her in half if he chose had taken charge of all her thought processes. There was no way she could break away. Talking her way free was the only option now.

'Climbing his way up from where, Edgar? Who is Rowan Leigh?'

The outlaw gulped. He knew he shouldn't answer, but then he shouldn't be holding a woman like this. He was already damned. 'The church. They did this. And the womn... they is the worst, they is... evil.'

His arm began to shake.

'Evil? The church? The women in the church?' Mathilda remembered how Edgar had closed his eyes so tightly when Leigh had made him hold her. Only now did she see that his manner hadn't been one of determination or concentration, but of revulsion.

'Hags. Cruel.'

'Cruel like Leigh?'

'Ha!' Edgar scoffed, 'Leigh is a beginner compared to 'em.'

Feeling unexpectedly sorry for Edgar, Mathilda was more wary than before. The man was clearly unstable as well as physically dangerous. 'Who made Leigh evil, Edgar? Was that the women too?'

'Church and a woman. One woman.'

'Do you know who?' Mathilda whispered, as alert as Edgar to the prospect of someone interrupting their conspiratorial chat.

'Not even he knows. They found 'im.'

'Who found him?'

'Church. Found 'im, raised 'im.'

Realisation dawned as Mathilda swallowed clumsily under the pressure of the hand. Edgar's fingers almost met around her slender neck as he became more tense; his grip began to get tighter again. Leigh had been a foundling.

Abandoned by a mother he'd never know and taught by the monks. Monks who, if Edgar was telling the truth, had abused their authority and taught him to be cruel and bitter rather than calm and forgiving.

If it was true it would explain Leigh's reaction when she'd referred to him as a bastard. But Edgar was obviously a muddled and troubled soul. He could be talking about himself.

'Did they, Edgar? Did the church find him and bring him up?'

'Beat 'im. Told 'im 'ee was nuffing.' Edgar sniffed, before adding, 'Women are bad luck. They bring trouble. Look at you. You've brought trouble. How dare you wear these?'

Unable to look down, Mathilda felt the tug of her skirts under his fingers. 'I don't want to wear them. I was freezing.'

'You're not worthy of 'im.'

'I don't want him.'

Edgar was quiet for a moment. Mathilda was increasingly scared he'd suddenly become aware of what he was doing and cut her throat. 'I'm promised to another.'

'A Folville!' Edgar's voice trembled now. 'Thieves and murderers.'

Mathilda didn't bother denying it. It was the truth after all. 'So is Leigh. He is making the same of you, Edgar. Why do you let him?'

'My Lord Leigh saved me.' Edgar stood a little taller, wrenching Mathilda's neck back as he did so, rocking her onto her toes.

Her words could only come out in strangled gasps now. 'He's not. He's sending you to a hangman's noose.'

'Already there.' Edgar's voice was strange, and with a mix of surprise and horror, Mathilda felt a hot tear splash against her shoulder. 'And damned now because of you.'

'Me?'

'Ee'd 'ave made me hold you while... while... If the messenger 'adn't come and interrupted us you'd be wedded by now.'

Clammy, sticky sweat engulfed Mathilda's body. So Leigh really had been about to rob her of her virtue. Never had she been more grateful for Allward. His bravery in pretending to be their messenger had saved her from marriage by rape. Wherever he was now, she fervently prayed he was safe.

'I didn't damn you, Edgar. Leigh did. Why do you call him your lord, when he is no more a lord than I am?'

Edgar bristled. 'Respect. 'Ee is my master.'

The words came out as if they'd been drummed into Edgar's head. 'Are you going to let me go, Edgar?'

'Go?'

'You said I was evil, and that it had all gone wrong because of me. Why don't you let me leave, or help me leave even? Then things could go back to how they were.'

''Ee'd know.'

'No, he wouldn't. 'Mathilda pushed the point home. 'If I'd run the other way, I'd never have come in here and found you. You wouldn't even know I'd left. You could pretend I didn't come here.'

'No, not 'im. The other man. '*Ee'd* know. 'Ee'd get my master to kill me. Leigh always does what 'ee says. Leigh thinks 'ee's a free man, but 'ee ain't now the other man 'as come with promises of power and influence. All a lie.'

'What other man?'

'Leigh thought 'ee'd caught 'im. Thought 'ee'd threatened 'im into working for us! The truth is the other way around, and only a fool can't see it. Unless of course, they choose not to see it because it suits their purpose to remain blind.'

Mathilda tottered to one side on her toes. 'What man?'

The noise came from nowhere. For a split second, Mathilda's heart soared. The feet crossing the workshop towards them had to be Robert. But then her hopes sank like a stone to her boots as she saw the blur of Rowan Leigh enter the workshop. He moved so fast that she was knocked to the floor before she'd registered his presence. A foot was placed on her chest as Edgar's knife was yanked from Leigh's belt and plunged into the bigger man's neck.

'Traitor!'

Edgar dropped like a stone. There were no demands as to why the outlaw had Mathilda in the workshop, no tortured questioning. Leigh had simply sliced his henchman's throat and left him clutching at the pumping wound, writhing on the dusty floor in his death throes.

Tears streamed down Mathilda's cheeks. 'He did no wrong. He stopped me fleeing.'

Clearly enjoying the view of the dying man, Leigh said, 'Edgar spoke too much.'

A creeping realisation came over her. 'You were listening.'

'I followed you from the stable. I'd been expecting your flight. I had hoped you'd be less obvious in your movements. I read your intentions to collect a weapon before running, rather than just fleeing through the open gate.

'I should credit you with the intention to swap the wedding clothes, however. Can you just imagine Robert Folville's face when he sees you looking so radiant in your bridal finery?'

Mathilda tried to rise, but Leigh's boot remained planted firmly in the centre of her stomach.

'No tart backchat from you this time, Mistress Twyford?'

Rowan's Leigh's smoothly angelic face blazed like fire as he stared at his captured prize. 'Shall we let Robert attend the ceremony? I'm sure he'll love it. After all, everyone likes a wedding, don't they?'

1320

Master Thomas the Carpenter was looking more ashen than ever. Surely, he wouldn't hold on much longer?

His patience was almost at breaking point. Once upon a time he'd thought he'd developed a way to make it last forever. Now, having so carefully orchestrated events, his capacity for waiting was close to running out.

It was time to start building his platform for vengeance.

~ *Chapter Twenty-six* ~

Sarah watched until the last man and horse disappeared from view. Feeling heavy with a responsibility she had no control over, the housekeeper bobbed her thanks to Walter de Folville as he took his turn to guard the manor's gates with his men.

Disappearing to her kitchen, Sarah looked around at her domain. Whoever came back would need feeding, whether it was a dawn supper or an early breakfast, and the food wouldn't prepare itself. Robert's tunics wouldn't clean themselves, nor would the beds magically make themselves. With all the men on guard and Mathilda missing, that just left Sarah to deal with everything.

Before Mathilda had so unceremoniously arrived in their lives, Sarah had revelled in her position as the only female in the house. Servants here had always been male and that had suited her fine. Now however, she craved Mathilda's company. Someone to talk to; to discuss the wedding with and to mull over her feelings for Adam. Sarah had reached this point in her life when she had no expectation of ever having a suitor, let alone a man she respected and liked. The thought of being the object of someone's affection, however gentle, had thrown her at a time when she needed to keep her head together more than ever before.

Common sense told Sarah that she should leave the household tasks and try to sleep. It was closing towards ten at night, and she had hours before she could realistically expect them to return. However, knowing sleep wasn't possible in her concerned state, she busied herself.

Her mind replayed the sight of Adam turning to wave to her as he rode through the manor's gateway behind Robert. His face had been set into stern determination and she'd mouthed the words, *Good luck, goodbye, come back to me*, to him before she'd realised she was going to.

In that one brief moment she'd allowed her feelings for Adam to become obvious, and she was furious with herself.

Pouring the water she'd been heating into the vast wooden wash tub and pounding the first dirty tunic with her good arm, Sarah began the almost impossible job of wishing away such thoughts. She didn't want to fall in love with someone whose body she might have to mourn in the morning.

The night sky was dotted with stars. Robert could see the moon staring down at them, providing as much light as it could. Sending up a prayer of thanks for its bright glow, Robert and his two comrades took their leave from the main group.

There was an hour before the time of the meeting with Leigh. The Folvilles were all in place. A quiet barrier of Eustace's men and horses, visible, threatening, but not moving, just outside the village of Lubbesthorpe, completely cutting the place off. No one could come in or out, as the silent force loomed in the moonlight.

On the orders of Lady Joan, the village had gone into a state of curfew. A combination of La Zouche and Folville men had visited every house and workshop in Lubbesthorpe. In every case, not only had they explained the non-negotiable fact that the entire household was to remain inside the property that evening and throughout the night, but that they would be staying within the premises as well until told to leave by their superiors.

Three of Robert's followers had established themselves inside the tavern, with strict orders not to drink more than was sensible. Everyone needed their wits about them.

Each man's orders were the same. No one was allowed in or out of the village, because no one knew which families were in Leigh's pay and which were just putting up with his presence because it was too dangerous not to.

As he dismounted his horse, preparing himself to leave the village of Lubbesthorpe behind, Robert asked his companions again if they were sure they wanted to risk their lives. Neither replied. Oswin and Adam simply pulled scarves over their faces, muffling the sound of their breathing as they moved silently though the dead of winter.

With a resigned but grateful nod, Robert instructed both men to think like Robyn Hode, and then bid them good luck. With a grim but knowing smile from each man, Robert mouthed a prayer of fortune in their direction, while weaving his own way along the narrow path to the meeting place alone. *It's time to get Mathilda back.*

Oswin could see a man in the tree above him. At least, he could see the soles of his boots. The vantage point the tree would give was perfect. Oswin could see why Leigh's man had selected it; it would provide a view right across the small clearing Robert was heading for.

Watching from below, Oswin listened to the quiet, almost deafening in its stillness. The act of removing the outlaw without making a sound was going to be impossible - and yet it had to be done. Taking his short bow, Oswin allowed his head to fill with images of his treasured sister.

Mathilda splashing with him and Matthew in the ford at home, picking apples in the orchard, washing the clothes, tending their mother during her illness. Her laughter, her rare tears; her bravery and intelligence which would have been the envy of many men. Oswin was sure there'd be many of Leigh's other's men in the clearing. To stand any chance of protecting Robert, he had to get amongst them.

Mumbling a quick prayer, Oswin aimed the arrow he'd notched to his string upwards.

The thud, scream and crashing of a body falling from the tree felt as loud as a cathedral tumbling to the ground. Oswin braced himself for shouts, for the rushing of feet in his direction. None came.

Either he'd been wrong and Leigh had no other lookouts on this side of the clearing, or the men were so disciplined that they weren't so stupid as to run towards arrow fire. Either way, Oswin hid for a full ten minutes before kicking the body into the undergrowth and shinning his way up the tree.

Adam took two steps before stopping to listen, then took another two. In this manner, keeping off the established path, he worked his way to a place to the far right of the clearing.

Hidden in the shelter of a closely packed group of ash trees, Adam was glad of the shelter of the intertwining branches in the absence of any leaves to conceal him properly. Never had he believed the skills he'd developed while on the run, staying silent and unnoticed, would be useful to him again so soon.

His hand gripped the knife in his belt. It felt fitting to him that it was the one he'd taken from Markham's kitchen in his haste to flee. He'd expected someone to have been in this space before him, but no one was there. Pressing his back to the nearest tree trunk, Adam moved his neck slowly so that he could survey the immediate area.

No one was visible in the clearing. That meant that Robert was waiting out of sight on the opposite side, although Adam couldn't see him.

It was possible that Leigh was hiding too, but if he was to keep his side of the bargain and bring Mathilda with him, Adam doubted quiet would be an option. Even if Mathilda was hog-tied and gagged, he was convinced she'd be doing something to make herself known - assuming she was alive. He shrugged off the image of Mathilda's cold lifeless body and scanned the trees. There had to be men hidden up there. Leigh wasn't a fool. If Robert had decided to come early to hide, there was no reason why Leigh wouldn't have done the same.

The fight had drained from Mathilda the second Edgar's body had stopped twitching, his life evaporating in front of her eyes. Leigh's indifference to the loss of a man who'd been loyal to him was more chilling than anything that had happened to her so far. The idea that there was no point in even trying to escape took hold. For the first time in her life she felt herself giving up.

Rowan laughed as he half-pushed, half-dragged Mathilda towards a cart that waited in the courtyard. She could hear him talking to Gamelyn, but not what was said.

'In!' Leigh ordered her to clamber into the cart.

Mathilda could feel his eyes burning into her flesh as she clumsily climbed aboard, her hands aching with cold, her whole body shaking. She wasn't surprised when he climbed up after her, but when he shoved her backwards, so that her back hit the bottom of the cart, Mathilda gasped, the air was knocked from her.

'Why? Why did you kill him?'

Leigh looked puzzled, before he said, 'Edgar?' As if he'd already forgotten about the murder he'd just committed. 'I told you, he talked too much.'

'Why did he think women are evil?' Mathilda was trying not to look at Rowan's eyes as she spoke, wondering how long it would be before he smacked her face if she asked the wrong question.

'The church.' The two words came out as an angry hiss. All the further questions Mathilda wanted to ask were silenced by the pure hate that crossed his face as he hauled himself up next to her.

Sitting astride Mathilda's body, Rowan leered down at her. 'I suggest you stay still. I'd hate any of the Folville scum to see my future bride with any more bruises on her pretty little face.'

Even through the layers of their winter clothes, she could feel the strength of Leigh's intentions pressing into her thigh. Revulsion, the strength of which she'd never known, flowed through Mathilda, as the cherubic face glowered at her without blinking. Stories of people being possessed by demons consumed her mind. She was too scared to struggle, too afraid to fight, as the stark reality of what he intended to do in the cart on the way to meet Robert hit her.

Time was ebbing away. Mathilda knew her only chance was to talk. Hoping he wouldn't gag her, she whispered from her chapped lips, 'Why Robert? Please, why are the Folvilles your target?'

Leigh pushed a hand hard against Mathilda's mouth. His face came down so close to hers as the cart rumbled towards Thwaite, that she couldn't help but shudder.

'I have good reason, girl. Good reason. There are many in this land of ours that would pay well to have every cursed one of your precious Folvilles wiped off the face of the earth. I am but one of them.'

~ *Chapter Twenty-seven* ~

Robert fought against the temptation to leave the safety of the hiding place he'd found while he waited for Leigh to arrive.

It was too peaceful. If he'd been Leigh he'd have had men here all day, waiting, watching, and making sure no traps had been set. Surely the one man he'd heard fall, which he was sure was the result of Oswin's handiwork, couldn't have been the only lookout? Was Leigh that sure of himself?

In a way Robert hoped he was. The arrogance of his own family had smacked him firmly in the face. They'd been foolish enough to relax into their position and the result had been that he and his brothers had left the door wide open for a newcomer. Robert hoped that Leigh was copying the Folvilles to the extent that he too had become over-confident.

Had Leigh *really* only sent one man to guard the clearing?

Robert settled himself in for a wait, his eyes permanently surveying the area before and behind him. Mercifully there was only a slight breeze, so the temperature wasn't as harsh as it had been and the shelter afforded by the trees, albeit in their naked winter state, gave him some protection. Keeping his ears and eyes on constant alert, Robert heard

Sarah's words repeat in his head. Would he still be able to love Mathilda if Leigh had sullied her?

Even though Mathilda was trapped beneath Leigh's body, the roughness of the track beneath the cart jarred and knocked her as they were driven along. Despite the feeling that she'd never be bruise-free again, Mathilda was glad of the rocking of the wagon. It meant that Leigh's initial attempts to break through her wedding clothes had become impossible because the road surface was sending them rolling all over the place. Even if he hadn't intended to molest her in the cart and was just enjoying frightening her further, she felt as though her chances were running out.

They had to be getting close to the meeting place.

Her eyes had been closed for some time. Leigh's unrelenting stare had become too much. Although he'd laughed at her for wishing him away, Mathilda had taken a few seconds' comfort from not being witness to his appearance. It was of no surprise to her that so many men followed him. His capacity to look innocent one moment and utterly ruthless the next was as compelling as it was terrifying.

Beneath the temporary safety of her closed eyelids, Mathilda began to speculate what might have happened to Rowan Leigh to make him this way.

Robert sensed they were nearby a second before he either heard or saw them. A subtle change in the air was quickly followed by the faint roll of wooden wheels over fallen leaves and twigs.

Wrapping the scarf tighter around his mouth to hide the puff of frozen air that would have made his position visible through the trees, Robert listened harder.

He heard the sound of an approaching cart moving,

and then it stopped. Whoever it was must be waiting just beyond the clearing. Robert wondered if Oswin could see them but didn't risk looking for Mathilda's brother. His eyes remained fixed on the perimeter of the clearing before him.

In his imagination Robert had played out how this moment was going to go. How Mathilda would be fighting to the last, her bravery and determination to get back to him keeping her going. He'd expected to hear shouts as Leigh dragged a struggling Mathilda into the clearing, but no voices could be made out.

Robert frowned. If Leigh hadn't brought Mathilda with him then he had given Oswin orders to shoot him on sight. Except, of course, Oswin didn't know what Leigh looked like - not yet, anyway.

Perhaps he'd been hearing things and he'd only heard a cart approaching because he was tired and desperate for the meeting to begin to see Mathilda, to make sure she was unharmed. Perhaps Eustace's men had intercepted the hostile party coming through the village itself? Although, Robert knew that was tactically very unlikely, it would explain why Leigh was late.

It was more likely, Robert thought as his toes began to numb within his boots, that Leigh was keeping them waiting on purpose. An additional underscoring to prove that he was the one in control of the situation. Robert had no choice but to be there if he wanted his future wife back. Leigh was clearly determined to make the most of that fact.

Remaining alert, Robert placed a palm over his sword's hilt. A silence had fallen again, but it felt lighter than before. A moment later it was broken.

His hand gripped the sword tighter, but he couldn't pull the weapon from its scabbard. Robert felt paralysed by the sight that had moved into the clearing.

Mathilda was in the middle of the roughly circular space. A man, who Robert presumed was Rowan Leigh, was gripping her around the waist. She was clamped so tightly against his front that there would have been no chance of her getting free, even if there wasn't a knife at her throat.

Her neck was tilted up. Her hair was uncovered. The plaits she usually wore coiled upon her head were undone. Robert didn't have time to register that he'd never seen Mathilda with her hair down before. He was too busy taking in the bruises that had turned her usual pale complexion to a patchwork of purple and green blotches. Even in the dimness of the moonlight, he could see that his belief that Mathilda would fight her captor was accurate.

However, it wasn't Mathilda's bruises and scars that had frozen his soul. It was her clothing that had stilled the hand upon the pommel of his sword and sapped his strength. Sarah had warned him. He'd known it was a very real possibility. But until now Robert had refused to accept the reality of it.

Mathilda was there. Captive and damaged, shivering with a combination of cold and fear, her wide eyes pleading for help, in a wedding dress provided by another man.

Roberts head filled with clouds of hate, rage and disgust. He wanted to rush at the gloating figure in the clearing. He wanted to run his sword through his miserable guts and kick his corpse away from Mathilda... but Robert didn't move. Hope drained from him. If Leigh had married Mathilda, there was no point. Even killing Leigh wouldn't stop the fact of the marriage. It wouldn't wash away his fingerprints from Mathilda's body...

A clouded mist of irrational incomprehension overtook him. How could Mathilda have let him touch her? Why hadn't she resisted?

Robert couldn't look at her as Rowan Leigh called across the woodland with clear calm confidence, 'You might as well make yourself visible, Folville. Come and see your former intended. She's in one piece as promised.'

It took all Robert's strength to step forward. Adam and Oswin's presence had been forgotten. The plans he'd made with his brothers had flown from his mind. All Robert could see were visions of the couple before him rutting together. Even the state of Mathilda's bruised face, which clearly indicated she'd resisted as hard as she could, wasn't enough to knock sense into his mind as he broke the agreement he'd made with Oswin and Adam that he'd stay in the shadows no matter what happened. He took a second step out of his hiding place into the clearing.

'At last!' Leigh's tone jeered, 'We were beginning to think you'd washed your hands of Mathilda here.'

Robert had been so transfixed on the state of Mathilda and the horror that was the man next to her, that he hadn't noticed that there was another man in the clearing as well.

Propped against a stout tree trunk, lounging in a relaxed manner, the man was playing a dagger through his fingers. Everything about him screamed out that he'd do anything his master told him. Absolutely anything.

Following the direction of Robert's eye line, Leigh said, 'I see you've spotted my associate. Let me introduce you to Gamelyn.'

'Named after a hero?' Robert spat on the ground in disgust

Leigh laughed more openly now, 'That is exactly what this lovely creature said. Almost word for word.'

Robert swallowed. He steeled himself to look at Mathilda's face. Her whole expression pleaded with him. Her eyes were urgent, imploring and for the first time since he saw her he began to wonder if he'd been hasty.

Cursing inwardly for allowing Leigh to make him break the cover they'd been depending on, Robert took a firmer hold of himself.

Mathilda had fought. Here and now, that was enough. Later... later he could say goodbye to her if he had to. But in private, away from the cruel crowing of this man.

Pulling himself together, Robert remembered what Eustace and John had agreed he should say. 'Rowan Leigh, I presume?'

'Correct.' Leigh moved the hand at Mathilda's throat, wrapping some of her hair around his fingers, dragging her head further back, so that her throat was more exposed to the blade of his knife. The small cry that escaped from Mathilda's lips pierced Robert's soul. He'd never seen her so afraid.

'I have spoken to my brothers. We have reluctantly agreed to let you have the rule of our lands in exchange for Mathilda's safe return.'

Rowan scoffed, 'Just like that! I'm astounded at such weakness from a Folville. You'd throw it all away for a woman.'

Robert felt bile rising in his throat. 'No, but we would for Mathilda. Let her go and we will negotiate.'

'There's nothing to negotiate. I can't believe the famous Eustace de Folville would allow you to exchange the Folville name for a chit like this one. I expected you to come and say you'd swap the girl for the lands and control. What made you so stupid as to think I'd believe a word that came from a Folville's tongue?'

'If you want to be regarded as a man of honour, then you should act like one!'

Rowan's laugh was more like a bark this time. 'Honour!

Honour, that's rich coming from the brother of such scum.'

Robert felt his fingers begin to unfreeze, and flex around the pommel of his sword handle. Adam and Oswin would be ready to strike. It was almost over.

'And anyway', Leigh sneered, pulling Mathilda backwards and licking her cheek in a way that made her face distort with disgust, 'the bargaining counter has altered. This pretty girl is mine now. As you can see, she wears the dress to prove it.'

~ *Chapter Twenty-eight* ~

Robert was running before he'd remembered how foolish it was to run.

The knife slashed across his left arm before he was close enough to grab Mathilda.

He'd reached out to pull her away from the monster holding her by the neck without thinking of the possible consequences. His all-consuming lust for action had cost Robert the safety of cover and changed the plan he'd shared with Adam and Oswin irrevocably.

Mathilda's mouth had opened to call out a warning, but if any sound had come from her lips he didn't hear it. All Robert saw was the woman he loved in another man's wedding gown. All he heard was the mocking laughter of Rowan Leigh. Nothing else existed. Nothing else mattered.

'You bastard!' Robert swore as he stumbled back a few paces, paying no heed to the wound Leigh had slashed into his skin. 'Look what you're done to her.'

Leigh's face contorted into a victorious grin, 'Is it obvious to you, what I've done to her? Is she still murmuring with guilty pleasure?'

Mathilda yelled, 'Lies!'

'Be quiet, wife, or I'll damage him beyond mending!'

Internally pleading for Robert to trust her, to believe her

mental screams that she hadn't got married, that the words Leigh uttered were lies, Mathilda began to tremble violently as Leigh kept up his gloating.

'I have to tell you, Folville, not only do I have the satisfaction of taking something so beautiful from you, but I've been able to enjoy the baser joys of married life. As it happens, you interrupted us in the middle of our first evening together and while the back of a cart was sufficient for our first ribald moment, I would like to get this meeting over with quickly, so I can get to know my wife better.'

Mathilda's throaty moan cracked with a single racking sob. Robert was so close, but she couldn't hear him move. Every fear in her was centring on the dread that he believed the evil Leigh spoke. She wanted to yell at the top of her voice, 'We aren't married. He hasn't touched me like that. I'm yours. I'll always be yours.' No words came though, for the blade of the knife was back in place, pressing harder against her flesh, Robert's blood making it sticky against her bruised skin. One step and she'd be mingling his blood with her own.

The night breeze had quietened to nothing. The frost that had begun to form on the trees branches had paused. It was as if Mother Nature herself was holding her breath to see what would happen next.

'I confess, Folville - your family has disappointed me. I'd heard so much. So many tales of defiance, of violence, of ruling the locality with uncompromising power. All of it has turned out to be but tales and fables. Even with one of the most evil men to walk the earth amongst your number, you're still nothing. Taking everything from you has been child's play.'

Robert kept his eyes on Mathilda's uplifted neck. The knife glistened in the moonlight. Leigh's taunts about his family couldn't hurt him now. It was too late for that. Clamping his right hand over the wound on his left arm Robert wondered if Oswin had a clear shot from his tree and if any of Leigh's men had a clear shot at him in return.

Sarah's warnings about what he might discover when he found Mathilda continued to circulate in Robert's head alongside the evidence of his own eyes. He was in danger of letting the reality be drowned out by the conflicting voices telling him Mathilda's disgrace was both true and untrue at the same time.

Blood had begun to seep through the layers of his sleeves. At first, Robert didn't notice that Leigh had changed the subject of his gloating from the conquest of Mathilda to the betrayal of Allward.

'He was quite a find, was Allward. I couldn't believe my luck when he turned so fast.'

Robert swallowed the hate rising faster within him. He had to control it; he'd need to use it for strength later. 'Allward was never your man, Leigh; just as Mathilda will never be your woman.'

Snorting, Leigh said, 'I can see why you'd want to believe that. But your lad betrayed you. He let us in to collect Mathilda, you know. It was his idea to make it appear as if he was being a spy for you, when in fact he was all for me from our first meeting.'

'So why have him killed?'

The sharp intake of breath from Mathilda told Robert she hadn't known her young friend was dead.

Leigh shrugged, as if it was obvious. 'His pathetic pride in being an orphan child caused his downfall. As if that was at thing to exalt in! Anyway, I'd finished with him. I couldn't rely on the boy not changing his mind again about where his loyalties lay.'

'Which goes to prove Allward was very much cleverer than you. He was *never* on your side and I doubt very much that he was the one who opened the manor gates to your felons.'

'You can doubt it all you like. But Allward let us in and he pulled your steward from his feet so that Gamelyn could finish him.'

The tiniest cry of 'Owen?' from Mathilda, made Leigh laugh louder.

'Sorry, my bride, but he was in the way of Gamelyn being able to fulfil my orders. Owen, if that's what his name was, stood between us and our happy future together.'

Robert was losing blood faster than he'd first thought. He needed a cloth to wrap around the wound to stem the bleeding. He needed Mathilda.

Knowing he had to keep Leigh talking so he didn't hurt Mathilda further, Robert continued, 'You can refer to Mathilda as your bride as much as you like Leigh, but I don't have to believe she is really yours. A bride who is so bruised from beatings is no bride. Your research into my family appears to be grossly inadequate. We are successful because we rule with loyalty. Yes, that loyalty may have an undercurrent of fear sometimes, but it lies heavy with respect. You just frighten people. What do you think that will achieve, long term?'

Scoffing, Leigh said, 'Well so far I have taken your future wife, your steward and your messenger. And I believe you are here to tell me I can have your connections. I'd say that frightening people is working very well so far. I did, after all, learn the skill from a master of the craft.'

'And that master would be?'

'You don't know?' Leigh shook his head, before continuing in more of a mumble, as if he was talking to himself for the moment. 'Of course, he'd never have said. That's how he works. Secrecy, pretence. I should use those skills more.'

Suddenly, he snapped his head up high and stared directly into Robert's eyes, 'So, you are ready to admit defeat?'

'Defeat? What are you talking about? All I can see is a kidnapper and murderer. You don't have the ability to run the Folville lands. And you have stupidly removed your main bargaining counter. If you have married Mathilda I'm hardly going to exchange our lands for her, am I?'

Mathilda whimpered into the dark cold sky. *Please, Robert, please...*

'I have no wish to bring damaged stock into the family and any woman unlucky enough to be implanted with your seed isn't worth having, is she.' Robert hated himself for sounding so convincing; hoping that one day Mathilda would forgive him. 'A Folville, should we ever stoop so low, would force marriage *after* we'd got we wanted, not before. A basic mistake, Leigh. Your overconfidence lets you down.'

Adam wasn't sure if he was still breathing. His ears were straining to listen as Leigh cleverly played Robert and Mathilda off against each other.

Keep him talking, my Lord, keep him talking. Adam begrudgingly admired Leigh's nerve. His ability to say precisely what was required to cause maximum pain and distrust was clear. Adam found himself reminded of another person he'd once known. A man with similar deceitful qualities...*What was his name?... Wilkin Sayer...*

A clammy sweat that should have been impossible on such a cold day, assailed Adam. *Surely Sayer didn't have a hand here...?* As a glimmer of an idea swept over him, the former steward doubled his concentration on the scene unfolding in the clearing.

Despite peering as hard as he could into the trees that surrounded him, Adam saw no sign of any of Leigh's followers. *If they aren't here, then where the hell are they?*

With a growing feeling that time was running out, spurred on by the horror of having to tell Sarah he'd failed to bring Mathilda home, Adam acted.

His taunting voice echoed round the clearing the clarity of the night air making it echo enough for its direction of origin to be disguised. 'You don't tell lies well, Leigh. Whoever taught you, whoever this master of the craft was, they let you down.'

Leigh turned sharply, dragging Mathilda with him as he twisted. 'I don't tell lies at all. Show yourself, you coward!'

'Coward? I think not. Merely sensible.' Adam marvelled at how sure his voice sounded compared with how apprehensive he was. 'Cowards hold women hostage. Cowards kill young men for no reason other than that they're no longer useful. I wonder if you were threatened by what Allward might have become one day. A better man than you, without doubt.'

'Says the man skulking in the shadows!'

Leigh sounded like a sulky child, as Robert realised what Adam was trying to do. Robert was about to speak, when Oswin beat him to it.

'My friend is right.'

Leigh's head snapped towards the sky, but he couldn't see anyone. 'Another coward!'

'Cowards use women as shields. I have no shield at all.'

Seeking to divide Rowan's attention further, Robert added, 'And to use a woman as a hostage... public shame will haunt you to your grave.'

'Eustace de Folville does!'

'Eustace does not. He has done many things of which I am not proud and has been accused, often falsely, of many more things. He is far rougher with woman than he should be, but he's never cowered behind a woman's skirts while fighting his battles.'

Adam shouted out again, making both Leigh and Gamelyn spin around again, 'So Eustace is the most evil Folville, is he?'

Oswin joined in, causing Leigh to shift his stance again, as he tried to work out where the voices were coming from, 'I don't think Eustace would ever win the prize for most evil Folville. Although I'm sure he'd be flattered by the viewpoint.'

Realising what the other were doing, Robert kept up the banter. 'He certainly would.' Robert nodded soberly. 'Eustace likes a bit of drama. He'll be sorry he couldn't attend tonight!'

Every time Rowan moved, Mathilda was dragged after him; this way and that as her warder spun in the rough direction of each voice, as the three men spoke faster, taking it in turns to surround him with sound. Her own mind worked fast as Gamelyn moved so that he stood at Leigh's side. *That was Adam's voice coming from behind, but the other man... Could that be my brother? How did Oswin get here?*

'And you call us cowards, and yet we have announced our presence' Adam called, 'I refuse to believe that you have no men here with you, Leigh. Only a fool would be arrogant enough to come here alone to meet a Folville.'

'Gamelyn!' Leigh almost shrieked the word, as his henchman moved forward into the clearing away from Adam, but not far below Oswin. 'Of course, I'm not alone, but nor am I such a coward that I need force of arms like you.'

Robert made a theatrical groan. 'You do like the word coward, don't you! Really, Rowan, two men hardly makes up a battalion, and it's common sense to arrive here light handed. A group would have been picked off in the trees, which, I suspect, is why you have also come along with minimal numbers, at least this far into the wood.' Robert stared at Gamelyn; the large man was dressed in dark grey and brown. He almost blended in with the trees themselves. *Were there others dressed and hidden in such a manner?*

Gamelyn said nothing, but the expression of concern he levelled towards his oblivious master spoke volumes. Robert could almost hear him wondering why he was serving a man who was so clearly sickening for madness.

A brief unnerving hush had fallen. The tension in the clearing then doubled as Gamelyn took his knife and pointed it towards Robert.

Adam silently eased his kitchen knife from his belt. He'd never killed with either a knife or a dagger, no matter what the gossips said. He didn't want to now, but if that's what it took... He took a single step forward but kept beneath the cover of the trees.

Oswin, also alert to the subtle change in atmosphere, knew it was now or never. Sighting his arrow along the bowstring, he aimed. It was no good trying to hit Leigh. The man was moving about too much and Mathilda with him. So Oswin aimed at Gamelyn, hoping with all his heart that if Leigh had any archers hidden, they'd be too slow to react.

Leigh's eyes darted wildly between Gamelyn and Robert.

'Now!'

1322

It was all his. The time had come. This was the moment to call in the favours he'd been careful to collect over the past decade.

First, though, he'd visit the abbey and make sure they understood precisely the extent of their neglect towards him and his fellow pupils.

He was the one in control now.

~ *Chapter Twenty-nine* ~

Mathilda wasn't sure what had happened first.

Had the arrow hit Gamelyn in the leg first, or had Robert dived at him first? Either way, the sound of Robert swearing at the wounded larger man as they fell into a fight vibrated though her. The clash of metal hitting metal pounded in her chest long after it had ended.

She couldn't see what was happening; couldn't check if Robert was winning or not. With her head yanked sharply upwards, Leigh was retreating with her towards the trees. Mathilda was sure he was aiming for the cart; and with his knife still at her throat, she'd never felt so useless in her life.

If Robert is killed... if Leigh moves the knife any closer... if he gets me back in that cart? Am I disposable like Allward now?

Not knowing where Adam or Oswin were, Mathilda braced herself for the end of the world as Leigh reversed her through the dark trees, away from the comparative safety of the moonlight.

All Mathilda was sure of was that they'd left the clearing.

The cart was only a few paces away, when Leigh whispered in her ear.

'I think it's time I was rewarded for putting up with

hearing you sniff and sob in my ear like a child!' Throwing Mathilda into the cart, Leigh lunged forward. His hands had grabbed either side of her cloak and, in his anger and humiliation he'd torn right through the thick fabric, making Mathilda scream into the night.

Weak from cold, hunger and fear, Mathilda had no fight left. Closing her eyes, praying to Our Lady that Robert, Oswin or Adam would hear her and come, she felt thick fingers grapple at her thighs.

And then, he was gone.

Mathilda opened her eyes and looked straight into those of Adam, who threw his cloak over her, putting a finger over his lips to tell her to remain silent, before he disappeared into the clearing. Seconds later he was back, with Robert and Oswin close behind him.

'Robert!' Mathilda's voice sounded too high, the semi-strangled pose Leigh had kept her in making her hoarse. 'Thank God! Is he dead? Is it safe now?'

The journey home was strained. So many questions needed asking and answering; yet no one spoke.

While Oswin headed to Lubbesthorpe to report to Eustace, Adam urged Mathilda to try and sleep in the cart, which he was driving to the manor. Robert sat silent and watchful. His eyes avoided her, staring instead into the woods on either side of them.

Mathilda felt sick with the weight of what Robert wasn't asking her. She wanted to reassure him, but she was afraid. If he didn't believe her, then she was even more lost than she had been before.

By the time they'd arrived at Ashby Folville, sleep had claimed her.

They told Mathilda later that nightmares had made her

twitch and cry out from the depths of her slumber all the way home.

Although aching to engulf Mathilda in a bone-crushing hug, just to make sure she was really there, Sarah's hands were gentle. 'I never thought we'd see you again.'

'Nor I you.' Mathilda's tears were as much of relief to see a face that held no accusation or suspicion, as they were of fear for her future. 'Are you whole, Sarah? No more harm came to you?'

'Not me, but others...'

'Allward and Owen.' Mathilda whispered the words through her cracked lips, 'I can't believe they're gone.'

Sarah carefully undid the tangled knots of her friend's hair, brushing each one out as they sat together in Mathilda's private chamber. 'Can you tell me what happened to you?'

With a sigh, Mathilda said, 'You're the only one who has been brave enough to ask me that. I want to tell Robert. I want to explain. He won't even look at me, and I didn't... there wasn't....'

'There was no marriage and no consummation?'

'No! Leigh tried, but, no! I got these bruises for a reason...'

Hearing her friend well up towards a new flood of tears, the housekeeper sighed at the stupidity of male pride. 'I know, child, I know. I believe you.'

'Robert doesn't though, does he? He hasn't even bothered to ask. He has assumed the worst. He's barely spoken to me since we returned. And would he trust my answers anyway?'

Mathilda clenched her fists, digging chipped nails into her palms in frustration. 'I'm not sure what happened at

The Thwaite in the end. Everything was so fast once Leigh dragged me to the cart.' Trying not to start shaking again, Mathilda murmured, 'Is Leigh dead now? Please tell me, Sarah. Is it over?'

Easing out a particularly persistent tangle in Mathilda's long blonde hair, the housekeeper said, 'I'm sorry my child, Leigh isn't dead as far as I know. Not unless one of Eustace's men got him; and I'm sure we'd have heard if they had. No one knows where Leigh went. It's not so hard for a man alone to slip into the forest unnoticed.'

Mathilda's forehead creased and the headache she'd been nursing for days thumped harder, 'But how did he get away?'

'I think you should hear that from the men. They were very brave going there, just the three of them.'

'Adam, especially.' Mathilda looked at the housekeeper, 'You should be proud of him.'

Sarah blushed, confirming Mathilda's suspicions.

'Good. I'm glad one of us will come out of these events happier than we were thrust into them.'

Recommencing her brushing, Sarah asked, 'How did you know, you haven't been here?'

'Adam was talking to himself in the cart on the way home. Something about making sure he got us here in one piece otherwise you'd succeed in killing him where Leigh had failed. The way he said it spoke of affection.'

'As Robert will speak of you again soon. He's had a lot of shocks in your absence as well as losing you. He didn't rest until he'd tracked you down.'

Mathilda opened her mouth to object, but Sarah held up her hand. 'Let's wait and see, shall we. Now we have those horrid clothes on the bonfire and you're clean and fed, we can work out what can be done. But first, you are going to stay in here, save your voice, rest, allow your bruises to heal and let me turn you back into the lady of the manor!'

Daniel had made the hall fire blaze as high as safety would allow. Sarah, concerned for the cold Mathilda couldn't seem to shake from her bones, had arranged her friend before it in the middle of a pile of animal skins and winter cloaks.

Feeling detached from the domestic scene around her, Mathilda watched as Daniel added a final log to the blaze and Sarah filled jugs with warmed wine she'd prepared for the meeting.

She heard the sound of Eustace arriving in the kitchen, his boots stamping along the connecting corridor towards the hall, accompanied by him calling to his groom to follow as soon as the horses were seen to.

Mathilda clenched her hands under the covers. *What if they didn't believe her?*

Adam was quietly adding tankards to the table. Mathilda wondered if Sarah was aware of how many times his eyes drifted in her direction. Knowing Sarah, she was probably more than aware, but was choosing to enjoy the attention without making a fuss. A tug of envy gnawed at Mathilda's heart. Robert used to do that. Now he couldn't face being in the same room as her.

Three days had passed and yet they hadn't spoken beyond polite greetings in the mornings and partings at night. Sarah had told Robert that there had been no marriage and no dent on Mathilda's virtue, but he remained withdrawn and distant.

The wedding was supposed to be in four days time.
Their wedding.
Mathilda was determined not to cry. Far too many tears had been shed since Leigh had ripped her life apart. Their

lives. Enough now. If Robert no longer wanted her, then so be it. She'd be devastated, but she'd survive. What was important was to track Leigh down and find out who was retaining him.

Thomas and Walter slunk through the door. Both grim and taciturn as ever, they sank into their favoured seats at the long table. Grabbing their drinks, they gave her a brief enquiring stare before dismissing her as unimportant.

Sarah had already informed Mathilda that John and Laurence were busy elsewhere, so it would only be a depleted gathering of the brothers today. Oswin should be there though, but so far, the round friendly face of Mathilda's younger brother was absent.

The only sounds in the hall were the pottering of Sarah and Daniel as they attended to pouring the wine, and the crackle of the fire behind Mathilda. Thomas and Walter gripped their cups and stared into the flames, each giving the impression that they were lost in their thoughts.

Mathilda licked her lips. The skin around her mouth was dry from the effects of cold and dehydration. Her bruises were healing and the tiny scar that she hadn't even noticed Leigh make at her throat, such was her terror in the wood, had crusted over.

Over the past couple of days, once the initial relief of being safe had overwhelmed her, Mathilda had done little but think over everything she'd gone through. She was hungry for information about what had happened here without her. Sarah had done her best to answer her questions, but there was so much that Mathilda needed to know before she could piece together what was going on.

The uneasy atmosphere was broken as Eustace entered the room, his gravel voice booming across the hall. 'Robert, where are you, brother? We've much to discuss. I've got my men acting as warders to six of his fiends hogtied and awaiting the law in his workshop, but Leigh needs tracking down. Fast.'

Followed by the burly figure of John Pykehose, Eustace was also accompanied by a woman Mathilda hadn't seen before. For a fleeting second, she considered that Eustace may have found a woman who'd put up with him, but she dismissed it as a fancy too far.

Then, at last, Robert came in with Adam at his side.

'I apologise, Lady Joan.' Robert bowed low, 'I hadn't realised you'd arrived. Please, take a seat.'

Eustace, unusually courteous, pulled out a tapestry cushioned chair next to the head of the table for their guest.

Mathilda went to rise at the sight of their strikingly beautiful visitor, but Lady Joan raised a hand in restraint. 'Please Mistress Twyford, I appreciate the offer of politeness, but you should rest. You've been through enough. Our Lady be praised you are safe.'

'Thank you, my Lady. Forgive me, but I'm rather behind with events. If you helped in my retrieval, then you have my wholehearted gratitude.'

'My pleasure. I, as you'll discover, gained from the situation myself.'

Mathilda wasn't sure she liked the hungry look Lady Joan was giving Robert but told herself it wasn't allowed to matter to her anymore. If she was to leave the Folville home after today, then the sooner she accepted the fact the better. But, if she could, Mathilda was determined to leave with dignity and with a parting shot at establishing justice for Allward and Owen.

~ *Chapter Thirty* ~

'I was sure he was going to kill her.'

Adam's darkly weathered pallor blanched as he relayed to the gathering how he'd followed Leigh and Mathilda as they'd backed out of the clearing.

'I thought I'd reached the point in my life when I'd witness no more unnatural death. But to see that evil man with a knife pricking the Lady Mathilda's flesh... I felt sick to my craw.

'I had no choice. He was so intent on deflowering Mathilda that I had to act. I dropped my knife for fear of accidentally stabbing Mathilda and wrapped an arm around Rowan's throat.

'Leigh is scrawny but strong. It didn't take long until he dropped Mathilda, but I'm ashamed to say that he twisted from my grip and punched me in the stomach. Leigh was gone into the trees before I'd regained my breath. I ran after him, but there were so many paths and I chose the wrong one. I'm not sorry to have been spared the act of murder; and yet I regret that he remains at large.'

Eustace addressed Adam with such sincerity, that the whole room stilled to hear what was to be said next, 'You claim you prevented Leigh from deflowering Mathilda, yet from what my brother tells me, Leigh took great pleasure in crowing about how that deed had already been done.'

Mathilda glanced at Robert, who had the decency to be red in the face.

'I'm pleased to report that was not the case. I have no doubt that Leigh was weaving lies to taunt my Lord Robert. I swear on the life of Our Lady herself that I overheard him talk to Mathilda. He was angry at how all his previous attempts to take her had been thwarted. The man is deranged. He was planning to take her there and then. I don't think, by this point, he even considered we'd be bound to stop him. It was as if only revenge against this family, through use of Mathilda, existed for him.'

A loaded silence hung in the air, before Eustace asked, 'Adam, are you sure about what you heard?'

'On my honour and my life, my Lord.'

'And you told Robert this?'

Adam looked at Robert, but his master was staring into the flick of the fire's flames. 'No, my Lord Eustace. My Lord Robert has not wished to discuss my Lady Mathilda. I have been unable to reassure him on this matter.'

'Robert?'

Despite the underlying threat in Eustace's voice, Robert ignored his brother, saying instead. 'And you, Oswin. Let's hear your account, please. It is important we hear all so we can put this puzzle together and track Leigh down.'

Keeping his eyes on his sister, Oswin responded, 'I disposed of what appeared to be Leigh's only lookout on my arrival. I can't believe there was only one, but as time went on, it became clear Leigh had lost his grip on reality and saw himself as unstoppable. The original plan for me to shoot Leigh had to change as he had Mathilda in his grip.'

Mathilda watched her brother carefully as he avoided mentioning that Robert had run into the clearing, making it impossible for Oswin to get a clear shot. That fact, Robert rushing to her side, had been the only thing that had kept Mathilda from completely giving up hope.

'Once Leigh's man, Gamelyn, came forward, I took the chance and shot him. To my shame my aim was poor and I only hit his leg. Leigh, who had my beloved sister by the neck, a knife to her throat, dragged Mathilda out of the clearing as soon as his man was injured. That is when Robert took his dagger to Gamelyn.'

Mathilda's eyes blazed; a heightened flare of interest pulling her from her misery. 'Forgive me interrupting, my Lords. Am I to understand that Gamelyn is dead?'

Oswin frowned, 'You did not know?'

'I did not.' Mathilda turned to Robert. 'Thank you, my Lord. His deeds were black.' She rubbed at the fading bruises that adorned her wrists. 'He was the one who murdered Owen.'

Robert held her eyes for the first time for days. Mathilda hoped she saw love there. She was certain she saw someone who wanted to love her but was no longer sure if he could.

Oswin, uncomfortable with the sudden silence, said, 'After that I dropped from the tree and ran to where I knew Adam to be hiding and followed Mathilda's cries. I reached the cart as Leigh threw his punch and winded Adam. I attended to my sister while Adam ran after Leigh and my Lord Robert fought Gamelyn. I could hear the curses coming from the clearing. Robert was in a fury, scolding Gamelyn for taking an outlaw hero's name as his own when it was so undeserved.'

Eustace snorted, 'That sounds like my brother.'

Recalling how she'd been disgusted by Gamelyn's choice of name for the same reason, Mathilda felt her palms prickle. Perhaps she and Robert had not drifted so far apart after all.

Lady Joan, who'd observed everything that had passed with a quiet interest, spoke. 'Leigh had more men than just Gamelyn. There were many. Where are they now?'

Eustace gave a semi-satisfied grunt. 'Six are penned up like pigs for slaughter. Many managed to flee. I'm glad you agreed to stay in Leicester's Abbey while we dealt with the situation. I would not have wished to have to worry about your safety as well as dealing with Leigh's miscreants.'

Lady Joan raised her eyebrows. 'You mean my father and my husband would have killed you if I'd been harmed.'

Mathilda couldn't believe she was hearing a woman talk to Eustace de Folville like that. She was even more stunned when he laughed.

'There is that as well; your father is not a man I'd cross. I make no comment about the Sheriff of Yorkshire, your husband. Nonetheless, I am glad you were out of harm's way.'

Robert coughed, 'You digress, brother. The village of Lubbesthorpe?'

Eustace scowled at his younger brother for talking to him in such a manner in front of Lady Joan. 'Leigh sent his men to guard the village itself. He had someone stationed at each corner of the place. However, he didn't do it early enough. Nor did he send men deep into the woods to surround the village as we did.'

Lady Joan was showing more interest in events now that Roger la Zouche's land was being discussed. 'Surely Leigh's men were in the village anyway, working, living and intimidating the villagers that have served my father well for years? Not to mention inhabiting his workshop on the outskirts of Lubbesthorpe.'

Eustace centred his attention on their guest in such a way that Mathilda began to wonder if Lady Joan's husband knew his wife was here. 'I take your point, Lady Joan, but Leigh appears to have been more concerned about stopping the locals leading us to him and therefore Mathilda. The lookouts were only sent out an hour before the meeting was due to take place.'

Preening slightly, Eustace went on, 'We, of course, were already in place and with far more men. Leigh's entourage was nothing like as big as he'd managed to make it appear.'

Eustace pulled his dagger out and started to trail it over the table, as was his habit. Begrudgingly he added, 'There I think Leigh was clever. He's moved his men around over the past few days, giving us all the illusion of him having a larger following than he does. And his men are all loyal, violent and have nothing left to lose except their lives anyway. The fact he was happy to leave Gamelyn's body where it fell in the woods speak volumes about how disposable his associates were to him.'

Mathilda had been listening carefully. She'd given up expecting the men to ask her anything, but she knew both Lady Joan and Sarah were champing at the bit to ask about what had happened behind the walls of the carpenter's workshop.

Robert was still stoically avoiding facing her unless he had to.

Oswin was staring unwaveringly in his sister's direction, his face a picture of concern.

Thomas and Walter looked vaguely bored. Mathilda was sure they were only there because they'd been detailed to report the events to Lord John in Huntingdon.

As the convivial glow of the fire seeped heat comfortingly into her back and the mulled wine Sarah had so lovingly prepared relaxed her insides, Mathilda found herself thinking back further. She'd been through so much since she'd met the Folville family. Kidnap, assault, the threat of a false murder charge and now, by luck and the help of Our Lady, she had narrowly escaped rape.

Every part of her body ached. Bruises and scars liberally dotted her skin, some of which she was beginning to think would never leave her.

The reason Mathilda was living in the manor at Ashby Folville in the first place was that she'd impressed the brothers with her astute way of thinking. She'd proved her worth to them again and again. If she wanted to stay; if she wanted to reassure the man she loved that she was the same girl she had been before Rowan Leigh crashed into their lives, then she was going to have to prove that worth all over again.

In the ballads the minstrels sang, love was enough to see them through, but as much as Mathilda adored the songs sung at the town's fairs, she wasn't naive enough to believe their romantic claims. She was a young woman from a lowly family. Her place in this household, however much she was cared for, would have to be earned again and again and again.

Against the backdrop of the crackling fire, Eustace was talking about how he'd placed his retinue under deep cover within the woodland that encircled the village of Lubbesthorpe, keeping a discreet, but watchful, distance from the carpenters so as not to endanger Mathilda further. It galled him that he'd slipped away from the workshop without his men noticing. His frustration that Leigh hadn't been taken was only outdone by his certainty that the man hadn't run in his direction. If he had, Leigh would certainly have been ensnared. From anyone else, Mathilda would have considered this belief pure arrogance. With Eustace, it was the truth - *and* pure arrogance.

Without giving their visitor the satisfaction of actually

turning in her direction, Mathilda could feel Lady Joan's green eyes challenging her. Their gaze seemed to call her a coward for not voicing her opinions.

The potter's daughter from Twyford had had enough. If she was to be removed from the household because some bastard had pretended he'd ruined her, she was going with her pride in place and her dignity returned.

Mathilda's voice abruptly cracked through Eustace's monologue. 'My Lords, if I may speak?'

~ *Chapter Thirty-one* ~

No one replied to Mathilda's request, yet every pair of eyes in the room swivelled in her direction.

Choosing not to look at anyone but Robert, Mathilda fixed her betrothed with an earnest expression, willing him to maintain their connection.

'My Lords, we have heard your accounts of what happened. If I'm permitted, I would like to add how brave Allward was. The news of his death...' Mathilda paused, the knot in her throat as she admitted her friend's murder out loud for the first time making her words croak, 'is particularly distressing to me. It was his act of trying to protect me; of trying to make sure you, my Lord Robert, knew where to find me, that caused his death.'

Sarah, without waiting to be asked, topped up Mathilda's cup so that the throat which was still sore from being throttled did not prevent her speaking. Giving her friend an almost imperceptible nod of encouragement, the housekeeper moved on round the table with the wine jug.

'I wasn't sure at first. I thought, may God forgive me, that Allward had betrayed us. He'd asked me to trust him, even though I might hear him say things I wouldn't want him to say. He swore he was doing what he was doing because he was loyal and that he wasn't throwing away all the love and care he had here. But hearing him say he'd deliver messages for that monster...' Mathilda paused, shuddering. 'It was hard, but in fact Allward was doing what he could to help. If it hadn't been for him, my injuries would have been considerably worse, and my virtue would have been ruined.'

Eustace dug his dagger deeper into the tabletop, so that it stood there without his assistance, quivering from the force of its embedding in the oak. 'I remain unconvinced. The boy led them to you. It must have been him who let them into this manor.'

'I suspect he did, my Lord, but he had no choice.' Mathilda's hand went to the scar on her neck. 'With a knife to the throat it is very difficult not to do what you're told.'

Eustace, who'd employed the same tactic when extracting money from debtors reluctant to pay their dues on a number of occasions, couldn't argue. 'You are claiming that Allward was compelled to go with them.'

'I am saying that I suspect this was the case. Allward told me he'd been manoeuvred into doing something he didn't want to do. He wouldn't say what, but he was clearly ashamed and determined to make amends. I think someone he trusted made him believe he was doing the right thing - a fact he soon realised was wrong.'

'Do you know who this someone was?'

'No.'

Robert, his pulse pounding with uncertainty, took a proper look at the woman he was to marry. Pale and bruised, red hair hidden away behind the dignity of a linen cover, she sat regally in the furs and blankets. He knew, for the first time since he'd seen Mathilda in the woods, that he still loved her.

Not wanting his brothers to think he'd weakened in the face of the potential personal loss, his voice wary, Robert broke his silence. 'And you know Allward felt ashamed, how, exactly, Mathilda?'

The accusation in his voice crushed Mathilda to the core. *He doesn't think I'm in league with Leigh after all that's happened, does he?*

Faltering for a second, the shock of this thought making her heartache worse than before, she said, 'On my arrival, after I was humiliated with freezing water, I was imprisoned with Allward in the stables.'

Forgetting her place for a second, Sarah sucked in her breath in a gasp, 'Freezing water! What did he do to -'

'Sarah!' Robert snapped. 'I'm sure you have chores in the kitchen.'

'I'm sorry, my Lord. I was...'

'Your liking for Mathilda is well known. Thanks to your clucking and care, she is in one piece, so you have no more need to worry. Return to your duties, Adam can attend to our needs here.'

Silently fuming, Sarah headed to the kitchen. Mathilda felt as though another chink had appeared in her armour.

It was Eustace who asked her the next question. 'What did Leigh do to you prior to your imprisonment with Allward?'

'I was foolish enough to stand up to him. And then, well, I was so frightened, I was sick. Some of it landed on Leigh's boots. He made me pay for this humiliation by soaking me to the bone with cold water and making me stand out in the night until I collapsed. In truth, my Lord, I thought I was to die of cold. I feared I'd never see my Lord Robert again.'

Mathilda felt Robert flinch before she saw it. She hoped he'd felt the truth of what she'd said. All she'd thought about as she'd stood there, doused in cold water, was her betrothed.

As the memory of her frigid fear came back to her, she started to shake. However, the proud tilt to her chin and the stiffness of her spine dared anyone to mention her tremors.

Lady Joan, appreciating the cost of Mathilda's dignity, asked a welcomingly frank question. 'You're lucky to have survived. How did you?'

'I was thrown into the stable with Allward. I was tied hand and foot, but Allward was only tied at the ankles. He had enough slack to his bonds to make sure my sodden cloak was removed. He covered me in dry warm straw, so I didn't freeze to death while I was unconscious.'

Robert's next words came out as a whisper. 'Allward saved your life.'

'He felt responsible for endangering it in the first place.' Mathilda sighed, 'If he'd lived, I don't think he'd ever have forgiven himself for believing whoever it was that convinced him to let Leigh's men into the manor. Allward's whole life would have revolved around making it up to me; to all of us. Yet, I never held it against him. The boy was terrified, yet he saved me more than once in that hellish place.'

Eustace looked at Robert, to see if he wanted to speak, but his brother was looking as if he wanted to destroy something, so Eustace carried on himself. 'How else did Allward save you, apart from limiting the level of the beatings you clearly sustained?'

'My Lords, despite what Leigh claimed, he *never* took from me what he really wanted. Allward stopped him the first time, and Adam stopped him the third time he tried.'

'And the second time?' Robert's eyes roamed over every inch of Mathilda as she continued to sit, her bearing proud, despite the slight quiver to her shoulders. He began to feel foolish for ever doubting her and yet he couldn't stop himself from asking the questions he wasn't sure he wanted answers to. 'How did you escape his grasp for the second time?'

'Believe it or not, it was one of Leigh's own men. Edgar. Leigh murdered him as a result. Right in front of me.' Mathilda squeezed her eyes shut for a moment. The image of Edgar's face as his master pierced him with the dagger filled her mind. 'I won't ever forget.'

No one spoke. Everyone waited for Robert to speak first. It had to be him who told Mathilda that they believed her.

With a glance at Eustace, who gave the tiniest inclination of his head, Robert came towards Mathilda, reaching a hand out to hers. 'Forgive me. I was afraid I'd lost you to that... That you'd lack the courage to fight. I should have known better.'

As his voice trailed away, the smile that Mathilda thought she'd had stolen from her for ever flashed across her face, to quickly be replaced by an expression of grim determination. 'My Lord Robert, I am to be married to a Folville. To you! If I lacked courage, then what sort of wife would I make for a household such as this?'

Seeing that the meeting was in danger of slipping into a display of sentiment, Eustace coughed, 'Well, thank God that's cleared up. You've been like a vengeful monk on heat, brother.'

The older Folville held out his flagon for Adam to refill. 'Mathilda, what did you learn about Leigh while you were his unwilling guest? Have you any idea where he might have fled to?' Eustace leant nearer to his future sister-in-law. 'This creature needs expunging from this earth. We need you to help us send him directly into the tender loving arms of Beelzebub.'

'How dare you? What idiocy makes you come here?'

'I'm not here for you, Sayer. I have to talk to de Cressy. Now!' Leigh was waving his knife before him as though he had very little control over it. Wilkin Sayer was beginning to wonder if his unwelcome visitor realised he was holding a weapon.

The recently appointed steward of the manor of John de Markham looked Rowan Leigh up and down. He'd never seen him looking do dishevelled. His face was scratched, as if he'd run blindly through brambles and branches. His clothes were stained, and his hands were shaking.

Sayer took a step back. The possibility that Leigh was deranged flashed into the steward's mind and refused to leave. 'Why are you here? We agreed never to meet again.'

'And I intended to keep that bargain, but it appears that your employer's assertion that capturing the Folvilles would be a straightforward matter was somewhat flawed.'

Checking over his shoulder to make sure that no one was listening, Sayer hissed under his breath. 'My employer is John de Markham. I have *no idea* what you are talking about.'

'No idea?' Leigh frowned, his usually unlined face creasing into ugly folds. 'It was *you*, it was your idea. *You* introduced us, you and de Cressy said...'

The slap landed on Leigh's face before got any further. Sayer knocked away Leigh's knife and drew his own weapon from his belt. 'You are mistaken. I have no notion of what you're talking about. As of this moment, I can surely say that I have never set eyes on you before.'

'What?' Leigh spluttered, 'but you...'

'I have put my past behind me. Anything you think I may have done, I can tell you without doubt, did not happen. I suggest you leave. Now.'

'We went through so much, when we were young, we....' Leigh recoiled with a mixture of betrayal and confusion. 'Where is de Cressy?'

Sayer held the other man's gaze. 'On his way to Leicestershire. I don't know where. Now leave. And, Rowan.'

'Yes?'

'Never come back here. Ever.'

~ *Chapter Thirty-two* ~

Robert knocked on the door to Mathilda's chamber.

He'd stood before men who wanted to kill him, thieves and some of the most corrupt officials in the land, but none of those encounters had filled him with the concern he felt as he waited for a reply to his polite knock.

It was no good pretending that he hadn't doubted Mathilda's word. That would have been a further insult, adding to the wrong he'd already done her.

The door opened and Mathilda bobbed a quick curtsey. 'My Lord.'

Now he was here, Robert felt robbed of everything he'd been going to say. Awkward, he took refuge in just looking at her for a moment.

They were opposite each other, their bodies so close. Mathilda waiting with a calm patience for him to speak.

Her face was fair but for the clusters of bruises which gave an inescapable reminder of what she'd been through while he'd fretted and paced, not knowing where to start hunting for her. Robert blamed himself bitterly for not finding Mathilda sooner, of not being at the manor when she was taken, of not doing something - anything - to stop the nightmare from happening in the first place.

Instead of saying all of these things Robert's eyes fell on

the plain brown leather belt she wore around her tunic. 'He took your butterfly girdle?'

'He did. But otherwise he did not take more than my clothes. Nor did he take all of those.'

'Mathilda, I...' Robert's words faltered. 'Damn it all! This is insane.'

She'd been about to tell him it was alright, that she understood he'd been scared for her, because if Leigh had taken her virtue they couldn't marry. Mathilda wasn't so naive as to be unaware of the rules where noble families were concerned; even within a family like the Folvilles, where laws were guidelines rather than rules, some lines were simply not to be crossed.

Mathilda didn't say any of this though, because Robert had turned around and walked away from her.

Storming into the kitchen like the wrath of God, Robert turned on Sarah. 'Has Eustace already escorted Lady Joan back to the La Zouche manor?'

Surprised by Robert's manner, Sarah said, 'Yes, my Lord. Eustace left not five minutes ago. Thomas and Walter have also departed for Huntingdon to report the details of the meeting to my Lord John.'

Unwilling to lessen his watch on the region until Leigh was securely under lock and key, Robert had detailed some of the family's retinue to remain on patrol across the family's lands, as well as in Melton. Eustace was going to deal with Lubbesthorpe, which meant that everyone he'd captured was about to be questioned.

'I'm going to join Eustace. There's something I need to find.'

'My Lord, is everything all right?'

'No, Sarah. Nothing is all right.' Robert stormed out into

the courtyard and grabbed his horse's saddle without calling to Adam or Daniel for help.

Eustace was standing in the courtyard of the carpenter's house when Robert's horse thundered up behind him.

'Brother, did you not trust me to finish the job here?'

Robert snorted, 'Far from it. But there is a task I must undertake myself.'

Gesturing to the workshop, whose doors were now closed and barred, with a burly man that Robert recognised as one of his brother's hired mercenaries on guard outside, Eustace said, 'Sheriff de Cressy is on his way. My men made sure the pretty birds didn't fly last night, but I'll be happier when I don't have to waste their time on guard duty when we have Leigh to track down.'

Tempted to visit the prisoners, his fists itching to imprint themselves into the felons' faces, Robert took a step away from the workshop. He wasn't sure he'd ever stop hitting them if he started. His rage was best saved for Leigh himself rather than for the men who'd worked for him.

'I'm here to see the stables and the house.'

'You want to see where he held Mathilda captive?'

Not wanting to reveal what he was looking for, Robert merely said, 'The more we know about Leigh the better.'

Eustace pointed towards the stable. 'The men inside the workshop have been persuaded to talk. They confirm what Mathilda told us about Allward and about her soaking. It seems Leigh had quite an audience when he threw the water over her. Truly brother, I am unsure how Mathilda survived without taking a death cold.'

'Allward did save her life then.'

'He did.' Eustace regarded his brother carefully. 'Will there be a wedding, Robert?'

Robert stared at his feet, before surveying the eerily quiet courtyard. 'Oh, yes. Before then, I intend for Leigh to have been wiped off the face of this earth.'

'Amen to that, Robert. Amen to that.'

Robert didn't linger in the stables. There was nothing to see beyond heaps of straw and the abandoned ropes and chains which had formed part of Mathilda's imprisonment. It was no good examining the scene, picturing Mathilda's distress; seeing her lying there, praying for him to come and save her. Thinking like that wouldn't change anything. All he could do now was make it up to her.

The door to the house was unlocked. The scene inside told of a household who'd intended to be back at work that day as usual. Leigh had clearly expected his mission in The Thwaite to be successful. Although, the more Robert thought, he couldn't imagine what it was that had made Leigh think he could succeed in his aim without even taking a number of armed guards with him last night.

Robert walked from the kitchen into a room that ran to its side and stopped dead.

This was clearly Rowan Leigh's private space.

A haphazard mix of tables and chairs, covered with bits of wood, clothing, and parchment, were scattered everywhere. There was a cot on the floor in the far corner. It was covered, not in blankets, but in Mathilda's clothes.

Dropping to his knees, Robert picked up her familiar tunic. It remained damp enough to tell Robert that when Mathilda had worn it, it must have been sodden. Small patches of mould had begun to form. It stank of mildew. How long had Leigh made her shiver to her very bones wearing these?

Revulsion like he'd never known swept through him as

he gathered up Mathilda's cloak, her boots and her surcoat. Shaking out each item carefully, Robert kept up his hunt. It had to be there somewhere.

Finally, he saw what he'd been searching for. Carefully wiping away the damp with his cloak, Robert placed the treasure into his bag, and quietly returned to Eustace.

~ *Chapter Thirty-three* ~

'I recognise that look on your face.' Sarah gave Mathilda a playful smile, 'You're plotting something.'

Mathilda, who'd been embroidering the corner of a hair net, lifted her eyes to the housekeeper from her place by the fire. 'Whatever makes you think that?'

'For a start, you're sewing in your chamber. Perfectly commonplace for the majority of ladies, but you only sew in here if you have to, or if you're thinking.'

Laying the pastel blue hair cover in her lap, Mathilda couldn't help but laugh. 'Does Adam realise he is falling in love with a soothsayer?'

Sarah was dismissive, but the gleam that had started to glow in her eyes didn't disappear. 'I have come to think he cares for me a little. We're both too old for more than that.'

'Don't be silly. No one is too old to be loved.' Mathilda smoothed the delicate material across her knees. 'Robert and I aren't exactly young to be getting wed.'

'You are still marrying, then?'

'I hope so. I think so.' Mathilda wiped the sleep from her eyes, 'But first there is something we have to do.'

'Catch Leigh.'

'More important than that. I need to find out why.'

'Why he took you?' Sarah selected a medium-sized log

and threw it onto the fire. 'We know that, don't we? He wanted to deprive Robert of you, so he could marry you himself.'

'He didn't know about me until the messenger came here. I was thinking more about why he wanted to target the Folvilles in the first place. This family isn't the only one using felonious behaviour to combat the corruption rife in this country. Nor are the Folvilles the only group who can be, shall we say, overzealous in their actions sometimes.'

'Diplomatically put.' Sarah laughed. 'Mathilda, you were born to be a Folville.'

'You're the second person to tell me that.' Mathilda held her needlework up to the candlelight. 'Do you think this will go with my wedding gown?'

'It's beautiful, and yes, I do.' Sarah was thoughtful. 'What exactly is it you have to find out before you can marry my Lord Robert?'

'The way Leigh spoke about the family; it made it feel as if this wasn't a political message, it wasn't even greed, it went deeper. Like the Folvilles had wronged him personally.'

'That can't be right. None of the brothers had heard of Rowan Leigh before this month; nor had Owen, Allward, Daniel or myself.'

'Not even when Roger Belers was killed by Lady Joan's father with the families help? Leigh was already the carpenter in Lubbesthorpe then, wasn't he?'

Sarah frowned. 'I hadn't considered that. It's unlikely Leigh could have been affected by that though, surely?'

'I don't know, but I mean to find out.'

'How?'

'Edgar, the man that Leigh killed in front of me.'

'One of the men who stole you away from here?'

'Yes. Edgar wasn't like the others. I got the impression he knew that what Leigh was doing was wrong, but he was afraid of not doing what he was told to do, even if it was bad.'

'Was he a simpleton?' Sarah busied herself lighting more candles to give better working light to the room.

'Not simple so much as terrified.' Mathilda picked up her sewing again, 'He talked about evil women and the church.'

'Nuns?'

'I assumed so. He could have been taken in by a nunnery as a child and mistreated.'

'By nuns! Surely not.'

'It happens.'

Looking profoundly uncomfortable at the thought, Sarah asked, 'How does speculating about Edgar's past help us find out what was behind Leigh's targeting of the Folvilles?'

'Something he said before Leigh killed him. I have been over and over everything that was said to me and all the conversations I heard while I was there. The more I consider it, the more I'm sure Edgar was murdered because of something he said, rather than because he was prepared to let me try and escape.'

Sarah was amazed. 'One of your kidnappers was going to help you get away?'

'It was more like he wasn't going to stop me leaving if I had the chance; but that's not what I mean. Leigh saw that Edgar wasn't going to stop me fleeing, but I don't think that was why he killed his man.'

'I don't understand.'

'I'm not sure I do either, but I'm sure it's to do with the church.'

Robert joined Eustace in time to see the local king's serjeant and his men round up the prisoners and escort them from the courtyard.

'Have any of them spoken?'

Eustace shook his head, 'Beyond a boisterous helping of blasphemy and cursing, not a word.

Robert looked at his brother with surprise. 'Not even when you tried to, shall we say, persuade them to tell us where Leigh has gone to ground?'

'Even a knife in the gullet wouldn't prise the words out of them.' Eustace oozed frustration. 'I would dearly love to have cut a throat or two in there. They must be very afraid of Leigh to risk death rather than sharing any information with me.'

'They will have seen Edgar's body. Word will have got around.' Scuffing his heels against the hard earth, Robert added, 'I think we need to talk to the sheriff. It's high time his lordship came around to our family's way of thinking about his place in our society, don't you think?'

'Time to implement some Folvilles Law, brother.' Slapping Robert heartily on the back, Eustace grinned. 'My thoughts precisely. Ingram was always of great assistance to us during his administration, it's time de Cressy was made aware of the benefits his predecessor enjoyed under our care.'

Robert unhooked his horse's reins from the fence. 'There's no time like the present. Leigh could be anywhere, and I want him found and legally disposed of before my marriage.'

Eustace's eyes narrowed. 'And you want his disposal to be out of our hands?'

'I want it done in a manner that casts no shadow of suspicion which could ruin the wedding Leigh had already done his damndest to destroy. Also, I want it to be public knowledge that *no one* crosses the Folvilles.'

'Well said, little brother. Well said indeed.'

Wilkin Sayer was not panicking. He had made a decision not to waste energy doing that; ever. This resolution however was being severely tested.

Of all the people he hoped never to see again, Rowan Leigh topped the list. Going through his daily tasks as steward, Sayer swallowed down the horror he'd felt at the sight of the foundling boy. The bastard child.

It was no good dwelling on the situation. He *had* turned up, and nothing could change that. What mattered now was getting to de Cressy before Leigh did.

But how to make his sudden absence from the Markham house seem normal?

Hunched over his work desk, making sure that the household lists were up to date, Wilkin sighed. How could he ever have hoped to leave his past behind?

Determined that he wouldn't be denied the position he had worked so hard to manoeuvre himself into, Wilkin scraped his chair across the stone floor and went to find John de Markham.

Excusing himself with news of a mythical messenger having arrived and departed with haste, with an urgent missive for the sheriff, Wilkin stood before his master. 'The messenger believed my Lord de Cressy to be here, my Lord. The message is serious indeed.'

Markham frowned. 'And it concerns?'

'The Folville family, my Lord.

'Did you send the messenger towards de Cressy's home?'

Glad that years of lying meant he never showed his deceit on his face, Wilkin replied, 'I did, my Lord, but since his departure I have recalled that my Lord High Sheriff's groom told me they were not going home, but to meet with his predecessor.'

'Ingram?'

'Indeed, my Lord, in Leicester.' Wilkin frowned, 'The messenger led me to believe that this was a matter of extreme gravity. Permission to try and catch the Lord High Sheriff up and pass on the message?'

'You could send Ulric.'

'The boy is already behind with his kitchen tasks, whereas I am up to date with my own, my Lord.'

'Granted.' Markham accepted Wilkin's gracious bow, but called after the fast retreating figure, 'You go no further than Leicester and you are to return by this time tomorrow.'

As he listened to the sound of his new steward's footfall rushing towards the stables, Markham tapped his fingers pensively on the table before him. He couldn't deny that Sayer was good at his job. He was efficient, prompt, good with letters and held the household together well even though he'd only been doing the job for a few weeks. And yet...

'What are you really up to, Wilkin Sayer?'

John opened the box on his desk. It held two of the objects which Adam Calvin had been accused of stealing. Ulric had found them two days ago, hidden in a bundle of blankets at the bottom of a rarely used wooden chest.

Ulric had only been getting blankets out because John's wife had been cold and asked for extra covers for their bed. If she hadn't been in the room at the same time, then John knew he might have thought the boy had planted the objects there himself, to cast suspicion away from Adam. After all, the lad had bravely stated on many occasions he believed the former steward to be innocent. An opinion that Markham was sure had caused him at least one beating from Sayer.

Although Ulric hadn't said anything about it, the bruises on his face hadn't appeared by magic.

Markham got up with a decisive bang of his fist against the desk. He was the king's serjeant, for goodness' sake. Sworn to uphold justice on behalf of the Crown. Ashamed of how long he'd let de Cressy mutely threaten him with the fact he had made one mistake, a mistake that had caused him to tiptoe into the realms of corruption. He knew it was time to act, even if he had to face some unpleasant consequences. After all, Wilkin Sayer had been recommended to him by de Cressy.

Markham called for Ulric.

It was time to put things right.

1326

They've killed a Baron of the Exchequer.

Roger de Belers is dead.

He imagined Richard's gloating face. He would have put money on Richard having been at the killing. He wouldn't have wanted to miss it.

The wait was beginning to make his fingers itch. The time wasn't right yet though. He had to wait for the right moment. And it would come.

It would.

~ *Chapter Thirty-four* ~

Mathilda climbed slowly off her knees. Her prayer to Our Lady had been long, soul searching and full of gratitude for her deliverance from the jaws of disgrace. It had also been a quest for guidance.

As she'd prayed, the words of one of Mathilda's favourite stories had come to mind. She could clearly hear her much-missed mother singing the lines as they'd swept out the pottery or scrubbed the clay stains from her father's cloths.

> *Lythe and Listen, gentlemen,*
> *That be of frebore blood,*
> *I shall you tell of a good yeoman,*
> *His name was Robyn Hode...*

The words gave Mathilda strength. And today she would need that strength.

Allward's body was to be taken to the churchyard to join Owen. They were to be buried side by side. Mathilda, as much as the thought of facing the body of the young man to whom she owed so much filled her with horror, wanted the chance to say goodbye. She also wanted to ask the men who came to collect the body some questions.

As soon as she'd suggested to Sarah that Leigh's actions towards the family may have been in some way tied up with the church, the housekeeper had gone pale. Sitting with a heavy thump, Sarah had whispered a single word so quietly, with such muted despair, that Mathilda had been forced to ask her to repeat it.

When she did hear the word the housekeeper had muttered, many things began to fall into place.

'Richard.'

'But how?' Mathilda sat next to her friend as the spectre of the family's most unpleasant brother hung over them once more.

'I have no idea. But if this is to do with the church, it has to be him. I mean, he is the only member of the family with clerical connections.'

Mathilda frowned. 'He isn't even here. Since he orchestrated the murder of Robert's friend, he's been abroad.'

Sarah's shoulders drooped. Mathilda was sure that memories of Richard de Folville, who blamed her for not loving him like his brothers and claimed that as the reason for his cruelty and cunning, had come to the forefront of her friend's mind.

'It wasn't your fault. You didn't make the decision to send Richard to the abbey to be educated while the others stayed at home.'

'I know. It doesn't stop him blaming me though, does it?'

'Richard is a master at making people feel guilty for the failings that are his alone. It is essential that you remember it is *not* your fault, Sarah. Richard de Folville managed to become the creature he is all on his own. He is the product of his own bitterness.'

Sarah gave Mathilda a weak smile. 'Thank you.' Brushing aside her feelings, she asked, 'Do you think this is Richard's fault, or are we being fanciful because this Edgar character mentioned the church?'

'I don't know. But I mean to find out.'

Robert and Eustace watched the soldiers take the prisoners away.

'Do you think that's all of them?'

Eustace frowned. 'What do you mean?'

'Do you think that's all of the people in the village who were working for Leigh? He can't have become so sure of himself without information coming from beyond here as well, surely.'

Nodding slowly, Eustace agreed. 'You think he had spies elsewhere?'

'Why not? He's modelled himself on us. We have spies everywhere. We call them friends, or informants, but you know as well as I do that they're spies.'

'True.'

'Leigh attacked the Melton and Ashby inns.'

Eustace could see his brother's thought process clearly. 'You know, Robert, I had begun to think you'd lost your edge when you went daft over that girl. I may have been hasty.'

'In truth, Eustace, thanks to Mathilda, my edge has never been sharper. That bastard almost took her from me and I am going to find him. And I'm going to start in Melton Mowbray.'

'Because?'

'Because it has suddenly occurred to me that when I went to the inn after Leigh had turned it over, the mess was very organised. Nothing too valuable had been broken. Elias wasn't making anything like enough fuss.'

'You think he was paid to stage being robbed?' Eustace was already mounting his horse as Robert jumped into his own saddle.

'I don't know yet, but if he wasn't, I still want to know why Leigh targeted Melton Mowbray. Of all the towns that we protect, it is hardly the most convenient for Leigh's men to get to.' Robert cursed into the cold air. 'I've been so blind, brother. I was caught up in the possible disgrace of the family name and then the loss of Mathilda, Owen and Allward. I stopped seeing the obvious. I had forgotten what it means to be a Folville.'

Eustace gave his sibling a grave look, 'I think it's high time we reminded people exactly how our family earned its reputation, don't you?'

The remains of the chicken house lay across the town's main street. Pieces of wood, wattle, straw and clay were strewn across the thoroughfare. It looked as if someone had taken their rage out on the fence with a sword. Eggs had been trampled on, as had the carcasses of the murdered fowl. The few chickens that had survived the onslaught flapped in a confused fashion all over the place.

As the Folville brothers rode into the town, the angry householder whose property had been attacked, while bemoaning the loss of both eggs and meat for the forthcoming weeks and months, frantically tried to corner his frightened livestock. He was throwing the hens into baskets, so he could rebuild the shattered pen.

Exchanging glances, Robert and Eustace said nothing as they passed by. They were both thinking the same thing: Leigh had been this way. And he was angry.

Three youths, despite the cold, were wading in the town's pond. Sleeves rolled up, muscles clenched, their lips blasted ungodly mutterings as they worked to retrieve a market stall which had been toppled into the water. From its chipped and fractured state, it looked like it had also been struck with the edge of a sword.

Other men were righting the stalls that had escaped a ducking but were littering the pathway, as if they were kindling rather than heavy wooden tables.

Sharing another knowing look with Eustace, Robert pointed along the road ahead. 'The chaos is leading us to the inn.'

Eustace pulled his horse to a standstill. Aware of the chances of being overheard by one of the locals and falling back on his usual stance of not trusting anyone, he lowered his gravel voice to a whisper. 'And when we get there, your plan is?'

'To persuade Elias to tell us where Leigh is.'

'And if he doesn't know?'

'Then he'd be well advised to make an educated guess.' Robert stared directly ahead as he spoke. 'Because Mathilda is going to have the peace of mind that Leigh can't ever hurt her again. Whatever it takes.'

Wilkin Sayer had almost given up.

De Cressy and his retinue had already passed the inn where he'd been convinced he'd find them taking refreshment before completing the journey home, as was his lordship's usual practise.

If the sheriff was intent on reaching Nottingham that night, where would he head? The castle, in which he had a suite of rooms, or his more comfortable and less draughty city dwelling?

With his head full of plans and ideas of what to say when he reached his former employer, Sayer realised that in his hurry to find de Cressy, he hadn't thought how he'd explain his arrival. In an inn, or on the road, he could pretend it was a coincidence, but heading to the sheriff's home or the castle was going to be more difficult to talk away.

The tavern no longer had a front door. Even the hinges, now free from their charge, were bent out of place. Whoever had ripped the solid oak from its position as guardian of the inn was either immensely strong or immensely angry, or both.

Eustace sprang from his horse. His sword was already drawn as he strode to the open doorway. 'I can smell ale.'

'That's hardly surprising here.' Robert, dagger to hand, was close at his brother's heels.

The aroma hit them harder only two more steps inside. The reason for the overpowering stench was all too apparent. A barrel has been placed in the middle of the floor and split open. The sickly sweet contents had drained onto the rush-covered floor.

'Elias!' Robert yelled, caring not one jot that the inn was currently closed, despite the open entrance. 'Elias Tavernier!'

As their eyes adjusted to the gloom of the place, usually so well lit with candles and a hearty fire, the brothers could see that this time the chairs had been kicked aside, not toppled with care. The tankards had been swept off the shelves, smashed into pieces and, by the looks of it, ground into dust beneath the weight of a boot.

'That's a new job for Mathilda's father if ever I saw one.' Robert said before he called the innkeeper's name again. Then he spotted something on the floor. It was blood. Not much, but a thin trickle that led from the bar to a door at the back of the room.

Striding to the door, the brothers tensed, each wondering

if they were about to find the body of the innkeeper behind it. Or perhaps Leigh himself.

Slamming the wooden door wide open with a crash, Eustace toppled yet more pots to the ground from the shelf behind it. This space was clearly a storeroom, or it had been. Now there wasn't much to store but broken cups and damaged barrels.

In the middle lay Elias. His face was blackened, his arm at an unnatural angle, but he was alive.

~ *Chapter Thirty-five* ~

Robert shoved the toe of his boot into Elias's gut. 'Talk.'

'He did this my Lord! You said you'd protect us.' Elias's groan was as accusing as it was pained.

'The agreement to protect your town was only extended while it remained loyal. And it only takes one person to destroy that loyalty.'

'One person, my Lord?' Elias lifted a bloodied hand to his face, rubbing an eye that was swelling fast.

'Just one, Elias. Although there may have been more traitors here. If there are, then we'll find out sooner or later. We always find out.'

Elias shifted slowly. He moved with the air of a man who wasn't sure if his ribs were broken or just badly bruised. 'I don't know what you mean.'

Robert gave a dramatic sigh. 'Elias, do I have to unleash Eustace on you? Do you really want another hand adding to the collection of injuries you're wearing so prettily?'

The innkeeper closed his eyes in response, making Eustace snort with false mirth as Robert nodded solemnly. Going back into the inn, Robert picked up two of the undamaged stools and carried them through to the storeroom, slamming them down in front of the prostrate Elias.

Sitting down, Eustace and Robert glared at the tavern

owner. 'I'm going to tell you what I think and then you can tell me if I'm right or not, OK?'

There was a faint wince as Elias hauled himself up to a sitting position. 'My Lord Robert?'

Eustace laid his sword across his lap, 'I'd advise against pretending that you don't know what's going on, Elias, we really aren't that stupid. And my brother here,' Eustace gestured towards Robert, 'is not in the mood for games.'

Saying nothing, Elias rested against a table leg, grunting as he stretched his long legs out in front of him, across the pottery covered floor.

Robert toyed his dagger between his fingers. 'I have many questions, Elias. The first and most important, being where is Rowan Leigh now?'

'I don't know, my Lord.'

Moving with blinding speed, Robert dropped from the stool to the floor. The sound of ceramic fragments cracking under his knees added to the menace of his tone, as he held the dagger under Elias's throat. 'I don't have time for lies!'

'I don't know.' Panic dripped from Elias's lips. 'I swear.'

'Did you know what he had planned for Mathilda?' Robert edged the blade higher up Elias's throat in the manner Leigh had held the knife to Mathilda's throat.

'No, my Lord.'

'And I suppose you swear to that too, don't you?'

'I didn't know. I thought, I just thought...'

'What did you think, Master Tavernier?' Robert relaxed his hand a fraction but didn't move it away. 'Perhaps I should ask my brother to help me persuade you to talk. I believe you have heard what happens to people who don't tell Eustace de Folville what he wants to know.'

'Please, my Lords!'

'Please what? Please hurt you more? It looks to me that

the consequences of working for Rowan Leigh have already been made apparent to you. Do you want to find out how much worse the consequences of letting a Folville down are as well?'

Elias was a picture of misery. 'No, my Lord.'

'I thought not.' Robert lowered his blade, 'In a few days time I am due to marry Mathilda of Twyford. It is my intention to give her the news that Rowan Leigh can't ever hurt her again as a wedding present. And you, Elias, are going to assist me in tracking the felon down so I can achieve this aim.'

The innkeeper's eyes remained on Eustace's sword. The older Folville was stroking the weapon with the sort of care normally reserved for a favoured hound. 'How can I help, my Lord? I truly have no idea where Leigh is now.'

'You can tell us what happened here.' Robert, rocked onto his haunches, but stayed within striking range.

'I heard him before I saw him.' Elias answered slowly, as if trying to arrange the events of the past few hours into some sort of sense. 'He attacked the chicken house at the end of the street.'

'Why?'

'No reason that I know beyond it was in the way of his march to my door.'

'And the market stall thrown in the pond?'

'My stand. It is always the first to be put up and the last to go down on market day, so it's on the edge of the stack.'

'And Leigh knew it was yours how?'

'The tavern crest is on the front. The lads like to have an ale or two while they set up the market.'

'And so obviously they put your stall up first. And I take it Leigh knew all this because he sold his woodwork at the market.'

'Yes, my Lord. He would have known it as my stall even if it hadn't got my mark on it. Leigh has been selling his goods here for years. Sometimes himself, sometimes he sends Gamelyn and Edgar.'

Eustace snorted. 'Well, those two gentlemen will not be bothering you again.'

Elias's bruise-mottled face blanched. 'Dead, my Lords?'

'Leigh doesn't take care of those who follow him. Edgar he murdered in cold blood. Gamelyn was sacrificed so Leigh could escape us when we retrieved Mathilda from him.' Robert's eyes narrowed. 'You knew about Mathilda being free, of course. You were not a bit surprised when I mentioned her earlier. So clearly you knew Leigh's plans had been disturbed.'

Hypnotised by the drawn blade, Elias mumbled, 'I knew, my Lord. Please forgive me. Leigh gave me no choice but to assist him.'

'That bit I can believe.' Robert traced the point of his dagger through the dust and fragments on the floor. 'What did he have over you? What did he threaten you with that was worse than disobeying me?'

'Not him, my Lords. It was Leigh who... He worked with another. They...' The innkeeper faltered. 'They made it clear I was to do what I was asked or I'd lose my business. My livelihood.'

Eustace raised the sword and rested it on a flinching Elias's shoulder. 'Are you going to tell us the easy way or the hard way?'

'If he finds out I told you, if he...'

'And if you don't tell us, then you'll be dead even sooner.'

Elias rubbed his hands over his face. 'Leigh was here not more than thirty minutes ago. He was like a man possessed. I knew he was coming, I'd heard the chaos outside and seen his progress. His face was... it was demonic. Dark with rage. He was deranged. Rambling, my Lords. He made little sense.'

'But he made himself clear to you.' Robert gestured about him. 'The damage speaks for itself. I assume the previous damage you claimed to have been committed here was arranged?'

'Yes, my Lord.'

'And did Leigh arrange it himself, or was this the work of his helper?'

'His men came. Edgar and another. They really did leave the message I gave you, but there was more to it than I said.'

'The additional bit being that you would receive a visit, bringing with it genuine destruction, if you failed to report to Leigh any information you came across about our family?'

'Yes, my Lord. If I didn't, then the consequences would be... well, you can see.'

'Does this damage mean you didn't betray us, or that you did, and it wasn't enough for Leigh to get his way?'

'I told them nothing. In truth, I had nothing to tell.'

Eustace had had enough. He lifted Elias up by the scruff of his neck so that he was standing on shaking legs. 'But you would have, wouldn't you, you snivelling coward, if you'd had something to say!'

'No! No, my Lord. But I made Leigh think I would. How could I not?'

Eustace opened his hand and Elias dropped like a stone to the floor. 'I suppose there is *some* sense in that. Robert, what do you say? It's your woman that's been wronged here.'

'I say,' Robert pushed his face into Elias's, 'that you

should have told us this sooner. However, *if* you give us the name of this benefactor of Leigh's, then you may live to tidy up your inn ready to serve the hard-working people of Melton Mowbray. If you do not... then you won't. Simple choice really.'

Elias swallowed, and he whimpered softly, 'Leigh will kill me.'

'He'd do it faster than I would. It would hurt less. It would also be later, not right now.'

The innkeeper nodded, the movement jarring his bruised head. 'The sheriff, my Lords.'

'De Cressy?' Eustace smiled. 'Well, Elias, you can breathe a little easier, for you have told us nothing we hadn't worked out. You have merely confirmed our hunch. Consequently, you have not betrayed Leigh, have you? Although I doubt he'd believe that...'

Robert stayed where he was, his expression not showing the grim satisfaction of his brother. 'The sheriff himself came and threatened you, did he? I can't see Edmund de Cressy sullying his hands in that way.'

'He sent his man.'

'Leigh?'

'No, my Lord. Another. I don't know his name. He knew yours though, and Leigh's. He knew everything.'

Eustace frowned. 'A spy?'

'I thought so, but I wasn't foolish enough to ask.' As if sensing the immediate danger had passed, Elias volunteered more information. 'He was small, this man. Skinny, and yet there was something about him, something that I knew was dangerous. Like Leigh, but with more intelligence and cunning.'

'Just the sort of man that would be useful to a sheriff.' Robert said as he held out a hand and helped pulled Elias to his feet. 'Especially to a corrupt sheriff.'

Almost forgetting the innkeeper's presence for a moment, the Folville brothers conferred. 'De Cressy could be anywhere. The castle in Nottingham, his manor, or anywhere in the county.'

Robert asked, 'Do you know where de Cressy is?'

'No, my Lord.' Fresh unease crossed Elias's face.

'Are you absolutely sure? Think carefully before you answer.' Robert drew the point of his dagger threw the dust in the floor next to the inn keeper's feet.

'Leigh mumbled something about the sheriff meeting an old friend.'

'Don't try our patience, man.' Eustace spat the words, as if he couldn't believe Elias would be so reckless as to hold out on them now. 'Which old friend?'

'I don't know. I swear I don't.'

Staring at Elias, scrutinizing his face, Robert said, 'He could be with John de Markham. Adam told me they were associates.'

'Adam Calvin?' Elias's ears pricked up.

Robert returned his attention to the limping man. 'You know Adam?'

'No, but he asked me about him. The messenger from de Cressy, I mean. The one who came here first and informed me in no uncertain terms that I had to assist Leigh by pretending the inn had been attacked. There has been a manhunt for this Adam Calvin. Apparently, he'd killed and stolen something. I know not who or what.'

Robert and Eustace looked at each other, both silent for a while, before Robert spoke to Elias. 'I suggest you get those wounds seen to and this place ready for opening. I also suggest you send a messenger of your own to Bertred's pottery in Twyford, placing an order to replace all your tankards.'

'But we have a good potter here, in Melton.'

'And yet, unless you want me to let Eustace practise his sword work on you, you will buy your replacement wares from Bertred of Twyford. Won't you, Elias?'

'Yes, my Lord Folville.'

'And now, if you'll excuse us, we have a sheriff to locate. And you, Elias, will keep your mouth shut, because we are coming back here very soon.'

Eustace leant forward and gently stroked some pottery dust from Elias's head, whispering, 'Very, very soon,' into the terrified man's ear.

1328

At last. He'd found the person he needed. A man with the ability to gift him the power he craved, and the status he deserved.

It wasn't just Richard who was going to suffer, but his whole family. It was his family that had made him what he was. It was their fault.

And soon they would understand what they'd done.

~ *Chapter Thirty-six* ~

'You can't mean to go alone?' Sarah suddenly looked like the annoyed housekeeper she had been when the kidnapped Mathilda had first been thrust upon her. 'Robert will be furious.'

'I'm going to take Daniel with me.'

Sarah shook her head angrily. 'You most certainly are not. If you are hell bent on this foolish errand, then you'll take Adam. At least he'll be able to protect you properly.'

Wrapping her travelling cloak around her shoulders before Sarah could talk her out of it, Mathilda said, 'I know you think I should wait, but I don't think we can. Not if we want to find out what's behind all this.'

'But it isn't your place to go chasing the felons now. You're to be the lady of the manor.'

Mathilda looked at Sarah with disbelief. 'This is the man that killed Owen and Allward. Maybe not with his own hand, but he was behind it without doubt. And he could have killed Adam and then he...'

Mathilda's shudder as she shut her eyes against the memory spoke volumes to the housekeeper.

'But Leigh's still out there. What if he's waiting for you?'

Mathilda lifted her chin. 'If he has any sense, then he'll be as far away from this family as he can get.' Softening her tone, she reassured her friend. 'Don't worry, I am not chasing Leigh. That job I am happy to leave to Robert and his brothers. I want answers. I have to know why. I want the nightmares to stop.'

Sarah smiled weakly, she'd heard Mathilda calling out in her sleep, but not mentioned it in case she didn't remembered the disturbing images that plagued her at night. 'Then please take Adam. I'll feel better knowing he's with you.'

'Alright, Sarah.' Mathilda headed to the chamber door.

The housekeeper felt a heavy wave of helplessness engulf her. 'What am I to do while you're gone?'

'Oh, that's easy!' Mathilda picked up the linen hair cover and gave it to Sarah. 'You can finish this for me. I'm going to need it very soon.'

'Are you certain that's where he'll be?' Robert asked Eustace as they trotted through the outskirts of Melton Mowbray, making a beeline towards the border of Nottinghamshire.

'No. But I am sure that the Lord Markham will have a better idea of where to start hunting than we do.'

Robert, who would normally have protested it was a waste of time riding so far, held his tongue. His promise to Adam, to discover what lay behind his banishment from his home, rose to his mind. He knew that when he'd originally made the promise he'd had little intention of keeping it, but now Adam's heroic actions in saving Mathilda, meant Robert felt he owed him. He was also more than a little curious as to how Adam's eviction from his post was related to what was happening. If the events hadn't been linked before, they certainly appeared to be connected now.

'My Lady, where are we going?'

Clicking his dagger into its sheath, Adam took the provisions Sarah held out to him for them both. The housekeeper didn't have to tell him to take care. He could read the words in every line of his face.

'The church.'

'St Mary's?'

Mathilda nodded, 'I am to be married there in a few days time. It seems logical to visit, does it not?'

'With respect, my Lady, I do not believe that is why we are visiting Ashby Folville's church this morning.'

Mathilda remained grave. 'Your natural suspicion serves you well. Shall we?'

As Daniel helped Mathilda onto her palfrey, she swallowed the wince that raced to her lips. Her sore bones throbbed with the effort of simply mounting her horse. Rather than put her off however, the pain drove her forwards. Leigh was never going to do this to anyone else.

'We should rest the horses.' Eustace reined in by the tavern on the edge of Willoughby on the Wolds.

Robert, whose body was keen to dismount, but whose brain wanted them to keep going, stayed in the saddle. 'There's a long way to go. We should press on before night falls.'

'The horses need a rest and we need a drink. Come on.'

Reluctantly, knowing Eustace was right, Robert dismounted. 'A few minutes only then.'

Calling to the stable lad to feed and water the horses, the brothers went into the inn. 'At least no one will recognise us in here.' Robert muttered. He, unlike Eustace, didn't bask in the fear that greeted the Folville brothers wherever they went.

'Actually, brother that is not entirely the case.' Eustace

gave Robert a meaningful look.

At the bar, Eustace paid the barman for the ale, and then held up an extra penny as if he was admiring how shiny it was. 'I wonder if you happen to know, just in passing of course, whether the Lord Sheriff has been this way recently.'

The man's eyes stayed on the unspoken promise of money for positive information. 'My Lord de Cressy is known to stop here sometimes. He likes his ale, does the Sheriff.'

Robert grinned into his ale. He knew Eustace had informers everywhere. This young man was clearly part of that merry band, happy to earn an extra penny when he could. It was always an education, seeing Eustace persuading someone to tell him things without the threat of violence. It felt wrong somehow.

'And would you recall when he last came and sampled the ale here?' Eustace took a second penny from his money bag and placed it next to the first in the palm of his hand.

'Today, my Lord. No harm is sharing that with you, he did not come in secret.'

'Does that mean he sometimes does come in secret?'

The young man's face flushed and he immediately blustered, 'I just meant I saw no harm in telling you what others could.'

Eustace held up a palm. 'So, he was here today. I don't suppose a keen-eared young lad like you overheard, purely by accident of course, where the sheriff was heading?'

Placing both coins on the bar in front of him, Eustace kept the tip of his finger on the edge of them both.

'He said nothing while here, my Lord, but his men talked of a place south of Leicester. I do not know where.'

Robert pushed away his empty tankard. 'South of Leicester? Eustace, we must go. Now.'

Taking up one of the coins, Eustace toyed with it before

sliding the other to the barman, who picked it up before the Folville could change his mind.

Before he turned to move away, Eustace said, 'Can you earn the other penny?'

'There was another man asking for the sheriff.'

'Today?'

'Not an hour ago. He didn't offer pennies. He offered me the chance to keep breathing.'

Robert and Eustace said at the same time, 'Leigh?'

'Slim, smooth face, unwashed and possibly blood-soiled?' Robert added.

'No, my Lord. This man was stocky, well-fed, and dressed with pride. Conceited and arrogant.'

'He gave no name?'

'No, my Lord, and I had better sense than to ask for it. Oh, and he was Welsh.'

'Welsh?' Eustace threw the second penny in the bar man's direction and ran after Robert.

'You're thinking he's going to Ashby Folville?'

'No, brother. I think they're heading to Lubbesthorpe. I doubt if word of Leigh's failure has reached the Sheriff's sensitive ears yet. I bet he is on his way to check on his investment.'

Eustace swung his long legs over the back of his mount. 'And this second man, this other enquirer after the good Edmund's whereabouts?'

'I'd say he was the same man who initially visited Elias.'

'Possibly.' Eustace looked into the darkening early afternoon sky, 'Daylight is not on our side, brother. We have about another three hours left if we are lucky.'

'Then let us not waste a minute of it.'

The rector of Ashby Folville climbed to his feet as he heard two sets of footsteps entering the vestry. On seeing the unknown lady and her escort he hurried from his position before the altar.

'My Lady, Sir, may I help you?'

'Father Herbert, thank you. I hope so.' Mathilda bowed her head a fraction in recognition of his clerical status. 'My name is Mathilda of Twyford.'

She got no further before a wide smile crossed the cleric's face. 'How wonderful to meet you, my Lady. I'm looking forward to performing your marriage ceremony.'

'Thank you again, Father, but sadly today, I come on a less happy matter. You will have heard of recent events?'

'I have. I was thanking God for your safe deliverance as you arrived.'

'You are most kind, however...' Mathilda paused. She wasn't sure how to continue. She hadn't expected the rector of the Folville's village church to be so pious. Then perhaps, she thought, he needs to be to survive here. 'The matter I am concerned with requires clearing up prior to my marriage to my Lord de Folville. I fear that unless some answers are uncovered, the wedding will be delayed.'

Pulling up a cushioned chair for his guest, Father Herbert gestured for Adam to also be seated as he prepared to answer any questions he could. 'What would you ask me, my child?'

'I am here in confidence to ask what you know, if anything, of the upbringing of Rowan Leigh. He is the man, I'm sure rumour has told you, who attempted what could have been my undoing.'

The rector frowned. 'I have heard the gossip, but his name, until a few days ago, meant nothing to me I'm afraid.'

'So you know nothing of Leigh's childhood?'

'Nothing. You have reason for thinking I might?'

Mathilda sighed. 'It was something one of his followers said. It appeared that Rowan Leigh had experienced ill treatment at the hands of the Church. Forgive me, I don't mean you or here, but if I could find out something - anything - about this man...'

'Then you might be a little closer to discovering why he did what he did.' Father Herbert smoothed his cassock down. 'Leigh worked at Lubbesthorpe as a carpenter I believe.'

'Yes.'

'Then the La Zouche family should know where he is from. They should know if he was blown in here like a leaf, rather than being home-grown.'

'I have spoken to Lady Joan, but all she knows is that Leigh was granted the position of carpenter after serving as apprentice to the previous carpenter some time ago, when her father was in a more favoured position.'

Father Herbert sat up straighter. 'Ah, then perhaps you should try my colleagues at Launde Priory.'

'The priory?'

'Many years ago, the carpenter at Lubbesthorpe took in one of the foundling children from Launde. He may not be the man you're looking for at all, but...'

'But he could be.' Mathilda was already on her feet, 'Thank you, Father. Thank you.'

A silent Adam rose with her as the Father added, 'The Prior is Henry of Braunseton. He is a gruff, elderly man, but his heart is kind. I can't promise he'll be able to help you, but if Leigh was taken in then he'll know if the child was raised there or sent to Leicester Abbey.'

Mathilda turned to Adam, her eyes dulled by concern. 'Sarah might have been right.'

'My Lady?' Adam frowned, 'What is it?'

Rather than answer the question, Mathilda merely thanked the clergyman. 'I hope to see you very soon, Father.'

'God go with you, Mathilda of Twyford.'

~ *Chapter Thirty-seven* ~

'My Lady, are you alright?'

This was the second time Adam had asked the question, but Mathilda wasn't sure how to answer. 'I am uncertain of how to proceed Adam. However, I do know that the information we need lies in wait for us at the Priory of Launde.'

'You know? You're sure?'

'I pray I am wrong, but every instinct in my body argues against that fact.'

Adam, whose eyes scoured the countryside around them as they travelled onwards, said, 'Then perhaps we should turn around? It is almost nine miles' ride to the Priory, and the night closes in early. It isn't safe.'

'It isn't, but now we are so close. I have to know. I have to know if Sarah was right.'

'What has Sarah to do with this?'

Mathilda slowed her mount so that she was level with Adam, 'He blamed her, you see. He always blamed her.'

'Who did?'

The hooves of their horses thundered across the frost-hardened ground. The cold air stung their faces, but there was no time to complain, and in truth, neither man had the energy left with which to grumble. They'd lost precious time going north when they should have travelled south.

Thankful that Eustace had made them rest the horses at the inn, Robert wiped his face with the sleeve of his cloak. They would get to Lubbesthorpe before de Cressy was warned of Leigh's failure. They would...

Wilkin Sayer almost turned west. It would have been easy to redirect his horse towards the border with Wales. It wasn't so very far away. A few days' ride and he'd be home. But he couldn't go back. He'd burnt his boats in Wales many years ago. Anyway, he'd worked too hard to get the stewardship. It was his. He'd earned it.

This, Sayer vowed to himself as he slowed his weary horse to a trot, was the last time he'd have to clear up after himself. He began persuading himself he was acting for the greater good; he was simply protecting the interests of his new master. After all, he was sure John de Markham didn't want it widely known that he'd once helped de Cressy pack and bribe a jury, something that he was prepared to let slip if he was ever threatened with dismissal.

Looking about him as he rode, Sayer felt the reassuring weight of the knife in his inside pocket as he travelled. It wasn't his knife. It had once belonged to Adam Calvin. Wilkin remembered how he'd had to restrain a chuckle as he'd taken it from the sleeping steward's belongings the night of his exodus; but that was then. And anyway, Adam Calvin was long gone.

'You must stay the night, my Lady. You cannot possibly travel abroad now, not with this felon still about, not to mention the other desperate men who live in our forests.'

Prior Henry was most insistent and although she knew Sarah would worry if they didn't return home that evening,

Mathilda accepted that the churchman was right.

'Thank you, Prior. We would be grateful to take up your offer. I only hesitated as we are expected to return home and I don't want my housekeeper to worry. She has been through enough lately.'

'I understand, my child.' The prior, as they'd been warned, was indeed a big gruff man with few of the airs and graces that were usually associated with clerics of such status. 'I can send a messenger if you would be easier in your mind.'

'You are most kind. But what would keep the messenger safe?' Mathilda smiled, 'If I can't travel because of the horrors of the night, I'll not send another in my wake.'

Temporarily taken aback, the prior the allowed himself a brief chuckle. 'You, my Lady, if you'll forgive the impertinence, are a most unusual young woman.'

'I will indeed forgive you, but there will be a price for that forgiveness.' Mathilda smiled, finding she rather liked the man's unfussy honesty.

'Isn't there always. So, what is the price?'

'Information.'

'Ah, well that is a price I will pay if I can.' The prior stood up from his throne-like chair and bid Mathilda and Adam to follow. 'If you can cope with the simple surroundings of our warming house, I will have Brother Dominic bring us food and drink while I hear what questions require answers.'

The crossroads lay before Wilkin Sayer. Did he turn towards Ashby Folville or Lubbesthorpe? Did de Cressy expect Leigh to meet him on home turf, or had the carpenter been arrogant enough to suggest they convene in the home of the family he'd intended to overthrow?

Luxuriating in the thought of having a hold over the sheriff for the rest of his life, Wilkin turned towards Lubbesthorpe.

Then a shadow crossed the former approver's face. Leigh had been looking for the sheriff as well. If he'd already found him, then any information he held on the man would be pointless. Because, without doubt, the man would be dead.

Robert's belly growled so loudly he was surprised it didn't spook his horse.

He'd gone over and over in his mind what he was going to do once he found Leigh. Now the very man he'd planned to hand Leigh over to sounded as though he might be the person harbouring him, Robert had to rethink the situation.

The image of Mathilda, small and pale, but with an iron-clad determination which would make a lesser mortal cower, kept him going. Slowly, as the prospect of his future bride's reward for him once Rowan Leigh was gone, filled him with a heat that had nothing to do with his winter cloak, Robert began to see a new way of making both Leigh and de Cressy pay.

Eustace, his horse a few paces ahead, as the crossroads came into view, began to slow down. 'You are sure it's Lubbesthorpe we should head to?'

'As I can be.'

'And if de Cressy isn't there?'

'Then we ride home, very, very fast.'

Edmund de Cressy stood in Rowan Leigh's courtyard and waited, his foot tapping impatiently on the stony ground. His groom had failed to find anyone to take their horses and the four men at arms who had travelled with him had reported the place was deserted.

Not wishing to bring attention to the fact that he was looking for Leigh by asking in the village, Edmund nodded to himself. If he wasn't here, then it must mean that he'd already been successful. 'Leigh will have gone on to the manor at Ashby Folville. This calls for a celebration. We must set out at once.'

The men at arms shifted their feet for a moment, before one was brave enough to speak. 'Forgive me, my Lord, but the horses are exhausted and the night closes fast. We would surely, if I may be so bold as to suggest it, be better off here overnight. A triumphant march on the manor in daylight would have more impact.'

Edmund had been ready to pounce on the man at arms, to label him a coward. Yet the second half of his statement made perfect sense. The idea of the spectacle of victory; of being seen to be the man who'd captured the Folvilles; to be the one to end their reign of terror... that was too strong an image to deny. It was what he'd wanted for so long.

'You speak sense. See to it that a chamber is made up for me and attend to the horses. I shall wait in the hall.' Edmund pointed to one of his other guards. 'You, go and light the fires.'

Wilkin Sayer watched and listened. He was an expert at listening and now he did so with ease as Edmund de Cressy's curt voice echoed across the evening, carrying far in the static air. Thankful that, despite temptation, he hadn't used his prime card against the sheriff before, Sayer allowed himself a stiff smile. The knowledge he held over de Cressy could be the only thing that kept the head on his shoulders.

He had been about to rush in, to tell the sheriff that Leigh had failed. To relish telling Edmund that Leigh was a broken man and that the Folvilles remained in charge - but Sayer's progress was halted.

A large palm wrapped itself around his mouth from behind, as a second man appeared before him. A man wearing a dark grey travelling cloak, who had the look of someone who'd fully embraced that his eventual place would be hell. The man's eyes alone informed Wilkin Sayer that if he didn't do what he was told, he'd get to visit its fires first.

Mathilda rested her head against the soft pillow and closed her eyes. She knew that although Sarah would be worried, what she had learnt over broth and bread with Prior Henry had been worth the temporary distress.

She just wished that it wasn't true.

There was no doubt in Mathilda's mind that it was. And although what she had learnt explained very little in itself, she was certain now of what had caused the underlying bubble of resentment which had burst into such a campaign of hate.

Sarah's eyes ached. She had finished embroidering the hair net for Mathilda some time ago and now she stood back to admire the last portion of stitching she'd applied to the wedding dress.

It was late. Very late. Telling herself repeatedly that Adam and Mathilda had not returned because they'd seen sense and stayed overnight with Father Herbert, the fact they'd been so long suggested Mathilda had discovered something about Leigh.

Or it could be that something has happened to them.

Sarah hung the dress against the doorframe. The golden thread she'd used to decorate the bodice panels shone in the firelight.

Tears pricked at the housekeeper's eyes as she sent up a silent prayer that the gown would be worn in two days' time as planned.

~ *Chapter Thirty-eight* ~

Sarah's body stiffened, unsure if she should be glad or afraid to hear hooves entering the courtyard.

Pulling herself together with a brisk, 'Don't be foolish, woman, Eustace's men are on guard outside,' Sarah made sure the stew in the cauldron over the fire was bubbling gently, and that the sweet pastries she'd begun to prepare, in the hope that they'd been needed for the wedding feast the following day, were cooking evenly, then headed into the early morning light of the yard.

Swinging down from his horse, Robert passed the reins to a waiting Daniel. 'Sarah, we have a guest.'

Eustace was still sat upon his horse. There was a smaller, stocky man thrown across his saddle's pommel. The man had his hands tied with rope. His eyes were closed, probably against the view of the land dashing by beneath him as the horse galloped.

The older Folville pulled up his prisoner's head while he awaited Robert's help to assist him in getting their guest down.

'Is that Leigh, my Lord?' Sarah's words came out as a whisper as a rush of cold tripped through her. She stared at the toad-like man's squashed countenance.

'No, Sarah. This is just a man with a lot of questions to

answer. Answers which we suspect are going to throw light on more than one issue.'

Knowing better than to ask any more questions yet, Sarah returned to her kitchen and prepared two tankards of ale and some food for the brothers. She could hear Eustace calling for Adam, but on getting no response, he issued orders to Daniel to open the cell for their visitor.

A short time later, Robert and Eustace sat side by side before the kitchen fire. Sarah tensed herself as she waited for the inevitable enquiry.

'Is Mathilda asleep?' Robert spoke through a big spoonful of broth.

'I-I don't know, my Lord. I'm afraid she isn't here.'

Robert was on his feet in seconds. 'Not here! What do you mean?'

'I did try to stop her, but my Lady Mathilda had an idea about Leigh's motivation and she wouldn't be diverted.'

Robert crashed into his wooden seat. 'Is that why there is no sign of Adam? You sent him with her?'

'I did, my Lord. If she was to go, I wanted her to be looked after.'

Eustace rolled his eyes. 'That woman of yours is too headstrong.'

Robert didn't bother arguing. 'Where did she go?'

'To speak to Father Herbert at St Mary's. I don't know what about, but Mathilda was determined to find out why Leigh had targeted your family. She remembered something that Edgar had told her about the effect the church had had on both his and Leigh's lives.'

'And she thought Father Herbert might have answers?'

'More that he might know where answers may be found.' Sarah felt uneasy, not sure if she should voice her fears about how long Mathilda and Adam had been gone.

Eustace grunted into his broth. 'At least Herbert will look after them. He's a good sort, as clerics go.'

Robert was far from happy. 'If Mathilda isn't home by noon I'm going to fetch her. I need to check the church is ready for tomorrow anyway.'

Sarah's eyes narrowed. This wasn't the reaction she'd expected from her master. She'd imagined he'd be furious that Mathilda had wandered off of her own accord. Sarah felt compelled to press the point. 'My Lady Mathilda said she wanted to discover why all this had happened before the wedding. She was also excited about meeting the rector who is to perform the ceremony.'

For the first time since Leigh had entered their lives, Robert looked happy at the mention of his forthcoming nuptials. 'Mathilda is keen to go ahead, then, despite my unworthy doubts?'

'Of course, my Lord. She bid me finish the gown last night. Mathilda will be the most beautiful bride there has ever been.'

'Mathilda would be the most beautiful bride if she wore her working clothes.' Robert laid his hand over the saddle-bag he'd brought in with him and tapped it lightly.

Sarah beamed. 'Yes, my Lord. She would.'

Busying herself contentedly for a minute while the brothers ate in thoughtful silence, the housekeeper enquired, 'Would you like the hall arranged for the questioning of our guest, or will you talk to him elsewhere? I only ask, my Lord, because I have been getting the manor ready for the wedding and solstice celebrations.'

Adam rode closer to Mathilda than his horse was really comfortable with, but if he lost her now, with only a mile left to ride home, he'd never forgive himself.

They'd left the priory the moment the dawn mist had lifted enough for them to be able to see the road ahead. Neither of them spoke. Adam knew his companion was lost in thought after what she'd learned from Prior Henry. If what he knew of Mathilda himself and what Sarah had told him, was to be believed, he was sure the future Lady de Folville was plotting something. The men of the household, Sarah had told him, were far from stupid, but Mathilda had the sharp intelligence to solve puzzles that the men would usually just punch their way out of.

While Mathilda thought about Robert, Leigh and the family, Adam thought of Sarah.

Despite everything that had happened over the past few weeks, the housekeeper had occupied far more space in his mind than he'd allowed himself to admit to until now. He'd long ago made peace with the fact he'd have no family of his own. With the country in such a mess, Adam had decided it was right not to add to its numbers. And yet, he'd be a liar to claim he'd never considered how nice it would be to have someone of his own to confide in. Someone to trust totally, someone to hold on cold winter nights. No one, unless you counted a petite French lass with whom he'd developed a short understanding over a decade ago, had tempted him to consider a lifetime's commitment. Until now.

Sarah was so set in her ways. She'd indirectly been a mother to seven boys and their housekeeper for most of her life. Would she really want someone coming along to disrupt her routine?

Chances were Sarah was just enjoying having someone of her own age to talk to and saw nothing beyond that. The looks Adam thought he'd seen pass between them were probably imagined.

He sighed. It was best to forget all romantic notions. Anyway, once this was over, the Folvilles would be asking him to move on. He was, after all, just a man on the run who'd robbed their food store.

'Don't get angry!' Mathilda put her hand up to stop the flow of recriminations that Robert was about to throw at her the minute she and Adam clattered into the courtyard. 'My reasons for leaving were sound and have paid off. Are the brothers all here yet?'

'Eustace is in the hall. My other brothers will be here this evening ready for the ceremony tomorrow.' Robert held out his hand to help Mathilda dismount. 'I take it you stayed over with Father Herbert, and you have news.'

'I have much news, but we stayed with the prior at Launde.'

A cloud passed over Robert's face. 'Launde, but that's where... Oh, no.'

Seeing Robert had made the same mental leap as she had, Mathilda nodded. 'I can't prove anything, but things are slowly fitting into place.' Gratefully passing her palfrey's reins to Adam, Mathilda asked, 'and you and Eustace, what news? Have you Leigh in your grasp?'

Hating to disappoint her, but having to anyway, Robert took Mathilda's arm, 'Not yet. We know that he is being supported by de Cressy, though.'

'The sheriff!'

'These are treacherous times, Mathilda.'

'And each day they grow more so.' Mathilda sighed as she recalled a few lines from a verse from her childhood. *'Who can truly tell, how cruel sheriffs are...'*

'I don't know that one. A song your mother sang?'

'Yes.' Mathilda gave Robert a bleak look, 'Any other news?'

'We have encountered someone who has information. He is currently awaiting our pleasure in the cell. Eustace and I were about to question him. Would you like to accompany us?'

'I think that would be a very good idea.' Mathilda tilted her chin in a familiar gesture of defiance.

As Robert regarded her, he could see that the worst of the bruises were at last fading and although they wouldn't be completely gone by tomorrow, they would no longer distract the eyes from her gown. With a stirring of pride, Robert escorted Mathilda into the warmth of the hall.

Eustace wasn't there, but the presence of three cups and a jug showed that Sarah had already predicted Mathilda would be attending the interview.

'My brother must have already gone to fetch our visitor.' Robert looked around the hall. 'Sarah has worked hard here.'

The tapestries had all been beaten and winter garlands of holly and ivy hung in bunches from each one. The aroma of delicious culinary temptations filled the air.

'She is determined that our wedding feast will not be forgotten.'

'And nor will it.' Robert smiled, 'I don't think I said how sorry I am that I doubted you. Leigh would never be a match for you.'

Matilda flushed with happiness. 'Thank you, my Lord.'

'And as a token, to prove I mean it, I have something for you.'

As Robert opened the scrip that hung at his waist Mathilda's mouth dropped open before it widened into a huge grin. 'I never thought I'd see it again!'

The belt Robert ran between his fingers was leather and patterned with a lattice of butterflies.

'Where did you find it?' Mathilda stroked it affectionately as her future husband ran it around her slender waist.

'In Leigh's chamber. That's where I raced off to.' Robert looked sheepish. 'He was sleeping on it, and your damp clothes.'

'Perhaps he did have a... genuine desire for me?'

'It is looking very much like it. I thought he was just greedy, or power mad, but now... his motives elude me.'

'But not me my Lord. I have much to tell.'

Robert was solemn for a moment; the sound of Eustace dragging their prisoner into the hall was growing louder. 'As soon as this interview is over, we will listen to your news.'

~ *Chapter Thirty-nine* ~

'That is what the messenger from Elias said? You are sure?'

Edmund de Cressy looked at the carefully blank expression on his man at arms' face. The sheriff could imagine how reluctant he'd been to deliver the message.

'Yes, my Lord. The man reports that during the night malefactors have been roaming the forest, including Robert de Folville and Simon de Folville. It is assumed they were in search of victims to beat, wound and hold to ransom.'

The sheriff slid his sword into its scabbard and began to attach it to his belt. 'There is no Simon de Folville, not that I've ever come across. The Folville brothers number seven, but there is no Simon amongst them.'

'A cousin perhaps?'

'Perhaps.' A black mood descended on Edmund. His night had been full of dreams of striding into the Ashby Folville manor to find Leigh in possession, the usual residents under lock and key and the associated land ready to be acquired. Now, if this report was to be believed, either Leigh had taken the manor while its lord was not at home, or he had failed to obtain his goal.

The man at arms coughed. 'My Lord Sheriff, do we make ready to leave?'

Coming to decision, the sheriff said, 'Make ready to ride

for Ashby Folville. Make sure it is known amongst the men that no mention of Rowan Leigh is to be made unless I say otherwise. As far as any of you are concerned Leigh is a man of whom you have never heard.'

'Yes, my Lord.'

The soldier turned to go when the sheriff asked, 'Any word from the villagers this morning concerning their carpenter?'

'No, my Lord. One minute he was here, the next he was gone.'

'And if anyone does know anything, they aren't saying.'

'Yes, my Lord. I thought it best not to draw further attention to ourselves by forcing the issue.'

Edmund dismissed his companion. Reminding himself there was no reason why the sheriff shouldn't visit one of the manor houses within his legal jurisdiction, especially one that had such an unruly reputation he made ready to leave the carpenter's house, muttering, 'Where are you, Rowan?'

'This gentleman was located listening at the window of the house of one Rowan Leigh, carpenter of Lubbesthorpe.'

Mathilda regarded the man as Eustace explained how he and Robert had come across him creeping around outside the carpenter's workshop. He was unwilling to tell them why he'd been there, so they'd decided to bring him here for additional questioning.

Just looking at him gave Mathilda the sensation that she needed a wash. There was something distinctly slimy about him. 'A spy?'

'We believe so. He claims otherwise.'

The man hadn't spoken. His tiny black eyes stayed firmly on Mathilda though. She could feel him appraising her;

weighing her up as if she was a piece of livestock for sale.

'And his name is?'

Robert took a slow drink of ale. 'Apparently he doesn't have one.'

'That must be very inconvenient.'

'Quite.' Robert agreed with Mathilda as she refilled his beaker. Making a play of how refreshing his drink was, when their prisoner had nothing, Robert added. 'He has been of some use to us however.'

'Really?'

'A message was requiring deliverance. He obliged.'

Eustace snorted from the other end of the table, 'Only with the threat of an arrow in his back if he didn't.'

Mathilda played along, 'Some people are so hard to persuade into helping. And did this message get delivered?'

'It did. And it should have been enough to make sure that our Lord High Sheriff of Nottinghamshire and Leicestershire pays us a visit today.'

'May I enquire as to the message?'

'That Robert, with a certain Simon de Folville, was busy causing havoc in the forest last night.'

'Simon?'

'Yes.'

Robert and Eustace's expressions remained blank, so Mathilda didn't enquire into their sudden decision to use the name of the fictitious brother she'd suggested to Robert when Adam had first entered their lives. 'That message should certainly oblige the sheriff to come here today in his official capacity, to make sure you are all behaving yourselves.'

Eustace nodded gravely. 'Indeed, it should.'

Mathilda pulled her shawl tighter around her shoulders, addressing the prisoner in her haughtiest tone. 'Your name, please?'

The man's black eyes blazed but said nothing.

'It is curious that you don't even proclaim your innocence, or that you have been wronged by your imprisonment here. I don't believe any particular grievance has been laid against you, beyond that, maybe, you know more than it is safe to know. You suffer from a guilty conscience perhaps?'

Eustace snorted again. 'More like no conscience at all. I think we should forget about him. We have better things to do.'

'Leave him in the cell until after the wedding, you mean?' Mathilda turned her back on the prisoner, looking at Robert as she spoke. 'It would be like an ice box in there now, though. No one could survive long without food and bedding in its damp confines.'

'A spy deserves no better.' Eustace grunted.

Robert agreed. 'We could leave him in there. Once our brothers arrive we'll have plenty to do to get ready for the ceremony in the morning. Do you think he'd survive a week in there while we make merry up here?'

The prisoner shifted a fraction, his short frame hunching further as he listened. He was clearly considering whether they were bluffing or not. Mathilda could almost see him thinking, *these are Folvilles. Do I really want to take that chance?*

The sound of hustle and bustle from along the corridor that linked the hall to the kitchen indicated that Sarah was busy cooking. The accompanying clatter of pottery cooking pots landing on wood told Mathilda that Adam was helping the housekeeper get the trays of sweetbreads out of the raging furnace of an oven.

In the hall, no one spoke. Eustace was carving another

line into the oak table with his dagger. Mathilda watched the reflection of the fire in the toad-like man's eyes. Robert leant back in his chair, his arms folded, the image of a man capable of waiting a lifetime to find out what he expects to discover. It was merely a question of how long their guest was willing to stand mute before he gave up his name.

Footsteps from behind the table heralded the approach of Adam, who Mathilda assumed would be coming to replace the ale jug.

The temporary steward was almost at Robert's side before he glanced at the face of the prisoner.

The jug fell from Adam's grip. Pottery splintered across the stone floor as the liquid sloshed everywhere, splashing everyone around the table.

Eustace exploded into anger at such clumsiness, but Robert and Mathilda had seen the look on Adam's face.

Not caring about the ale that had spattered her, Mathilda reached out a hand and grabbed Adam's arm, 'You know him?'

'Sayer. Wilkin Sayer.'

The prisoner said nothing but licked his lips nervously, as he wiped a stray black hair from his forehead. The first sign of an emotion other than contempt showed on his face.

Eustace's ire cooled as fast as it had boiled over when he saw how much discomfort Adam's presence had on their guest. 'What can you tell us, Master Calvin?'

Adam's hand was on the handle of his knife, but his eyes were on the empty scabbard that hung at Sayer's waist. 'He is, or was, approver to Sheriff Edmund de Cressy. An arrangement that preceded de Cressy's elevation to sheriff and I suspect, helped him obtain that position in the first place.'

Robert put out an arm to stop Eustace diving forward to finish the prisoner off there and then, saying. 'You may notice, Sayer, that my brother Eustace is not keen on people who make a living out of sending others to the noose, often when they are innocent of everything except being a convenient figure to accuse. I advise you to answer everything asked of you - and to do so truthfully.'

Wilkin remained silent, but Adam spoke with slow deliberation. 'My Lord Robert, did this *person* have a dagger with him when he arrived?'

'He did.'

'May I see it?'

Mathilda rose to her feet on a signal from Robert and went to find Daniel, to get him to fetch the dagger which had been stored safely.

Moments later she returned, not only with the dagger, but in the company of a young boy.

'Ulric!' Adam rubbed his eyes to make sure he wasn't seeing things. 'Why are you here?'

The boy grinned widely as he saw Adam, but when his eyes fell on the figure of Wilkin Sayer he stopped in his tracks. Ulric's smile dissolved and his shoulders stiffened.

'It's alright, Ulric.' Adam clasped the boy to his side, 'Sayer is a prisoner here.'

The boy's voice was a whisper of wonder. 'His deeds have finally caught him up?'

'They are close to doing so. Now you are here with your own story to tell, I am sure Sayer will be further speared by his own evil.'

Mathilda saw Wilkin look to either side less covertly than she suspected he thought he was. 'You can search for a way out if you like, but I assure you, there isn't one.'

Eustace was getting restless. 'Boy, who are you and why are you here?'

Ulric, with Adam's reassuring palm on his shoulder and

a drink from Mathilda in his hands, began his tale. 'My Lords, my Lady, I am come from West Markham in Nottinghamshire, sent by my master, John de Markham, King's Serjeant, with urgent news concerning the sheriff. I hadn't expected to find Adam here. Nor him.'

The boy averted his eyes from Wilkin's glare and noticed the weapon in Mathilda's hand for the first time. 'How did Adam's dagger get here?' Ulric looked up at his friend, 'It was missing? Did you find it before you fled after all, Adam?'

Tilting his head towards Sayer, Adam said, 'He had it.'

'I knew it!' Ulric looked grim. 'Forgive me, my Lords; it seems in coming with a message for you, I will be delivering an equally important one back to my Lord. He never believed Adam guilty of the crimes laid at his door. Now I can present him with proof that his suspicions were correct. You'll be able to come home, Adam and he,' Ulric pointed accusingly at Wilkin Sayer, 'can stop bullying the household into obeying him.'

'He is steward now?' Adam's brow creased as he abruptly turned to Robert. 'I have to thank you, my Lord. You promised you'd get to the bottom of finding who blackened my name and you have done just that.'

Robert regarded the man before them again. 'Thank you, Adam, but we can't take credit for this. Another reason brings this felon to our house. Perhaps we should deposit Sayer back in the cell now. Suddenly we have more to consider than we realised and I'd rather he was not in a position to possibly profit from what he learns at a later date.'

'No.'

The word was spoken without volume, but with a finality that made everyone in the hall turn towards the speaker.

'No?' Robert took a step towards Wilkin. 'And why

should we not place you in our gaol and forget about you? You framed Adam, so you could take his position. Or do you deny that?'

'I meant, no, because I can be of use to you.'

Adam bristled, pointing a finger firmly in Wilkin's direction. 'If I may be so bold, my Lords, this man is not to be trusted.'

'I believe you, Adam.' Robert held his ground before the approver. 'Make haste to prove your point, Sayer. Tell us how you can be of use. I suggest what you say has a great deal to do with why we found you skulking outside of the workshop and home of Rowan Leigh.'

'It has everything to do with Rowan Leigh and Edmund de Cressy and their shared obsession.'

Mathilda, who was growing impatient to share her own findings with Robert, marched up to Sayer. 'And their shared obsession is?'

'The Folvilles. Or should I say; the destruction of the Folvilles.'

~ *Chapter Forty* ~

'Do we believe him?' Mathilda asked the group in general.

Adam was the first to answer. 'I would normally assume Sayer is lying, but what he said makes sense in relation to my Lord Markham and de Cressy.'

'You think that Markham was afraid of being blackmailed by the sheriff?'

'Yes. Unlike Sayer, I do not make it my business to listen at keyholes, but I knew that my old master did not like the sheriff. He put up with his acquaintance because he had no choice. I believe Lord Markham was once put in a position he couldn't get out of, a position where the sheriff had tricked him into corruption by packing a jury and de Cressy has never let him forget it.'

Eustace slammed a hand onto the table, making everyone jump. 'That's history! We need to think about the here and now.'

The elder brother swung round to face his future sister-in-law. 'Does what Sayer said about Leigh make sense to you? You spent more time with the felon than anyone and you remain oddly quiet for a woman with so many opinions.'

When Wilkin had been speaking, Robert had slipped his hand into Mathilda's. She'd been grateful for its comfort and supporting presence. With every word it had become clearer that her instincts about what had triggered Leigh's campaign had been correct and that her trip to see Prior Henry had been more than justified.

'Mathilda?'

'Sorry, my Lord Eustace.' She sat upright as she considered where to begin. 'I don't know why de Cressy has a dislike for this family. The motive behind Leigh's hatred is on the other hand is sadly very simple. It is built on a childhood suffering, a festering resentment which was seeded within this very family.'

'Here?'

'Richard.'

Eustace's complexion darkened as Robert shouted, 'By Our Lady! The man is abroad, avoiding a noose around his neck. What has our unholy reverend brother done this time?'

Mathilda sighed. 'This is an old, old crime, my Lords. A childhood crime he probably has no memory of inflicting. I'm sure it would have been nothing but sport to Richard.

'Prior Henry was able to tell be that even within the confines of Leicester Abbey, Richard was a bully. His primary target had been a foundling child, one the monks named Rowan Leigh because he was found in a field beneath a rowan tree.'

Robert spoke gently as he tightened his grasp on Mathilda's palm. She had gone cold at the mention of the clerical Folville brother. 'Why should Richard's bullying produce this reaction so long after the event?'

'According to Prior Henry, the monks at the abbey didn't notice the damage until it was done. Leigh returned to the abbey some years after he'd left, full of bile for what the monks had forced him to put up with. That was when it was reported in the almonry records. With hindsight, it was clear, but it took until the crime was over to see the cost of the felony.

'Richard was clever. He never let any blame fall on him for the cruelties he inflicted on the other boys, never got caught in an act of unkindness and never had any cause to be admonished by the monks. Instead he made sure that punishment for every wrong he did fell on another, and his favourite target was Rowan Leigh.

'Leigh grew up thinking that the only way to be successful was to be part of a powerful household and that goodness was something that made you weak. Richard turned a small shy boy into a monster with a grudge that grew with every word of this family's success, despite its involvement in murder, ransoms and other crimes.'

'But those deeds were always, are always, for the greater good,' Robert growled.

'It rarely looks like that to the outside world, Robert, and it wouldn't matter to Leigh if it did. His wounds go too deep. Look at his actions. He gathered others about him, he makes them call him "my Lord"; he copies your acts, although on his own terms. And all of it is designed to damage this family. The family of the man who ruined his life and who constantly rubbed his nose in the fact that he was unwanted and unloved.'

'And the monks realised their blindness to this matter?' Robert laid his palm over Mathilda's, on his knee.

'When Leigh secured the carpentry shop. Only when he was settled in his own house did Leigh let poor Brother Mark, who'd done so much to care for him as a babe, know in the harshest terms what Richard had put him through.'

Eustace ran a hand through his hair. 'This is all very interesting, but it does not tell us where Leigh is, nor how we will act when Edmund arrives.'

'Do you think de Cressy knows where Leigh is?'

'No, or he'd have gone to him yesterday.'

Mathilda took a steadying breath. 'I suggest we invite Edmund de Cressy to stay for the wedding.'

'What!' Robert was stunned.

'Think about it. Leigh has overplayed his hand. According to Sayer, Leigh went all the way to West Markham looking for de Cressy. To get rid of him, Sayer told Leigh that the sheriff was in Leicestershire. It is only a matter of time before Leigh tracks him down and what is more natural than a sheriff being present at a nobleman's wedding.'

Robert's eyes narrowed. 'But we haven't invited him.'

'Leigh doesn't know that. The man is paranoid. He thinks he's failed because someone betrayed him. He has killed Edgar, Gamelyn is dead; his remaining men have been imprisoned. There's only de Cressy left. If we could get Leigh to believe... if someone could get him to believe that this had been the sheriff's plan all along, that de Cressy had intended to set Leigh up and then pretend there was no connection between them, can you imagine how Leigh would react to that? And can you imagine the prestige de Cressy would have heaped upon him if he apprehended a man such as Leigh?'

There was a hush around the table as the men considered what Mathilda had said.

It was Adam who, coughing politely, broke the silence. 'This does sound like something the Lord Sheriff would do. His loyalty to the Crown has been questioned in the past. A plan like this, to be seen to catch the man who was a threat to us - even though he'd set up the treachery himself - would elevate him in the eyes of the throne without question.'

Robert nodded. 'You don't know this to be true though, Mathilda. It is a guess at what may be?'

Mathilda raised her hand from his leg and pressed her palms against the table, pushing herself to her feet. 'It is a fiction of my own making, although it could be true. My point is that we should make Leigh believe it to be true.'

'How? We don't even know where he is?'

'As I said, I think he's looking for the sheriff. He'll be heading here.'

There was no time for Mathilda to expand on her thoughts however, for the sound of horses thundering into the courtyard rose the brothers to their feet.

Edmund de Cressy had arrived.

Bundling Ulric into Adam's care, and getting both of them out of sight, Mathilda issued a plea to Robert and Eustace. 'Please, my Lords; act as though we are simply getting ready for the Winter Solstice and our wedding. There is no prisoner here. There has been no trouble here. All is normal.'

'But why?' Eustace's brow furrowed, he'd clearly been looking forward to venting his anger on the sheriff.

'Because with any luck, if I'm right, Leigh *will* turn up, and de Cressy's expression on seeing him will be enough to condemn both of them.'

'My Lord Sheriff, what a delightful surprise.' Robert bowed low as Edmund dismounted from his horse. 'I'm heartened that the invitation found you. You are the first wedding guest to arrive, although I'm sure my brothers will soon be behind you.'

If Edmund de Cressy was unsettled by the fact he was about to be surrounded by the entire Folville clan, then he managed to hide it well. 'Robert, my congratulations. I fear however that I may not be able to stay for the ceremony. Duty calls me here. I'm sorry to report that I've had word that you and a certain Simon de Folville have been out roaming the forests looking for victims to hold to ransom.'

Robert laughed and clapped a friendly hand on the Sheriff's shoulder. 'I think you need a draught of Sarah's most excellent mulled ale. I fear someone has been leading you astray.'

'The source was a respected one.' Edmund followed Robert into the manor, 'And you have to admit, it wouldn't be the first time.'

'It would be the first time for me, in the company of a person who does not exist and on the eve of my wedding. What do you suppose I was doing out there in the forest, my Lord, herding wedding guests? Hunting enough money to buy a gift for Mathilda, perhaps?'

'I would advise you not to mock your sheriff, Robert.'

'Forgive me, my Lord. I'm curious that is all. Who is it that has played you for a fool?'

Edmund bristled. 'I am no fool, Folville.'

'You are not. But nonetheless you have been fooled. I have been in no forest these past few nights, and I have neither brother, uncle, cousin, nor father called Simon.'

Sarah came into the hall and with a curtsey, brought forth the promised ale. As she poured, Robert said, 'Is the sheriff's room ready? He is to be the honoured guest at the wedding.'

'It is, my Lord.' Curtsying again Sarah left them to it.

The second she reached the kitchen she ran to Mathilda. 'Quick, my Lady, can you help me? I'm to have a room ready for the sheriff to spend the night!'

Mathilda beamed. 'With pleasure Sarah.'

It appeared that Robert had baited the trap.

~ *Chapter Forty-one* ~

The time Adam and Ulric had spent avoiding the sheriff had been employed in talking to Wilkin Sayer.

Adam, who had never previously found satisfaction in violence, had experienced an unsettling sensation as he'd sat next to the spy. This was the second time since entering the Folville household that he'd held a dagger to another man's throat. And on this occasion, he'd almost enjoyed it.

Now, leaving Sayer under lock and key in the very storeroom where he'd been kept on his arrival at the manor, and having made sure that the sheriff and his men were otherwise occupied, Adam, with Ulric, set about grooming the horses, ready to carry the wedding party to the church the following morning. While they worked, Ulric explained what had happened after Adam had been thrust out into the night, filling his friend in on all the information that Wilkin either didn't know, or had failed to mention.

Gossip had spread quickly about Adam's disappearance, the boy said, and each tale was slightly different from the next. Looking back, it was clear that Wilkin had intended there to be enough confusion for no one to quite know what had happened. John de Markham now suspected that Sayer had planted the seed of suspicion in many ears around both the household and the village in advance; that so that when the time came to act, it would be easily believed that Adam was the felon.

Sayer had become the steward after de Cressy, who'd just happened to be passing that same night, recommended him for the post. The sheriff had sworn to Sayer's trustworthiness and vouched how good a servant he'd been for his previous master before his death. A master whom Markham and his household now suspected had never existed.

The rumours of a death left in Adam's wake had referred to a hunting dog, not a man. That hounds slaughter, as well as the petty thefts that had happened over the previous weeks, had all been set up and committed by Wilkin himself.

Ulric told Adam that Lord Markham suspected that, having been primed with details of how to get in and out by the sheriff himself, Sayer had crept around the manor with no one being any the wiser for weeks before his employment there.

It had been Ulric's finding of the trinkets his steward was alleged to have stolen which swayed his master into believing Adam had been framed. The only reason Markham could see for that to happen was that de Cressy wanted to manoeuvre Wilkin Sayer into the role of steward in his home.

'Whether the sheriff wanted Sayer in the house as a spy, or whether it really was, as Sayer has just claimed, that he wished simply to give up the approver's life, we may never know.'

Adam looked grave. 'My Lord John wouldn't want to take the chance, though. To have a spy loyal to the sheriff in his home would be unthinkable.'

'That's why he sent me here.'

'But, Ulric, how did my Lord John know I was here?'

'He didn't tell me.'

Adam continued to brush the horse's mane. 'Will you stay for a while, Ulric, or are you expected to go back today?'

'I was told to recover after the journey. I will set off tomorrow, if there is room for me, and no one minds my presence.'

'You may stay gladly.' A smile crossed the older man's face. 'Would you mind helping me? Sarah has presented me with a list as long as your arm of things to do and this place is about to fill with Folvilles. Once the wedding is over, all the guests will assemble here for a joint wedding and Winter Solstice celebration.'

The circumstances of their reunion temporarily forgotten, Ulric glowed with joy at working by the side of his friend again, adding with a cheeky wink, 'She's nice. Sarah, I mean.'

Mathilda had never prepared for a wedding before. She'd been to one in the village where she'd grown up, but if she'd ever considered marrying one day, the idea had been dismissed on the death of her mother. Nothing had been said, but it was understood that she'd remain at the pottery, looking after her father and two brothers until such a time as they married and had wives to take over. After that, she'd have either been made to feel she was in the way, or remained as a skivvy, cleaning and cooking for everyone.

Now she was the focal point of a noble household's wedding and was to be a nobleman's wife. It could have been the stuff of ballads, except the journey from meeting Robert to the night before her nuptials had hardly been a fairytale.

'Maybe that does make it the stuff of ballads.' Mathilda smiled quietly as she flexed her arms, easing out the recurring stiffness she'd felt since her ordeal.

The Folville brothers were all in residence now. Sayer had been returned to the cell on John de Folville's orders, and it was just as well. With the sheriff unexpectedly in residence, as well as six of the brothers currently in the manor, and Mathilda's family on the way, there was barely room for everyone to sleep.

Daniel and Ulric had spent ages putting out spare cots along the sides of the main hall so that all the attendants to the brothers and the sheriff could sleep in relative comfort.

As she laid her gown across her bed, Mathilda ran her fingertips over the delicate needlework. Sarah, despite still suffering from occasional stiffness to her arm, had produced a garment a queen would have been proud to wear.

A small tear ran down Mathilda's cheek. She knew she didn't think of her mother as often as she should. Somehow her early grief had been consumed in a landslide of household tasks that were suddenly hers and hers alone, leaving Mathilda as resentful as she was sad. Now though, as the hour of her wedding approached, Mathilda craved her mother's presence.

A knock at the door heralded Sarah's arrival. Flushed and tired after very little sleep in her quest to out-cook even the royal household for this occasion, the housekeeper's eyes travelled from Mathilda to the dress. Seeing the sheen of sadness to the younger woman's eyes, she asked gently, 'Are you ready to put it on?'

'Yes.' Mathilda hugged her friend, 'But I wish you could come. It seems wrong not having you with me at the ceremony. You've been as much a mother to me as I've had in years.'

'Thank you. That means a great deal to me.' Giving a brave smile, Sarah laid a hand on Mathilda's shoulder. 'I do feel as if I have a son marrying today, for sure. But I know my place and I have the feast to prepare. I'll be thinking of you both and welcoming you back with open arms and a roasted hog.'

Feeling lighter now, Mathilda laughed as she hugged Sarah. Then, as they began the long process of arranging her into her wedding garments, Mathilda asked, 'any news yet?'

'Not yet.' The housekeeper frowned. 'You are sure he will come.'

'I'm sure.'

'Prior Henry, how wonderful to see you.' Robert dismounted, his brother's horses fanning around him in formation, as they came to a halt outside the church of St Mary's in Ashby Folville. 'I hope your presence is a nice surprise, rather than an indication that something has befallen Father Herbert.'

'Not at all, my son. He awaits you within.' The prior waved a stocky arm towards the ironstone and limestone building behind him. The recently added north and south aisles had left an aroma of fresh clay and grout in the air. The starkness of the new structures stood out against the weathered stone that had already supported St Mary's for the past hundred years. 'I was so enchanted by your bride, a lovely, caring, brave woman, that I thought I'd indulge myself and witness a wedding I wasn't presiding over for a change.'

'I'm honoured. Prior Henry.' Robert bowed his head reverently, 'And yes, Mathilda is certainly all of those things. Thank you for helping her. You gave her useful information in these troubled times. She received the answers she expected to hear.'

'But not the answers she wanted.'

'No one wants to hear that the evils which have befallen

them are of their family's own making, however unintentionally.'

The prior nodded sagely. 'Your family has always ploughed its own furrow, my Lord Robert. Occasionally a seed or two is going to blow from the rest of the row. And while I cannot condone much of what you do, I know that the motives behind your family's actions are often good. If not, the methods employed to carry out your deeds.'

Robert laughed. 'As I say, you're a good man, Prior.'

'As is your brother Eustace.' Prior Henry pointed up to the latest area of construction, 'The window he paid for last year is looking wonderful in the winter sun, don't you think?'

A rueful grin crossed Robert's face as he regarded the clever churchman. 'One of the King's wisest moves; making Eustace pay for Belers' death via a hefty donation to the church.'

'Indeed.' The prior gave Robert a mischievous wink just as Father Herbert came from the church.

The priest took in the large numbers of guests. 'My goodness, you have almost a full congregation's worth here already.'

The entire village had arrived to see the wedding but mingled amongst them was the majority of the Folville brothers' hired retinue. Robert shrugged.

'Sadly, many of these men are more guards than guests. With Rowan Leigh at large, we can take no chances with Mathilda's safety, nor your own, Father, Prior. That's why we've ridden ahead of the wedding procession.'

'Our safety?' The prior tilted his head questioningly.

'The Church, in Leigh's eyes, let him down. Especially this church, your priory and the abbey to which you are affiliated.'

The clerics shared a look of surprised concern, before Father Herbert spoke. 'Then we thank you for your caution. I will not allow arms drawn inside St Mary's though.'

'I am hoping that no arms will be drawn at all, but better to be cautious.'

'Quiet so.' The prior waved in greeting to many of the villagers as they began to gather around the church steps. That was when he noticed de Cressy.

'My Lord Sheriff! Please forgive me, I had no idea we had such an eminent guest amongst us.'

'Prior.' Edmund stiffly greeted the churchman. 'The Folville family kindly invited me to attend as I was in the area.'

'An honour for them, I'm sure.'

Robert allowed himself a private smile. The Prior of Launde was no fool. He knew that if de Cressy was there, then trouble really was in the air.

Seeing some more welcome and expected guests arriving across the church green, Robert said, 'If you'll forgive me, Sheriff, Prior, Father, if my eyes do not deceive me, Robert Ingram has arrived.'

If the prior noticed the brief flash of dislike cross de Cressy's face, then he didn't acknowledge it. Robert noticed it, though, and another piece of the puzzle dropped into place as he turned to join the heavily guarded wedding procession which was now approaching.

~ *Chapter Forty-two* ~

The balladeers were in fine voice. Mathilda could hear them entertaining the crowd around St Mary's as the small entourage crested the hill upon which the church had been built, at the edge of the village.

She wondered if someone had told them of Robert's love of the outlaw tales, for the first minstrel she heard was in fine voice, retelling the tale of *Robyn Hode and the Monk*. It was a far cry from the usual tales of love against the odds that such men usually sang at weddings and the choice made her smile. Her mother had sung that to her. Perhaps she was here today after all.

Bertred had joined Mathilda at the manor house and the procession had begun.

Lord John and his brothers had ridden ahead with Robert, and then Mathilda, with her father at her side, and her two brothers behind her, had ventured forth. The villagers from Mathilda's former home at Twyford merrily streamed up the hill to the church behind them.

Sarah had been left at home with a guard of Eustace's men. Eustace himself, chosen as the best man by virtue of him being the finest swordsman of all the brothers, was next to Robert, with his younger brothers just behind him.

Lady Joan la Zouche stood by the church steps with

Lord John de Folville and his wife. On either side of the main group, grooms, servants and villagers walked to the church, all laughing and joking, as they enjoyed a rare day off from their usual labours. Yet, as the family's men at arms wandered through the crowds, there was still an air of people waiting for something unpleasant to happen.

The winter sun shone with benevolence upon the wedding party as it travelled the last few yards to the church. Mathilda felt that Our Lady had decided to smile on her, to bless the day with a brightness which couldn't fail to lift her anxious mood. The attack from Rowan Leigh, which she'd been convinced would happen between the manor house and the church, hadn't happened.

As they arrived outside St Mary's, Bertred gave his daughter a look of such pride that Mathilda felt a sense of intense happiness. The sunshine made the golden threads Sarah had woven through Mathilda's light green wedding dress shimmer. The gold and silver stitching through the cornflower blue hair net caught the light as Mathilda gracefully slid from her horse.

She could see Father Herbert waiting as Robert greeted her with a low bow, a wide grin on his handsome face. As Mathilda ran her eyes over his new tunic and cloak, her stomach knotted into a ball of love and longing. Had this man really chosen her for his wife? Reflecting on Robert's love, Mathilda allowed her father to lead her to the church steps, where her future husband and Eustace awaited them.

As Father Herbert mounted the steps, Mathilda forgot all about Leigh, de Cressy, Sayer and the legacy of violent resentment Richard de Folville had left behind him.

With Eustace to his left, Robert gave Mathilda an encouraging nudge as Father Herbert raised his arms to indicate the need for silence from the crowd. A happy tranquillity fell on those gathered as the cleric asked Robert and Mathilda for their ages, and if they had the blessing of their parents and elder siblings.

Then, asking for confirmation that they were not related, Father Herbert paused for Eustace to read the dowry involved, which in this case consisted of very little but pottery, some trinkets of Mathilda's mother and the love of a good woman.

As Mathilda and Robert then distributed the contents of a small bag of coins to the waiting villagers, the crowd cheered, as the initial formalities were completed.

With a gentle word from Father Herbert, the villagers calmed once more. Next came a sermon which made Mathilda and Robert smile so much they had to stop themselves from laughing. As Herbert extolled the virtues of wifely obedience, Mathilda could almost hear Robert thinking, 'Some hope!' as he looked at her fondly.

Father Herbert, the amusement in his eyes saying that he knew he was preaching into the wind, ended his address with a request for Eustace to present Robert with a ring to place upon Mathilda's finger.

Mathilda, her palm cold in Robert's hands, beamed as the band of gold slid onto her finger and suddenly, unbidden tears pricked at the corner of her eyes. As the ring found its resting place, how close she'd come to this moment never coming hit her. Although she smiled through her tears, it took all her willpower not to step closer to Robert and become engulfed in the comfort of his height and weight. Instead, Mathilda looked around her with joy and pride as the church doors were thrown open for all to enter.

As the prayers began, followed by a mass, Mathilda found she wasn't really listening to Father Herbert anymore. Her head was a mixture of what might have been and what was to come. It came as quite a surprise when Father Herbert closed the ceremony by placing the traditional kiss of peace on Robert's cheek. A kiss which Robert then passed to her; his new wife.

Taking Robert's hand as Father Herbert blessed any children they may have in the future, Mathilda was swept up in the loving reassurance of her husband's arms and the service ended.

Outside of the church, the villagers were in full fete as the balladeers struck up their tales once again. The ever resourceful innkeeper, Jacob Lock, recovered from his encounter with Leigh, was wandering through the crowd with jugs of beer in hand. His wife distributed cups from a tray with one hand, while taking a penny for each sale from the fast-growing crowd of onlookers, who were stamping their booted feet against the crisp cold of the winter solstice.

Robert, his arm now linked in Mathilda's, bent to her wife as she waved to the crowd. 'You look beautiful.'

Blushing, Mathilda beamed, 'Thank you, my Lord. You look most handsome yourself.'

'Why thank you, Lady Folville.'

Mathilda's eyes widened in surprise, as she heard her official title for the first time. 'Lady Folville. That's going to take some getting used to!'

Robert winked, 'I'll be sure to help you adjust, my Lady.'

A rather darker pink hue flushed over Mathilda's complexion as the horses were gathered for the procession back to the manor and Sarah's wedding feast.

As they rode, Mathilda tried not to make her survey of the crowd look like anything beyond a greeting to all who'd turned out to see if a Folville really would marry a mere potter's daughter.

Robert was not fooled. 'He isn't here my love. For once,

I'm pleased to say that your instincts were wrong. If he had ruined our wedding ceremony I don't think there would be any forgiveness left in the world for him.'

Under her breath, so no one else could hear but Robert, Mathilda said, 'Do you think Sarah is alright at the house?'

'We left her with more guards than we have here. And Adam would no more let a soul lay a hand on her than I would you.'

Adam strode into the hall and passed Sarah a cup of weak ale.

'Woman, will you sit down for a minute or two and drink this. You look so hot and flustered that you're beginning to take on the colour of the hog you've got young Daniel roasting on the spit.'

Rolling her eyes, Sarah took the offered cup. 'Stop with your compliments and help me make sure that every place at the table has a drinking vessel.'

Taking the tray of cups that Sarah had been balancing in her arms, Adam began to walk the length of the three long tables Daniel and Ulric had erected as soon as the wedding party had left for the church.

Grateful that Ulric had stayed to help, Adam couldn't help but reflect on the boy's earlier comment on Sarah's kindness. She was firm but gentle and fair of face. Adam felt his insides contract at the thought that she too had suffered at the hands of Leigh's man. So much had happened in so short a time that his own arrival into the household and Sarah's stabbing had all but been forgotten.

The way Sarah's arm tired easily as she worked showed that the wound troubled her. The cold wouldn't help either. Adam speculated that the winter months ahead would continue to niggle at the scar and the incident would be fresh in her mind each time she worked too hard or faced illness.

The urge to look after her became overwhelming, an unshakable desire to care for her and ensure no further harm ever befell her. It was a strange sensation.

Adam paused as Sarah returned to the hall, her arms full of winter roses which she began to spread upon the floor in a floral carpet, to celebrate the happy couple's return. The desire to embrace her was beginning to make his palms itch.

Sensing she was being watched, Sarah looked up from her work. 'They'll be here soon, Adam. Could you help me with placing the last few dishes on the tables?'

'I could.' He wanted to add, 'if you'll let me hold your hand, and kiss your cheek, and keep you safe for ever,' but he merely placed the final tankard on the table and joined Sarah to admire the spread before them.

Countless freshly baked loaves adorned the tables. There were over a hundred boiled and shelled eggs, pounds of cheese, a carved quarter of an ox, galleons of mutton broth, fifteen capons, eight chickens, three geese and, over the fire, a spit-roasted hog, which was filling the hall with an aroma as delicious as any Adam had ever smelt.

With wine as well as ale available at the top table and ale at the other two, the scene was set, with just enough space left for the sweetmeats Sarah now gave to Adam to jostle into position.

Adam had just manoeuvred two roasted chickens a fraction to make space for some jellied boars' feet, when Ulric, his face full of delight and his mouth watering, rushed into the hall.

'They approach! The Lord and Lady Folville are but a moment away!'

~ *Chapter Forty-three* ~

The noise was deafening. The two balladeers had followed the procession from the church, in the hope of being asked to play at the feast and so earn enough for their supper. To their surprise they'd both been invited in, on the understanding that they either took it in turns to perform or sang together.

Sarah, clearly exhausted, but proudly standing by to help serve the feast to the honoured guests, waited at the doorway to the hall, curtseying to master and mistress, as Bertred and Eustace escorted man and wife to pride of place in front of the fire.

Robert, as Adam bowed in greeting, asked out of the corner of his mouth, 'Any sign?'

'Nothing, my Lord, but your brother's men remain vigilant. No one has slipped in. No one has even tried.'

Flushed from the heat of the fire behind them, with the delicious aromas of roasting meat and heady spices mingling in the air, Robert took Mathilda's hand. 'Sarah has done us proud.'

The food was half gone, the wine and ale flowed, and the balladeers could barely be heard above the chatter and laughter from all three tables. The atmosphere was so different from that of the last few weeks. Light and relaxed,

Mathilda could feel the stresses of recent events pouring away from her. She had clearly been wrong. Leigh would have struck by now if he was going to. The church had been the obvious place, largely undefended, with everyone's concentration on the marriage rather than a potential attack by a revengeful madman. He hadn't taken that opportunity, so maybe Leigh had simply gone away.

Lord John, who'd willingly sacrificed his usual place at the head of the table for Robert and Mathilda, Father Herbert and Prior Henry, got to his feet.

'I am delighted to welcome you all here today to celebrate the union of my brother, Robert de Folville, and his new wife, Mathilda of Twyford.' A cheer erupted around the room, accompanied by a clattering of tankards, until John reclaimed his audience. 'Mathilda, as many of you will know, came to this household through a most unorthodox route, and to our collective surprise, she swiftly proved her worth to the entire family and unexpectedly won her way into Robert's heart.'

Another cheer rose as Robert leant over and kissed his bride on the cheek, before getting to his feet. 'Thank you, my Lord. And, thank you all for coming, especially Bertred of Twyford, father to my wife, and his sons Matthew and Oswin. Mathilda and I would like, if you'll forgive us, to somewhat break with tradition and thank someone else very special as well. We would like to thank Sarah. Our loyal housekeeper, the woman who had the upbringing of my brothers and myself thrust upon her, and who has taken Mathilda under her wing and made her part of this household. She has also provided us with this incredible wedding feast.'

Talking through the shouts of appreciation for a blushing Sarah's food and drink, Robert continued, 'These last few days have been more testing than any that my family has faced before. Sarah was attacked, and my beloved Mathilda was almost lost to me, a thought which now, more than ever, is unthinkable.' He reached a hand out for Mathilda to hold as he spoke. 'I know well that I am a very lucky man. Few noblemen get to marry for love. My good fortune astounds me. Please join me in rising to your feet and toasting the good health and long life to, Lady Mathilda de Folville.'

Adam smiled along with the rest, his own heart souring as Sarah's role in the proceedings was so graciously and unexpectedly acknowledged. He had not partaken of the ale or wine on offer however. Nor had he overeaten.

The general mood in the hall was relaxed. Too relaxed.

The brothers seem to have forgotten about the threat that remained outside, not to mention the man who currently resided in the cell. Then there was the sour faced sheriff at the far end of the high table.

De Cressy had been sat directly opposite the former sheriff, Robert Ingram. Adam couldn't help but be amused by the tactical placement of the two men. It couldn't be lost on de Cressy on how welcome Ingram was here. His association with the Folvilles had always been civil, if sometimes brittle. Yet respect had always been held on both sides, and now Ingram was no longer in power, the relationship had drifted into a friendship that remained useful on both sides. A friendship which was crystal clear now as Ingram, sat next to Eustace and Lady Joan la Zouche, laughed and feasted in style.

The current sheriff however ate little and sat quietly. Adam could see de Cressy watching everyone. It wouldn't be long, Adam knew, before the sheriff's eyes fell on him. When that happened, Adam wasn't sure what his reaction would be. Would the sheriff demand Adam's arrest? He was, after all, unaware that Wilkin Sayer was currently under lock and key within this very manor.

As he observed the official, Adam was more convinced than ever that de Cressy must know there was a chance Rowan Leigh could turn up. Perhaps Leigh was already nearby, planning how to get past the guards.

Maybe they were all wrong. Perhaps Leigh had decided to flee into Wales or Scotland, or head down to London to try his luck in the capital city.

Running his eyes along the tables as he picked up two jugs of ale, topping up any tankards thrust in his direction, Adam saw Jacob and his family from the local inn. He was sat next to a badly bruised Elias Tavernier from Melton. The two innkeepers were engaged in an intense conversation; both looking as if they were at a funeral rather than a wedding feast. Adam's eyes narrowed.

What was Elias doing there? Surely Robert hadn't invited him after what he'd done?

Deciding to keep a careful eye on Elias as well as de Cressy, Adam gestured to Daniel to have a break from carving meat from the spit now that the majority of people had moved onto Sarah's splendid supply of pies and cheese. Pulling the boy to one side, he whispered into his ear, 'Can you go and check that the gaol door remains secure?'

Daniel frowned, but said nothing as he slipped from the hall.

Ulric, who was collecting empty platters from the tables, recognised the concerned sheen to Adam's eyes. 'Are you alright?'

'Has de Cressy noticed you yet?'

'Why would he? I'm nothing to him. The sheriff is the type of man who doesn't notice servants.'

'True.' Adam nodded. 'I don't like this, Ulric. Everyone

is too relaxed. I know they should be having fun, but...'

'But they seem to have forgotten all that has happened.'

'Indeed. Daniel has gone to check Sayer is secure. Would you take out those platters and check the courtyard for me? It's very loud in here, the perfect cover for hiding how quiet it might have gone out there.'

'But there are loads of Eustace's men out there.'

'Yes, there are, but Eustace's men are mercenaries.'

'Is that a problem?'

'It is if someone comes along and offers them more money to disappear than they are getting to stay.'

The minstrels had struck up a new tune. Each of their tales was becoming more robust than the one before as the drink flowed faster amongst the wedding guests.

Adam edged around to the top table where Sarah was making sure the happy couple had enough food. 'A most wonderful spread, Sarah.'

'Thank you. How are the ale supplies holding out?'

'We have enough for another two hours, but after that we'll need to go easy. I've had Daniel adding water to each jug for some time. We don't want the brothers' edge to be completely blunted, just in case.'

Sarah's face glowed beetroot with exertion, 'Good. I can't help thinking something is still going to happen.'

'Daniel and Ulric are checking the cell and the courtyard for me. They'll be back in a minute. So far, I've managed to avoid serving de Cressy, but even amongst all these people, it's only a matter of time until he spots me.'

'Would he arrest you?'

'I think he'd try.'

Sarah's flushed expression paled. 'Adam, I don't want...' She couldn't go any further. They were too busy for any sort of conversation - certainly for one that concerned how much she dreaded him returning to Markham, let alone him being wrongly arrested for the crimes of another.

Understanding what she wasn't saying, Adam held Sarah's gaze for longer than usual, willing her to understand that he didn't want to leave either.

Sarah was just steeling herself to say something to Adam when she became aware of Mathilda waving to her. As the housekeeper hurried to her side, the new Lady Folville said, 'Sarah, could Robert have another drink? He's about to do an extra speech and it's so hot here by the fire.'

'Certainly. Is everything alright with the feast, my Lady?'

'It s beyond perfect.' Mathilda laughed, 'Sarah, you'd better call me my Lady in front of all these people, but you will call me Mathilda when we're alone, won't you?'

Beaming, the housekeeper inclined her head. 'You look beautiful. If I didn't know better, I'd say you were already aglow with child.'

Mathilda giggled, 'give us a chance. We've not finished your feast yet!'

Slyly winking at her mistress, Sarah turned to top up Robert's tankard, in time to see Daniel re-enter to the hall and gesture to Adam that the lock on the cell door was exactly as it should be.

With a slight relaxing of her shoulders, Sarah continued her never ending ale topping up duties along the top table as Robert returned to his feet.

'My lords, Lady Joan, and welcome guests, I find I cannot let this occasion pass without raising a cup to those who recent events have so cruelly stolen from us.'

A murmur of agreement echoed around the room and a quietening fell over the revellers. From his position at the back of the hall, Adam watched de Cressy like a hawk as

Robert continued.

'My loyal steward Owen, and my faithful messenger and stable lad, Allward, were murdered. Stolen from us by hands unknown, but under the orders of the renegade carpenter, Rowan Leigh of Lubbesthorpe, these men died trying to keep my wife safe. I would like you to stand and raise your drink in memory of two good men, whose deaths, I can herby promise...' Robert turned his gaze, fixing his eyes directly into those of the current Sheriff of Nottinghamshire and Leicestershire, 'will be avenged.'

Adam waited. Edmund de Cressy hadn't even flinched, but he couldn't fail to be aware that it wasn't just Robert who held his cold stare. Every member of the Folville household held his gaze, whether they were family or not.

But not Ulric's. A prickle of fear shot down Adam's spine.

Where was Ulric? He hadn't come back from the yard.

The sheriff and the two men at arms behind him hadn't moved.

Adam ran has eyes over the muddled chaos of the hall, frantically looking to see if the young lad from Markham was busy attending to the needs of a guest.

He couldn't see him anywhere.

Nor was there any sign of Jacob Lock or Elias Tavernier.

~ *Chapter Forty-four* ~

Edging out of the hall, gesturing to Daniel to come too, Adam tapped discreetly on Walter, Laurence and Thomas's shoulders. Mouthing a quick, 'Forgive me, my Lords,' as he did so, Adam hoped the urgent concern on his face would excuse him for interrupting their revelry and explain what was needed without the time-consuming necessity of words.

Understanding at once, the three Folvilles rose quietly from their position at the head of the second table and followed Adam to the corridor between the hall and the kitchen.

The group's daggers were drawn before they crept from the boisterousness of the hall, but the brothers hadn't even reached the kitchen before Adam discovered why Ulric had been gone so long.

Leigh, a dead expression on his face, had Ulric by the scruff of the neck, his trademark knife at the boy's belly. 'I believe the messenger carrying my wedding invitation must have got lost. Perhaps this boy's life will guarantee me an audience with the new Lord and Lady Folville.'

Nobody spoke as, waiting just long enough for Daniel and Adam to disappear into the hall, they took a few steps backwards to let the deranged man through. There was no way Leigh could know that Laurence and Thomas were part of the family; and they knew better than to reveal their hand too soon.

Urging Daniel towards the high table to alert the wedding party, Adam, his stomach churning with rage, picked a jug up off the nearest table. He sped to where Edmund de Cressy sat, so far unaware that his prodigy had arrived on the scene.

Trying not to think about how scared Ulric must be, Adam checked to make sure the knife Sayer had returned to him was in place on his belt. Then, doing his best to make it look as if he was pouring wine, Adam placed himself between the sheriff and his men at arms.

Every hair on Adam's head prickled with tension. Any second now the family would know. Any second now and Prior Henry would see the pupil that his almoner had saved from perishing in the open air as a baby, only to have his spirit broken at the hands of another child. Adam kept his eyes peeled as he busied himself with tidying plates that needed no tidying. He could see Daniel whispering something into Lord John's ear.

Folville was on his feet in an instant and Daniel ran on to Robert and Mathilda. There was no need for him to pass on the ill tidings. It was obvious now what was happening.

Every Folville jumped to their feet, Mathilda included.

Then Ingram leapt up, a bellow of outrage hissing from his lips, as to Adam's side de Cressy scraped his own chair back and got to his feet.

Adam had the point of his discreetly drawn knife held against the sheriff's ample belly before anyone had noticed. With a hiss of, 'Say nothing if you know what's good for you,' Adam took immense satisfaction as de Cressy registered who was stood next to him in such a way that only the two of them knew one held a dagger to the other's gut.

'How did this lunatic get in here?' John de Folville's roar silenced the last of the oblivious revellers and the minstrels broke off their singing mid stanza.

Mathilda's face blanched white, the heat of the fire behind her suddenly having no effect. Cold consumed her from the toes up, as her entire physical being reacted to the horror of seeing the man who'd tried to rape her and freeze her to death. It was only Ulric's frightened face, as he was shuffled along before Leigh like a living shield, that kept Mathilda's feet firmly glued to the floor, rather than fleeing for the nearest lockable door.

Daniel, his voice almost lost in the eruption of chaos that turned to an icy quiet, said, 'My Lord John, the innkeepers Jacob Lock of Ashby Folville and Elias Tavernier of Melton are gone. They must have distracted the guards and let Leigh in.'

'Our innkeepers! Trusted men!' The lord of the manor's expression illustrated the full heat of his rage.

Leigh's snort of mirth lacked humour as he sneered, 'I think you'll find they were mistrusted men. As men with everything to lose often are.'

John de Folville held Leigh's ghost like gaze, 'You forced them? How?'

'Their businesses are on land I was promised as my own. If they wanted to keep working on those lands, and if they wanted their families to survive the changeover of ownership... and Lock has already lost a nephew.' Leigh spat upon the floor, 'And he pretended to be a foundling! He dared to pretend he knew what it was like to be discarded... how...'

John shouted across the man's babbling, 'What outrage is this you're babbling?' He gripped the hilt of his sword, struggling not to swipe at the man's knees and tip this unwanted drama into chaos.

Leigh's unnaturally high voice cracked as he drew Ulric before the high table, uncaring, or possibly not noticing, that he'd effectively surrounded himself with armed men. 'Outrage. Yes, a good word for what has happened here. For what has *always* happened within these walls.'

The sound of drawing swords filled the room, but Leigh merely laughed. 'You'd risk the death of another suckling pig, would you? Isn't having one servant boy's death on your conscience enough, Folville?'

Robert looked at his elder brother. John understood at once. The bridegroom was asking permission to do the talking. John granted his request with the lightest of blinks.

'And which Folville would you be talking about, Leigh?' Robert fixed his gaze onto that of the intruders, 'My brother Richard is not here. Nor would he be welcome. It is him, I assume, that you are referring to?'

Leigh gasped, before pulling himself together, 'You're not as stupid as you look.'

'But, clearly, you are.'

'I think you underestimate me. Your brother always did that, now I suggest you call him.'

'Richard would certainly underestimate you, that particular brother of mine underestimated everyone.' Robert squeezed his wife's palm as he addressed her abductor, 'He made that same mistake with Mathilda. In this instance, however, it is you who have misjudged the situation. Not only is Richard not here, but there are over fifty armed men in this hall, including one former sheriff of the county,' Robert gestured towards Ingram to the right, 'and, more pertinently perhaps, the current sheriff sits at that end. He could have you in gaol within the day and dead within the month.'

Mathilda tensed. She was waiting for Leigh's reaction as his eyes fell on the sheriff. Would Leigh assume de Cressy was there as a guest? Would he feel betrayed again? Paranoia was his main driving force. Would Leigh assume the sheriff had tricked his way to the table to await his presence?

The expression of the serving sheriff gave more away that Leigh's did as their gazes met. His bearded face darkened, and for a second Edmund's eyes flashed a warning in the fugitive's direction, as if he was daring him to be so foolish to speak against him.

It was soon clear why Leigh had not yet reacted to de Cressy's presence.

It hadn't been the sheriff that his gaze had fallen upon. It was the man who was so close to the sheriff, that he almost had an arm around the man which held the outlaw's attention.

'You!' The thought of finally catching up with Richard forgotten, Leigh staggered sideways at the sight of the man who'd wrestled Mathilda from him. As he moved, he ripped up Ulric's tunic so that the dagger blade he held was pressed directly against the flesh of the boy's stomach. 'Don't move!'

Adam said nothing, looking instead at Robert, who said, 'So it isn't just the Folvilles that Leigh's afraid of then.'

'Afraid!' Leigh spat onto the trampled floor, 'I fear no one, least of all a servant.'

Robert opened his mouth, but Mathilda got in first.

'Adam saved me from you. He showed great bravery. You *should* fear him.' Her voice was so quiet, so soft by comparison to those that had gone before, that it seemed to ring out all the clearer in the uneasy quiet that had descended upon the hall. 'You say you fear no one, but that hasn't always been the case has it?'

'What?'

'You were happy once. A good pupil, wasn't that how

Brother Mark described the young Rowan, Prior Henry?'

Leigh's head snapped around so fast that Ulric was dragged closer to the weapon, causing him to yelp as the sharp point pricked his skin.

'Yes, my child,' Prior Henry's voice rose with unfazed authority, 'that is how you, Master Leigh, used to be.'

The remaining colour drained from Leigh's face as he noticed the churchman for the first time. 'You!'

Ulric crashed to the floor as Leigh leapt the table and wrapped his sinewy arm around the prior's neck before anyone had blinked. Then, tugging the corpulent cleric off his seat, Leigh growled, 'Treachery everywhere!'

The prior, who appeared remarkably unruffled at having an elbow digging into his throat and a knife at his stomach, said 'If you are determined to see treachery and betrayal everywhere, then you will. It will appear in every face, every glance. Rowan, my son, you have it as a disease and we are partly to blame for that.'

Mathilda didn't miss the moment of shock that crossed Leigh's face as the prior admitted some responsibility for what his former pupil had become.

Henry's great chest pumped like a bellows to counteract the restriction at his throat, 'Brother Mark couldn't forgive himself. He left, you know. After your visit as an adult explaining how your young life had been lived once our backs were turned. He gave up working in the almonry and moved to an abbey many miles away. He couldn't get past it you see; that Richard had deceived him. Deceived us all. And that you, his favourite pupil, had been his main victim.'

'I don't believe you.'

'That is your right. It is not, in this case, the accurate belief to take. However, as you have a knife at my belly, I will not argue with you.'

Mathilda didn't know who to observe first. Leigh and the prior, Adam and the sheriff, or Robert and his brothers.

She could feel the tension of helplessness rising from her father and brothers.

Keep Leigh talking. Just keep him talking.

Leigh didn't reply to the prior as his dark eyes flashed around the hall. Not wanting him to have the chance to settle his gaze on anyone else, Mathilda licked her dry lips. She had to distract him.

Rolling up the arm of her wedding gown, Mathilda said, 'Do you see these bruises, Rowan?'

The unexpected use of his Christian name made the outlaw turn his dark eyes onto her.

'Do you see them? You made these. The fact they are here still shows how bad they were upon infliction.' Mathilda could hear her father's chair legs move violently against the stone floor as he stood with haste. Putting a hand out, warning Bertred to stay where he was, Mathilda continued. 'The bruises will go, but the scars won't. They will knit, they will fade, but a couple of them are never going to leave me. Does it make you proud that you did that? That you have damaged the property of a Folville? Are they enough revenge for you?'

Leigh said nothing, but his chin tilted upwards, as if he was indeed proud of what he'd done.

'Because that's what this was all about, wasn't it. You didn't want me because you desired a wife. You took me so that Robert couldn't have me. You had Owen killed for the same reason. To deprive this family of his friendship and loyalty. Allward and his connection to Jacob was a real find though, was it not! You'd be able to make Jacob Lock your puppet, with no choice but to do whatever you said, just to keep the boy alive. Then, when Jacob wavered, you ordered

Allward's death. No wonder Jacob and Elias helped you here today; who would you have murdered if they hadn't? And of course, all of that was to deceive us into thinking you were in control of the area.'

'I *was* in control. And in case you hadn't noticed,' Leigh tugged at the prior until he stumbled to his knees, 'I still am.'

'No, Rowan.' Mathilda shook her head kindly. There was pity on her face, 'Richard de Folville is in control. He has been controlling you since you were a child. And what is worse, you are letting him. I am beginning to think you enjoy his power over you.'

~ *Chapter Forty-five* ~

No one in the hall would ever forget Leigh's scream. It ricocheted around the oak beams long after it had left his mouth.

Mathilda feared for Prior Henry's life as Leigh's knife hand began to shake. She could see the outlaw's knuckles whiten as he twisted the fabric of the churchman's hood. There was a danger of Henry's clothing being turned into a tourniquet.

Ever since the last time she'd seen him, Mathilda had been trying to forget the spectral expression that lived on Leigh's face. Now it was before her in horribly sharp focus; but worse.

The smooth face had sagged into dark pockets under the eyes. The eyes themselves looked huge; as if Leigh was forcing them as wide open as possible. There was a scratch across his neck, making Mathilda wonder if he'd become entangled in brambles when he'd run from The Thwaite.

Despite the quivering of his knife hand and the madness in his eyes, Leigh still appeared very much aware of where he was and how easy it would be for his audience to overcome him.

Mathilda had to begrudgingly congratulate him. Dropping Ulric and replacing him with the prior might well have brought a sigh of relief for the boy and Adam, but Ulric meant nothing to the Folvilles. There was every chance that Eustace and John would have considered the boy's injury or death as acceptable damage in the quest to rid the world of Rowan Leigh and attacked him whether he held Ulric or not. Few would miss Ulric, fewer would grieve for him.

With Prior Henry it was another matter. He was a man whose murder would be questioned; and so it was stalemate.

Mathilda was about to speak again, but Robert got there first. 'Why are you here, Leigh? Why haven't you run as far away as possible?'

Leigh appeared bemused by Robert's question. He acted as if the answer was so obvious, that the question hadn't even been worth asking. 'To get what I'm owed.'

Robert immediately put his arm out to Mathilda. 'You're too late. She's my wife!'

Leigh laughed. 'Not your slut, Folville! She wasn't my prize; just an interesting way in which to annoy your family, an extra thorn in your side.'

Squirming to hear herself described in such a dismissive way after all she'd been through, Mathilda looked away from Leigh for the first time since he'd invaded her new home. Looking at her lap, for a split second, Mathilda was surprised to find she was still wearing her wedding dress.

Anger filled her slowly. As it consumed her, it warmed her toes from within her insubstantial wedding slippers and curled upwards, through every bone of her body.

This is my wedding day! How dare he?

Rowan Leigh had so nearly sabotaged the entire event and now, here he was, ruining everything... and yet, at the same time she was surrounded by some of the most feared swordsmen in the country. And not one of them was doing anything!

Enough.

Without turning her head, Mathilda swivelled her eyes so that she could see Adam. The sheriff hadn't moved. Then she saw why.

Adam's eyes were clearly telling her to say nothing about the knife he held at the mute sheriff's gut. The men at arms behind them, whose own swords were drawn, the blades glinting in the fire and candlelight, couldn't have seen Adam's dagger. At least, not yet.

Mathilda's fingers began to tingle with the urge to act, to do something, anything to end this. If someone didn't act soon, there would be another death, but she wasn't sure whose.

Her eyes moved away from Adam and de Cressy and sought out Sarah.

The housekeeper was by the entrance to the kitchen corridor. She was rubbing her arm where she'd been stabbed. Her face was bleak. Sarah was staring straight at Adam. She had obviously also noticed that the man she had fallen for was holding a weapon to the stomach of the sheriff of the county. That act alone was enough to condemn Adam as a dead man.

Enough.

Robert put his hand out to his wife as he heard her take a step forward. Mathilda nodded to him, silently telling him she knew what she was doing. Then, hoping Leigh was too intent on keeping the prior secure to notice, Mathilda darted her eyes to Adam and back again. To her relief, Robert followed her eyes, and a second later she saw his expression darken further. He'd seen the position of Adam's dagger too.

Robert subtly nodded his assent to Mathilda as she addressed Leigh again. 'What is it you've come for, then?'

'I told you! For what I was promised.'

'And was that promise made by someone in this room?'

If the atmosphere in the hall had been tense before, it was bristling with uncertainty now. Every guest regarded their neighbour with a new air of suspicion, as from their positions behind Leigh, Walter, Thomas and Laurence made their way to where the sheriff stood, shifting uneasily from foot to foot.

'And that man', Mathilda went on, 'for I assume it was a man; he promised you what exactly? And for what services?'

'To rid the world of the men who killed his friend and a family with far too much control for a group of murderers.'

Someone dropped a plate. The clatter echoed around the room as Mathilda said, 'That sounds like you are repeating what someone has said to you. Am I right?'

Leigh said nothing, but his eyes landed on the figure of Edmund de Cressy.

Wondering who 'the friend' Leigh referred to had been, but coming up with only one possible contender, Mathilda, her heart pounding in her chest, pushed on. Any gap in the conversation could prove fatal. 'I bet this man couldn't believe his luck when he encountered you; someone who hated this family as much as he did?'

Leigh didn't answer. He wasn't looking at her at all now. Just at Adam and the sheriff.

'The chances of you meeting him, though, this man who wished to avenge a death arranged by this family, they were slim for a bastard carpenter.'

Leigh flinched, and the prior gave his first cry of pain as the dagger pricked his skin; but the outlaw said nothing.

'Forgive me, Rowan,' Mathilda turned to Robert, 'I think, husband, that our unwanted guest isn't fond of being reminded of his lack of parents. A fact that Richard, the rector of Teigh, took glee in rubbing in on a great many occasions.'

Robert looked solemn. 'That would be in line with my unholy brother's behaviour. He always finds such taunts amusing.'

Ensuring Robert's hand was firmly in hers; Mathilda began to walk them both away from the fire, getting nearer to Leigh as she kept talking.

'When you met this man, a man of power, and you discovered he had a mutual axe to grind with this family, you must have been overjoyed. At last, you had someone to help you direct all that hate. A real chance to extract some sort of revenge, if not on Richard, the culprit himself, but on his family.'

Robert touched Lord John's arm as he moved; indicating that he should follow.

Leigh gaze was transfixed upon the figure of the sheriff. Although the name de Cressy hadn't been spoken, Mathilda knew it wouldn't be long before it was obvious to everyone present who was really responsible for the disruption of the wedding feast.

Mathilda permitted herself a hollow laugh. 'But, Rowan, didn't you realise, that whatever you did to me or his brothers, however bad, it would be applauded by Richard? From the look on your face, I can tell you truly believed you'd find him here. Now you are beginning to wonder, though, aren't you?

'Richard de Folville is in France. He hates me in particular. Me even more than you, because I sent him there. I am the one who had him condemned for arranging the murder of Hugo of Bakewell. He suffers a life fighting for the King because of me. My persecution, and Robert's, would delight Richard de Folville, not aggrieve him. When he hears of this, you'll have made him incredibly happy.'

'No!' Lunging forward, Leigh dragged the prior off his knees as if he weighed nothing. Marching the cleric towards the sheriff, Leigh scattered any guests who hadn't been sharp-witted enough to move out of his way. 'Richard would hate it! He bragged, he bragged all the time about having a family who worshipped him.'

Robert's roar was more indignation than anger. 'Worshipped him? That brother of ours has been a thorn in this household's boots since the day he was born. He was trouble from the moment he opened his eyes.'

'What?' For the first time, Leigh sounded uncertain.

'And what's more,' Robert added, 'the man who talked you into all this knew that. He has always known there was no love lost for the rector of Teigh in this family. Richard is our brother by birth, but that is where it ends. He waived his right to family loyalty a long time ago.' Robert and held Leigh's dull gaze. 'And yet, knowing that, this benefactor of yours still persuaded you to set your life on a course of destruction just so you could cast vengeance upon him. How kind of you to do the dirty work of another!'

Leigh swallowed hard. 'You lie. All Folvilles lie.'

Mathilda kept moving, softly and quietly so as not to startle the man with the drawn blade. 'Your benefactor lied to you, Rowan. If he was telling you the truth, why hadn't he told you that Richard isn't here? The rector's removal from England wasn't widely known, but *he* knew. The man who swore to help you. *He knew.* I bet he told you that if you helped him rid the country of the Folvilles, if you disgraced them; if you made it appear that they were not worthy of the reputation they have built for themselves, you would be rewarded.

'But look at where you are, Rowan. You're surrounded.

Even if you kill the good prior, then where will you go? How will you escape from here? You can't. The innkeepers who let you in here are not stupid - foolish and afraid, but not stupid. They will have fled as far as they can from this place. Although for their sakes I hope they reach a foreign border before my husband's family get to them, for they will not survive long otherwise.'

Leigh was shaking his head violently. 'I am not the one who's trapped.'

'Oh, Rowan,' Mathilda sighed, 'did you think I wouldn't want to find out why you'd done what you'd done? Why you'd hurt me and allowed my friends to die. And who it was that helped you?'

'Why didn't anyone tell me about Richard being gone?'

'I doubt those who knew were brave enough to face the ire in you which that news would bring. You'd have murdered the messenger on the spot.'

Robert was now so close to Leigh that one strike could knock the knife from his hand - but only if he was quick enough to do so before Leigh retaliated by stabbing Prior Henry.

'You bluff.' Leigh's words came out in a whine now, as Mathilda kept talking.

'Bluff? With you here right now, staring into the eyes of your ally. The man who has been festering with the need for revenge since the death of his corrupt friend, Roger Belers.'

A gasp shot around the room, and Lady Joan la Zouche, whose father had been the killer of Belers, rose with dignity, and said without a hint of fear. 'Roger Belers was a slug.'

Eustace was at Lady Joan's side in seconds. 'He was less than a slug.'

While Leigh was staring at the sheriff, and all other eyes in the hall were on Leigh himself, Robert pointed to Adam.

Speaking in a clear loud voice, Robert announced, 'the dagger you have at de Cressy's gut, Adam - now might be the time to drive it home.'

1329

The girl is beautiful.

I wasn't going to keep her at first, but then... There's just so much fire in her soul. I thought maybe I would have her for my wife after all. I would never have damaged her too much.

A few scars would have been essential though. A message of my intent. A reminder to her to remain loyal once she was wedded to me and was truly mine. A wedding gift of wounds. Only on her thighs, though, so only I could gaze on them whenever I wished.

Her clothes are soft.

She smells of fear and rose petals.

She'd have made me children. Strong powerful sons.

Then I'd have showed off our offspring to them. Sons to make the brothers Folville look like piglets scrapping in the mud.

I would have...

~ *Chapter Forty-six* ~

De Cressy's shout of denial was almost as loud as the one Lord John counteracted it with, as the head of the Folville household ordered every person in the hall to remain precisely where they were.

'This is my brother's wedding day! There will be no bloodshed here.' The men at arms behind the sheriff took one step back each, but both of them kept their hands on their swords.

'Explain yourself, de Cressy.'

His demeanour haughty with outrageous indignation, the sheriff bellowed, 'I have nothing to explain and no inclination to do so while your ruffian has a knife at my flesh.'

John tilted his head towards Adam. 'You may relax now, Master Calvin. Perhaps you could attend to young Ulric. The boy is badly shaken.'

Part relieved, part disappointed, Adam lowered his weapon and turned to Ulric, who sat on the stone floor, his knees tucked under his chin. Bundling the boy against his stockier body, Adam pushed his way through the crowd that had thickened around the drama unfolding in the centre of the hall. Heading to Sarah, he got Ulric to the kitchen corridor in time to hear the sheriff attempt to deflect the room's attention.

'You allow that man, Calvin,' de Cressy spat, 'to hold me at knifepoint. An outlaw, a felon! Adam Calvin is a man guilty of theft and murder in the Nottinghamshire town of West Markham. Perhaps I should not be so surprised to see such a man has been welcomed into the heart of this particular family.'

Sarah put an urgent hand on Adam's arm to stop him from racing back across the hall. 'Let the brothers' deal with this. Trust them. Trust Mathilda.'

Adam was about to argue, but then Sarah added, 'Please, I need you here. Don't give him an excuse to arrest you.'

Sarah looked as if a lifetime of being strong was about to collapse around her. 'Alright, lass. It's alright.' Adam placed a hand in Sarah's, 'I'll stay by your side unless bidden otherwise by their lordships. Come on. Let's get Ulric somewhere safe to lie down.'

In the background, Adam and Sarah heard Robert laughing. It was an empty sound of someone finding amusement where there was none.

'Nice try, Sheriff. I believe my brother asked you to explain yourself. You are a guest here. May I suggest that if you want to leave here in the same manner, rather than as a fugitive, you talk.'

'You don't have the power, you're just...'

'The family that has already sent one corrupt official into his grave. Belers was a man so wrapped in sin that the King himself pardoned us the act in exchange for my Lord Eustace bestowing a stained glass window on our beloved St Mary's church.'

'Are you threatening me, Folville?'

'Yes. I am. *We* are.' Robert gestured to his family around him, 'Because it was you. You who encouraged Rowan Leigh into this enterprise. You took advantage of his hurt and used it. You promised him things that weren't yours to give, in return for getting rid of us, for blackening a name even King Edward himself showed begrudging respect for.'

'How dare you! I would never...'

Robert ignored de Cressy and turned to Leigh, whose grip at the prior's throat hadn't lessened. He was growing concerned for the welfare of the elderly cleric. 'What did the sheriff offer you, Rowan?'

The felon didn't hesitate. The hunger in his eyes for this to work out well burnt in his eyes. 'This place. A home and lands, in exchange for freeing the land of you all.'

Surprised by the willingness of Leigh's answer, Robert asked, 'An act you were going to achieve how? By disgracing us? An unlikely prospect, surely, when the king has acknowledged our usefulness?'

Leigh's face went puce. Words of rage tumbled out of his mouth in a torrent of disbelief, treachery, and disappointment.

'You said, you said...' He rounded on de Cressy. For a moment he dropped the prior, who gagged and spluttered for air, until Leigh suddenly remembered he held a hostage.

Raising his knife from the monk's belly to his throat, he pulled Henry along until they were both directly in front of the sheriff. 'This was to be mine. All of it. The home I was denied by my bitch mother, who abandoned me! She left me to die in a field...'

Leigh started to shake his head as he spoke, pointing the tip of the dagger at the sheriff, his elbow squashing the prior's neck instead. 'I was clearly of noble birth, *you* said. Born to greater things than carpentry. I should have a manor, and lands and a name. A proper name, with respect and loyal followers. You, you...'

Mathilda watched the unfolding tableau carefully. As

Rowan Leigh's rage ran into incoherent ramblings, the guests were forming themselves into a circle of knife-wielding men surrounding him. She wasn't sure Leigh had noticed. He was so wrapped up in the space between himself and de Cressy, that he was becoming blind to everything else. Only John, Eustace Lady Joan, the prior, Robert and she remained close to Leigh.

Edmund de Cressy, his men at arms elbowed away by Walter, Thomas and Laurence, who had explained the benefits of them finding new employment fairly soon, stood towards the circle's edge.

Moments ago, the hall had been full of winter decorations and jubilation. Now it bristled with weaponry and nervous expectation, as the sheriff finally responded to Leigh's accusations.

'I make no bones about my dislike for the Folvilles. However, I am the sheriff! I have a duty to uphold the law, not flout it as I see fit. This man,' he stabbed a finger in Leigh's direction, 'is clearly deranged. I have no knowledge of him beyond what you have told me. As soon as this charade is over, I will be having him arrested and removed.'

Leigh lunged forward to strike the sheriff, but was encumbered by the prior, whose weight prevented him moving quickly.

De Cressy looked smug, 'You see! He is even trying to assault me before an audience. Whatever makes you think I'd consort with such a dolt as this? And how am I ever supposed to have met this felon before anyway? Leigh pins his hopes on blaming me because I was the first man he laid eyes on with any official power or influence in this place.'

Leigh was shaking his head faster than ever, as if trying to dislodge the knowledge that he'd been used and played for a fool. 'You do know me. You do. This was your idea!'

'I hardly think I could have orchestrated your gang of felons and the kidnap of a woman from so many miles away.'

'But you...'

'Enough!' Mathilda's voice eclipsed the sheriff's. 'You can out-deny each other until you're old and grey. Or we could prove your connection beyond all doubt here and now and rescue what is left of our wedding feast!'

'Oh really!' Edmund scoffed, 'And you can do that, can you? You have the audacity to attempt to prove the un-provable?'

'Yes, I do.' Mathilda smoothed down her gown, 'However, I like to think of it as bravery rather than audacity.'

The sheriff's shock was far more satisfying than the stunned expression which adorned Leigh's, face as Mathilda called to Daniel. 'Could you ask Adam to bring our prisoner in here, please, Daniel?'

'Prisoner?' The sheriff's eyes narrowed, 'What prisoner?'

'Wait and see.' Mathilda crossed her arms, 'Leigh may have committed unforgivable felonies. Crimes that will see him hang, but you, Sheriff, *you* are the bigger criminal. And yet you'll probably go free, merely because you were born into a noble family and Rowan wasn't.'

Leigh's bluster of 'I might have been!' was lost as de Cressy responded through gritted teeth. 'I repeat, Miss Twyford, I have committed no crime.'

Robert snapped, 'That's Lady Folville. I will thank you to address my wife properly.'

'A potter's daughter rises to become a murderer's wench.' Edmund's sneered, 'Is that supposed to impress me?'

Ingram, who'd so far listened without comment, stepped forward. 'You aren't supposed to be impressed, de Cressy.

Afraid, maybe. You offered Leigh the chance for betterment where there was none, just so that you could gain land and win vengeance that only you care about. And yet you claim that he's the fool!'

'Says the sheriff who took Folville pay!'

'I never did that.' Ingram spoke quietly, with a menace that would have made a better man shudder. 'I agreed with many of their methods. Methods a wise sheriff would investigate thoroughly, before making his mind up about how to deal with the more influential families within his jurisdiction.'

Knowing that Ingram was buying them time while they waited for Adam to return, Mathilda sent up a silent prayer of thanks to Our Lady, grateful for the former sheriff's cool calm presence.

The sound of approaching feet revealed that Adam and Daniel were returning dragging someone reluctant to leave the safety of his nice cold cell.

A gap opened up in the far end of the enclosed ring of guests, to let the two servants and the struggling prisoner through.

Mathilda watched as the people who'd been wedding feast guests only half an hour before, played their part as warders to the outlaw and his holy hostage - and possibly their sheriff. It was no wonder that the overriding sense in the room was one of unease.

Leigh's eyes bulged in their sockets as he saw who was being led towards him.

'More treachery? Is there not one person in my life who I can trust?'

De Cressy ignored Leigh and turned to Lord John. 'Is this magically conjured man supposed to worry me, my Lord?'

'Frankly, yes.' John looked grave. 'And you can bluff, bluster and pretend all you like, de Cressy, but I'd advise you not to waste my time.'

'How dare...'

'Oh, save it!' Mathilda shouted, making everyone gasp at the way she'd just addressed an officer of the Crown, even if he was as corrupt as they came.

'Wilkin Sayer is your spy. Your approver. Recently, he decided that he was getting a little old for the hazards which accompany such a role, so he asked you to find him a position that would keep him safe, housed and fed in his remaining years. And lo and behold, you knew of a suitable role. Unfortunately, someone was already filling it. But that wasn't a problem, was it. You knew how that could be sorted out, and so, between yourself and Sayer, it got sorted.'

Mathilda lowered her voice, gesturing her hand towards Adam. 'And in the process, Adam Calvin lost not only his position and his home, but the respect of a master to whom he'd always been loyal - and his personal safety.'

Adam thrust Wilkin forward, so he was only a few strides from Leigh and de Cressy. The three men formed a triangle of hate as each eyed the other, wondering who had said what to whom.

A whimper from Prior Henry broke the spell.

Robert dived forward. Smashing his elbow into Leigh, he knocked the fugitive flying. Dropping his knife, Leigh let go of the churchman, who landed against the crushed roses with a dull thud.

In a blur of only seconds, Eustace and John had their right feet pressed against Rowan Leigh's legs; their swords at his chest.

Mathilda smiled quietly at her husband before gently taking his dagger from his belt.

Then, to the astonishment of the onlookers, the bride knelt down and placed the knife at Leigh's throat.

'Give me one good reason why I shouldn't use this?'

~ *Chapter Forty-seven* ~

'Lady Mathilda.'

The voice of the prior cut through the babble of the crowd. 'My Lady, you are better than this. You are better than him.'

Expelling a slow breath, Mathilda rocked onto her haunches and let the dagger fall to the floor.

Robert pulled her to his side. 'Are you alright?'

Quickly reassuring Robert, Mathilda addressed Prior Henry, 'I'm sorry, my Lord. Thank you. I would have regretted that.' Stepping away from her husband, Mathilda gently helped the churchman to his feet. 'Are you hurt?'

Henry ran a hand around his throat. 'A little sore.' The prior found a seat, 'A drink would be welcome if any remains un-spilt.'

Daniel immediately proffered the nearest jug and tankard from the table behind him, as Eustace kicked Leigh sharply in the ribs. 'I'm bored of this now. Let's just shove all three of them in the cell and let them fight it out amongst themselves.'

'Tempting, brother.' John gave a thin grimace, 'However, I think we should hear from Sayer here. We require you to tie the threads together for us, Master Spy. I would suggest you do so with haste.'

'And if I do?'

Eustace barked a laugh. 'Spoken like a true approver, always on the lookout for financial gain.'

Wilkin was unmoved, 'And if I do, my Lords, I will walk away from here now and I will not be followed.'

John looked at Robert and Mathilda. 'Your opinion, please?'

Mathilda was firm. 'With respect, my Lord, this has to be Adam's decision. He is the one who has been most wronged by this man.'

'Well said.' John de Folville turned to Adam, 'What say you, Master Calvin?'

Searching out Sarah's face, Adam stepped forward. 'May I ask Sayer a question first, my Lord?'

'You may.'

Adam took a step nearer to Wilkin. 'Why?'

'Which *why* do you require an answer to?'

'Clever answer. I would expect no less from you.' Adam resisted the temptation to pull his knife again, the promise he'd made to Sarah about giving the sheriff no excuse to arrest him large in his mind. 'Why did de Cressy want a spy in the Markham household? That will be the reason why, out of all the households where the sheriff holds sway, my position was chosen for you.'

Sayer turned his piercing gaze to the sheriff. 'John de Markham is a king's serjeant and a lawyer. He is a powerful and useful man; an excellent ally to have, albeit an unwilling one, for a man who holds wide ambitions.'

'You lie!' De Cressy shouted, and then he laughed uneasily, 'of course you lie. That's your job, and you are so good at it. Here and now, though, the lie is worthless, because they know.'

Robert played his knife between his palms. 'Would you care to elaborate on that?'

'Sayer wanted a cosy job for his old age. He used the fact that I was a friend of a known corrupt official, Roger Belers, as a tool to ensure I gave him what he wanted.'

Leigh, from his trapped position on the floor, whimpered as he listened.

'That wasn't all though, was it?' Mathilda looked at Prior Henry, who nodded as if to say it was alright to go on.

'However, it answers your question.'

'I will tell you.' Leigh's voice was defeated. He looked skinnier than ever beneath the boots of the two Folville brothers, and for the briefest of moments Mathilda felt sorry for him. A feeling that melted away when he added, 'I will tell you if you let me go.'

'Let you go?' Robert sounded incredulous. 'Let you go?'

'I can tell you how I met Sheriff de Cressy.'

Mathilda glanced at her husband briefly before saying, 'Very well.'

Leigh frowned. 'And you'll let me walk out of here?'

'Yes.'

A cry of outrage rose from the wedding guests, but Robert put his hand up. 'Silence. Speak, Leigh.'

'And I can walk out of here?'

Mathilda pick her words carefully. 'You will be allowed to rise from the floor and walk from this hall untouched.'

Rowan gave an audible sigh of relief, 'as I suspect the prior was about to tell you, Sayer was also a foundling child. He was briefly at Leicester Abbey almonry as well, before a troop of Welsh acrobats came and took him as one of their own.'

'So you knew Wilkin when he was young?'

'I knew him, and he knew of the hate I harboured for Richard.'

'And?'

'Sayer came across me years later as part of his work for de Cressy. He was seeking information concerning Lady Joan's father, after Belers' death. He came to my workshop asking questions.'

Mathilda began to understand what Leigh was saying. 'And one glimpse of you in adulthood was enough to remind Sayer that there was another man who hated this family as much as his new master did. And as Sayer wanted to impress de Cressy, then using you as a weapon against us, as well as being the one who knew enough about the situation to have some influence over the sheriff in case he ever needed to talk his way out of trouble, must have felt like a gift from Heaven.'

'Yes.'

'You must already have been planning revenge though, Rowan?'

'Only by surrounding myself with people who might encroach on your lands a little. I was just going to be there, a thorn in your side. Anything that hurt Richard's family had to be a good thing.'

Mathilda frowned. 'And then, there you were, face to face with another man from the past. Someone who knew the truth of your suffering at the end of Richard's vicious tongue. And more than that, Sayer was a man who claimed he could give you the backing you needed to not only humiliate Richard's family, but who could actually give you their lands.'

Leigh, speaking to the beamed ceiling, murmured, 'Sayer and De Cressy must have thought they'd found a pot of gold.'

'And they had. You were to do all the dirty work, commit all the crimes.'

'I would have been rewarded.'

'No, Rowan, you would have been arrested or murdered, or both. You would never have lived here, you would never have been granted the titles the Folvilles were born to.'

Closing his eyes, Leigh said nothing more. Mathilda got the impression he'd have curled into a ball and wept if there hadn't been two large feet on his chest.

Feeling some of tension drain from her shoulders, Mathilda asked another question. 'Sayer, tell us, was Adam Calvin in anyway responsible for the thefts and the death of a hunting dog at West Markham?'

'No. He was not.'

Turning to Lord John, Mathilda curtseyed. 'Forgive me, my Lord; I had not intended the wedding feast to turn into such a spectacle.'

'The apology is not yours to make, Mathilda, but I thank you for it anyway.' John de Folville drew himself up to his full height, 'Ladies and gentlemen, this has been, I think you'll agree, a most unusual wedding feast. If you would be so kind as to return to your seats, then my brothers and I will despatch the few problems remaining. Adam, Sarah, Daniel; would you attend to the fallen plates and jugs and look after our guests.'

With a nod to his family, John swept out of the room with Ingram and Prior Henry at his heels. Eustace grabbed Leigh by the throat and, with Laurence taking Sayer, and Walter and Thomas escorting de Cressy, the exclusive party adjourned to the kitchen; Robert and Mathilda were right behind them.

John stood with his back to the kitchen fire. His brothers

had a firm hold of the three prisoners, while the prior and Mathilda waited in the doorway.

Speaking as if the spy was unable to hear him, John spoke to Laurence first. 'Take Sayer to the cell. He will do well to have a few days to stew before I hand him over to the authorities.'

With a satisfied grunt, Laurence removed Wilkin Sayer from the room.

Pivoting on the balls of his feet, John fixed his sights on Leigh. 'Now, then, we had an agreement.'

Leigh looked anxiously at Mathilda, 'I don't deserve your mercy.'

'Indeed, you do not.' John looked him squarely in the eyes. 'I trust when you get to hell you will pay.' He turned to Walter and Thomas. 'You will hold Leigh here. Under no circumstances is he to leave this room until I return.'

Then with Mathilda, Robert, Eustace, and the prior, John de Folville headed to his private chamber.

~ *Chapter Forty-eight* ~

Mathilda couldn't believe what she was being offered.

Robert looked more than satisfied, and the prior, who nursed the wound Leigh had made at his neck, said it was the only way. That there was no liveable life which could hold any peace for Leigh now.

Rowan Leigh had caused the deaths of Allward and Owen and many others. Somehow, he had forced Jacob and Elias to act against their own kind; an act that condemned them to spend the rest of their lives living outside the law. He'd frightened her to the point of rape and death.

His only excuse was that another man had made him unhappy.

Mathilda closed her eyes. She could see the young Rowan, lost and afraid in a place he'd come to think of as safe until Richard de Folville had arrived with his untouchable manner and self-assured arrogance. A bully from birth. It angered Mathilda to the core that he'd never know how much damage his *fun* had caused.

'Then it is agreed.' John de Folville got to his feet. 'Robert, could you ask Thomas and Walter to escort the sheriff into our company.'

Sarah, Adam, and Daniel righted scattered platters, refilled ale jugs and persuaded the minstrels that they were in no danger, and that they should continue to play.

Rather than feel aggrieved by what had happened, the guests had seen the incident as high drama of the sort expected from the Folville house.

Adam had joked that many of them probably thought it was all just invented as some sort of show. Sarah however continued to appear worried.

As soon as everyone at the tables looked settled, Adam led her to the far end of the hall. 'What is it?'

'You name is cleared, and I'm most pleased. Really I am.'

'But?'

'Will you return with Ulric? Lord Markham has need of a steward, and now you are proven innocent...' The housekeeper found she couldn't finish her sentence. Her cheeks had bloomed into red points of embarrassment.

Adam smiled. 'Sarah, my Lord Robert has already asked me to stay here, as this household's steward. I have accepted.'

'What? When?'

'While I was assisting him into his wedding garb and polishing his sword. You were busy with Mathilda. I was going to tell you, but today hasn't afforded many opportunities for private conversation.'

'Oh.' Sarah wasn't sure where to look. 'Well, good.'

Adam gestured towards the restored merriment around the hall. 'If Lord Robert and Lady Mathilda allow it, and if you would consider marrying me, do you think it would be acceptable to have a rather quieter wedding day?'

Sarah's mouth opened to tell Adam that he had no right to be so presumptuous but shut it again. 'I think that would be perfect. If you are asking me, of course.'

'I am asking you.'

'Then, yes.' Sarah grinned, 'Now, stop staring at me as if my gown has become see-through and help me find more ale. This lot are drinking us dry!'

Mathilda didn't think he'd do it. She wasn't sure which feeling was stronger. Relief that it was over or revulsion at the ease with which the sheriff had accepted the payment for his sins.

Lord John had told Edmund de Cressy that there was only one thing he could do which would prevent the king from hearing of his recent misdeeds. All of his lands in Leicestershire were to be given over to the Folville family, with a parcel of that land being gifted to one Bertred of Twyford.

That was fair and was in line with how a court of law might have dealt with the issue. Mathilda had been full of pride that her brother-in-law considered her father worthy of such a gift.

The second part of the bargain made Mathilda feel sick, until the prior had reassured her that it was kinder than leaving Leigh to the cruelty of the life that waited for him if he survived.

Henry had spoken softly, describing how Leigh would have been hunted, caught and sent to wait in a stinking cell until such a time that the gaols were delivered of all criminals and the noose could be put around his neck. Better this way, a quick death by the hand that had orchestrated his crimes and played him as a puppet. It would also, he'd added, free Leigh from the torment of his own mind.

A punishment for them both, that's how Prior Henry had labelled it. The Folvilles had agreed. And, to her horror, she realised she had seen it almost as a kindness to Leigh. Mathilda had stated there and then, though, that she didn't want to be there, a wish that was granted willingly. This was, after all, her wedding day.

De Cressy had been ashen when they'd led him to the kitchen. For the first time in her life Mathilda had wished she hadn't been granted such a good imagination. Left alone in Lord John's chamber, she had dropped to her knees, her wedding gown crushed against the floor, as she prayed to Our Lady for forgiveness and deliverance from the sin she felt she was committing, albeit third-hand.

As she rose again, light-headed, Mathilda wondered how many more times she'd have to pray in that way now she'd married a Folville.

She'd married a Folville. A small flutter in her heart made her smile despite everything Leigh had tried to ruin. A hopeful warmth filled Mathilda, who thanked Our Lady aloud. Perhaps, as the prior had declared, this was the kindest way.

The door to the chamber opened, and Robert stepped inside.

'Is it over?' Her voice quavered as she regarded her husband.

'It is.' Robert took her hands in his, 'De Cressy is a good shot with a short bow. It was quick. Leigh is no threat to anyone anymore.'

'And now the Folvilles have the ability to accuse the sheriff of murder if he ever steps out of line again. Correct?'

'Correct.' Robert wrapped his arms around her, 'I'm so sorry, Mathilda, so very sorry. I regret I couldn't protect you from Leigh in the first place and for allowing him to ruin our day. I do love you.'

'I love you too.' She felt Robert kiss the top of her head and cursed the fact that duty would force them to return to their guests. 'You have no need to be sorry. I can't pretend I like how it ended, but I am glad it ended.'

Reluctantly letting Mathilda go, Robert held out an arm, 'Then come, wife, we have a feast to return to. I don't know about you, but I think asking the balladeers to sing *The Lytell Geste of Robyn Hode* would lighten the mood no end.'

Mathilda laughed. 'But it goes on forever!'

'But you love it don't you.'

'Well yes, I do.'

'Then you shall have it.'

Epilogue

'I almost felt sorry for him in the end.'

'Sorry? For Rowan Leigh? The man was unspeakable! A monster even. He has scarred you for life.

'I said *almost*.' Mathilda stood with her husband as the last of the wedding guests departed. 'Not a celebration they'll forget in a hurry.'

'It all adds to the Folville legend.'

Mathilda laughed, 'Maybe the minstrels who attended will be singing about us in the future.'

'You never know. Perhaps we'll be singing of it to our children one day?'

'Perhaps.' Mathilda looked up at Robert. 'An heir to the Folville dynasty is yet to arrive. A heavy responsibility for a potter's daughter and a noble's younger son.'

'It is a burden of a duty indeed.' Gently pulling his wife from the courtyard towards their private chamber, Robert added, 'and one that will need practise to perfect.'

Mathilda flushed. 'Shouldn't I help Sarah and Adam clear the hall?'

Cupping her face, Robert kissed Mathilda firmly on the lips. 'It's our wedding day, woman.'

Mathilda beamed. 'It is, isn't it!'

Allowing her husband to manoeuvre her nervously into

their room, she looked down at the butterfly girdle she'd insisted on wearing around her wedding dress. 'I should warn you, my Lord, it is the devil itself to undo those buckles.'

'Is it now?' Robert laughed, before setting himself to the challenge.

THE END

Historical Notes and References

The ballads and political songs mentioned within this story come from the following sources.

The Outlaw's Song of Trailbaston, Dobson & Taylor, <u>Rymes of Robyn Hood: An Introduction to the English Outlaw</u> (Gloucester, 1989,)

Piers the Plowman, Langland, W., <u>The Vision of Piers the Plowman; A Complete Edition of the B-Text</u> (London,1987), Passus XIX, line 245.

Robin Hood and the Monk, Dobson & Taylor, <u>Rymes of Robyn Hood: An Introduction to the English Outlaw</u> (Gloucester, 1989).

A Song on the Times is recorded in the '*Harley Manuscript*' No.913, folio 44. Wright, T., <u>The Political Songs of England, From the Reign of King John to that of Edward II</u> (Camden Society, First Series, Vol. 6, London, 1839)

A Geste of Robyn Hode, Dobson & Taylor, <u>Rymes of Robyn Hood: An Introduction to the English Outlaw</u> (Gloucester, 1989), p.112, stanza 456

Robin Hood and the Potter, Dobson & Taylor, <u>Rymes of Robyn Hood: An Introduction to the English Outlaw</u> (Gloucester, 1989), p.127, stanza 17

***

Roger Belers was murdered by La Zouche and others, in 1326 in the field of Brokesby, Leicestershire. The incident was recorded in the Assize Rolls – *Just1/470*

The steward of the Folville Manor at Ashby-Folville was John de Sproxton. I have only named the steward Owen for the purposes of this story.

The one and only mention of a 'Simon de Folville' occurred in the in <u>Calendar of the Close Rolls, 1327-1330</u>, p.213. There it reports that a group of malefactors, *"including Robert de Folville and Simon de Folville were roaming abroad in search of victims to beat, wound and to hold ransom."*

Sir Robert Ingram was sheriff of Nottinghamshire and Derbyshire on four occasions between 1322 and 1334. <u>Lists of Sheriffs for England and Wales from the earliest times to AD 1831 Preserved in the Public Record Office</u> (List and Index Society 9, New York, 1963) p.102

Henry of Braunseton was Prior of Launde in Leicestershire between 1319-1334. <u>A History of the County of Leicestershire: Volume 2</u> (1954), pp. 10-13.

Edmund de Cressy was the Sheriff of Nottinghamshire and Derbyshire in 1329. Hughes, <u>A. List of Sheriffs for England and Wales from the Earliest Times to A.D. 1831.</u> London: Eyre & Spottiswoode, (1898)

***

If you are interested in learning more about Robin Hood and the historical felons of the English Middle Ages, there are many excellent references available. Here a few of my personal favourites.

Books

Dobson & Taylor, Rymes of Robyn Hood: An Introduction to the English Outlaw (Gloucester, 1989)
Hanawalt, B.A., Crime and Conflict in the English Communities 1330-1348 (London, 1979)
Holt, J., Robin Hood (London, 1982)
Keen, M., The Outlaws of Medieval Legend (London, 1987)
Knight, S., Robin Hood: A Complete Study of the English Outlaw (Oxford, 1994)
Leyser, H., Medieval Women: A Social History of Women in England 450-1500, (London 1995)
Morris, W.A., The Medieval English Sheriff to 1300 (Manchester, 1927)
Nichols, ed., History and Antiquity of Leicester, Vol. 3, Part 1
Pollard, A.J., Imaging Robin Hood (London, 2004)
Prestwich, M., The Three Edwards: War and State in England 1272-1377 (London, 1980)

Periodicals

Bellamy, J., '*The Coterel Gang: An Anatomy of a Band of Fourteenth Century Crime*', English Historical Review Vol. 79, (1964)
Scattergood, J., '*The Tale of Gamelyn: The Noble Robber as Provincial Hero,*' ed. C Meale, Readings in Medieval English Romance (Cambridge, 1994)
Stones, E., '*The Folvilles of Ashby Folville, Leicestershire,*

and their associates in crime, 1326-1347'. <u>Transactions of the Royal Historical Society 77</u> (1956)

Lightning Source UK Ltd.
Milton Keynes UK
UKHW040625260519
343327UK00001B/16/P